CRAVING HEAT

STEELE RIDGE: THE KINGSTONS

ADRIENNE GIORDANO

STEELE RIDGE
www.SteeleRidgeSeries.com

Print Edition, July 2018, ISBN: 978-1-948075-06-0
For more information contact: adrienneg@adriennegiordano.com

ALSO BY ADRIENNE GIORDANO

PRIVATE PROTECTORS SERIES

Romantic suspense

Risking Trust

Man Law

A Just Deception

Negotiating Point

Relentless Pursuit

Opposing Forces

HARLEQUIN INTRIGUES

Romantic suspense

The Prosecutor

The Defender

The Marshall

The Detective

The Rebel

JUSTIFIABLE CAUSE SERIES

Romantic suspense novellas

The Chase

The Evasion

The Capture

BOOKS AVAILABLE BY CO-AUTHORS OF THE STEELE RIDGE SERIES

Books Available by Tracey Devlyn

NEXUS SERIES

Historical romantic suspense

A Lady's Revenge

Checkmate, My Lord

A Lady's Secret Weapon

Latymer

Shev

BONES & GEMSTONES SERIES

Historical romantic mystery

Night Storm

TEA TIME SHORTS & NOVELLAS

Sweet historical romance

His Secret Desire

Books Available by Kelsey Browning

Prophecy of Love series

Sexy contemporary romance

Stay with Me

Hard to Love

Texas Nights series

Sexy contemporary romance

Personal Assets

Running the Red Light

Problems in Paradise

Designed for Love

The G Team Series

Southern cozy mystery co-written with Nancy Naigle

In For a Penny

Fit to Be Tied

In High Cotton

Under the Gun

Gimme Some Sugar

Jenny & Teague Novellas

Spin off contemporary romances from the G Team Mysteries

Always on My Mind

Come a Little Closer

Novellas

Sexy contemporary romance

Amazed by You

Love So Sweet

STEELE RIDGE CHARACTERS

The Steeles

Britt Steele - Eldest Steele sibling. Construction worker who has a passion for the environment and head of Steele-Shepherd Wildlife Research Center.

Miranda "Randi" Shepherd - Owner of Blues, Brews and Books aka Triple B and Britt Steele's love interest.

Grif Steele - Steele sibling. Works as a sports agent and Steele Ridge's city manager.

Carlie Beth Parrish - Steele Ridge's only blacksmith and Grif Steele's love interest.

Reid Steele - Steele sibling. Former Green Beret and head of Steele Ridge Training Academy.

Brynne Whitfield - Owner of La Belle Style boutique in Steele Ridge and love interest of Reid Steele.

Mikayla "Micki" Steele - Steele sibling and Jonah's twin. Master hacker.

Gage Barber - Injured Green Beret and Reid Steele's close friend who comes to Steele Ridge to help run the training center. Love interest of Micki Steele.

Jonah Steele - Steele sibling and Micki's twin. Video game mogul and former owner of the billion-dollar company, Steele Trap. Responsible for saving the town of Steele Ridge, formerly known as Canyon Ridge.

Tessa Martin - Former in-house psychologist at Steele Trap and Jonah Steele's love interest.

Evie Steele - Youngest Steele sibling. Travel nurse.

Derek "Deke" Conrad - Commander of SONR (Special Operations for Natural Resources) group and love interest of Evie Steele.

Joan Steele - Mother of the six Steele siblings.

Eddy Steele - Father of the six Steele siblings.

CRAVING HEAT

STEELE RIDGE: THE KINGSTONS

ADRIENNE GIORDANO

STEELE RIDGE

www.SteeleRidgeSeries.com

1

"You *cannot* be serious."

Jayson slid a sideways glance at his agent and his rare use of a condescending tone. During negotiations, Grif generally voiced his opinions in a direct, unquestioning manner. Something Jay admired in the man. Never a runaround. Only truth. Reality as seen by Grif Steele.

This reality sucked.

Big-time.

Sitting across from Jay at the oversized conference table, Drew Chandler wouldn't—or couldn't—meet his eye. The hand-painted Knights logo on the wall behind Jay monopolized his attention.

The guy always was a spineless weasel and this episode proved it. When wrecking a man's life, the least he could do was look that man in the eye.

"I assure you," Drew said, "we're very serious."

Not I. We. As in an entire organization. One that Jayson had spent the whole of his professional football career representing.

All those years and this is what he got?

Beside Drew, Eli Paskins, the team's major shareholder, held up both hands.

The Knights held the distinction of being the United States Football Federation's only publicly owned team and being the major shareholder, Eli participated in potentially high-impact decisions.

Like releasing a franchise player.

One Paskins himself had recruited. His word was rule, but he also took the unenviable heat from shareholders when profits were down.

Over the years, Jay had assisted Eli in any number of team-related activities. Everything from player issues to press briefings to charity events, Jayson Tucker, superstar quarterback, had been right there, stumping for his team, letting everyone know the Knights were *the* team to watch.

"Gentlemen, please," Eli said.

Grif huffed out a breath, his frustration with the proceedings evident.

"Grif," Drew said, "you've put the screws to me for years. Don't play like you're horrified."

"I may have put the screws to you, but I'm not playing. I *am* horrified."

At certain times, Jay didn't mind his agent speaking for him. Right now? No way. He'd spent years leading this team, on and off the field, getting his head beat in and maintaining a *cool under fire* image under a brutal spotlight, and the front office wanted him gone. Fast.

A knife slice ripped at him. His career.

Over.

Everything. Gone, gone, gone.

Before he'd experienced a championship.

And that pissed Jay off.

Grif leaned in, ready to launch into an argument, but Jay

gave him a backhanded flick on the arm. "Don't bother." He faced Drew and Paskins again, his direct glare leveled on Drew. He'd deal with Paskins, his *friend,* in a minute. "You're releasing me after everything I've done for this team—all the dog and pony shows, keeping your locker room in check, which hell, that's no picnic, and oh, right, grooming that *pain in the ass* rookie quarterback for *my* job. And you're not asking for my side of this thing. What the fuck does that say?"

"Tuck," Paskins said, "take it easy."

Tuck, my ass.

From the second Jay had walked in here, it had been all formal use of his name. Now, with him getting, as Paskins liked to say, a little hot, his boss wanted to knock the edge off things by using Jay's nickname.

Jay wasn't having it. Not for a second. Not for the tiniest fucking tenth of a second.

"You're destroying my career *and* reputation. We're not talking just football. There are endorsements, too. This is my goddamned livelihood. Why the hell would I take it easy?"

Paskins's dark eyebrows hitched up and his mouth hung open, expressing the fake revulsion he wanted Jay to buy.

Finally, he forced a choppy breath. "*I'm* destroying your career. *I* gave you your first big-league contract. And when that contract was up, I made you the highest-paid quarterback in the league. When have I not supported you?"

Uh, how about now? "Check your calendar. It's Tuesday. The press has been dogging me since Sunday night and management has shown zero support. Aside from long-standing teammates, there's been radio silence from an organization I've spent fifteen years pimping myself out for.

Am I the highest-paid quarterback? You bet. I earn every cent."

"He's right," Grif said, "you know this is crap. If you release him, I'll find a way to sue you. Count on it."

Drew ignored Grif's threat, and for the first time, looked at Jayson. Dead on. "You *attacked* a player. In a locker room full of reporters. He's a first-round draft pick. How do I defend that?"

Fighting to keep his temper in check—and avoid saying something stupid—Jay drove his heel into the carpet. After two days of his superiors failing him, he was smart enough to not take a chance on them leaking the events of this meeting to the press. Lifting one hip, he reached into his pocket for his phone and retrieved the video he'd watched at least a hundred times. "You tell the truth," he said. "Say you benched Eric Webb, your golden boy rookie quarterback, and he retaliated by nearly having my head knocked off." He tossed the phone on the table. "Take a look. Real close. That's Rajae Evans and his illegal hit that could have paralyzed me, and all the guy gets is a one-game suspension. And Golden Boy, a guy I've put more man-hours into than I can count, set me up."

"You don't know that," Drew said.

"The hell I don't. Evans was Golden Boy's college roommate. You think that's a coincidence?"

Jay pulled air through his nose, forced himself to breathe and settle his thumping heart. Retreating to the logo behind Jay, Drew broke eye contact. Of course he did.

Time to deal with his *friend*. Jay shifted to Paskins. "We've shared meals. You've asked me for favors. Did you even look into it? Maybe do an investigation to see if the Golden Boy and Rajae had a phone conversation on Saturday? Before they tried to end my career. Or don't you care?"

Never one to shy away from an argument, Paskins leaned in. "Making an accusation like that won't help your career."

After this fuck-fest, did he even want to be in this league? "What I did was wrong. I'll own that. But I wasn't alone in it."

Paskins shook his head. "Webb is threatening to press charges. You should be thanking me for keeping you out of jail. He may sue you yet."

"Let him. I'll call every reporter I know—and that's a busload—and tell them what he tried to do to me. Maybe you should have thought of that before you decided I was the dispensable one." Jay stood. "But you didn't. You let the press think I'd lost my mind and randomly attacked my teammate. Thanks for the loyalty, boys."

Unfuckingbelievable. He had to get out. Remove himself from the toxicity before he gave them more ammunition to use in the destruction of his marketability.

"Wait," Grif said, obviously intending to try and save Jay's job.

"No." Jay stood. "I'm done. After what I've done for this organization, this is how they treat me? Bullshit. I won't play for people who refuse to protect their players. The right players, anyway."

Jaw locked, Jay strode from the conference room. He'd attended endless mind-numbing meetings here with team executives and now they were throwing him out.

Betrayal. A vicious bitch.

He kept moving, past Veronica and Sally who, unlike Drew, met his eye. They both shook their heads. Two admins understood the insanity, but the team's president couldn't. Or wouldn't. Either way, it stunk.

"Tuck," Grif said, hustling to keep up as Jayson pushed

through the doors leading out of the executive suite. "Let me talk to Paskins privately."

Paskins. A guy Jay had hoped would find him a front office job once he retired. "Don't bother," he said. "Drew doesn't take a shit without asking Paskins. If he wasn't on board with this decision, that meeting wouldn't have happened."

Jay got to the elevator and tapped the button. "Even if you talked them into letting me stay, how's that gonna work? We'll have chaos in the locker room and I'll feel like the charity case they kept on. After this shit show, nothing good will come of me staying."

The elevator doors slid open and they stepped on. Grif already had his phone out. "We'll need spin control. Let's get your PR people to put out a press release. Keep it short and sweet. Due to recent incidents, you're leaving the team, yada, yada. We'll beat them to the media, then give it a week. By the time I get you a new team, everyone will know you got screwed. For now, lie low. We'll make a statement and tuck you away somewhere."

His agent. Always working the angles. "Are you handling me, Grif?"

Grif met his eye. "If it keeps your head on straight, you know it. It's the middle of the season and there are three teams needing leadership to get them to the playoffs. You focus on football, I'll do the rest."

Lying low. Not a bad idea if he intended on salvaging his career. He'd hunker down, hit the gym, and get his mind right about his future. The elevator came to a stop, the doors sliding open, and Jay held the door for Grif. "I'll find a private place to work out. It'll be fine."

Grif stepped into the cavernous lobby of the New York Knights headquarters and Jay followed, the heels of his dress shoes clapping against the marble. He'd heard that sound thousands of times, each a mundane occurrence. One of the comforting sounds of a secure existence.

Not this time.

He fought the punch to his chest, reeled in the spurting anger and sadness. He'd had a plan for ending his career. The generous leader going out on top while helping his team stay competitive. Now he had...nothing.

Before stepping outside, Grif turned to him, one hand on the door. "Come to Steele Ridge. It'll be quiet there and we have the facilities to keep you out of the public eye. You can work out with my brother. Reid is an animal. If you can put up with his arrogance and constant mouthing off, he'd love to beat the crap out of you for a few weeks."

VACATION: T MINUS FIVE DAYS, TEN HOURS, AND FORTY-TWO minutes.

Maggie brought her cruiser to a stop on Main Street right behind Mrs. Royce's parked and extremely ancient Lincoln. The land yacht. How the woman navigated the streets of Steele Ridge in that thing was still a mystery. On the sidewalk, Mrs. Royce and Mr. Greene, quite possibly the town's oldest resident, squared off.

Right in front of the Triple B where folks streamed in for a quick breakfast and the best damned coffee in three counties.

To think the day had started off so well, with Maggie gaining a whole second on Reid's obstacle course record. If she shaved two measly seconds off her time, she'd beat her much bigger and stronger cousin.

And never let him forget it.

That damned high wall. Of all the obstacles, that one

slowed her down the most. She had to figure out how to get over that thing faster.

Later.

Right now, she had a geriatric smackdown to break up and joined the Old Folk's Brigade on the sidewalk.

Ignoring Maggie, Mr. Greene banged his cane on the sidewalk as he jabbed his free hand's gnarly index finger at Mrs. Royce. "Now listen, you old bat, you know I've been parking in that dang spot for...for...Well, hell, since Randi opened her doors."

The parking spot. Every morning Maggie drove by the B, where Mr. Greene's car sat snugly in the space just outside the front door. She'd known, right down to her thick-soled boots, it would eventually be a problem. Bound to happen.

"Who are you calling an old bat?" Mrs. Royce shrieked. "You're older than me!"

Maggie checked her watch: 9:05. Vacation: T minus five days, ten hours, and thirty-nine minutes. *Just hang on.* That's all she needed to do. But being a sheriff in a small town sometimes tested her. Like now. Was it sick that she occasionally craved a good, savage crime? Something that required investigative skills that went beyond enough patience to deal with ornery residents.

"My spot!" Mr. Greene hollered.

Enough already. Maggie whistled through her teeth, sending enough of a shrill to shatter cheap windows in a three-block radius.

Mrs. Royce covered her ears. "My ears! I have my hearing aids in. Are you *trying* to kill me?"

Oh, the drama. "No, ma'am. But you two are blocking this sidewalk. I need you both to calm down so we can fix this."

Mr. Greene banged the cane again. "We'll fix it by you ordering her to move that damned boat out of my spot."

"Bah!" Mrs. Royce said. "It's not *your* spot. I don't see a sign. And why should I park across the street when there's an empty space right here in front? My hip is killing me. The less I have to walk, the better."

Ah. The hip. That explained it. After all this time of Mr. Greene monopolizing the closest spot, Mrs. Royce's bad hip cried foul. And it had a point.

Maggie held her hands up. "Mr. Greene, the residents have given you latitude when it comes to parking. You have to agree with that."

"Well, sure. Because it's my spot."

"No, sir. Technically it belongs to the town."

Mrs. Royce bobbed her head and the loose skin at her neck wobbled. "That's right. And I don't see no sign reserving it for you. I'm old, too. We need to take turns or something."

A sign. Hmmm. Maggie faced Mrs. Royce. "Ma'am. Please. I'm talking."

"Sorry." She swung a fist at Mr. Greene. "He makes me so mad."

"I understand, but that's not helping."

"My spot!"

A dull thump erupted behind Maggie's right eye. Usually, if she got a headache, it waited until lunchtime. The day's nonsense had started early today.

Randi poked her head out the door. "Y'all are making a spectacle of yourselves. And you're disturbing the customers. Either come inside and let me buy you a coffee while you talk this out or move it along."

"Randi," Maggie said, "would you join us for a second, please?"

Randi speared her with a look. "I'm in the middle of a rush and the new barista is struggling."

"I'll be quick. Mr. Greene and Mrs. Royce are arguing over the parking spot."

"Because it's my damned spot."

In her mind, Maggie sighed. Too darned early to feel this tired. "No," she said, her voice carrying the rough edge that came with strained patience. "You're lucky you've been given liberties this long."

Before Mr. Greene could launch into a counterattack, Maggie pressed on. "I have a solution. A compromise that should make you both happy."

Clearly needing to be on her way, Randi peeked over her shoulder. "Mags, can we move this along?"

"Yes. What do you think about reserving this spot for a customer of the week? You have regulars that come in every morning. Maybe you do a raffle to make it fair. We'll rotate the names and whoever has a certain week has the spot reserved between 9 and 9:30 every day. If they don't get here by then, first come first serve."

Randi pondered the idea. "I like it. I could even do a discount for that customer for the week."

Excellent.

Mr. Greene tapped his cane. "How often would I get the spot?"

"We'll come up with a fair rotation," Maggie said. "That's the best we can do."

Mrs. Royce nodded. "I'm in favor. Thank you, Randi."

"Don't thank me. It was the sheriff's idea. Now, I need to get inside. Breakfast for you three is on me this morning. Just quit blocking my foot traffic!"

At the thought of one of Randi's ham-and-egg breakfast croissants, Maggie's headache backed off a smidge. "It's settled then. Randi and I will work out the particulars. In the meantime, whoever gets into town first, gets the spot. No arguments."

"But—"

"Mags, I'm glad you're here."

Maggie looked over Randi's shoulder and spotted Grif exiting the B. Saved by her cousin. *Thank you, kind sir.*

She faced Mr. Greene. "No arguments or I'll ban you from the spot altogether. Now head inside and get your coffee while I talk to our esteemed city manager."

Randi escorted Mr. Greene and Mrs. Royce inside and Maggie met Grif's eye. "Thank you for saving me."

"What were they fighting about?"

"The damned parking spot. It was bound to happen. I can't believe this is the first time. And, by the way, we're making it a reward. Customer of the week. You good with that?"

Grif shrugged. "Whatever you and Randi want. I need to talk to you."

Apparently her cousin had bigger fish to fry. "What's up?"

"Can you come up to my office? I have a client coming in who you'll need to meet."

Since when did Grif have clients come to Steele Ridge? He'd become the king of video conferencing since moving home.

And why, unless it somehow involved her, would Grif want her to meet his client?

Vacation: T minus five days, ten hours, and twenty-two minutes.

Across the street, a shiny black Range Rover pulled into one of the spaces in front of the Murchison building.

"This is him," Grif said.

They jaywalked across the street and earned themselves a honk from a passing car. *So, arrest me*. It wasn't as if Main Street suddenly needed a stoplight to control congestion. Still, Maggie offered an apologetic wave.

"Grif, I'm leaving on vacation on Monday."

"I know. I know. You've reminded me no less than five times. Where are you going again?"

"Bahamas. A women-in-law-enforcement retreat. By Monday afternoon, I'll be sipping drinks with silly umbrellas in them. Nothing is keeping me from those umbrellas."

She hadn't taken a vacation in the last three years. Not even a weekend away since she'd become sheriff. She deserved this trip. She needed this trip. She *wanted* this trip. And that didn't happen all that often.

Grif was oddly silent. Her cousin. The master negotiator. A smooth-talker, he chose his moments of silence carefully. Grif's silence was usually packed with a whole slew of messages.

As long as one of those messages wasn't her canceled vacation, she had no problem with it.

2

JAY SAT IN HIS SUV STARING AT THE SUN-DAPPLED FRONT OF A brick building that, if he knew his agent at all, Grif had had recently painted. But this was Grif and plain old beige wouldn't cut it. This color had a hint of...something. Red or orange maybe. Just enough to give it a rustic look. Whatever it was, it managed to maintain the charm inherent with buildings about to hit birthday number 125, according to new-looking bronze plaque beside the front door.

Grif. The magic man.

Said magic man had his work cut out for him when it came to salvaging Jay's career. The ring of his cell trumped Stevie Ray Vaughan and filled the car. His phone had been blowing up since yesterday with calls from the press, his sister and unhappy teammates. He appreciated the support from his sister and teammates, but the idea of having to return every call and explain how his career imploded gutted him.

He checked the dashboard for the caller ID. Mom.

"Crap."

The week kept getting better. He didn't need her brand

of crazy right now. He looked out at the building again, where the sun's rays showered over it. That's what he'd focus on. Sunshine on a nice fall day.

Resigned to dealing with his mother, he picked up the call. "Mom, what's up?"

"Only *youuuuuu*," she said, "would be dumb enough to wreck your career by puh ... puh ... *punch*ing someone."

Barely 9:30 and his mother was already tripping over her words. "What can I say? I learned from the best."

Damn. When would he learn not to take the bait?

A sharp intake of breath sounded and the telltale clink of ice in a glass confirmed Jay's suspicions. On a good day, Sober Marlene was a mouthy handful. On a bad day, Drunk Marlene raged hard enough to send innocents scrambling for cover.

"How many have you had?"

"You know," she said, "all the years I put into you—"

Game over.

He stabbed at the button on his steering wheel and immediately turned his cell to do not disturb. It wouldn't be the first time he'd hung up on his mother. She'd never remember it anyway. He'd developed an adeptness to ending their phone calls at precisely the right time. That time being right before she got *really* wound up, spewing about what losers she'd raised and how he and his sister weren't fit to carry her name.

Which, technically speaking, wasn't even hers anymore. Over two decades later and she still paraded around, signing the Tucker name all over the place as if Dad hadn't shacked up with another socialite. One who definitely did not drink.

His parents. What a pair. Jay rested his hand on the top of the steering wheel. "How the fuck did this get to be my life?"

A knock on the window jerked him from his mind travel and he swung his head left.

Grif.

Christ. He hadn't even seen him.

Call it fatigue from last night's long drive and one hell of a week, but Jay was off his game. In a big way.

He killed the engine and opened the door. At the rear bumper stood a tall woman with hair that was a cross between honey blond and light brown. All of it in a tight ponytail. She wore a police uniform and Jay's exhausted mind went to a bachelor party five years ago when the stripper put the groom in handcuffs.

This one had the body, no doubt, but her demeanor didn't say stripper. Her pressed uniform shirt was tucked in neatly, the buttons all aligned. Even the creases in her uniform pants were straight.

She locked her eyes on him for a long few seconds. Given his experience as a professional athlete, he'd seen that look before and it usually meant good things for a man ready to get laid.

"Hi," Jay said, immediately extending his hand.

She nodded and shook his hand. Like the rest of her, the handshake was a quick, efficient affair. "Maggie Kingston."

"My cousin," Grif said. "She's the sheriff here."

There went the stripper fantasy. More interesting might be the dynamics in play with Grif being the city manager and his cousin the sheriff. Small towns. Always fascinating. Growing up on the upper East Side of Manhattan, Jay learned a different way to get things done. A way that included money—a lot of it—and regular smacks with a belt from his mother.

Maybe small-town life wouldn't have been so bad.

"I trust you slept well," Grif said. "I told Mrs. Tasky to

give you the best room. Figured since you got in late, you could crash at the B and B last night and avoid my mother's fussing."

"All good. I slept hard."

After the meeting with Drew and Paskins the day before, Jay had gone home, packed a suitcase, and hauled ass out of town before the press had mobilized on the street in front of his condo. By the time they'd gotten there, he'd been forty minutes into a ten-hour drive that let him be alone and think. One thing about him, he could bug out quick when necessary. Years of ducking his mother's fists and then running from rabid fans and reporters had taught him evasion skills.

Grif jerked his chin at the brick building. "Let's head to my office. You hungry? We can grab you something."

"I ate. Thanks."

Mrs. Tasky had offered a hell of a spread that morning. He'd stuck to proteins and avoided carbs and starches, but the potatoes had looked damned good. The realization hit him that being an unemployed professional athlete meant not having to worry about his carb intake as much.

Grif stood back, waved his extremely hot cousin ahead of him. "Let's go to my office."

All right then. The sheriff joining their meeting.

Jay must have made a face because Grif met his eye. "We're bringing Maggie up to speed in case the press shows up."

As much as they'd like to keep his location quiet, thanks to endless *Sports Illustrated* covers and various men's magazines Jay's mug wasn't exactly unrecognizable. Hell, the attention from the sexiest man alive gig took him to a level of fame that had blown his mind. Who knew *that* was such a big deal?

The sheriff shot Grif a look. "Vacation," she said. "Silly umbrellas."

What the hell did that mean?

Grif flashed a smile. "I got it, Mags."

Inside the building, Grif ushered them to his first-floor office, a simple deal, with minimal accessories and a large desk for Grif to do his magic. Jay waited for the sheriff to take a seat at the small, round conference table, then sat across from her, leaving the seat between for Grif, who dropped a legal pad and pen in front of him.

"Mags, here's the short of it. Jayson and the Knights have parted ways."

"I saw that on ESPN last night." She looked at Jayson. "I'm sorry. Sounds like you got a bum deal."

"I'm the old guy. Replaceable. Welcome to professional sports."

"He won't be on the market long." Grif faced Jay again. "I've had a few calls already."

That sounded promising for a thirty-six-year-old quarterback who, in his humble opinion, still had a few good years left. Thanks to smart investing and the fact that he'd get paid the rest of his contract, he had enough money to last him four lifetimes. This wasn't about money, though. This was about not being slapped with an assault charge. This was about passion. For the game. For leadership.

For his identity.

Since high school, football had been the goal. Sure, he'd graduated from college with a solid 3.5 GPA, but the degree was an afterthought. Football had been the dream. One he'd achieved.

At this point, he'd only just begun thinking about what life after football would look like. And when it came to a career? Dead loss. No clue.

"We'll talk about that when we're through here," Grif said. "Mags, we're keeping Jay's location under wraps. So far, the media thinks he's holed up in his condo in New York. My thought is we'll put him up at the training center. There's security up there. He can stay in Jonah's old room at the house rather than the hotel. I don't know if Reid has a group coming in and I'd rather Tuck have privacy. In case fans start showing up."

"And," the sheriff said, "the press."

"Sorry, Sheriff," Jay said.

She shook it off. "Don't apologize. A surge of people needing to sleep and eat is never a bad thing. Still, you're a guest here and we'll want to keep you safe."

"Exactly," Grif said.

"Obviously," the sheriff said, "given your high profile, I'd imagine you get unwanted attention. Is there anything I should be aware of?"

"As in wack-jobs?"

Her slow, curving smile brought him back to that damned stripper fantasy. "I was trying to be polite about it, but yes."

Polite? He'd given up on that long ago. At least behind closed doors. In public? He'd become the master of ignoring idiots. People who threatened and called him foul names didn't deserve polite.

Jay shrugged. "It's run-of-the-mill stuff. After the past few days, a few threatening e-mails and tweets are expected. My security team is on it."

She gave him a look like he'd lost his mind. Maybe he had, but if he had a meltdown every time he got hate mail he'd be in a mental ward by now.

"What do you consider *run-of-the-mill* threats?"

Yep, the hot sheriff thought he was loco. "It sounds flip, but we take them seriously. Every threat is vetted by my security team. I'm informed when I need to be. I can't have the details in my face all the time. If I did, I'd be afraid to walk outside. I'm not living that way." He waved it away. "This week's threats included someone explaining how he'd break my throwing arm. The other was from a woman claiming she and Eric Webb—he's the rookie I've been grooming—were meant for everlasting love. That they were soulmates. A rare and beautiful thing, she claimed. Guess she discounted the fact that he's married."

The sheriff's brows drew together. "What was the threat?"

"Since I dared to put my hands on her beloved, she intended to do me bodily harm."

"What kind of bodily harm?"

Jay glanced at Grif. Really, he didn't need to use coarse language in mixed company, but Grif urged him on with a brief nod.

"She...uh...told me she knew where I lived and could gain access to my building. Where she would tie me up and carve my pecker to pieces."

The sheriff didn't flinch. This chick took total deadpan to another level, which, oddly enough, released some of the tension locking up his shoulders. Talking about this crap was never easy. Forget telling a female about how someone wanted to make sushi out of his dick.

"I see," Sheriff Kingston said.

"Yeah. This is my life."

"All right." She faced Grif. "We'll increase patrols around Tupelo Hill."

"Thank you," Jay said, already anticipating making a sizable donation to the Sheriff's Department. He'd dig around, see what fancy new equipment Sheriff Maggie wished for, but couldn't afford on the city's budget.

Grif smiled at Jay. "Reid is anxious to get his hands on you. I believe he said, 'Send me the superstar. We'll see what he's got.'"

"Lord," the sheriff said. "He's such an ass."

For the first time in at least twenty-four hours, Jay laughed. "Nice. This should be fun."

"That's one way to put it," she said. "Have you met Reid?"

"No."

"He's...entertaining."

Grif snorted. "Annoying is more like it."

The sheriff's face split into a smile that bunched her cheeks and lit her eyes and...whoa...suddenly this buttoned-up sheriff sparked of dangerously female. And not the *in your face*, sultry female. This was all wholesome country girl with a subtle undercurrent of heat. And sex.

"Just make sure you get there fifteen minutes early to warm up," she said. "He doesn't like wasting workout time on warm-ups."

Grif cleared his throat. "If you're on time," he said in a gruff voice, clearly imitating his brother, "you're late."

The sheriff pushed out of her chair. "You sound *just* like him. Which terrifies me on several levels. Gentlemen, thank you for keeping me informed." She turned to Jay. "Great meeting you. Please update me on any further threats or odd occurrences, no matter how silly it seems. We're a small town with limited resources. I'd rather get ahead of it."

"Understood. And thank you."

"Of course. Let me know if you need anything while you're here."

Oh, he might need something...

He met her gaze for a few seconds, letting her know he was interested, but he'd keep it light. He wouldn't be that guy. The aggressive knuckle-dragger. He understood the trappings of being a professional athlete. Temptations, when it came to women, were constant. His looks didn't hurt. He'd been touted as everything from roguishly sexy to blond-haired farm boy. None of which he was, but it helped feed his bank account, so why not?

"Thank you, Sheriff."

"You're welcome. Grif, I'll talk to you later about the parking space."

"Great fun," Grif muttered.

Jay waited for the office door to close, then met his agent's eye. Enough with the distractions. He needed a job. "Who were the calls from?"

"Dallas, LA, and Portland."

Crap. Cross-country moves, all of them. LA wouldn't be horrible. Good ownership, good coaching. A young team that could use his experience.

Grif rolled his bottom lip out. "It's early, though. I know you'd like to stay on the East Coast."

"I would, but if the situation is right, I'll suck it up for a few years."

Because, realistically, that's all he had left in football. He'd hoped to finish those years in New York, with the one and only team he'd ever played for.

This mess, his nosediving career, he hadn't anticipated. Released by the Knights and so far two of his sponsors had dumped him, with possibly a third about to.

"I got a call," he said, "from Will Burns."

Grif eyed him. A call from the executive director of the domestic abuse charity Jayson represented might not, at this particular time, be a good thing.

Celebrate Hope, the nation's largest advocate for abuse victims, not to mention his sister's employer, currently had a spokesman who had attacked a teammate. Not a stellar example of a nonviolent, compassionate individual.

For the first time, Jayson Tucker was a liability. Absolute poison.

Grif sat back. "What'd he say?"

"He wanted to set up a meeting. Since I'm only three hours away, I'm heading down there tomorrow afternoon."

"That's a good sign. If he wants to meet in person, maybe they're still on board."

"You, my dedicated agent, are delusional. They should have jettisoned me Sunday night."

The weight of it surrounded him. After everything he'd been through, he'd managed to blow the one sponsorship gig that gave him the most satisfaction.

"Tuck, you've been with them a long time. You do good —great—work for them. And they like you. Go to the meeting. Make nice. Maybe they'll hold on for the ride."

"Would you?"

In lieu of an answer, his agent blew out a breath. "See what they say. Do you want me to go?"

"No. Let's keep it informal. Bringing my agent sets a tone."

"I agree."

"And, by the way, Paskins called last night."

"*Really?* That fucker. All communication should be going through me. In case we decide to sue their ass for some contract violation I've yet to come up with."

Good old Grif. Always ready for battle. "Relax. He was doing a temperature check." He flashed the magazine-cover smile. "He knows we might sue them for some reason you've yet to come up with."

"Don't count that out."

"Never. He gave me the whole song and dance about his untenable position. They can't support violence in the locker room, yada, yada." Jay twisted his mouth. "It's all too damned bad. Paskins and I were friends. At least I thought so. Drew was always a douche, but Paskins helped me."

The man's lack of support stung. Badly. Being the major shareholder, he wielded a big stick. If he'd wanted to keep Jay, to try and understand the situation, they'd have found a way. Instead, his so-called friend and mentor hadn't even bothered to pick up the phone and ask Jay for his side of the story.

"Well," Grif said, "he said his piece. Any other calls from them, send to me. For now, let's get you up to the training center. You can settle in and meet my mother. She's excited to have the sexiest man alive over for dinner."

3

AT 6:05, IN THE DARKNESS THAT CAME WITH AN OCTOBER dawn, Maggie made her way up the long mountain road to Tupelo Hill, a sprawling twenty thousand acres containing her aunt's Victorian plus the training center where Reid, her beloved cousin, would do his best to make her puke.

He would fail.

Always did.

As a former Green Beret, Reid understood what it meant to push the human body. He'd broken many determined men with his body-blasting workouts, but not her. Never. Even if she'd come close to losing her breakfast a couple of times, she'd refused to give in.

The ring of her phone blared through her Explorer's Bluetooth—no doubt who this was. She hit the button. "I know. I'm late."

On time means you're late. When it came to the schedule, her taskmaster wanted her warming up at 5:50. Torture began at six sharp.

Well, not today.

Today, the wasted fourteen-year-old son of one of Steele Ridge's town council members had decided to pass out in the middle of the high school football field.

At 3:00 a.m.

To say the situation needed to be handled delicately would be an understatement. Maggie had received the call from her panicked deputy, who'd seen the kid stumbling around and decided to follow him. Maggie dragged her butt out of bed, had her deputy help load the errant teenager into her vehicle, and then drove him home. Where his father had the pleasure of carrying his son to bed with a promise from Maggie to keep the situation on the downlow.

Small-town politics. A never-ending cycle.

And she was good at it. 1-800-Call-Mag. That was her. Fixer of all messes.

"You're late." Reid, of course, repeated what she'd already stated.

"I'm turning in now. I was up at three o'clock dealing with a situation."

Reid let out a low whistle. "I'm impressed you're here. Good for you."

"See you in two."

Yes. She was here. Ready to work because breaking a sweat every day, pushing her body to its unholy limits, kept her from going insane. Kept her from wondering what police work outside of Steele Ridge—outside of drunk teenagers and squabbles over parking spaces—might look like.

Thanks to the Steele boys, she'd had her share of unusual cases in the past couple of years and as much as she bitched and moaned, she'd loved it. Loved digging in and feeling...what? Useful. More than a babysitter? Something.

She roared up the drive, swung into the small visitor lot in front of the training center. Her headlights smacked against the glass front of the building where Reid stood waiting in his usual attire of track pants and a zip-up pullover that wasn't exactly tight, but hugged his torso enough to indicate the muscles beneath.

In short, Reid was a badass. In addition to his physicality, he had the *fuck with me and die* attitude Maggie craved. When it came to describing a woman, the terms ambitious and bitch were often interchangeable. Learning to navigate the duties of her job meant avoiding tripping into bitch territory. Had a man been in this job, no one would question his authority. Her? If she raised her voice, folks murmured about it being that time of the month.

And yet, they wanted her to keep them safe.

Go figure.

She shut off the engine and hopped out, her mind already advancing to the warm-up. Spidermans and inch-worms. Karaokes and shuffles. She enjoyed the routine of it, those few minutes of being alone, the quiet morning air that let her breathe and be in the moment.

And maybe, if she got really lucky, she'd get a bonus of seeing the hot jock who'd shown up to take temporary refuge at Tupelo Hill.

The sheriff in her detested the headaches that came with a celebrity visit. The hadn't *been touched in months* female? Well, she couldn't resist staring. A lot. Ripped, ripped, and more ripped. That was Jayson Tucker. She'd be an idiot not to notice it, even through his shirt. Pair his body with a face teetering on the glorious edge of movie star handsome and the close-cropped beard she wanted to touch and Maggie would have to be blind—and stupid—not to appreciate him.

"Hey," Reid said.

He held the door open, led her through the lobby and down the hallway to the back door. Outside, massive flood-lights illuminated the obstacle course her insane cousin had designed and built. He, of course, owned the family record, something he reminded everyone of on a regular basis. The course record was held by some SWAT guy from LA who'd been here training with his unit. As far as family? Reid had the record. And Maggie, only two seconds behind, wanted it.

Today, given her fatigue, probably wouldn't be the day she'd achieve her goal. That much, she'd accept.

"You wanna skip the course today? Just do cardio and weights?"

"Heck no. I may suck, but let's run it. Practice makes perfect."

"Attagirl. Get warmed up."

An hour later, her body sufficiently warm from her workout, Mags stood at the obstacle course starting line.

If she had to be here, she might as well bust it out. Even if the jock hadn't yet given her a glimpse of him.

She peered downrange, focusing on the log mounted a few feet in the air. With one good leap, she'd vault over that, sprint to the low wall, and then reach the insanity of a twenty-foot vertical ladder jutting straight up. She'd navigate each rung to the top, coming down the other side and dropping the last six feet. All without breaking her neck.

Those were easy compared to that damned high wall. In Maggie's mind, ten feet shouldn't be that high. Unless you were trying to climb over it. Which she was. And stunk at.

If she intended on shattering Reid's record, she had to improve her time getting over the wall.

It'll come.

Reid held up his stopwatch. "You ready?"

"Yep."

"Go!"

Jay walked from the main house toward the training center, spotted the floodlights—who could miss those?—out back, and detoured through the grass to the rear of the building.

Reid sat on a picnic table off to the right, his gaze on something in his hand. Stopwatch.

Out on the course, a woman in snug tights and a long-sleeved fitted shirt swung across monkey bars, her body moving with the fluid motion of an athlete.

Damn. That was hot. Understanding the nuances of the body, Jay appreciated the stamina it took to complete an obstacle course and the woman on the bars attacked it.

She rounded the turn, her ponytail flying and...wait. *Is that...?*

"Three tenths behind!" Reid bellowed.

"Fuck you!" the woman yelled back.

Yeah. Definitely Hot Sheriff Maggie. Jay burst out laughing. Had to love a girl with gumption.

Reid glanced back at him. "Superstar. You're early."

"I wanted to warm up before we got to it."

This brought a smile to Reid's face and Jay said a silent thanks to Maggie.

"Good. Give me Spidermans and inchworms. I'll be with you in twenty. Finishing up with Mags."

On the course, Maggie dropped and army-crawled under a bed of barbed wire. "She's good, huh?"

"Hell, yes. She might wind up breaking my record,

which'll piss me off, but she deserves it. She's working her ass off."

He checked his stopwatch. "Damn, she's fast on the crawl. She's got a full half second on me there."

After clearing the wire, Maggie popped to her feet, her long legs moving with the speed of a sprinter to the finish line. Wow, she could move. She slowed to a walk, then bent low for a second before straightening up and realizing she had an additional set of eyes on her.

"Hi." She huffed out a breath that made her chest—and very nice tits—rise and fall.

Hey, he was a guy and she was a woman dressed in skintight clothing. Sue him.

Jay pointed to the course. "You look great out there."

"Thanks, but not my best work. I was slow today."

"Only by two tenths," Reid added. "You made up time on the crawl."

She looked back over the course and waved a hand. "It's that damned wall. I can't get over it fast enough."

"You're tired today. You'll get it. Go in and cool down. Then roll out and you're done. I'm gonna see how I can torture the superstar here." Reid faced him with a vicious grin. "I'm still waiting on those Spidermans. Do it while I get coffee."

Spidermans. Right. The big man lumbered off toward the main building, leaving Jay still staring at Maggie and in no rush to warm up.

She scooped a towel from the table and quickly ran it over her face and neck. Nothing about her movements could be considered sexual, but Jay's body warmed up before he'd even hit the ground for those Spidermans.

"Any updates for me?" Maggie asked.

The only update he had was the one about possibly seeing her naked. Something he'd keep to himself, thank you very much. At least for a little while, until he could convince her he was a decent guy. He wouldn't be staying, but maybe, while he was here, the sheriff wouldn't mind handcuffing him.

"Updates?"

She laughed. "How soon they forget. Threats, worrisome e-mails, anything I should be aware of?"

Oh. That. "No. I'll have my security people call you if you want."

"That'd be great. Then I don't have to bug you."

He smiled. "Bug me anytime."

She tossed the towel over her shoulder. "No offense, Mr. Sexiest Man Alive, you can lay off the charm. I'm not a groupie. I'm doing my job."

Alrighty then. After the last few days, he shouldn't be shocked that the hot sheriff had shut him down faster than a good defensive back about to sack him. "I thought I was being nice. And, really, if I were laying on the charm, I'd do it a lot better than that, but, hey, message received. Sheriff." He jerked a thumb. "I gotta warm up."

Shit. Now he sounded pissy. To her, he must look like a douchebag who got pissed when a woman shot him down. Which, yeah, it sucked because what little of her he knew, he liked, but said pissiness wasn't about her rejection. This was about him and his inability to control a single damned thing in his life.

Like figuring out how to get Maggie to go to dinner with him. *Idiot.*

"Sorry," he said. "That sounded crappy. I'm uh…" How to explain it? Would she even care? "I should go."

He started for the building, more than ready to work off his bad mood.

"Jayson?"

He stopped walking, but didn't turn.

"I was rude," she said. "I had a long night. Not that it excuses bad behavior, but I'm tired and...Well, I'm sorry, too."

Jay angled back. Maggie stood, hands on hips and shaking her head.

"Hey," he said, "it's all right. I'm no better. Call it flirting gone bad on my part. My brain is short-circuiting on me just in time for a meeting where one of my sponsors will dump me."

Hell. Why would he say *that*? Way to impress a girl.

Maggie's mouth dropped open. "Really?"

"It happens when you lose your temper and torch your career."

"It's one incident. It shouldn't define you."

He shrugged. "I'll manage."

"Still, to be in the middle of it has to be stressful."

Did he even know what he felt anymore? For years, he'd been dealing with fame, hysterical fans, the lack of privacy, all of which he'd welcomed because it came with chasing his dream. This was his life. One he was damned grateful for.

His silence prompted Maggie to twist her lips. A sure sign that someone, a woman usually, was about to ask him about his feelings. *Please, God, no.* One thing he didn't need was to *talk*.

"I see you showed up early for your workout," she said.

He let out a relieved breath. This woman. Too good. She'd read his signals and backed off. "I did. Thanks for the tip, Sheriff."

"You're welcome. Call me Maggie. I'm not a stickler on the title."

It wasn't an invitation to bump uglies, but it was forward motion. "Sounds good. Maggie."

"Superstar!" Reid hollered from the building. "You warming up or making time with my cousin?"

He met Maggie's gaze for a long few seconds. "Well," he said, "I'm not warming up."

"You son of a bitch," Reid said. "Get your ass in here!"

THE CELEBRATE HOPE HEADQUARTERS, JUST OVER THE SOUTH Carolina border, was everything a charity's corporate office should be. Small, low-key, and budget friendly with commercial-grade carpeting and furniture the staff generally put together themselves. Even the reception area, a place the Knights had gone all out with, had been kept to the basics. Where the Knights splurged on marble floors, high-end leather seating, and original Warhols, Celebrate Hope got by with four metal-framed chairs, an L-shaped desk for the office assistant, and inspirational posters. The whole setup probably ran them under five hundred bucks. The board did everything right when it came to keeping administrative costs to a minimum.

The office assistant ushered Jay into Will Burns's office, where he rose from his desk and met Jay at the door. "Tuck, thanks for coming in."

As always, they shook hands. "No problem. I'm glad you called."

Will wore his typical navy suit and his thinning gray hair gelled back. Will didn't have that slick East Coast vibe about him, but when it came to business? Knife-edge sharp.

Burns waved Jay to the sofa. Every meeting Jay had

attended in the office, the seating arrangements had been the same. Jay on the sofa and Will in the adjacent chair. The man liked his chair. He sat back, crossing one leg over the other while pretending this would be like all those other meetings.

Jay knew better. His churning stomach knew better. He should have popped an antacid before coming in.

He'd do them both a favor and make this quick. Jay sat forward, rested his elbows on his knees and linked his hands together, staring at bare fingers he'd like to see an over-the-top championship ring on.

He put thoughts of his hopes and dreams from his mind and met Will's gaze. "You called me here to dump me."

If Will's wince was any indication, Jay's word choice might have been a bust. Semantics aside, they needed to own it.

"I'm assuming," Will said, "you understand the conflict. I mean, Jesus, what were you thinking?"

What was he *thinking*? Jay cocked his head. Well aware of his own infractions, he didn't need to be scolded by Will Burns and it set him on edge. It was bad enough he had to keep quiet as the sports world denigrated him; now this?

"After five years of working with me, do you think I was even marginally coherent when I punched a teammate in front of half a dozen reporters?"

"Tuck, I have to let you go. You've been—" He broke off. Shook his head. "Everyone loves you. Women, men. On some level, you connect with everyone who comes through our doors."

Thanks to a mother who used him to vent her frustrations.

"If it were just me," Will said, "I'd spin it somehow. It's the board."

Jay held up a hand. They didn't need to drag this out. He could do his thing by smiling at the right time and offering a string of reasons for Celebrate Hope to stand behind him. He'd do a damned fine job, too. All while the acid in his gut tore through his flesh because another organization, people he'd worked hard for, couldn't find a way to stand by him. All of it, the firing, the dumping blame on the board, seemed way too familiar.

"Obviously," Will said, "we'll make a brief statement, but we don't intend on making this a focal point. Or damaging your reputation."

Might be too late for that, chief. Rather than prolong the inevitable, Jay stood and waited for Will to do the same. "Thank you for everything. I'm assuming this won't impact Sam at all?"

Sam. His baby sister. She sat right down the hall in an office no bigger than his closet. Upon hearing of an opening in the finance department three years earlier, Jay greased the wheels for her. Up to this point, she'd done well and he'd hoped they'd be smart and keep her on.

Will gave him a puzzled look. "She's an exemplary employee."

"Good."

Intent on being a gentleman to the end, he shook Will's hand, then walked to the door, pointing to the far end of the hallway. "You mind if I stop and see her?"

"Not at all."

Shoulders locked tight from the collapse of yet another of his professional relationships, he strode the length of the hall to Sam's office. He'd have preferred to walk out and put the damned mess behind him, but his sister was the most important person in his life and he wouldn't ignore her. He knocked on the half-open door and stuck his head in. Three rows of four-high boxes lined the wall of the already tight space.

Sam—Samantha—sat behind her desk, her funky black-framed glasses in place as she studied her computer screen. She'd whacked a few inches of her dirty blond hair off a few weeks ago and it now fell to her chin in the front and got progressively shorter at the back. A modified bob she'd called it. It looked good on her. Emphasized her cheekbones.

She glanced up and the stern look of concentration morphed to a wide, relieved smile that reminded him of their teenage years when he'd smuggle her out of the house to shield her from Drunk Marlene's terror.

He pointed at the boxes. "You going somewhere?"

"Only if you are."

She'd do it too. Quit a job she loved because he'd been fired. His baby sister came around her desk and extended her arms for their customary hug. "Are you okay?" she asked. "I'm worried about you."

"You mean since the last time you asked me on the phone thirty minutes ago?"

"Don't be a jerk. And yes, since the last time I asked."

"I'm good. They fired me. I expected it."

"So much for standing by their man."

"It's business. Some things we might be able to spin. This one? It's a big ask."

"I know you loved this work, though."

Given their history? Yeah, he did.

"It'll blow over and I'll find something else. Something similar. Will assured me you wouldn't be affected." He backed away, held her at arm's length. "And don't think you're going to do some crazy-assed form of protest and quit.

This has nothing to do with you. Stay focused. Now what's with the boxes?"

"Jack Hill quit last night."

Holy shit. Major doings around here. First the CFO leaves and now Jay gets dumped. "Seems Will has been busy. What happened with Jack?"

Sam shook her head. "I have no idea. I guess he quit and it got heated, so the big shots decided it would be better if he just left."

"Did he call you?"

"Not a peep."

"Is that odd?"

She shrugged. "He always kept his distance, but the whole thing still seems odd. None of it makes sense. Even if he wasn't the type to socialize or make small talk, normally, you get a sense when someone is unhappy at work. Which makes me think they gave him an option to quit or be terminated. Either way," she waved a hand, "they asked me to box up his office and no one is to take any calls from him. Or call him. I'm waiting for Will to get all that stuff out of here."

Behind them, her desk phone rang. She ignored it, but the acid in his stomach reminded him of his frayed nerves. "I'm gonna let you get back to it. But, hey, I'm only three hours away now. Maybe I'll see you this weekend?"

"I'd love that. We could meet somewhere. Maybe in Asheville."

He nodded. "I'll call you tomorrow. Be careful." He pointed at the boxes. "Don't break a leg tripping on all that crap."

"For the love of God."

Maggie hit the brakes on her cruiser and stared out at

the mounting traffic jam on Main Street. Pedestrians stood on the sidewalks, apparently dumbstruck by the snarl of bumper-to-bumper cars. Jam? Forget that. This was a dead stop. One further mired by the inability of her residents to give in and back up so traffic could clear.

Last time this happened, it was caused by two of the elders taking to the street in protest of new streetlamps. Taxes were high enough, they'd said.

This wasn't streetlamps, though. The news van three vehicles ahead told her that much. Dammit.

Vacation: T-minus three days, five hours, and twenty-five minutes.

She jumped on her radio. "Dispatch, do we have a problem on Main?"

"Aside from all the reporters?" Joelle's snarky voice shot back. "No, ma'am. Appears the world has discovered Jayson Tucker is here. Locals have lost their minds over at the B."

"Terrific," Maggie muttered.

The car in front of her inched forward enough for her to hook a U-turn. She'd take the side streets to her office and walk back to clear the mess on Main.

Unbelievable.

She pulled into her reserved space in front of the sheriff's office, tucked her car keys in her pocket, and hoofed it to the middle of Main Street, where bulky news vans monopolized every available space.

"Maggie!" Mr. Trambly said from in front of the B. "Shit's gonna get wild if you don't clear this out."

No kidding there. "I'm on it."

She approached the closest news van double-parked behind other vehicles. A young guy with short, reddish hair sat behind the wheel, one arm propped in the open window frame.

Maggie kept her hands at her sides. No folded arms or pissy look. This would take finesse. "Hello."

"Hi," the guy said.

"I'm Sheriff Kingston."

The guy had the balls to check her out from head to toe, then smiled like she'd want to do him in the back of the van. Men.

Still, she matched his smile. "I'll need you to get this van off the street. You're blocking traffic and with the fire department just around the corner, it's a safety hazard."

"Um," the kid said. "We're trying to get an interview with Tuck's agent."

"That's fine. But you need to get this vehicle off my street. Pronto. Before I start writing tickets."

Assuming the kid got her message, she moved to the next news van. On her way, she glanced over at the Murchison building and found Grif standing in the window. Just staring out at the street like he had nothing better to do. Well, that was about to change. His client had caused this chaos. He'd help her fix it.

She whipped out her cell and punched him up.

"Hey," he said.

"What are you doing about this?"

"Me?"

"Yes, you. The kid from CBS wants an interview with you. Get out here and give it to him. Or let him in. I don't care. I need these reporters off the street."

"They don't want me, they want Tuck. They're trying to get to him through me."

"So your plan is to ignore them while they turn our town into a circus? Pardon me for judging, but that plan sucks."

Her comment was met with silence. Pissed-off Grif or

thinking Grif? At this point, she didn't give a rat's patootie as long as he got those damned reporters off the street.

"Hey, dumb-ass!"

Maggie whipped around to see Mr. Jacoby screaming at one of the news vans from the front seat of his pickup.

"I'm fixing to get to the hardware store. Move it before I come up there and move it for you!"

"Crap," Maggie muttered into the phone.

"What?"

"I gotta go. Mr. Jacoby just threatened one of the news-people. Grif, you need to do something about these reporters."

"Like what? Take them up to the Hill? Lead them straight to him? So much for hiding."

Maggie gritted her teeth. She loved her Steele cousins, but they were a stubborn bunch. "Of course not. Do a press conference or something. Obviously, they know he's here. Somewhere. And they're probably not going away until they get a sound bite or two. You don't have to tell them where Jayson is, but give them something and send them on their way."

Mr. Jacoby exited his vehicle. *Oh, no you don't.* A former boxer, the sixty-five year-old Mr. Jacoby had no issues getting into a street brawl. Heaven knew he'd spent a night or two in Maggie's temporary holding cell for mixing it up with tourists.

"Mr. Jacoby"—she pointed at his truck— "get back in your vehicle. *Right* now."

"Sheriff! What are you standing around for while these assholes muck up traffic?"

From the other end of the phone line, Grif sighed. "I heard that. All right. I'll call the fire chief and let him know we'll need their community room for a press conference.

Give me thirty minutes to give the chief a heads-up and to figure out what the fuck that press conference will be about. I hate press conferences. I'm the behind-the-scenes guy."

"Not anymore, cuz. Mr. Jacoby! I'm taking care of it as we speak. Now get *back* in your vehicle before I arrest you."

Clearly getting the message, he threw his hands up and stomped back to his truck.

Good. Last thing she needed was him causing a ruckus with a bunch of reporters and cameramen milling about.

Welcome to Jayson Tucker being in town. If this continued, she'd be blowing up her budget with temporary officers to keep the peace.

And more than likely not going on vacation. In three days, five hours, and twelve minutes.

Ten miles outside of town, Mozart was overpowered by the ring of Jay's phone via the car speaker. The god of phone-silence had just sent him a solid thirty minutes of peace while the sun's rays and quiet mountain roads settled his mind. For the first time in days, his thoughts weren't taking him five steps ahead, obsessing over the future. Or ruminating over the past.

This might be what all the Zen folks of the world preached about.

Huh. Who knew?

The phone rang again. Grif.

As much as he'd like everyone to leave him alone for a damned minute, ignoring the man trying to find him a job wouldn't cut it. He tapped the steering wheel. "Hey."

"Where are you?"

"On my way back. Another ten miles. You need me?"

"No, but bypass Main Street on your way back to Tupelo Hill."

This didn't sound good. "All right. Want to tell me why?"

"Press everywhere."

So much for living in the moment. He'd known it would eventually happen. A scandal like his was raw meat to hungry media lions. "I'll call Pam, see what she suggests."

Pam, the wonder PR girl, had been dealing with drafting and releasing a few press statements since this mess began. She'd advised him to keep his mouth shut and not feed the beast, which he'd gladly done.

"I'm on it already," Grif said. "Maggie is about to take my head off. Main Street looks like a goddamned parking lot. I'm doing a press conference at the fire station. They have the space."

Hold tight here. "You're—" Jayson shook his head. What the hell was happening? "What's the press conference about?"

"I have no fucking idea."

At that Jayson laughed. He knew the feeling. But his agent talking to the press wouldn't take care of the problem. "Settle down, Ace. They want me. And if they came for me, they're not leaving without a statement."

"The point of you being here is to keep you out of the public eye."

"Well, yeah, but I think you'd agree that horse has left the barn. Clearly, someone in town tipped them off because they know I'm here. Let's deal with them and maybe they'll go."

Which could only score him points with the hot sheriff.

"When is this press conference?" Jay asked.

"Twenty minutes."

Twenty... *Holy shit.* His agent didn't fool around. In the

last fifteen years, Jay had answered thousands of press inquiries. Most of those answers unprepared and straight from the hip. Now? No way. Given the precarious public situation, and possible career-ending implications, this wouldn't be a good time to wing a press briefing. Someone needed to draft a statement for him.

And fast.

"I have to find Pam. I'll meet you at the fire station."

4

PAM—PR WHIZ, SPIN DOCTOR EXTRAORDINAIRE—WAS IN A meeting. Wasn't that always the way?

Jay swung his Range Rover into the fire station parking lot, where a line of news vans with clunky satellite equipment rising from their roofs cluttered the area. Shit, that was a lot of press.

A few seconds of panic gripped him before he spotted Maggie talking to a guy near the station's side door. His hair was dirty blond and he wore navy pants and a blue T-shirt. Firefighter, no doubt. A couple inches taller than Maggie, he stood with his shoulders pushed back, his confidence sparking like a downed wire. Nothing about their body language said intimate, but there was something there. A knowing that pinged Jay's chest.

He might have to ask Grif—or Reid—about this guy.

As the guy talked, he pointed to a hand-written sign on the door proclaiming Press Entrance.

Talk about grass roots. Totally free-balling this one. Jay cruised by Maggie and threw out a wave on his way to the only open parking on the grass.

Packed house. And him unable to contact his PR person, not that there was enough time for her to do much at this point, anyway.

Jesus. This week kept topping itself.

He flipped his visor down, checked his look. At least he had the suit on.

In his rearview, Maggie approached. Not ready to be seen by anyone hanging by the door hoping for the jump on him, he rolled the window down.

Her rubber-soled boots crunched over gravel, the sound getting louder, reminding him he wasn't in the Knights' pressroom with their PR folks standing by.

Maggie appeared in his window and the scent of her soap, something light and musky, made him think of sex and skin and touching her, despite her buttoned-up demeanor. She leaned in, bending over a bit to see inside the car, her pretty eyes focused.

Shaking off the X-rated thoughts, he faced her. "Maggie, I'm sorry."

"As if it's your fault? I should have anticipated it. But . . ." She scanned the parking lot. "Wow. You draw a crowd."

He snorted. "Everyone inside?"

"Yeah. We've checked everyone's credentials. I was hoping to have Blaine, one of my deputies, posted outside the door during the press conference, but we just got a call and I sent him to check it out. I'll stand inside and if anyone new comes in, I'll screen them. I also just heard from one of my other deputies. Main Street is finally clear. Are you ready? I'll walk you in." She smiled. "Play the muscle."

A vision of his mother bearing down on him flashed and his breath caught.

Maggie's eyebrows arched, wrinkling the skin on her forehead. "Whoa, cowboy. It was a joke."

"What?"

"Playing the muscle. It was a joke. This crowd is ornery, but I checked their credentials and talked to all of them going in. They'll be civil."

"It's..." What? How would he explain this? The big bad football star scared of the media? "No," he said. "It's not them."

Damned Marlene. Her fists might not pummel him anymore, but she still rattled him. "It's..." He waved it off. "Nothing."

"Okay." She glanced at the door. "Do you need a second? Is your statement ready?"

He slipped from the car and snagged his jacket from the back, sliding it on and adjusting the cuffs, all under Maggie's watchful eye. At six foot four he had a good six inches on her and peered down, taking in her deep brown eyes and the tiny crease between her brows he itched to smooth away. Which brought his mind to her curling into him and tucking her head under his chin. These thoughts. Not good. It might have been the eighty-degree day, but the heat storming between them couldn't be denied.

"My PR guru is MIA. I'm on my own. How do I look?"

Gaze glued to his, a small smile played on her lips. "I think you know how you look. You'll have them eating out of your hands. But are you sure you want to wing this?"

"I'm a big boy," he said. And, man, that sounded like a seriously bad come-on. One that shattered the amazing energy between them. He should have kept his damned mouth shut.

He winced. "Did that sound as bad as I thought?"

She lifted her hand and—*please let her touch me*—poked his chest. Not exactly the touch he was hoping for, but...

"Relax. *Big* boy. It wasn't as if you'd commented on the size of your feet."

He barked out a laugh. God, that felt good. Twice today, Maggie had made him laugh. And it wasn't the sarcastic, resigned one he'd perfected.

"Thank you."

"For what?"

"For being the only person to make me laugh in days."

"Eh. I do what I can. We need to get in there before someone spots you. What are your thoughts about your statement?"

He shut the car door and hit the lock. "Trying something new."

"What's that?"

"I'm gonna be myself. Just answer the damned questions and try not to totally blow it."

JAYSON TUCKER. SMOOTH, CHARMING, HANDSOME. HE SAT front and center at a folding table, complete with the Triple B borrowed tablecloth Grif insisted on. Grif, always worrying about the details.

Jayson—seemingly unfazed by the microphone and crowd—fielded rapid-fire questions while Maggie stood to his right conjuring images of him doing naughty things to her. Oh, these thoughts. So not good when she was supposed to be protecting him. But, hello? She had needs.

And 20/20 vision.

Forget the lust and do your job.

She scanned the room, sweeping back and forth a few times. So far, everyone had behaved.

"Tuck." An older man held up a pen. "What about anger management? Are you checking yourself in?"

Anger management. For throwing one punch. If every person she encountered throwing a punch was shipped off to anger management, there'd be one heck of a shortage on counselors. Mr. Jacoby would be a full-time resident.

"Guys," Jay said. "I'm not minimizing what happened. No one should ever behave the way I did. Let's keep it in perspective. It was one incident. I'm not perfect. I get mad."

By now, thirty minutes in, Maggie would have lost all patience. Her mind would be blown, and yet, he answered every question, no matter how insulting or personal, in a calm, direct manner. Another vision of him—naked this time—flashed and she peeled her gaze away. All that charm. Too damned distracting.

"No anger management, then?"

"Next question," Grif said from his spot on the side wall near the door.

A platinum blonde with too much makeup waved a notepad. "Rumor has it Dallas is interested. Have they made an offer?"

"I can't discuss that. Sorry."

"Have there been any offers?"

Jay laughed. "Believe me, when a decision has been made about my future, you'll be the first to know. Next question."

A slew of questions sent the noise level skyrocketing and Jayson pointed to a man in the back. "Joe, let's hear it."

"Thank you," the reporter said. "Have you heard from Eric Webb? Is he pressing charges?"

"I haven't heard from him. On any matters."

The entrance door came open and a woman with stringy dark hair entered. She wore jeans, leather boots, and a blue sweater topped off with a baggy jacket.

Jacket.

On an unusually warm day.

Jayson answered another question that Maggie had missed, but he must have nailed it because the room broke out in laughter. The man was good.

She scanned the crowd again, bringing her attention back to the woman at the door. Every female in the room was either a reporter or a camera operator. The reporters were dressed for television in suits or dresses or some form of business attire. The camera operators dressed more casually, their appearance similar to the woman at the door. Only she was missing one thing.

A camera.

Maggie tilted her head. Someone's assistant, perhaps.

If so, why would she still be at the door and not finding her coworkers?

Time to check her out.

Maggie pushed off the wall and strode toward the woman, her movements direct, but not aggressive. The woman, without a doubt, spotted her and shifted left, refusing to make eye contact.

Uncomfortable.

Another reporter called out a question. Something about how many more years Jayson hoped to play. Once again, the sound of his voice registered, but Maggie didn't catch the words. Her focus was on the woman, who saw Maggie bearing down. She took two steps before Maggie caught up and casually herded her toward the wall, away from the crowd.

"Hello," Maggie said. "Are you looking for someone?"

"I..." Eye shift. "Um..." Another shift. "Yes."

Whoever this woman was, she tripped every one of Maggie's tension meters. "Which station are you with?"

She peered over Maggie's shoulder. To Jayson.

Maggie shifted right, blocking the woman's view. "Stay with me here. What station are you with?"

The woman's lips pinched and she angled left—now she wanted to be a PITA?—where she gazed at Jay with an odd mix of desire and...

Don't know.

The woman met Maggie's gaze again and Maggie homed in on sea-green eyes that glowed. A hard, vicious glow that came with crackheads and junkies bent on causing trouble.

Whoa.

Maggie moved sideways so she could keep her eye on the room, the odd woman, and Jayson. She held her arm out, gesturing to the door the woman had entered through. "Let's move outside and talk."

The woman's gaze shifted to Jayson, still doing his thing with the reporters, then back to Maggie.

"I can't," she said. "I have to watch him."

Him.

She bobbed her head, then slid sideways, moving closer to the crowd. The last damned thing Maggie wanted.

Get her out. Too many options existed for what this woman might be doing here. Until Maggie ascertained whether this was a television station employee, an innocent —albeit creepy—fan, or a psycho stalker, Maggie couldn't chance it. Better to clear her and risk the wrath of a news network than have a situation.

"Please step outside," Maggie said. "Everyone in this room has had a credential check. I'll need to do that with you and I don't want to interrupt the press conference."

Come on. Get outside.

AGAIN THE WOMAN'S EYES SHIFTED. THIS TIME TO THE CROWD.

Then to Jayson. And Grif. Who was on the move, walking toward them. Inevitable, considering his vantage point and his view of the room.

When the woman's shoulders flew back, Maggie put her hand up, halting Grif mid-stride. His presence put their visitor on edge, made her squirrelly.

Maggie didn't like it.

The woman reminded her of a guy she'd arrested six months ago. He'd been passing through and squatted in an empty house just outside of town. One of the neighbors spotted him and called it in. Maggie figured he was a homeless guy looking for shelter on a stormy night and when she questioned him, his ping-ponging gaze indicated his nerves coming apart. His panic didn't come until she'd gotten the first cuff on him. That's when the fun started and he went batshit crazy, taking a swing at her and connecting with her right eye. Before he could run, she'd trained her service weapon on him and brought about a change in his attitude. Imagine that.

The pain of her battered eye hadn't been so bad. The humiliation? Way worse. Days of swelling and bruising served as a constant reminder.

Enough so that Maggie, refusing to accept vulnerability, started Krav Maga lessons with Reid.

Lessons that might pay off if this woman turned crazy on her.

Maggie jerked her head toward the door. "Outside."

Seeming to comply, the woman took a few steps, then whirled back, raising her right hand.

Knife!

At the sight of the six-inch kitchen knife, Maggie's mind exploded. *Weapon, hands, feet.* Instinct urged her to rip her weapon from the holster. *Too close.* By the time she got the gun out, her suspect could plunge the knife into her.

"Mags!" Grif said, his hushed voice smothered by Jayson's answer to a question.

Jayson must have unleashed his charm again, sending the room into a burst of laughter. Maggie kept her back to the room and her eyes on the knife pointed at her. She snapped her right hand out and locked her fingers around the woman's hand, squeezing the knuckles and thumb. With her free hand, Maggie caught the wrist at the pivot point, bending the woman's hand back. The attacker's face twisted.

Maggie applied more pressure and the woman loosened her grip on the knife.

"Drop it."

Nothing. Dammit. *More pressure.* She bent the hand farther back, pressing it to an angle that shouldn't even be possible without snapping it. Their eyes locked, the challenge evident in those creepy, glowing eyes.

She might be high.

What a nightmare.

"Come on, guys," Jayson said. "I can't believe you haven't asked about my endorsements yet. Let's do it and get it done."

Good man.

The reporters shouted questions while Jayson did his thing, keeping all eyes on him. All they needed was the attention of one reporter on Maggie. That would lead to another and another and soon they'd all forget about superstar Jayson and tromp on over to the crazy woman holding a knife on the sheriff.

As Maggie's brother, Way, would say, Jesus Hotel Christ.

Add that to Jayson's recent media frenzy and this episode

might put Steele Ridge on every evening news segment on the East Coast.

Maggie didn't have the staff for the attention that would bring.

She pushed harder, increasing the pressure until the woman's hand should have popped right off.

Give the girl credit for toughness. Finally, she blinked. Scrunched her nose and bowed back, releasing her grip enough for Maggie to let go. The knife clattered to the floor while Jayson upped his game, saying something that resulted in another eruption of laughter.

Maggie spun the woman around, kicked the knife out the door, and shoved her into the streaming sunlight.

"Hands against the wall. Now."

The woman put her hands up, placed them against the side of the building and Maggie stepped up behind her to pat her down. "Do you have anything in your pockets that can hurt me? Needles?"

The woman didn't answer. Excellent. Leave it to Maggie to arrest a mute.

Grif appeared in the doorway, his jaw tight, but otherwise looking Grif smooth. "People are noticing. What do you need?"

"Shut that door and keep everyone inside."

"I warned him," the woman finally said.

"What?" This from Grif.

"Grif," Maggie said. "Inside. Please. If those reporters come out here, we've got a bigger problem."

Her cousin never did like being ordered around, but he, of all people, understood the situation. He turned away, shutting the door behind him.

The woman rested her head against the wall. "He should have just gone away. Left Eric alone."

Maggie Mirandized the woman while carefully patting her down, checking the pockets of her coat and jeans, searching for any more possible weapons she'd yank from under that jacket. Damn. She'd known that seemed off.

She finished her pat down, finding nothing exciting or threatening. The sole discovery was thirty-three cents from the right pocket of the coat. "What's your name?"

"I don't have to tell you."

"I'm still arresting you. Eventually, you'll have to give me your name."

"I want a lawyer. I get a phone call."

"You sure do. When I get you processed, you can make your call."

"I warned him," she said again. "He's so fucking selfish. He should have just gone away."

Oh, boy.

Maggie handcuffed the woman and led her to the cruiser. Jayson Tucker was in residence less than three days and they already had bedlam on Main Street and a deranged fan.

Amazing the havoc one hot football player could create. And something told her this was just the beginning.

5

AFTER THE SHIT-SHOW PRESS CONFERENCE, JAYSON, MAGGIE, and Grif huddled up in Grif's office to get everyone updated on the woman who'd pulled the knife. Grif sat at his desk with Jayson in one of the guest chairs. Maggie had yet to sit. She'd marched in and gone straight to the window, where she continued to check traffic on Main Street by peeping through the lowered blinds. More than likely making sure the news vans didn't blockade her town again.

And this was supposed to be a quiet stay. Jay should have known better.

He shifted in his seat to face Maggie. "Where is this nutcase now?"

"On her way to the county lockup. She'll be arraigned tomorrow."

"Do we know who she is?"

Maggie didn't bother checking her notepad. Nor did she peel her gaze from the window. "Ariel Bowman. Twenty-four years old. Lives in Brooklyn. Do you know her?"

"No."

Finally, she gave up on the window and looked at him. "She certainly knows you."

Not unusual considering he couldn't take a dump without media coverage.

She peered through the blinds again, watching for a few seconds before bringing her attention back. "The street is clear. Not a news van in sight. You must have satisfied them."

"For today, at least," Grif added.

Maggie abandoned the window and stood behind the empty guest chair, resting both hands on the back, her long fingers curving over the cushion. Her neatly trimmed and unpainted nails grabbed his attention. Most of the women in his orbit kept weekly manicure appointments. His last girlfriend went for a fill, whatever the hell that was, every ten days. Without fail. Somehow, he didn't think Maggie messed with fills.

She drummed her fingers against the cushion. "I'd like to connect with your security people. I believe she's the woman you told me about yesterday."

"The one who wanted to carve me up?"

"Yes. Your run-of-the-mill hater could have put a knife through you. Or me."

Touché. If she'd wanted to prove he'd become too casual about wackos, she'd succeeded. Jay ran his hands over his face. Jesus. He'd almost gotten her hurt. Or worse. He dropped his hands, let them rest on his legs. "Maggie, I'm sorry. I didn't—" He stopped talking. Anything he said right now wouldn't matter.

"Unless you put the knife in her hand, it's not your fault. The problem is, I don't know how many like her are running around our town." She turned to Grif. "You know we don't have the staff for this."

That, Jay could fix. Money he had. "I'll hire people. I

don't want anyone getting hurt. I'll move out of Tupelo Hill and rent a place on my own. Or better yet, go back to New York."

Grif shook his head. "Not happening. New York will be ten times worse. Down here, not everyone knows you. Up there you'll be hounded day and night."

"I can't put your mom in danger. I won't have that."

"Of course not. I'd never put my mother in harm's way. The safest place is Tupelo Hill. With all the training equipment and ammunition Reid keeps there, the entire property is a fortress. To be safe, you'll hire extra security people. If Reid wants to bring in his own people, you'll cover the cost." He looked back at Maggie. "Can we get temporary help from the state police?"

"Sure, but it's not in my budget."

"I'll cover it," Jay said.

Maggie narrowed her eyes as she considered it. "I'll see what we can do and get you cost estimates."

"It doesn't matter."

"Well, isn't that my dream come true?" She let out a long sigh that sent his mind places she probably hadn't intended. At least not at the moment. What the hell was wrong with him, thinking these thoughts when he'd caused this mess?

"All right," she said, "we're good for now and I need to get back."

She strode to the door, not bothering with a glance their way.

Maggie was pissed. At him? Or the situation? His presence caused a major disruption in her town and had almost gotten her attacked.

Once she was out the door, Grif picked up a folder. "I had two more calls today."

Grif wanted to talk football. Now? When Jay had groveling to do? He pushed out of his chair. "Hang on."

A conversation with Maggie needed to be had. To... what? Plead his case? Good luck there. This thing was a hot-ass mess.

He headed out the door and jogged down the hall after her. She'd already made her way through the building exit to falling darkness and streetlamps illuminating the sidewalk. By the time he got outside, Maggie had just stepped off the curb.

"Maggie, hold up."

She paused under the glare of the streetlamp and slowly eased her shoulders back. Confrontation ready. He must have seriously pissed her off. *Good work, Ace.* He'd fix that. She turned just as he reached her car door.

"Hey," he said, "can we talk?"

When she didn't respond, he took that as a green light. Of course he did. One thing about Marlene Tucker, she'd taught him how to capitalize on situations. Besides, by now Maggie could have hopped into the cruiser and taken off. Which she didn't.

"I'm sorry," he said. "My crazy life put you in danger. You have no idea how much I hate that. And, let's be honest, I like you. You're funny and smart and, well, you carry a big gun. I'd rather you not be mad at me."

She shook her head, but the smile tugging at her lips couldn't be denied. Score one for the jock. He pointed to the corner of her mouth. "I think you're smiling."

Pushing his luck—what the hell?—he inched his hand closer. Close enough that the tip of his finger brushed the insanely soft skin at the corner of her mouth and he wanted...Jesus, he wanted his lips there. Right at that spot.

She wrapped her hand around his finger and—wow—if

she'd wanted to get his mind out of the gutter that wasn't the way to do it.

"That woman," she said, still holding his finger, "is stone-cold nuts. None of this is your fault."

"Then why are you mad at me?"

Finally, she let go of him. "I'm not."

"Yeah, you are."

"You don't even know me. How would you know if I'm mad or not?"

He'd spent half his life surrounded by amped-up football players. More than anything, he recognized when people were pissed. "I've spent a career working in a team environment. Learning people's signals and moods. You're right, I don't know you, but I know when someone is angry. At least talk to me. Not that you owe it to me after today, but —" Damn. He shook his head. How to say this without sounding like a douche?

"But what?"

"Nothing."

Which, of course, was total bullshit. It was definitely something. Something that began with him looking at Maggie and liking it more and more. He met her gaze and inched close enough to hook his finger into her belt loop, pull her forward and ...

He dipped his head, studied the slope of her top lip and the air stopped moving. Everything froze. Including his lungs.

"I..." She peered down at her feet, dug the toe of her boot into the ground, then rocked back.

He took a hard inhale, held it until his chest slammed, and blew it out. Lord, he felt like a middle-schooler trying to steal his first kiss. "You what?"

She lifted her chin and the street lamp shined in her

lush brown eyes and he was gone. Totally smitten with this beautiful, strong woman so unlike the soft-spoken females he went for. The ones who let him call the shots.

Maggie, Maggie, Maggie, what are you doing to me?

"I got distracted," she said. "During the press conference."

"There was a lot going on."

"That doesn't matter. I had a job to do."

"Maggie—"

She squeezed her eyes closed, jabbed her open palms at him. "Shut up."

Whoa. Shut up? "I'm trying to—"

"My lack of attention could have gotten you hurt." She pressed the fingers of both hands into her forehead. "I've been shredding myself over this, thinking about all the things I did wrong, every second I could have done something differently and yet," she dropped her hands "I stand here, looking at you and thinking, 'Gee, I'd bet he looks mighty tasty fresh out of a shower.' How stupid can I be? That's what I'm pissed about. It has to stop."

Not one to let a grade A opportunity pass him by, Jay tipped his head closer. "If you're thinking those thoughts, I don't want it to stop. In fact, I'd throw myself off the top of this building to make it *not* stop."

She gawked at him. Literally stood there, mouth agape, and instinct kicked in. "Honey," he whispered, "if you want me, I'm all yours."

Something in the air changed and a charge big enough to light the town whipped between them. She gripped his shirt, squeezing the fabric and yanking him the last inch toward her, slamming her lips against his. *Well, all right.*

He slid his hand to her hip, the one without the gun—he was no dummy—and pulled her close, forcing himself not to drive his tongue into her mouth. This was her doing, he'd let her control it, but damn, she'd surprised him. In a stupendous, *little man hardening*, and totally ready for a body slam kind of way.

One thing was for sure, Maggie Kingston knew how to kiss a man.

WHAT THE *HELL* WAS SHE DOING?

Kissing the hot football star. That's what.

In the middle of Main Street.

Holy crap.

Stressful day. That's all. Stress and her need to connect, to be touched by safe hands rather than one holding a weapon.

And, well, how often does one Jayson Tucker come to town and *want* her kissing him?

But in the middle of Main Street? Really, Maggie? *Really?* She broke away, nearly leaped back and did a quick scan of the street to see exactly who saw her amazing display of mauling. Across the street, a couple wandered toward the Triple B. One thing about small towns, the sidewalks shut down early. Lucky for her.

The B, though.

The place might be loaded with town criers ready to spread the news about Sheriff Kingston and the football star. Total humiliation.

She couldn't worry about it now. She had to figure out what to say that might salvage even a speck of professionalism. She'd already failed once by allowing an unstable woman with a weapon near him.

Buck up, Mags. "That kiss," she said, "amazeballs."

No sense in denying it. The way he'd jumped right into the fray indicated he didn't exactly hate it.

He hit her with a flashing smile that had probably incinerated any number of women's panties. "Can we try again? I mean, you kinda shocked me there. I *know* I can do better."

Oh, this one was dangerous. Too good. He'd simultaneously relieved her of any weirdness *and* asked for a replay. Brilliant. "You seem to be forgetting I'm the sheriff and swapping spit with a superstar in public won't make my residents very happy."

"But will it make *you* happy?"

As if that mattered. "I'm an elected official. Nobody cares about my feelings. My job is to make everyone else happy."

"Then your job is impossible. I've had my performance reviewed by every media outlet in the tristate area. Not that I'm comparing sports to law enforcement, but I get it. People constantly judging you, not giving a shit if you're functioning with a 103-degree fever or a banged-up back. Nobody cares when you have a responsibility to the public."

She waved her arm. "This town, the people in it, are my responsibility. I blew it today."

"By disarming a psycho with a knife? Honey, if that's your idea of blowing it, your standards are unreasonably high."

Gah. Jayson Tucker might be working her last nerve. And wasn't this interesting? The athlete who held the record for most passing yards in a season, enlightening her on standards. Some would consider it ironic. Maggie wasn't sure what she considered it. "Everyone in that room was in danger and I didn't know it."

"How could you?"

"Jayson! *That's* the problem. I should have known. I *should* have had *two* deputies—not just one—helping me do bag checks and had people remove everything from their pockets. I didn't do that. All I did was check credentials. I knew something was off when she walked in wearing that coat, but I was slow to act. As a result, I put everyone, including you, in danger."

"When did you have time to set all that up? You didn't and still handled the situation. You got the knife out of her hands and removed her. As far as I'm concerned, you did what you were supposed to."

She locked her jaw to keep her frustration from spilling out and stared up at the darkening sky. He didn't get it and maybe never would. Clearly, she'd done a crappy job of explaining it. She inhaled through her nose and counted to three. *One more try.*

"And what about tomorrow? What if the knife-wielding psycho gets released on bond? Or what about the other crackpots out there who want to make a name for themselves? Going forward, when it comes to your safety, and the safety of the people in this town, we need to make changes. I'm not pissed"—God, how could she even admit this? —"because of the psycho with the knife. That's on her. This is not New York, where you can lock yourself away in your secure building. This is Steele Ridge and these folks depend on me. I let them down today."

There, she'd said it. Laid it right out for him. Go-to Maggie had failed. Epically.

He continued to stare at her like she'd grown a second head. "Wow. I thought I was tough on myself. You're downright brutal."

Whatever. When it came to people's safety, including his, brutality was necessary. "Maybe so, but I need you to not disregard any threat and pass every one of them along. After today, staring at the knife in her hand, I'm not risking another situation like that. I don't care how run-of-the-mill you think it is. For me, for us, in Steele Ridge, none of this is normal. We're way outside our comfort zone."

In short, she didn't know what the hell she was doing—personally or professionally—when it came to Jayson Tucker.

He held up his hands. "You're right. I'm sorry. I guess I'm used to the kooks. I figured being down here, I could lie low and I got lazy about having security with me. How about I set up a call with my people. I'll have them walk through everything with you. Even the ones they think aren't real threats."

Whether he finally understood or was simply humoring her, he'd said exactly what she'd wanted. "Yes. That would help. I can't protect you if I don't know what might be coming our way."

"Understood."

"Good. Thank you."

"You're welcome." He hit her with another devastating smile. "Can we make out more?"

Maggie laughed. *Men.* "Not on the street."

"Interesting. You're not saying no. Just not on the street."

True that. She pulled the cruiser door open. "Who said jocks weren't smart?"

An hour later and still in her uniform, Maggie hopped out of her Explorer and ran to the front door of her childhood home.

After the chat and amazeballs kiss with Jayson, she'd barely gotten here on time. If she knew her father, dinner would be ready to roll at seven sharp. They'd been told to be there at six so they could do their normal family updates and, well, Jayson. Her entire afternoon had revolved around him. After making a spectacle of herself on Main Street, she'd gone back to the office to clean up some e-mail and before she knew it, she was late for family night.

She swung through the front door and the sound of her brothers' voices from the kitchen drew her down the hallway where Mom and Dad's border collie, Nicksie, met her. Maggie's parents—bless their hearts—had a thing about naming their children, including the dog, after their favorite singers. Thus, Stevie Nicks was a regular part of life in the Kingston household. Nicksie cocked her head and waited. She knew this game. If she did it right, there'd be a treat in it for her.

"Ooh, you're a good girl." Maggie squatted. "Go!"

Nicksie charged, stopping just short of Maggie before lifting her paw for a high five.

"You're late," Shep said.

Lacking a filter, her youngest brother never hesitated to point out the obvious.

"The hot football player must be distracting her." This from her sister, Riley, who was also no slouch in pointing out the obvious.

Riley may have been a smart-ass, but she nailed it.

Nicksie in tow, Maggie entered the kitchen where her siblings gathered around the table. Puck, Shep's always observant golden retriever, hopped to his feet, already anticipating a treat being thrown his way. These dogs. So darned smart. Maggie moved to the cabinet near the sink and grabbed a couple of treats, tossing them to the already sitting dogs.

"Ry," Maggie said, "you're not blind. What woman wouldn't be distracted?"

"I know I am." Mom's voice carried from the mudroom

and everyone laughed. A second later, Mom appeared in the doorway. She wore loose khakis and a cashmere sweater with a pair of black flats and Maggie marveled at her mother's ability to make casual clothes so elegant.

Recently retired, Mom's transition from the corporate world to housewife hadn't been as smooth as everyone hoped. As an environmental engineer, Mom had climbed the ladder at a major oil company. As a result, she'd become used to managing thousands of people and expecting her word to be gospel. As a retiree dealing with her husband and grown children, she'd had to adjust to life as a peon like the rest of them.

"Where's Dad?"

"Outside," Mom said. "He has ribs in the smoker. He's feeling confident about tonight."

Maggie glanced at Riley. "Thank you for your help before."

"Sure."

After her day had gone to hell and knowing she didn't have time to stop home, Maggie had called Riley and asked her to stop by her house and pick up her contribution to dinner.

Contender was more like it.

Food in this house was a pure and potent thing. Her father, from a young age, loved to cook. Dissatisfied with the vegetables he'd find at the market, he'd started his own organic farm right on their property. As kids, they'd sit around and moan when he'd ramble on about taking chicken from a basic meal to a feast.

So much so that every person in the house learned to cook. And be competitive about it. Except Mom. Lord, she was god-awful in the kitchen. In secret, Cash swore she might be trying to kill them all. Still, they loved how hard she tried and encouraged her by choking down whatever disaster she came up with.

"He's not beating my bread tonight," Shep said. "I'm locked in."

Confidence. Good for him. "We'll see," Maggie said. "My sweet potatoes will be tough to beat. There's enough brown sugar that it could qualify as a dessert."

"Yay," Riley said.

The back door came open and Dad pushed through wearing his Kiss the Cook apron. His normally combed dark hair, more salt than pepper these days, hung over his forehead in a messy windblown look.

He walked straight to her and pecked her cheek. "Hello, favorite older daughter."

Riley rolled her eyes. When they were kids and Dad played Mr. Mom—before it was cool—he'd refer to Riley as his favorite younger daughter. He'd figured out how to not play favorites while making each of his daughters feel special.

Something she'd always love him for. "Hi, Dad."

He perused the various food items on the counter. "Looks good. Who was brave with Brussels sprouts?"

Cash pounded a fist against his chest. "That's me. I'm not afraid of this bunch. I threw bacon in there."

Bacon. Great. And she thought she'd been slick with the sugar overload. "That's so wrong, Cash. You know we love bacon."

"Look who's complaining? *You* brought potatoes that double as dessert."

Dad laughed and moved to the sink to wash his hands. "How was work today?"

As usual, the question was directed to the room at large.

Considering Maggie had faced down a knife-wielding crackpot, she'd let her siblings carry this conversation.

Cash met her eye and she shook her head. He'd left the fire station before the incident, but he'd called to check on her and informed her that half of Steele Ridge was already in the know.

Dad looked at each of them and when no one volunteered, he went straight to Maggie. "How was your day?"

Of course, he'd singled her out. "Typical day," she said, hoping to sound casual.

Shep, still sitting at the kitchen table, tipped his head up at Maggie. "I heard someone tried to kill Jayson Tucker at some press conference."

Mom whirled from the cabinet where she dug out a platter for the ribs. "What?"

Still drying his hands, Dad focused on her. "Mags?"

Ooh, she hated when he gave her the stern-dad look. Even as an adult she couldn't stand the pressure. Sensing the thickness in the air, or maybe it was Maggie's growing anxiety, Cash cleared his throat. Maggie gave him the wide-eyed, help-me stare.

"Dad," he said, "how are those ribs doing?"

Dad ignored him, keeping his gaze firmly on Maggie. "What happened?"

"Relax. Shep is misinformed. No one tried to kill Jayson."

"No," Shep said, "I stopped in town on my way over here and I heard some maniac walked in there with a knife."

In general, they all tried to cut Shep some slack when it came to his bluntness, but this was pushing the boundaries of sibling devotion.

"A knife," Mom said. "My God. Is everyone all right?"

Finally, Maggie gritted her teeth at Shep. Maybe that would get him to shut the hell up. "Everyone is fine."

"So," Riley said, "was there a knife or not?"

Maggie sighed. The way the news pipeline ran in this town, they'd all hear it soon enough. Small-town living could be a major pain in the ass. She waved one hand. "This is a police matter so I can't give details. I can tell you what's public knowledge. "

Mom folded her arms. The pissed-off executive stance. "Which is?"

"There was a woman with a knife. I removed her from the press conference and arrested her. She was nowhere near the football hunk."

"*You* removed her? With the *knife*?"

"I'm fine, Mom."

Mom threw her hands up. "Which means that knife was near you."

Maggie pointed at Shep. "You. Are a dead man."

"I'm just repeating what I heard. I didn't know it was you."

Always the gentle one, Dad set his hand on Mom's shoulder. "She said she's fine. If she'd gotten hurt, she would have alerted us."

Right. *Thanks, Dad.* "Exactly. Plus, Cash would have been the one to stitch me up." Attempting to lighten the mood, she flashed a grand smile. "We like to keep it all in the family."

Cash snorted. "Anyway, can we get back to my Brussels sprouts? I'm thinking you're all toast tonight. The sprouts are epic."

Later, she'd give her little brother a smooch. The other little brother?

He was in the doghouse.

Maggie wandered to the fridge, patting her brother's shoulder on her way by. "Good luck there. If there's one thing this family loves more than bacon, it's brown sugar and there's a mountain of it in my potatoes."

Across the room, Dad eyed her, then nudged his chin toward the door. Now came the private interrogation.

He picked up the platter Mom had set on the counter near the door. "I'll get the ribs. Y'all head in and get settled."

Any hope Maggie had of escaping a private chat with Dad, died fast when he looked over at her. "Mags, give me a hand."

Yep. Interrogation time.

She followed her father out the door and down the steps into the cool night air that tickled her cheeks. The smell of cooking meat mixed with the smoky scent of burning wood from the fire pit and she inhaled, let the joy of being outside settle her. Perfect night. She zipped her jacket and stared out at the twenty acres of farmland her father intended on filling with organic produce. His dream. Only part of the land had been planted on, but each year Dad added to his crops, testing different varieties and slowly expanding his small, locally known business to a North Carolina success story.

How different they were. She wanted to fight bad guys and her father wanted to dig in the earth.

Dad set the platter on the small table next to the smoker and checked the timer. Satisfied with the progress, he stood in front of her, one hand on his hip. "What happened today?"

"It wasn't a—"

"Don't tell me it wasn't a big deal. That's what we tell your mother. Me? I want to know."

Arguing wouldn't help her. This she knew. Dad might be

the Zen guy around here, but when he wanted answers, he got them. So Maggie gave in and relayed what details she could, leaving out anything that might jeopardize legal proceedings. For his purposes, Dad got the version the reporters had, plus a few extra facts.

"I had it under control."

Mostly.

"Of course you did. Your self-defense lessons are paying off."

That was an understatement. "They are. It's been a good time investment."

Considering that the knife could have gone through her. But Dad wouldn't comment on that. He left those conversations to Mom. The one who encouraged Maggie to pursue an academic career, possibly as a police academy instructor. Anything that got her out of situations like the one she faced today.

Dad? When it came to his kids and their choices, he offered rational pros and cons and supported final decisions. Given Mom's career and the time she'd spent building it, Dad had been the more present parent. His role, as he saw it, wasn't to be the heavy. That was Mom's job. She was out of the house fourteen hours a day. She could escape the wrath of obstinate teenagers. Dad didn't want to deal with the load of nonsense five kids could throw his way.

He checked the ribs again. "Another two minutes."

"They smell great."

"I mixed up some different spices. We'll see. Tell me about Jayson Tucker."

Uh-oh. Why would he ask that? Someone at the B must have burned up the phone lines about Maggie and Jayson whoring it up on the street.

Shep.

He'd just said he was in town. Her brother had a knack for saying inappropriate things, but telling their father she sucked face with a hot guy?

Nah.

Even he wouldn't go that far. He might threaten her with it privately just to be annoying, but certain lines didn't get crossed.

"I don't know that much."

Dad circled one hand. "Give me the top-line. Is he a decent man? Until a week ago, he'd been the USFF's premier player. On and off the field. Now they're crucifying him."

"From what I can tell, he's a good guy. Normal, I guess. Which seems weird, given his lifestyle."

"Maybe he keeps his ego in check. Or has people in his life who help him with that."

"I don't know. He has a sister. She works a few hours from here."

Maggie wouldn't mention the research she'd done after her workout this morning. The research she'd convinced herself was for background purposes only. She'd learned that Jayson Tucker grew up in Manhattan. Wealthy family. His parents divorced when he was ten and his father had moved overseas. And yet, even without his father present on a daily basis, Jayson grew into one heck of an alpha male.

No wonder she stuck her tongue in his mouth.

Her cheeks burned and she thanked the stars above that it was too dark for her father to see.

"How long will he be in town?" Dad asked.

"I suppose until Grif finds him another team. As nice as he is, his being here is a logistics nightmare. Were you in town today? Did you see that traffic?"

Call her slick, because that question was meant to

ensure her father hadn't been in town today. Possibly watching his slut of a daughter put on a show on Main Street.

"No. But I heard it was a mess."

Phew.

"The impromptu press conference saved us, but we can't be doing that every day. Particularly after the, uh, incident. Between clearing traffic and handling the press conference, I don't have the manpower for this. And I'm supposed to leave on vacation in a few days. I have no idea what to do about that."

Dad eyed her. "You *are* leaving on vacation. You've been looking forward to this for months. When's the last time you did anything for yourself?"

"Dad, in case you forgot, the citizens of Steele Ridge don't care. I have responsibilities. I can't leave with this going on."

"Why do you have to decide now? You're not leaving until Monday. If things calm down over the weekend, you'll go. If the deputies can't handle this town until you get back, you need better deputies."

The organic farmer telling her how to manage her town. Priceless. "Now I need better deputies?"

"Hey, you're the one doubting them. Not me."

"How am I doubting them?"

He shrugged. "You're concerned they can't handle things while you're away. If you were confident in their management skills it wouldn't be an issue."

"You are totally twisting my words."

"Am I?"

"Dad!"

He shook his head, let out a sigh. "Look, honey, I think

you're worrying prematurely. Give it the weekend, then decide. That's all I'm saying."

"You two," Mom called from the screen door. "Everyone is at the table. Those ribs have to be done. Let's eat."

Dad scooped the platter from the table. "Be right there."

The first rib hit the platter and Dad jerked his head toward the door. "Go in and wash up. Get those sweet potatoes prepped for the Brussels sprout battle."

6

REID STEELE WAS NO JOKE.

Jay might even call him a sadist. The more pain the guy inflicted during a workout, the happier he got. This morning, though, he'd surprised Jay—in a fairly stupendous way —by bringing in Maggie's brother, Cash, formerly a high-school football player, to take catches and keep Jay sharp. Short passes mixed with long passes, they'd worked together with Cash doing a damned fine job of keeping up. When Reid tired of barking out orders from his spot on the picnic table, he jumped in, taking handoffs while Cash played defensive tackle.

After the stress of the week, blowing off some steam with a football in hand and a couple of guys willing to take hits wasn't a bad way to end a week.

And, hello, the bonus of the whole thing wound up being that the firefighter Jay had seen Maggie getting chummy with had been Cash. Her brother.

Not a boyfriend.

Yep. Great day so far.

Cash had even managed to bloody Reid's forehead after

hauling his ass to the ground. Reid was beefier, but Cash had the speed and competitiveness that made him a pain in the ass on a football field.

All of which Jay enjoyed the fuck out of, considering the abuse he'd taken from Reid on their last session.

"Girlfriend," Jay said to a bloodied Reid, "you want me to call your mommy? Get her down here to kiss it and make it better?"

Reid pressed one of the clean towels he'd brought outside to his still bleeding forehead. "Keep talking, Superstar. Don't forget, you're mine again soon."

Shit.

The two exchanged smiles that were all *I'll fuck you up.* "Bring it on, man. Bring it on."

Jay may have been talking big, but in the name of all things holy, his body was beat to hell. Hamstrings, quads, traps. Even his abs—muscles he'd worked tirelessly for years, to build core strength—despised Reid right now.

But all this soreness made Jay think maybe he'd gone soft.

Maybe not soft, but easier on himself. Sure, he worked out with a trainer regularly, but that was in a gym. In a controlled environment with machines and free weights. The stuff Reid had him doing? This outdoorsy stuff of throwing logs, hanging off the side of a flat roof doing sit-ups, and flipping the biggest goddamned tractor tires Jay had ever seen had taken him to another level. Upped his game.

Something, despite the pain, he'd always be grateful for.

Reid's head stopped bleeding and he and Cash spent a solid five minutes smack-talking and wrestling like ten-year-olds while Jay sat on the picnic table guzzling water and laughing.

Couple of idiots, they were. Still, it looked like fun. Clearly something they engaged in regularly and probably had been doing since childhood. Jay knew nothing of that. Having grown up with only Sam and no extended family nearby, he'd never had a Cash to play war with.

All he'd had was his mother. And there was nothing fun about her wars.

When he started playing football, all that pent-up rage tore from him like a derailing high-speed train.

"Oh, you fucker."

Jay glanced up, found Reid about to put Cash into a headlock.

"Tap out, cuz," Reid said. "I've got you."

"Yeah, but I made you bleed."

Reid laughed. "You got lucky."

"My ass."

Jay shook his head. "Call it a draw before one of you gets hurt."

Another minute of negotiating ensued until, yes, perhaps the two most competitive people Jay had encountered—and that was saying something, considering what he did for a living—called a truce.

Both men lumbered toward him and Jay handed over water bottles and a clean towel for Reid's once-again bleeding head. "You're assholes."

Cash took the bottle and twisted the cap off. "What's your point?"

"Dang it." Reid stared at the splotches of blood on the towel. "The lecture I'll get from Brynne will turn me to stone."

"Poor baby," Cash said. "I got a first-aid kit in the car. I'll clean you up. Tell her you hit your head on a cabinet door. Happens all the time."

"Lie to my Brynnie?"

"It's either that or turn to stone. Pick your poison."

Reid curled his lip just as Jay's phone rang. Sam.

He scooped the phone up and hopped off the table. "This is my sister."

He tapped the screen and told Sam to hang on a second before offering his hand to Cash, then to Reid. "Thank you. Both of you. I needed to get a football in my hands. Cash, if you wouldn't mind getting out here early with me a few days a week, I'd appreciate it. We'll work out a fee structure."

Cash waved it off. "Are you kidding me? You're not paying. This is a dream come true for me. Plus, I get to beat the crap out of Reid. It doesn't get any better."

"Fuck off," Reid said.

Cash ignored his cousin. "We'll have to work around my shifts, but I'm up for it."

These people. Beyond generous. Anyone else would be looking to capitalize on Jay's name. Using it for bragging rights or some sort of endorsement.

Cash Kingston? He wanted to play ball.

"Excellent. Thanks again. I'll call you."

He left the two at the table, putting the phone to his ear while he walked toward the door leading inside the training center. "Hey," he said to Sam. "Sorry. I was finishing up my workout."

"No prob. How's that going?"

"Surprisingly well. It's...different. Challenging. They're nice people. A good family. Makes me realize what we missed."

"Oh, let's not go there. Please. Glad it's working out, though."

"What's up?"

"A couple of things. Since you're so close, I thought I'd

take a half day today and visit you for the weekend. Would that be okay?"

He stopped at the door to the training center and looked back over his shoulder to the acres and acres of towering trees. She'd love this place. Plus, it gave him a weekend with the one person who knew his secrets. With Sam came acceptance. Together, they'd lived the life of Drunk Marlene and shared a level of trust that allowed Jay to talk freely and not measure his words. In short, Sam let him relax.

"That'd be great. We can catch up."

"Awesome. I'll leave here around noon."

"That'll get you here about three o'clock. I'll text you the address."

He'd have to speak with Miss Joan about having another visitor. On his way out the door yesterday, he'd mentioned he'd seen his sister. Miss Joan assured him Sam would be welcome anytime, but he'd check with her just in case.

"I need to go home and pack a bag, so it'll be closer to four o'clock. You can buy me dinner later."

"Happy to do it."

"Before I let you go," she said, "I'm digging through some reports from Jack's files."

Jack. The CFO who'd left without warning. Why she'd be talking to Jay about Jack's reports, he had no idea.

"And?"

"You pay your own expenses, right? I mean, when you do events on our behalf."

From the start, Jay had refused any form of payments from Celebrate Hope. Given his background of abuse and the ridiculous amount of money he made every year, he didn't see the point in taking money from an organization that could use every cent to change people's lives.

"Yeah. Always have. Why?"

"These reports are funky. There's a marketing account that's showing payments to you. Reimbursements for travel expenses. I assumed it was an error. Maybe someone plugged in the wrong name." He sister let out a huff. "I'll download the folders and figure it out on Sunday when I get home. I wanted to check with you before I spent hours trying to track which employee's expense it was."

Another call beeped in and—welcome back to the real world—Jay checked the caller ID. Eric Webb. The Golden Boy.

After the week he'd had, not a lot would shock him ever again, but this one was up there on the holy-fuck factor.

"Sam, I gotta go. I'll text you the address."

"Go," she said.

He disconnected and picked up the Golden Boy's call before it went to voice mail. "This is Jay."

"It's not enough," Webb said, "you're sticking your nose into my business, now you're fucking my wife?"

The accusation zapped him. What the *hell*? Jay had dealt with a lot of media-created lies during his career, but he'd sue anyone who accused him of adultery. That, he wouldn't suck up.

"Watch yourself, Webb. I'm done with your nonsense. I haven't touched your wife and you know it."

"I don't know shit."

Really, what he should do is hang up. Eric Webb had nearly wrecked his career. Might still wreck his career. Even being in the same country as this douchebag posed risks. The kid had been a cancer from the start. Management knew his history when they drafted him. Sexual abuse allegations, bar fights, DUIs. All of it shuffled away by a Division I university unwilling to lose their star quarterback.

And then the Knights dumped him off on Jay, blowing

all kinds of smoke up his ass about how he could mentor the troubled rookie. How Jay's teammates looked up to him. A born leader, they'd said. All to convince Jay he'd make a difference in Eric Webb's career.

He'd made a difference all right. He'd made the guy a household name. For all the wrong reasons.

Jay opened the door to the training center and stepped inside. "Webb, if you don't know shit, then where's this coming from?"

"I was told."

"Then whoever said it is a liar."

Webb let out a growling laugh that was half sarcasm, half anger. "Among other things. I'll bury you with this one. You and my bitch of a wife. You deserve each other."

Jay locked his teeth together. Calm. That's what he needed right now. He'd never put a hand on Webb's wife. Outside of that damned party, he'd barely had a private conversation with her. Whatever was said to Eric, was, without a doubt, meant to get his attention. Jay doubted it came from Eric's wife. Why the hell would she want to poke that bear and possibly get herself a beating?

No way.

The Golden Boy had to be making this up. Goading him into a fight. Classic end run of trying to make Jay look like a shitty teammate. If—when—the story behind the locker room brawl came out, Eric Webb would finally be held accountable for his abusive behavior.

But goddammit, this was a hell of an accusation and in the court of public opinion, right now, Jay was the enemy.

He strode to Reid's office, grabbed his jacket from the chair, and headed to the front door. "Webb, it's not true. And you won't *bury* me with it because I will sue your ass."

Not wanting to waste any more of his energy—the daily

bucket was only so full—he punched the screen and disconnected.

Fucker.

Lying, scheming fucker.

Feet pounding the tile, he walked out the front door already lining up a to-do list. Shower first. It would give him a few minutes to calm down. Get the initial anger to a low boil so he could think straight.

Grif.

After getting cleaned up, he'd drive into town and speak to his agent about this latest bombshell.

"Goddammit!"

Focus here.

Keeping his head on straight had never hurt him. Losing his shit always did.

Lies.

All lies. He knew it. There'd be no proof anywhere. But that damned court of public opinion. It didn't need proof. Rumors were enough to tarnish a career.

He'd had enough of that.

Concentrate. Work the plan.

Shower first. Talk to Grif. Maybe, if he got really lucky, he'd see Maggie in town.

After that smoking kiss yesterday, she'd brighten his day, without a doubt.

AT 7:00 SHARP, MAGGIE PUSHED THROUGH THE FRIDAY NIGHT crowd in the Triple B. As usual on the weekend, bodies pressed in—some of them way too sweaty and sending various odors into the atmosphere—while country rock music thumped and reverberated against the floor.

Freshly showered, a face full of makeup, and wearing

her favorite jeans and cowboy boots, Maggie squeezed to the back of the bar where she'd find her family and oxygen. Britt better have opened that back door.

What had started as a Steele family tradition of meeting at the B on a Friday night had grown to a Steele-Kingston event. Pretty soon, they'd be occupying half the seats in the place. All Maggie knew was that she looked forward to it every weekend. Time with her family, immediate and extended, gave her a few hours to laugh and unwind from the week. A chance to ground herself again and be thankful for the love of good people.

"Maggie," someone called over the music.

She turned and spotted a man in a black baseball cap pulled low and a graphic T-shirt that probably cost more than she made in a week. And the way his shoulders filled out that T-shirt left no doubt who wore it. Jayson. Every yummy, ripped-muscle inch of him.

If the baseball cap was his idea of a disguise, he needed to work harder. A man that good looking wouldn't stay hidden for long. Something he should have realized since he'd already attracted the petite blonde beside him.

A spurt of something dark and searing shot down Maggie's torso. Years had gone by since she'd experienced the nasty hold of jealousy. She hadn't missed it, this stab of disappointment. What she had missed was feeling a strong enough attraction to a man that it would incite this reaction.

What am I doing?

Being a fool, that's what. Jayson Tucker? Total player. And why not, when women threw themselves at him?

He was an unattached adult. Who could blame him? She didn't need to see it, though. She'd do as her parents taught her and be cordial. Especially to the cutesy blond witch who made Mags look like an Amazon.

Be nice, Sheriff.

Couldn't have guests commenting on the lack of hospitality from Steele Ridge officials.

Mags slapped on what had to be an over-bright smile and detoured to Jayson and the bitch of a blonde. Now she was a bitch? *Get it together here, Mags.*

As she maneuvered around people, Jayson reached for her, gently pulling her to his side. The simple touch set her already teetering nerves skittering. "Hi," she said. "Are you hiding?"

"A little bit. Yeah."

A drunk jackass stumbled behind her, nearly plowing her over and Jay tugged her closer.

"The place is nuts," he said.

"Friday night. It's always like this."

"Good for Randi. I'm glad we ran into you. I wanted to introduce you to my sister. This is Samantha. Sam, meet Maggie. She's the sheriff here."

Under the cover of loud music, Maggie unleashed a snort. She'd flown into a bout of jealousy for no reason. As a law enforcement professional, hadn't she learned not to prejudge a situation?

"No way," Sam said. "Seriously? A female sheriff. You go, girl."

A smile lit Jay's face. "Cool, right?"

As much as she didn't want to feel a rush from a man's approval, well, yes, it got her hot in places that hadn't been hot in way—way—too long. "Thank you," she said. "A female sheriff is different for some folks, but they treat me all right. Are you two having dinner?"

"Trying to. Sam cut out of work earlier and drove up for the weekend. Britt told me to come in the back door so no one would see me, but there's not a table to be had."

Thus, why he stood huddled in the corner. She couldn't leave the two of them standing here. Her mother would never survive the shock of one of her children exhibiting bad manners.

She'd blame it on Mom instead of her own wild, apparently insatiable hormones.

The crowd shifted and a young woman stepped back, pressing Maggie closer to Jayson, who slid his arm behind her, drawing her flush against him. "Switch spots with me," he said. "You keep getting bumped."

She shook her head. "You can't stand here all night. Someone will spot you and you'll be mobbed. Come join us."

"Who?"

"All of us. The whole Steele clan and my brothers and sister. Randi reserves us a table. We'll put you in the corner so no one can bug you."

"Maggie is right," Sam said above the music. "You'll draw a crowd. At least back there you're closer to the door and can make a run for it."

All of this was said with a straight face and Maggie took a second, contemplated the idea that Sam was serious. That Jayson spent his life, at least part of it, running.

So not a good way to live. She swung her thumb over her shoulder. "Both of you, follow me."

Staying close to the wall, Maggie led them to the back corner. The Steele section, as it had been dubbed. At the table sat Britt, Reid, Reid's fiancée, Brynne, Evie, and her man, Deke. At the opposite end, Cash and Riley were in a heads-down, deep conversation with Jonah. More than likely, Cash was bending Jonah's ear about funding a new tactical medical team that Cash, of course, intended on running.

"Hey, y'all." Maggie held up her hand. "Look who I found."

Introductions were made, handshakes exchanged, and everyone went back to their business. No starstruck, wide-eyed fans here. Just people wanting to connect with each other.

Against the wall, Britt slid over two places. "Jay, you and Sam sit on this side. Grif and Carlie Beth will be here in a bit and they can have the two end spots."

"I'll sit on the end until they get here."

Maggie dropped into the chair on the end while Jayson sat in the spot against the wall. Sam settled between him and Britt.

With Maggie anchoring and Reid beside her, no one would get by to hound Jayson.

"Man," Jay said, "you guys rock."

"You really should have security when you're in crowded places like this."

"I do."

"Where?"

He pointed to a guy leaning against the wall nursing a bottled water. "He stays close enough to react, but tries to give me space."

Maggie, once again caught up in her lust for the hot jock, hadn't even sensed the bodyguard. *Maggie, Maggie, Maggie.*

"You don't always take security, though," Sam said.

"No. But I'm smart about it in public places. After the press conference, I brought them in. Common sense."

Maggie smacked a hand on his shoulder. "As the sheriff, I thank you."

Jayson responded with a fast smile that turned up the heat on Maggie's privates. His eyes shot to her hand, then back up to meet hers and the heat wasn't only in Maggie's privates. It shot off Jayson like a jackrabbit.

Oh, she wanted to do this guy. Just slam him down and let loose. *Wicked, wicked girl.*

But hey, even the good ones were entitled to a little wickedness.

Kris McKay, the assistant manager at the B, appeared, notepad in hand. On busy nights, Kris often helped the waitresses by taking orders. Plus, she'd known the Kingstons and Steeles her entire life, so taking their food orders wasn't so much a job as a friendly gesture.

After food had been ordered, Sam squeezed behind Jayson and Maggie to hit the ladies' room. Britt walked away with Sam and Reid was busy talking to some beefy guy about working out at the training center. Which left Jayson and Maggie somewhat to themselves. How very sad for her. *Not.*

"Hey," Jayson said.

"Hey, yourself. Having fun?"

"I am. Which is pretty much a miracle. Thank you for the invite."

Jayson glanced up as his sister emerged from the crowd. He waved her around to the empty chair beside him, making it clear he wouldn't be moving again. Before she sat, he leaned over, got right up to Maggie's ear. "And, I wanted to mention, you look amazing tonight."

Another hot flash erupted. Dang it. Was she actually blushing?

"Thank you," she said. "Jeans are just about my favorite piece of clothing."

"Maggie, these last few days, I've liked everything on you." He shot off a grin. "Forgive me for being a pig, but the tights are my favorite."

"Oh, Lord. You're *such* a man."

He cracked up. "Why, thank you."

Sam squeezed back into the chair. "This place is great. Everyone is so nice. It's a good switch from the crabs in my office." She laughed. "And I work for a charity."

"She works for the charity that just dumped me," Jay added.

Talk about awkward. "Eww, that's rough."

"Not really," Sam said. "Everyone there loves Jayson. It's the situation."

Jay nodded. "They're a domestic abuse charity."

"Celebrate Hope? The one you do all the commercials for?"

"That's them." He ran a finger over the condensation on his beer mug and after a few seconds of silence, turned to Sam. "Did you figure out that issue you called me about?"

"Not yet. But I will. It's probably something dumb. There are a few things that look wacky." She leaned in closer to avoid yelling over the crowd. "I had to prep a financial summary for Will." She glanced at Maggie. "He's our director. I couldn't make sense of the marketing expenses, so I called the bank and asked for copies of all statements. I figured I'd start there so I'd at least know how much money we had. It took all morning, but the bank finally sent over the statements."

"And?"

"Well, there's an account I've never seen."

"Is that odd?" Maggie asked.

"I don't know. Our CFO just left. He kept things close, so I suppose it's not completely odd. It's creating a mess for us, trying to figure out how funds are processed. Not a good look for a charity."

"No kidding," Maggie said.

"Hey, you three."

Reid walked off to talk to someone just as Britt wandered back to the table. He squeezed between the end of the table and the wall and Maggie stood and hugged the big lug. "I haven't seen you all week. Where've you been?"

"On the mountain. I had a bathroom remodel."

Typically, she ran into him in town when he dropped in on Randi at the B. If Maggie's instincts served her, after Brynne and Reid's wedding, Britt and Randi wouldn't be far behind.

Which left some hope for Maggie, a woman feeling her eggs drying up by the hour. Randi and Britt were well into their thirties when they found each other, so why couldn't it happen for Maggie? Even if it didn't, she'd freeze her eggs and have a baby on her own. She didn't even need a penis for that. She'd find a baby daddy, hijack his sperm, and be artificially inseminated. Although, a little sex wouldn't hurt.

She slid a glance to Jayson. Definitely a candidate. On both fronts. Premium sperm to be hijacked here.

Man, oh, man, she was losing it. Lonely. That's all. She needed a life. Or at least a diversion from her life.

Britt leaned forward to speak to Jayson. "We still on for tomorrow?"

"Hell, yes," Jay said. "Do you mind if Sam joins us?"

"Not at all."

What was this now? "I see you've been plotting with Britt."

Jayson nodded. "Yeah. He stopped by Tupelo Hill yesterday."

A waitress pushed through the crowd just as a guy leaning on the wall near the table caught her attention to place an order. Maggie studied his profile. The straight nose and his hair, an inch too long in the back and curling.

Whether he recognized Jayson, Maggie couldn't tell, but so far, he hadn't made an attempt to get closer. She'd have to keep an eye on him.

The waitress jotted a note, then turned from him and handed Britt a rock glass with his usual whisky.

Randi had mentioned Britt was making her a little nuts with constantly critiquing the different whisky brands she brought in. Still, Maggie thought it more than slightly adorable that he wanted to help.

Britt set the glass on the table and leaned over so they could hear him. "I'm taking Jay to see the wolves."

It had been months since Maggie had been up on the ridge where Britt discovered a pack of nearly extinct red wolves on Steele property. Given their rarity, he'd applied for grants to protect them. Jonah's deep pockets didn't hurt either.

"Wow," Maggie said. "I'm impressed." She turned to Jay. "He's secretive about them. I'm shocked he's taking you up there."

"He likes hiking," Britt said. "The fat donation check he wrote me didn't hurt."

Ha. She liked Jayson more and more. The man knew how to get things done. "You bribed him?"

Jay splayed a hand over his heart. "I made a *donation*. Big difference."

"He bribed him," Sam said and they all laughed.

"Maggie, why don't you join us?" Jay angled his head to Britt. "Is it okay? I'm turning this into a circus."

Britt waved it off. "It's fine. She's been there. We'll head up around ten. The wolves tend to be more nocturnal, but we'll see."

Ten o'clock? She could do that. She'd run her normal Saturday errands a little earlier and then meet up with them. "I haven't hiked that part of the mountain in a long time. It'll be fun. Plus," she elbowed Jay, "we can see what kind of shape the superstar is in."

"Oh, honey," he said, "you are *on*."

"Great," Sam said. "Surrounded by competitive people."

"Sorry, Sis. You're screwed on that one. You should see Maggie run that crazy obstacle course I showed you."

Maggie slouched back. "Ugh. That damned thing. I may die trying to break Reid's record, but I'll do it."

Britt laughed. "You two are funny with that."

"Funny my butt. I know he doesn't think a woman can break it. He's about to get schooled. It's that wall. I can't get over it fast enough."

Jay took a long gulp from the water glass the waitress had set in front of him, then set it down. "He has the upper body strength and he's taller. He'll always be faster."

"Great. Thanks for the pep talk, Mr. Sunshine."

He shrugged. "It's human physiology. You have to come up with another way."

Maggie flapped her arms. "I'm trying."

"Forget the wall. You'll never beat his time there. Improve on the other obstacles. The army crawl. You're faster than he is on that."

That piqued her interest. What now? "How do you know?"

"He told me. That first day when I watched you. Improve your time on that and you'll beat him." He gave her one of his charming smiles. "And, being the competitive sort, I'd be happy to help you. He kicked the crap out of me this morning. Revenge is in order."

The army crawl. Reid—the competitive little shit— never told her she'd beat him on that. Now, he'd pay. "You're on, mister."

He held up a hand for a high-five. "Let's do this."
Yes. Let's.

By 10:30 Saturday morning, the sun had burned through the clouds and Jay and Sam rode with Britt on a road Jay didn't quite consider a road, but apparently Britt did.

The morning hadn't started out so promising. It had greeted Jay with gloomy gray skies and forty-five degrees. Being the dedicated career guy, he hauled his ass from bed and logged five miles around the property before Sam had even rolled out of bed.

After which, Miss Joan treated them to ham and eggs. This kind of living, he could get used to. Miss Joan deserved a nice gift for putting up with him. And his sister. The woman opened her home to strangers, trusting they wouldn't walk off with valuables. Or family secrets.

Finally, Britt pulled into a clearing where Maggie leaned against her SUV, face tipped to the sky. She wore lightweight cargo pants and a long-sleeved shirt layered over what looked like a white T-shirt. She'd pulled her honey-blond hair into a ponytail revealing the long column of her neck and Jay was hit with a gut shot that brought back thoughts of handcuffs.

Maggie looked over at them and smiled. *Handcuffs.*

Of all the women he'd dated, none of them were...

Maggie.

Independent. Strong. Tough in some ways. Not like his mother tough, but enough that... He shook it off.

"Let's hit it, people," Britt said.

Putting thoughts of his mother from his head, Jay pushed the truck door open. Nice morning, good company, and nature.

That's what he'd focus on.

An hour into their hike, with sunshine knocking the edge off the crisp morning air, they climbed higher toward the top of a bluff where the gentle burble of water sounded. Creek. Dead ahead. Jay peered up at the sky, taking it all in. The beauty of the day, the land. Perfection.

He'd never been a church guy, but days like this he believed, without a doubt, in God's work.

After events most people would consider total horseshit, being outside, listening to the crackle of branches and leaves under his boots, this wasn't a bad way to spend a day.

Britt turned and held his finger to his lips. He'd warned them before they started hiking to stay quiet when they neared the den. Which meant...*close*. A burst of excitement filled him.

Behind him, Sam huffed and puffed with each step. His baby sister needed to up her cardio. Get in better shape.

Maggie took up the rear, more than likely making sure they didn't lose Sam, because one thing was for sure. Everything in these woods looked the same. If one of them got lost, it'd take a day to figure out how the hell to get back.

They'd need a damned search party.

Britt dropped to peer through binoculars, then waved them down.

They all hit their knees just as Britt handed Jay the binoculars. "Through those trees on the other side of the creek. Stay quiet. The babies are big now. Almost as high as their mama."

And there they were. A half dozen wolves, a few standing, the rest lazing around, their red fur bright against the dull brown bark of the trees.

Jay drew a breath. Damn, they were beautiful.

One of the wolves swung his head, seeming to stare

straight at Jay with tawny eyes screaming of suspicion. Before the animal spooked and took off, he handed the binoculars to Sam.

"Wow," she breathed. "Stunning."

Pop-pop-pop.

Three rapid shots cracked the air and Jay froze. What the hell?

Pop-pop.

Two more.

"Goddammit!" Britt said.

A hunk of the tree sheared off behind Jay's head and old instincts kicked in. He tackled Sam, smothering her with his twice bigger body.

"Everyone run!" Maggie grabbed the back of Jay's jacket. "Behind those trees. Now!"

She let go and Jay swung his head around, found her on the move, weapon in hand. The hem of her long-sleeved shirt caught on a waist holster that had been hidden while they walked.

"Britt," she said, "stay with them. And don't touch that tree. We might get the bullet."

"Take these." Britt tossed her the binoculars.

Jay hopped to his feet, shielding Sam while they ducked low and ran for the cover of the thick clump of trees twenty feet to their left.

Jay shoved Sam behind a thick-trunked oak tree. "Don't move." He squatted behind another huge tree. "What the hell was that?"

"Hunters," Britt said, pulling his own handgun from a waist holster.

"Should they be up here?"

"Hell no. But we've had problems before. The wolves are endangered and it's no secret they're here."

"Trophy hunters?" Sam asked.

"Might be. You okay here? I don't want Mags out there alone."

Jay waved him off. "We're fine. Go."

MAGGIE SQUATTED BEHIND A TOWERING HICKORY TREE AND scanned the area where the shots came from. At least she thought it was. At the time, she'd been busy fantasizing about Jayson's voice whispering naughty things to her.

Idiot, Maggie. Letting her stupid hormones distract her—again—when they all could have been killed.

A low whistle sounded behind her. Britt's whistle. Smart man knowing not to sneak up on her. She glanced back. Ten yards behind, Britt duckwalked under the cover of a clump of trees.

He moved closer, his boots crunching over leaves and twigs. "Get behind that tree." She pointed to an oak wide enough to shield him. "I think the shots came from the ridge across the creek."

"Did you see anything?"

She shook her head. "Only the tip of a hat. The person was running and then ducked into the brush."

"Male?"

"No idea. All I saw was the hat before he—assuming it was a male—ducked away."

"What do you want to do?"

"I called it in. Blaine's coming up the other side. Maybe we'll get lucky."

"I'll call Reid. If he's at the training center, we'll have him check the backside of the property."

A nice idea, but by the time Reid saddled up and got here, their shooter would be gone.

She stared out over the bluff, then checked the binoculars again. *Where are you, you little shit?* Two minutes of scanning the area resulted in zero movement and she lowered the binoculars. "I think he's gone." She handed the binoculars back to Britt. "Let's head back."

With Britt in tow, Maggie strode through the trees to Jayson and Sam, still huddled behind the protection of the ancient oaks.

"You two okay?"

"We're fine," Jay said. "But your wolves took off. I don't think they were hit."

"They'll be back," Britt said.

Sam, sitting with her back against the tree, got to her feet. "Did you find anyone?"

Maggie shook her head. "We called down to one of my deputies and to Reid and told them to check the roads around the property. Whoever was out there, they got up here somehow."

Her mind tripped back to the shots. *Pop, pop, pop.*

Not a shotgun.

Maggie stayed quiet, her instincts drawing her a few feet to the right. Scanning the trees, she visualized the trajectory if the bullet ricocheted.

That way. She whirled around.

"Maggie," Jay said.

She held up a finger. "Give me a second."

Where are you? Where are you?

A sliver of sunlight sliced through a puffy cloud and illuminated the area to her right.

"There," Britt said. "See it?"

Her cousin pointed and she followed his direction, spotting the splintered surface of a tree. She moved closer, studying the marred flesh and—there. Lodged inside was a mushroomed bullet. "Got a bullet," she said. "I'm calling it in. We'll get the forensics team up here."

Jayson's head jutted forward. "What do you mean forensics? I thought the shooter was a hunter."

She paused for a few seconds. No sense sugarcoating it. If her instincts served, the man had a right to know. "Jayson," she said, "that was rapid semiauto fire. Most hunters don't use semiautomatics. At least not when they're hunting animals."

7

AFTER OVERSEEING THE COLLECTION OF THE BULLET, MAGGIE
worked her way down the mountain, moving fast and
cutting through trees to shorten the trip to her vehicle. For
safety, Britt and one of her deputies had taken Jayson and
Sam to Maggie's office. If someone wanted another shot at
Jayson, they'd have to do it in the sheriff's office.

Fresh air filled her lungs, sharpening her senses as she
moved. Whoever took that shot wasn't aiming for a wolf.
Too far off. That, or the shooter needed to work on his aim.

Security team. She'd have to check in with Jayson's
people. See if any of the threats indicated this level of
violence. If so, they'd have some leads. And Reid could
check video footage from his security system. Maybe he
caught a plate or something.

She hit the dirt path leading to the road and grunted.
Crap. Beside her vehicle stood Alexander Westlake, the one
and only full-time reporter for the *Steele Ridge News,* circula-
tion 2,505 after picking up five readers last month. Growth
spurt.

Xander met her at the rear bumper of her SUV. "Xander,

what are you doing here? You know you're trespassing on Steele property, right?"

The reporter waved his notepad. "Heard the call on the police scanner. Shots fired up here. What's that about?"

Hoping to brush him off, Maggie marched by and opened her driver's side door. "It's nothing."

"If it's nothing, why did I see Jayson Tucker and a woman hightailing it out of here with Blaine? Does this have something to do with him?"

"Xander, I have nothing for you."

"Well, then I'll have to go with what I have."

"Which is nothing."

Before hopping into her SUV, she gave him the same *you dopey boy* smile, she'd given him when he thought it would be fun to announce Mr. and Mrs. Hopkins spent Friday evenings doing the nasty in the park.

He held up his notepad. "What I have is Jayson Tucker and an unknown female hiking on Steele property at the same time someone with a semiautomatic fired shots. That gun isn't generally used for hunting, Maggie."

Now the persistent little weasel was pissing her off.

After the press caught wind of the knife-wielding nut, they'd sent social media buzzing. She shut the door. "Xander, you need to be careful here. You saw the chaos created in town by Mr. Tucker's presence. You were also at the press conference where a woman showed up with a knife. What we don't want are further incidents that might prove dangerous. To Mr. Tucker or the residents of our town. And we certainly don't want to create widespread panic due to irresponsible, sensationalized reporting. Am I clear?"

Xander twisted his face, pinching everything tight. "I never report anything but the facts."

"Maybe so. But *I* don't even have all the facts. How could you?"

"Look, Maggie. I'm not the only one who listens to the police scanner. I know the area and got here first. Everyone will be chasing this thing. Give me something I can run with."

What didn't he get about this? "Xander, you're not listening. I don't have anything for you."

"I'll go with what I have."

Maggie bit off a curse she'd love to unleash. This must be what major-metropolitan law enforcement dealt with. The constant press inquiries. She'd only had a few days of it and it irritated the crap out of her.

"How about I give you a heads-up if there's anything interesting?"

"What? Like an exclusive?"

Nice try, buddy. "Not an exclusive. But if there's a press statement, I'll get it to you first. That's the best I can do."

Xander clicked his tongue while mulling it over and Maggie made a show of checking her watch.

"Okay," he said. "How much of a head start?"

"Thirty minutes. Long enough for you to load it onto the newspaper's website."

Ah, the digital age.

"An hour."

Having had enough of Xander, Maggie opened her car door and hopped in. "This isn't a negotiation," she called back. "Thirty minutes is all you're getting. And get off Steele property before I slap you with that trespassing charge."

With that, she fired the engine and hit the gas before any other reporters showed up. They weren't the only ones with questions. She had them, too. A lot of them. In their first meeting, Jayson had been flip about hate mail. Hopefully, after her discussion with him about not putting her town in a dangerous position, he'd heeded her advice and not held anything back.

She'd find out when she got to her office.

She dialed Reid.

"Mags, what's happening?"

Exactly what she'd like to know. "I just found Xander roaming around near that path where Britt parks to check on the wolves. I informed him he was trespassing, but if I were you, I'd send someone up here in case he decides to play dumb and wasn't clear on the message."

"I've got two men heading up. I wanna know how the fuck this guy got on the property."

"The shot definitely came from higher ground, so he must have been on the ridge. Do you have video surveillance up there? Please say yes."

Reid hesitated and Maggie huffed. Could she get one tiny break here? "Cuz," she said, "you're not instilling confidence."

"Eh," Reid said. "We might get lucky."

Might? Zero confidence. "Meaning?"

"We have video surveillance on all physical structures on the property, but there's a shit-ton of land up there, Mags."

"What about that shack at the base of the ridge? Is there a camera on it?"

Her cousin, having been stranded in the wilderness as a Green Beret, understood the need for emergency supplies. He'd asked Britt to rebuild an old shack on the northwest side of the property and stocked it with what seemed a month's supply of water, protein bars, and ready-to-eat meals.

"Yeah," Reid said. "We're looking at the footage now. If

the shooter used that path, we should get some kind of visual."

"Good. How soon will you know?"

"Mags, I'm on it. Give me five minutes and I'll call you back."

"Thank you."

She disconnected and hooked a hairpin turn that would lead her into town. If they worked quickly, she might be able to find this shooter before he got too far.

Upon entering the station, Maggie breezed past the reception desk where Shari, their office assistant and girl wonder manned the phones Monday through Friday. On the weekends, it was every man for himself and Deputy Blaine now sat at his desk with the phone to his ear.

Blaine pointed down the short hallway. The sheriff's office wasn't fancy, but she'd managed to squeak enough out of the budget to give the building fresh beige paint and new floors that replaced cracked laminate. Given what she had to work with, the place at least had some warmth rather than the tired, worn look she'd inherited.

She made her way to the windowless conference room next to her office. The door stood open and inside Jayson and Sam sat at the table playing with their cell phones. The muted sound of Blaine's voice drifted from the bullpen, but otherwise a tension-filled quiet settled over the room.

Apparently sensing her presence, Jayson set his phone down and brought his gaze to her. He wore the bombed-out look of a man desperate for sleep.

Maggie stepped into the room, closing the door behind her. "Are you both okay?"

He glanced at his sister and she nodded. "We're good. Did you find anything?"

"Nothing new. I sent the bullet to the lab. I just got off the phone with Reid. He checked their surveillance video."

Jay's eyebrows hitched up. "Good news?"

"Debatable. Reid had cameras installed on all physical structures. There's a shack along the path our alleged shooter may have taken and the guy—it's a man—walked by. The angle is bad, though. We only have a partial profile view. I'll send it to someone I know at the FBI and ask him to run it through their facial recognition program."

"You have a friend at the FBI?"

She nodded. "I do. Technically he's Reid's cousin—on his father's side. No relation to me, but he's a good guy."

A good guy living the life she'd wanted. Once upon a time, she'd had dreams of Quantico. Dreams that blew up when her mother, the career woman, earned the promotion of a lifetime and was forced to relocate to South Dakota. Riley either had to go with them or stay put and be chaperoned. The obvious candidate had been Maggie. Being the oldest sibling—and female—she'd been more settled into her career and a routine than her brothers. Plus, she could have said no, but Riley only had six months of high school left and it hadn't seemed fair to uproot her baby sister. Which left Maggie putting off her application to the FBI and eventually being promoted to Chief Deputy. Fate, being a fickle sort, decided to further complicate things by having the then-sheriff drop dead of a heart attack and leave Maggie as interim sheriff. Soon after, she'd been elected to the job.

And here she was. Seven years after moving back into her childhood home to play guardian, she still hadn't applied to Quantico.

"And we're sure it's not a hunter?"

Huh?

Hunter. Jayson.

Focusing might be an option, Mags. "I can't say for certain. As I mentioned, semiautomatics aren't generally used by hunters. But Britt's already had a run-in with trophy hunters so it's possible."

Jay glanced at an owl-eyed Sam. The woman was completely spooked. And really, she might not need the particulars. If Jay chose to clue her in, that was on him. She'd let him make that decision.

"Sam," Maggie said, "I need to speak with Jayson privately. Could you give us a minute?"

Sam's gaze shifted to Jay for a long few seconds. "If it's okay with Jay."

When her brother nodded, Maggie opened the door again and stepped out into the hallway. She listened for a few seconds. Nothing. "Blaine?"

"I'm here," came his reply.

"I'm sending Sam out while I talk to Jayson. Would you do me a favor and see if Randi has anyone who can run us over some food?"

Sam and Jay had to be starving. Besides, the food might offer some comfort by getting their minds off the sound of a semiauto rifle.

Maggie reentered the conference room where Jayson sat with his head down and arms crossed. She slid the chair next to him out and sat facing him. Inches away, he bounced one knee up and down, up and down, up and down and she itched to set her hand on it. To still him.

Being the sheriff didn't give her that luxury.

She rested one arm on the table. "You're sure you're all right? Can I get you anything?"

He finally looked up at her and dug his palms into his eyes before letting them fall against his jeans with a *fwap*. "I'm fine. You think they were after me?"

"I think it's a possibility. You've had a long week with a lot of negative attention. We know from the woman at the press conference that people are highly charged right now. Have there been any other threats in the last day or so? Anything you haven't had a chance to share?"

"No. I've given you everything. I didn't speak to my security people today, though."

"When did you hear from them last?"

"Yesterday. Daily e-mail updates. Unless they need to talk to me."

"All right." She pointed at his phone. "Let's see if we can raise them."

THE SECURITY TEAM WAS A BUST.

Nothing new to report. That news should have brought Jay relief. Should have. Instead it left frustration and help-lessness. For a guy who thrived on controlling his surroundings, not a good combination.

Maggie set the phone in its cradle and pushed it back to the middle of the table. Everything nice and neat and in its spot. That was Maggie.

"At least we know there's been nothing new," she said.

Jayson grunted. "Someone almost killing us is nothing new?"

The look she hit him with may have been a cross between *fuck off* and *don't be an ass*.

"I'm trying to find the upshot," she said.

The intercom buzzed. "Maggie?"

"Yes, Blaine?"

"Uh, we got a problem?"

Maggie rolled her eyes. A problem. What else was new? She rolled her hand at the phone. "What is it, Blaine?"

"News van. Outside."

"Shit," Jayson said.

Maggie held up her hand, cutting off anything further he might say.

"Are they blocking the road?"

"No."

"Then there's nothing we can do. The second they impede traffic, it's a safety violation and we can move them along."

"Got it, boss."

"Do me a favor and find Grif. If he doesn't answer his cell, run over to the high school. Aubrey is involved with some kind of fundraiser over there. Tell him I'm sorry, but we need to talk."

"Yes, ma'am."

Maggie hit the button and Jay cocked his head. "What were you saying about upshots?"

"A couple of news vans is nothing. And, full disclosure, there was a local reporter waiting for me when I came down the mountain. He caught the incident on his police scanner."

Goddammit. How did this become his life? But, like everything else, he'd work the problem.

"I held him off," Maggie said, "but I had to promise him a head start on any media releases."

She had to promise? Without consulting him. Since when did she run his PR? "You shouldn't have done that. My media team handles press inquiries. There's a hierarchy when it comes to reporters."

"Well, Jay, as sheriff, I'm not obliged to run *anything* by your people. Tell your team I'm working on the fly and the *Steele Ridge News* was about to go with a story about you getting shot at—with a *semiautomatic*—while hiking. Maybe they'd prefer that to the deal I made?"

One thing about Maggie, she didn't resort to pouting or yelling when pissed. Her brand of torture? Expertly aimed sarcasm.

Before firing back with his own smart-ass comment, he took a second to settle his mind. Fighting with Maggie wouldn't help the situation. And as much as it pained him to admit he'd lost total control of the situation, she was right. "You may not believe it, but this isn't my life. Not normally anyway. This is a circus. I'm high-profile, but not like this. It's not relentless."

"You don't owe me an explanation."

"I want you to feel safe around me. That's important to me. Vital, in fact, for the people I care about to feel safe."

She leaned in and the movement stretched the fabric of her shirt tight across her breasts and—*handcuffs*. God, her body, all that tight muscle mixed with female curves, drove him to a level of need that should kill him.

"You may have noticed," she said, "I can take care of myself. I also carry a fairly big gun."

Oh, he'd noticed.

Mirroring her body language, he leaned in, brought his lips inches from hers. Close enough that if one of them puckered—game over. He studied her lips for a few seconds, then met her gaze. "This is crazy shit. No one has ever taken a shot at me. Never. They almost hit my sister."

The one he'd watched over for years now. The one he'd protected by sleeping flush against her bedroom door so his mother couldn't push it open.

The thought snapped him from thoughts of Maggie, in

handcuffs, on his bed, to the fucked-up mess that had become his life.

A buzzing sound echoed in the quiet room. Intercom.

"I have Grif."

Maggie sat back, breaking the eye contact, and all he wanted was to rewind, go back thirty seconds to right before he thought about the hell of his childhood.

The intercom buzzed again. "Grif?" Jay said.

"Yeah." Grif's strained voice shot from the speaker. "What the hell's going on?"

"Well, my hard-working agent, we got a situation."

"Again? What now?"

"I'm here with Maggie and—"

"Grif," she cut him off, "we were up on the northwest side of Britt's conservation area. You know that clearing where the wolves are?"

Jay sat, arms folded waiting for her to finish. Something inside him pinged again to Drunk Marlene, constantly interrupting him.

"What happened? Is everyone okay?"

"Everyone is fine, but someone took a shot at us."

"A shot!" Grif let out a creative group of swear words. "Hunters again?"

"Doubtful," Maggie said. "How many hunters use semi-automatics?"

"Get the fuck out?"

"The bullet we dug out of a tree was a thirty caliber. Our SWAT snipers use those. We called Reid and he has a visual of a guy from a surveillance camera."

"Did you recognize him?"

Maggie shook her head for no one's benefit but her own, since Grif couldn't see her and Jay already knew the answer.

"I haven't seen it yet. Reid said it's only a partial and

nobody he knew. I'm sending it to the FBI. I'm hoping Cam will run it for us as a favor. Otherwise, it'll blow up my budget."

"I'll cover it," Jayson said.

She finally looked over at him. *Yeah, babe, I'm still here.* Her forehead creased and she blinked a couple of times.

"That works," Grif said. "Tuck can reimburse us." A slew of voices broke into a shout on Grif's end. "Hang on." He paused for a few seconds, obviously in search of quieter space. "Okay, Mags, what else do you need from me?"

"We already have a news van outside. Xander was up at the site."

"Police scanner," Grif said.

"As usual. I talked him down by promising him a thirty-minute lead on any updates we do. Jay says his media team won't be happy with me, but—"

"I'll take care of it. What else?"

"I have a feeling more reporters are on the way."

Finally, Jay's chance to actually say something. "I can do another press conference," he said.

Maggie shook her head. "I don't think that's a good idea."

Now she wanted to tell him how to manage the media?

"I agree," Grif said. "We'll release a statement saying you're fine and police are investigating. Hopefully, we'll find this guy and he'll be a hunter that we'll rule out of anything sinister."

Why Jayson was even in on this call, he didn't know. Considering his agent and Maggie had no interest in his thoughts.

Maggie tapped a finger on the table and he looked up, found her eyeing him. "Grif," she said, "if you'll connect with the media team, I'll deal with the reporters on the street. I'll get with Reid and see where we are on the video."

"Sounds good. Keep me posted."

Maggie stood, leaned over the table, and punched off the call while he tilted his head and made a show of appreciating the way her hiking pants outlined her ass.

Shitty?

Yeah. But he'd learned early on the best way to get a woman's attention was to piss her off.

He wanted to believe he'd grown up some and that years of therapy had taught him another way, but in the last five minutes she'd tripped every goddamned one of his triggers.

And he was a stupid son of a bitch for allowing fucked-up, emotional garbage to dictate his actions. Worse, none of it had to do with Maggie being good at her job and everything to do with him being emasculated by strong women.

Thanks, Ma.

Maggie dropped back into the chair and met his stare. "I'm not sure what your problem is right now, but if you're pissed that I interrupted you, I'm sorry. I know that mountain. I thought I could explain it faster."

"Not a problem."

Liar. The burn in his intestines proved it.

He needed to cool off. Get his head together. He pushed out of his chair and paced the length of the room. He stopped in front of a photo hanging on the far wall. A statue of a soldier. Civil War, maybe? The uniform looked about right.

What the hell am I doing here? She didn't need him. If anything, he needed her and none of that sat right with a guy who'd spent years figuring out life on his own.

"I'm no use to you here. I'll head back to Miss Joan's with Sam. See if we can salvage this little familial visit."

"Sure. If that's how we're going to play this," she said from behind him, "go ahead."

Having had enough of the soldier, he turned back to Maggie. "What?"

"I've irritated you. Rather than talk about it, you're going to walk out. If that's how you handle conflict, we'll have to find a compromise, because it's not my style."

He shrugged. "All due respect, you don't want a compromise. You want it your way."

For a solid five seconds she sat still. No twitch, no wide-eyed stare or pressed lips. Zippo body language. By now, his mother would be coming at him with her fists—and anything else within reach—flying.

But Maggie? Nothing.

Great. Now he'd have to brush up on mind-reading skills.

Still seated, she crossed her legs and propped one hand on the arm of her chair. "I have been running my ass off cleaning up the messes left in your wake and you think *I* have *control* issues? Pardon my language, but you are out of your *fucking* mind."

Yep. *Here we go*. The situation itself sucked and he couldn't keep from screwing it up more. Total mess. That was him. Confused and angry and way too in his own head to work through this with her. Best to leave now and get grounded again before this thing went nuclear. He walked to the door and opened it. "I'm not talking about this now."

Finally, she stood. "I don't even know what we're talking about!"

The harsh tone tore at him, scraped against every last working nerve. He whipped back, pointed at her. "Do *not* raise your voice to me."

"Jay?"

Behind him, Sam stood in the hallway, her wide gaze shooting between Jayson and Maggie. Yelling, for his sister, meant hiding. Running for cover. Between the two of them, they were a hot-ass mess.

"It's fine," he told her. "We're having a discussion. That's all." He held one arm out, ushering her toward the exit. "Let's head back to Miss Joan's. We can all use a break."

8

AFTER REVIEWING THE SNIPPET OF SECURITY VIDEO REID HAD sent her, Maggie walked into his office at the training center ready for a look at the entire segment.

Reid looked up from his computer and stared at her with glazed eyes. She stole a peek at the monitor. Ah. Spreadsheets were not his favorite thing, to say the least. As a former Green Beret, her cousin preferred the adrenaline rush of action.

"Hey," he said. "Did you get it?"

"I did. Now I want the rest."

"The rest?"

Oh, boy. Laughing, she snapped her fingers. "Focus here. That spreadsheet is frying your brain. All you sent me was the part of the video with his profile. I'd like to see every frame with him in it."

Reid shrugged one shoulder and Maggie imagined his T-shirt crying for mercy. That shrug from Mr. Muscles might have pushed those seams to their limits.

"Sure." He stood, patted the sides of his cargo shorts and

snatched a set of keys from his right pocket. "Surveillance room. You can watch it on the wall monitors."

"Thank you."

"You could have called me."

"I could have."

"But you didn't."

She grinned at him. "Very astute for a knuckle-dragger."

As usual, he laughed. Being in this family meant plenty of practice at taking a joke. The Kingstons and Steeles played hard and loved equally hard. They may have all been nuts, but with that came unflinching acceptance.

He waved her to follow him the short walk to the surveillance room two doors down from his office. "What happened with the superstar?"

"You mean after someone tried to shoot him?"

"He came back to the house all crabby."

Of course he did. Had he calmed down and talked to her like a reasonable adult, they might have avoided the whole argument. If it was even an argument. Who the heck knew? "I think he's pissed at me."

"You don't say."

"Oh, ha, ha. We were on the phone with Grif and I interrupted him. I'm not sure he liked that, but I know the area. What would have taken him five minutes to explain took me one."

As he walked, Reid offered up a slow nod. "So you took over."

Oh, please. Now he wanted to make this an alpha thing? "I didn't *take over*. I was trying to save us time. I *did* apologize for being rude."

Why was she explaining herself? Again. She apologized. That should have been the end of it. Instead they had drama.

Reid stopped in front of the surveillance room door and shoved the key in the lock. He hadn't looked at her. Had barely turned his head, but his stiff posture and slightly pursed lips told her he had something to say. When it came to opinions, Reid always had one.

"Go ahead," she said. "Say it. I know you want to."

He laughed. "Of course I want to. You probably won't like it."

"As if that ever stopped you? Let's hear it."

"He's a quarterback. He's used to being in charge."

"Not in a criminal case, he's not."

Rather than answer, Reid opened the door for her. Since their teens, they'd been confidantes, sounding boards for any number of situations. Which, she supposed, was the real reason she'd driven up here instead of calling him.

He tossed the keys on the desk and dropped his big body into one of the three chairs. On the wall hung six oversized monitors that came to life as soon as he touched the keyboard. For a guy with huge hands, his fingers moved easily.

"Mags, you're no dummy. You've seen the way he looks at you."

With his military background, Reid understood body language. And apparently she and Jayson were doing a crappy job of hiding whatever—*hopefully sex*—it was they had going on.

"Well, if you'd seen the way he looked at me an hour ago, you'd feel differently."

He clicked a file and within seconds a video popped up. A few more clicks brought them to a timestamp of 10:55 a.m. Forty-five minutes prior to the shooting.

Before hitting play, Reid sat back and swiveled to face

her. "Here's the thing about guys. Guys like him specifically,"

"This should be good."

"Actually, it is. I'm going to enlighten you." He hit her with the cocky smile. "I get this guy. We have a lot in common."

Didn't that just scare the hell out of her?

"We're twisted," Reid said. "We want a strong woman, but not too strong. We like being the hero."

Maggie snorted and Reid put up his hands. "We're also, in some ways, control freaks. When I was in the Army, I never knew when a mission would go sideways. It freaked me out for a while. Then I figured out I could control other aspects of my life. My clothing, my shaving habits, how I put my socks on. Easy, routine stuff. I see a lot of that in Tuck. He's neat. Orderly. When he works out, he's shows up fifteen minutes early and is ready to go when I say. The exception was the day you distracted him. Basically, he's a control freak with a hero complex."

Had she been paying attention, she'd have realized it. She'd have realized that Jayson, who'd almost gotten blown away earlier today, might be suffering some emotional stress from the disruption to his environment. Then, to further complicate that stress, she'd rushed off to chase the bad guy. Leaving him behind.

Did it make her wrong in her actions?

No.

But at least now she understood.

Maggie blew out a long breath. "Well, shoot."

Reid hit play on the video. "Now she's getting it."

Absently, she watched the video scroll. "Not only wasn't he in control of his environment, he was the intended victim. Then I shanghaied the conversation with Grif."

On screen, the shooter appeared in profile, casually walking with a soft gun case hung over his shoulder and something dinged in Maggie's brain.

Hang on. Something about him was familiar. Had she seen him before? She studied him for a long few seconds, but...nothing. This guy could have been any average Joe.

She shook it off as Reid zoomed in.

"No," Maggie said. "Leave the wide view. I want to see his hands."

He panned wider, getting the shooter's hands into view. She tilted her head. "Can you zoom in on his right hand?"

"Sure."

"I hear what you're saying about Jayson, but I can't apologize for doing my job."

"Not saying that. People rely on you. Same goes with him. Once in a while, you gotta throw the guy a bone. Let him be a hero."

Oh, whatever.

This had been her problem with every male suitor in her life. They loved her independence, but hated her lack of neediness. How the hell was she supposed to deal with that?

No way to win.

She pointed at the monitor. "Right hand. He's a smoker." She backhanded Reid on the shoulder. "Do me a favor and keep watching that. See if he tosses the cigarette on the path."

"I'll kill the fucker myself. I mean, trashing our property? What the hell?"

"I'm hoping he did." Maggie headed for the door. "Call me if he tosses it."

"Where are you going?"

"To find Jayson and then hopefully retrieve that cigarette butt."

Jayson stood at Miss Joan's counter mixing Sam's favorite meatloaf for dinner. His cooking lessons taught him that prepping it early allowed the meat to absorb the spices and enhanced the flavor. Since Sam liked onions and green peppers he'd mix one for her and one for him. Minus the onions.

The activity got his mind off the stupid ass argument with Maggie. He still couldn't process what the hell happened there. All he knew was that he'd walked out pissed and hurt.

"Did you put onions in it?"

Behind him, Sam sat at the large farm table messing with her laptop.

"Don't I always?"

She smiled. "Yes, you do. Thank you."

"You're welcome. What are you working on?"

Jeez-a-lou let it be something mildly interesting that wouldn't involve thoughts of a hot sheriff and her handcuffs.

"While you're busy there, I'm trying to figure out what these weird marketing expenses are. I know Will is going to hit me with it on Monday and I want to be ready."

"As opposed to standing around with your thumb up your ass?"

"Something like that, big brother."

The back door came open and in walked Maggie. She wore the same hiking clothes as earlier, but had stripped off the long-sleeved shirt revealing a body-hugging T-shirt and the sculpted masterpiece known as her body.

"Hi." She halted at the door, jerking a thumb over her shoulder. "Um, sorry to interrupt. I usually just walk in."

Instead of begging forgiveness, as he should have, Jay

118   ADRIENNE GIORDANO

continued mixing meat. He'd had two hours to think this through and had yet to come up with a satisfactory explanation. At least for Maggie. He knew how and why he was fucked up. Admitting it to someone else? No way.

So, being the asshole he knew he could be, he shrugged. "Don't apologize. It's not my house. Miss Joan isn't here, though. She went up to the cabin with your uncle."

"I'm not here to see her." She held up her phone so he could see it. "I have a photo of our shooter. Do you recognize him?"

Jay stopped mixing and peered at the screen. Damn. That would have been too easy. He shook his head. "Not ringing any bells."

Maggie shifted to Sam, holding the phone for her as well. "I don't know him," she said. "I'm sorry."

"Don't be sorry. We'll run it through facial recognition and see if anything pops."

"Thanks," Jay said.

Thanks? Really? He shook his head and resumed mixing meat with a ferocity that should have popped a few knuckles.

A heavy, awkward silence filled the few feet between him and Maggie and he finally found the balls to look at her. She met his gaze, then glanced at Sam, who abandoned her laptop in favor of the weirdness between her brother and the sheriff.

"You know," she said, closing her laptop. "I could use a nap. Jay, do you mind?"

His sister. So perceptive. "Go ahead. It's been a rough day."

Sam exited with a backhanded wave while Jayson washed his hands and put foil over the two meat loaves.

"You're cooking," Maggie said. "What's on the menu?"

"Meat loaf."

"Nice."

Never one to leave a mess, he wiped down the counters and set the meat in the fridge.

Time to face it. The one mess he couldn't clean up with kitchen spray.

He leaned against the counter, shoving his hands in his pockets rather than crossing his arms. After his behavior earlier, he'd focus on keeping his body language casual and his words kind.

Looking at her, he saw all the possibilities. Their commonalities, their shared love of the outdoors, their need to be doers. All of it made Maggie great company.

Great company with one minor issue. His days of letting a woman push him around had ended on his fifteenth birthday when he told his mother if she hit him again, he'd hit her back. At that point, he'd given up on his father flying in to save them from their mother. Besides, Jay had already grown bigger and stronger than Drunk Marlene. She'd taken his warning seriously and never raised her fists to him again. Whether he'd actually be able to hit her still haunted him. He doubted it. Which, had she beat him again, would have created a whole other monster because then he'd be the weakling who didn't have the balls to stick to his threat. No way to win.

Maggie rested one hip against the counter, then drummed her fingers against it.

"What's up, Maggie?"

"About interrupting you before—"

"—It's fine."

"I could have handled it better."

"You were doing your job."

Something he hadn't considered at the time. In the span

of a few days, he'd stopped thinking about her as the sheriff and started thinking about her as Maggie, a girl he wanted to get naked with while doing wicked things.

What an asshole I am. The woman was trying to keep him safe and all he could think about was his fucking ego.

He shook his head. "I'm sorry. I acted like an idiot. I'm not used to..." He sighed.

"You like being in charge," she said.

"Yeah. I do."

"Controlling your environment."

She got him. Maybe there was hope for him yet. "Exactly. This morning rocked me. A lot of my life is out of my control, between the paparazzi, the fans, getting my head beat in during games. I can't change any of that. The stuff I can change, that's what I focus on. When it comes to Grif, I lead those conversations. I tell him what I want and he usually gets it for me. The plan might wind up altered, but he manages that for me. Bottom line is, we usually do what I want."

Maggie boosted off the counter and closed the space between them. "I understand that. We may not have big city crime here, but Steele Ridge is in my care. You're in my town and have had two potentially life-threatening situations. And"—she rolled one hand—"we're circling something here on a personal level, so I'm dealing with a major conflict of interest."

He smiled. "What? You don't think it's smart for me to want to screw your lights out when someone is trying to kill me on your watch?"

She nudged him with her shoulder. "I do like you, Jayson Tucker."

"I like you, Maggie Kingston. I'm fantasizing about your handcuffs."

Her lips puckered and she eased out a quiet breath. He didn't hear a whole lot of rejecting the idea.

"Yeah," he said, "handcuffs."

"Okay. We'll get back to that. Let's deal with what happened earlier. In a lot of ways, we're the same animal. We're bound to piss each other off. Can we cut each other some slack on this control stuff?"

Slack. Based on his family history, slack was often too much. Every time his mother apologized, he wanted to believe it. At least until he found the empty scotch bottles.

All of it had groomed him for women who'd fit nicely into three categories. Quiet, sweet, and moldable.

Compared to Maggie, sweet and moldable felt predictable. Boring.

But...he wanted her. So screwed.

He took a chance by dragging his fingers along the underside of her chin, over her jaw, and down the soft slope of her neck. "I like touching you."

She tangled her fingers in his. "Good. I like when you do it."

"Slack," he said. "I'll do better with that and give you space to operate."

"Thank you. That leads me to the second reason I'm here. I reviewed the security video of our shooter. He's a smoker. He walked by the camera puffing away. I'm hoping he ditched his cigarette butt on the path."

"DNA."

She touched his nose. "Bingo. I'm about to go search for it."

"You're going up there? Alone?"

No way. He couldn't have that.

And Sam *was* taking a nap.

"Let me change my shoes and we'll go."

Before he took a second step, she locked on to his arm. "Uh, no. You're staying here."

"Maggie, I'm not letting you go alone. What if the guy is still up there?"

"Um, you're not *letting* me do anything. I decide what I do. That aside, if you're his target, you'll give him a second chance. I'd be an idiot to bring you up there with me. Reid's security guys blocked and checked all the access roads. There are no vehicles. Unless the shooter walked in from town, he's gone."

Jayson peeled her hand from his arm and squeezed it. "Slack."

"Yes, but—"

"If he's gone, we have nothing to worry about. I'll get my shoes."

UNDER THE WANING RAYS OF LATE AFTERNOON SUN, JAY hoofed it up the path with Maggie easily keeping pace. If she were at all intimidated by hiking with a professional athlete, he didn't sense it.

Their boots crunched over loose gravel and Jay gazed up at the towering trees, backlit by a blanket of pure blue. Fresh air, clear skies. Maggie. His crappy day didn't seem so crappy.

Tucked under a clump of trees that could have been spruces sat a structure no bigger than an oversized shed. "Is that where the camera caught the guy?"

Maggie nodded. "Reid keeps emergency supplies in there."

A good idea, but seeing the perfection of this land, even after the shooting this morning, Jay couldn't wrap his mind around it being anything but peaceful. "It's amazing up here."

"This morning aside, there's sanctuary here. I try to hike every weekend."

Every weekend? Did that mean... Forget asking around about her dating habits. She'd given him the opening he'd walk right through. "Who do you hike with?"

Was he fishing? You bet. Pathetic? You bet. Did he care? Not a lick.

"Usually, I'm alone."

Could there be a more perfect answer? Not in this lifetime. "That's a shame."

Even if it did make him damned happy.

She shrugged. "I used to hike with others, but I'm not a leisurely hiker."

"And you don't like slowing down."

"Is that horrible?"

"Not to me. I've spent a career weeding out people who can't make the climb. It's a mindset."

"*Exactly*. Thank you. I don't mind slowing down once in a while, like with Sam today. I want everyone to enjoy this place as much as I do. But week after week after week made me crazy. Then I felt bad about it making me crazy. I mean, I can't expect everyone to like pushing their bodies, right?"

"No, but you have the right to hang with people performing at your level. There's no shame in that."

On her next step, her boot caught the edge of a large rock that knocked her off balance. She tilted sideways, bumping him, and he grabbed her arm before she went over.

"You okay?"

"I'm good. Too busy talking to pay attention." She glanced down at his arm. "You can let go. I won't fall."

Pity, that.

He released her and immediately regretted it. Whatever it was about her, he loved touching her, feeling the heat of her skin, fantasizing about his fingers moving over every inch.

Handcuffs.

She swooped one hand in front of her. "I started losing the joy in this. Can you imagine being in this amazing place and feeling irritated? The one place that de-stresses me and I was stressed. After that, I gave up hiking with others. It was easier than beating myself up."

"Do you do that a lot? Beat yourself up?"

She snorted. "Of course. I'm the youngest sheriff Steele Ridge has seen. And a woman to boot. Add to that a reputation for being a fixer and there's some self-induced pressure. My brothers have a running joke about me needing my own 1-800 number. If there's a problem, Mags can fix it."

"I get that. Some days you want people asking how the hell *you're* doing before they dump their shit on you."

She stopped, smacked him on the shoulder. "Yes! Thank you. It's completely insane. People barge into my office and spill their problems. No one ever asks if I have time or if I'm in the middle of something or if, heaven forbid, I'm having a bad day."

"Start locking your door."

She laughed. When he stayed stone-faced, she rolled her bottom lip.

"Set boundaries, Maggie. People can't respect them if they don't know where they are. My mother taught me that the hard way."

She halted in the middle of the path and her shoulders sunk a mile. "Wow."

"What? Too up in your business? Sorry."

He had a tendency for that. To jump in and save everyone. Some, he knew, couldn't be saved. Or didn't want to be.

"Not at all," she said. "I'm...shocked. You summarized my life in one sentence. Where've *you* been, Jayson Tucker?"

Oh, honey.

The things he'd do for her. He stepped closer, tilted his head and focused on her top lip and that sexy curve that always stole his attention. Two perfect peaks he wanted to lick. "I'm here now."

Those lovely lips twisted into a wicked smile. "Yes, you are."

She leaned in—green light if he ever saw one—and he dipped his head, sliding his lips over hers, gently touching his tongue to hers. Testing. Giving her a minute to decide how far she'd like to take it.

Apparently, pretty far.

She increased the urgency, her tongue matching his stroke for stroke and holy shit, he got hard. Arching into him, she drove her tongue deeper into his mouth, turning up the sex factor a thousand amps. He pulled her in, holding her hips flush against him—*all yours, sweetheart.* God, her body. Amazing.

Her arms came around him and tightened. Maggie, it seemed, gave as good as she got.

At least until her phone chirped. *No, no, no.*

"Ignore it," he said, gripping her tighter. "Please. I'm begging."

Jayson's phone beep-beeped. *No. Please, no.*

She arched back, her brown eyes hot and crazy and, screw it, if she'd let him, he'd do her right here. Right on the damned path. Or against that shack wall. His breath caught and his mind immediately went to the damned handcuffs. *Please, let her have them on her.*

"We're both getting texts," she said. "That can't be a coincidence."

Both phones went off again and Maggie damn near leaped from his arms.

She slipped her phone from her pocket just as he reached for his.

"It's Reid," Maggie said.

"Me, too."

She tapped the message and dipped her head back. This couldn't be good. He peered down at his own phone and read the text.

You're aware I can see you, yes? You fucker.

He burst out laughing. Each day, he liked this guy more and more.

Maggie glanced up and found Jay smiling. "What'd he say?"

He held up the phone and let her read the message.

"What a maniac," she said. "He sent me a nicer version. He's such a butthead. If I didn't love him so much, I'd kill him. Hang on."

She turned away and marched to the shed, her lovely ass swaying in the fitted hiking pants.

She scanned the structure, checking overhead and along the edges. After a minute, she paused and pointed at something on the roofline.

Then she flashed a bright smile straight into the camera. And flipped it the bird.

9

An hour of searching netted nothing. Zippo.

Jay set his hands on his hips and stared up at a darkening sky. "We're losing daylight."

"We can try again tomorrow."

That might be an idea. Maggie peered out over the property, her face long with disappointment. He admired her determination, but they were literally looking for a needle in a haystack.

"But we could be out here for days," she said. "There's too much land. Plus, we don't know if he cut across to the bluff from here"—she pointed straight ahead—"or over there." She pointed again, this time twenty yards to her right.

Her phone chirped and she checked it. "It's Reid. Telling us to get off the mountain before it gets dark."

She tapped out a quick response.

"Let's take a break," Jayson said. "It's been a long day."

"I know we should stop, but I want that damned cigarette butt."

She tucked her phone back in her pocket, took a slug of

water, and handed the bottle to Jay. Hell, she'd had his tongue in her mouth an hour ago, sharing a water bottle obviously wasn't a big deal.

After taking a long drink, he held the bottle out to her. "Finding that cigarette butt is a long shot."

"But if the shooter kept to the path, I'm hoping he wouldn't want to risk a fire and dropped the butt on the path before stomping it out."

"So, he'll kill me but save the trees."

"God knows, I've seen crazier." She shook her head. "Let's call it a night. Maybe I'll run back up here tomorrow and check that other section. Besides, you have Sam waiting for her meat loaf."

"She's probably not even up yet. She'd sleep all night if she could. Major napper."

They trudged along the path, once again reaching the shack where Maggie paused to moon the camera. She didn't actually pull her pants down, but she still left Jay smiling at her antics.

On her way back to him, she turned and blew a kiss to the camera. "My hound of a cousin is probably still watching."

"I'm sure. And I can't wait to get back there and have him kick my ass. Won't that be fun?"

"Nah. He just likes to beat on his chest."

Didn't they all. "Hey," he said, "It's been a long day, why don't you have dinner with us? I might even invite Reid and Brynne."

"And have us crash your time with Sam?"

"Please. She'd love it. We never had big family meals."

"Really? I can't imagine that. My dad owns an organic produce farm. He's always been a foodie. It's a way for us all to connect. Dinner was the one time we'd have together. My parents insisted on it."

Jealousy pinged him. Before his father left, his parents ate out most evenings, leaving Jay and Sam with the housekeeper.

"I'd have liked that," he said. "My father was too busy making deals and my mother..." He took a second to get his thoughts together. For years he'd been protecting Drunk Marlene, giving the public a view of a privileged childhood and loving parents rather than the reality of an insane divorce, a wasted mother, and a father who'd failed to protect his kids.

He faced Maggie, met her eye.

"Your mother what?"

Could he do it? Spill the nasty secrets that had held him and Sam hostage all these years. He'd been obsessed with protecting his family's image. His own image. Now? His reputation was shot anyway.

"If she'd tried to cook dinner she'd have burned the place down."

"Not a chef, huh?"

"Actually, I don't know."

"I'm sorry?"

"She can't stay sober long enough to handle a stove."

Jay wasn't sure what he expected. He'd always wondered about this moment. The time when he finally admitted his secrets to someone outside of Sam. He'd imagined an outpouring of sympathy, people fussing over how horrible it must have been and suggestions of twelve-step programs. None of which he wanted.

Pity, he didn't need.

Maggie shook her head. "That's stressful. We have a family in town dealing with that. I get calls about arguments and it breaks my heart. His kids are terrified half the time, but he won't get help. He says he will and then when he sleeps it off, he changes his mind. It's a vicious cycle."

"That's rough on the kids. After my dad left, she got worse. The drinking, the beatings, everything went to another level."

"Beatings? Oh my God. Your dad *left* you with her? Who protected you?"

He grunted. "Me."

She stepped forward and locked her arms around him. *No, no, no.* A burst of panic rattled his mind. This right here? Weakness grabbing hold, reminding him of all he had to lose. Strong men didn't moan about less than stellar childhoods. Everyone had shit to deal with, why shouldn't he?

He should step back. Dismiss her. Assure her he was fine and over it, by now.

Who he'd be convincing, he wasn't sure.

"I'm so sorry," she said. "How old were you?"

Right about when he should've been pushing her away, he brought his hands around, settled them at the base of her spine, and inhaled. Maggie, all clean air and soft skin might be exactly what he needed. "My dad walked when I was ten. Can't say I blame him with a wife like that, but he left us to deal with her. Then the bitterness got to her and she took to the bottle. It's a brutal combo, alcohol and anger. The trifecta was that I look like him."

She backed away, but slid her hands down his arms, settling them at his wrists. "Oh no."

"I was her main target until I got too big. Then she turned to Sam and I wasn't having any of that. With my mitts being the size of frying pans, my mother and I came to an understanding about her abuse." He shook his head. "I don't think I could have actually hit her. Although, I wonder about that. If I have it in me."

"You don't."

He shrugged. "Luckily, she didn't test me. She never put a hand on us again. It drove her deeper into the bottle, though."

"She didn't have an outlet."

"Nope."

"Which is why you like controlling your environment."

He stayed silent, but patted her hip hoping she'd understand it as acknowledgment. "I've never shared that with anyone."

Jesus, what had he done? A few seconds of the receding panic sparked again and then...nothing but lightness. Which he sure as shit never experienced when it came to his mother.

His ongoing silence equaled Marlene keeping her social status. It worked for him. Her charities and snooty black-tie events occupied her. And freed him.

If he let it slip about the abuse, if he admitted it, his mother would lose friends. That would, like everything else, be his fault and she'd roar back into his life, calling him every ten minutes, raging about what a selfish bastard he was.

"You've been holding it in all these years?"

"I have. It didn't fit the image. The league liked the idea of the blue-blood quarterback. It played better than the wealthy drunk's kid."

"That's awful."

"Don't blame them, I went along with it. With my dad gone, I've spent my life trying to keep my mother calm. If she's calm, she's not bugging me. That's what I want. For Drunk Marlene to stay out of my business."

"I won't share it with anyone."

"Thank you. I'd appreciate that." Having given Marlene more than her deserved attention today, he pointed down the path. "Getting closer."

What he needed was a few minutes of silence. Time to absorb what he'd just done. His family's secrets finally spilled, laid out there. All this time he'd imagined the day when he'd finally admit it, the courage it would take.

Truth was, it hadn't been that hard. Not with Maggie. Probably because of her job. With the shit she saw in a day, his issues hardly shocked her. Maybe that made it easier to admit.

He didn't know. All he knew was that it felt right.

JAYSON WAS QUIET. THE MAN HADN'T UTTERED A WORD IN— she casually checked her watch—nearly fifteen minutes. He'd dropped that bombshell about his family and then went silent.

Typical male.

Then again, what was left to say? Particularly since he'd trusted her enough to confide something so personal. He'd trusted her not to sell that juicy tidbit to the press.

Whether it said something about her character or his— maybe both—she wouldn't analyze. It didn't matter. He'd kept his painful past a secret, managing to avoid bitterness while growing into Jayson Tucker, football hero.

Maggie peered ahead where the path widened toward the road. She drew a long breath and reminded herself to call her parents. Tell them how thankful she was for them. Growing up, her situation was not the norm—Dad being the stay-at-home parent, while Mom conquered corporate America—and Maggie, many times, found herself...embarrassed. *What does your father do?* In her youth, that question had become a landmine. At first, she'd freely admitted her father was a stay-at-home dad. At least until a classmate's mother gave her the *oh* face. The one where she opened her mouth, but nothing came out. That had been the first indication something was different about Maggie's parents.

And she'd resented it. Resented that her father wasn't the stereotypical dad, working outside the home while his wife ran carpool.

"End of the road," Jay finally said.

"It is, indeed."

He kept walking, his pace steady, but not fast. "Thank you."

"For?"

"Being you." He pointed to a hole in the ground, then latched on to her elbow. "Watch your step."

"Got it."

Rather than let go, he moved his hand down the length of her arm. Sensing what he wanted, she slid her fingers into his and found herself the recipient of Jayson Tucker's movie-star smile.

"Maggie," he said, "you're the best thing about this week."

She squeezed his hand, then bumped him with her shoulder. "Thank you. You're creating chaos in my town, but..."

"What?"

"I don't know. You bring out something in me that reminds me I'm female."

He snorted. "Oh, you're definitely female."

Now she bumped him harder. "Listen, smart-ass. In my job, being female is a handicap. It's a boys' club and I've worked hard to be accepted. It's not easy."

"I understand that. You don't want them to see you as hot."

"Exactly. Even on traffic stops, men flirt with me. At least until I give them the ticket they tried to charm their way out of."

"It must limit your dating choices."

"Lord, you have no idea. Can't date cops because half of them—at least the ones I find— are intimidated by a woman with a higher rank. They all want to be in charge. Which is fine. I'm smart enough to know when to let that happen and when to tell a man he's full of crap. It's about choosing my battles."

He stopped walking and faced her. "You need a guy confident enough to accept your strength."

Once again, he got her. How the hell did he know this stuff? "That's exactly what I need. Are you that guy?"

"Without a doubt."

She smiled. Couldn't help it. It all sounded good—too good. Jay had enough cocky, pro athlete swagger to pull it off. To make himself believe it. Could he handle her and her life for the long haul? For nights when her phone rang at all hours and times when she couldn't pick up and follow him around the country to watch his games because she had responsibilities beyond making him happy? Sharing her life wouldn't be easy. Particularly for a man used to getting things his way. "I guess we'll see."

"I guess we will."

They reached the end of the path where the mouth of the road opened to two narrow lanes, then they turned left toward Maggie's vehicle.

Wait.

She froze. Stopped right in the middle of the road because...oh, my.

"What?"

She'd parked her SUV so it straddled the road and part of the shoulder, leaving enough room for another vehicle to maneuver around it. Anyone parking on this road would realize they'd have to do the same or risk blocking other vehicles from passing. "The shooter. He had to have left his car here. Just like us. It's the only path with enough room to park."

She moved ahead, scanning the ground as she walked. "Help me look."

"Oh-kay. What am I looking for?"

"I have a friend who smokes. She won't do it in her car. It's a lease and she's afraid of burn holes."

"So, she tosses the cigarette butts before she gets in."

Maggie pointed two fingers at him. "Boom."

A sudden energy zipped between them and Jayson broke away, his long legs tearing up the space heading the opposite direction. "I'll check down here."

Maggie strode across the two lanes, moving slowly as she scanned the ground. Tire tracks. In the dirt on the shoulder. New? If not, they'd have to be recent to still be intact. And Britt hadn't parked here earlier.

Wide tires. A truck. Possibly a pickup. She snatched her phone from her pocket and snapped a few pics. Couldn't hurt.

After checking the photos, she inched sideways, farther into the road, and continued her study of the pavement.

Come on, come on. *Be there for me.*

"Anything?" Jayson called.

"Not yet. Tire tracks, though."

She took two more steps and the track curved toward the street. As if pulling onto the road.

Maggie stopped and slowly turned. If he'd parked where

the tracks were, the driver's side door would be...right...
about...She stepped left.

Here.

Her gaze swept the ground, back and forth, back and
forth and...whoa.

Barely a foot in front of her sat a cigarette butt burned
clear to the filter and her pulse slammed so hard her
head spun.

"Jayson! I've got something."

"No shit?"

She swung her head right, found Jay jogging toward her.
"No shit, fella. Do me a favor. There are gloves and baggies
in my center console. Grab them. I'll take pictures of where
we found the cigarette butt and then we're sending that
baby off to the lab."

AFTER TAKING JAYSON UP ON HIS INVITATION TO SHARE THE
meat loaf she'd watched him mix, Maggie walked through
her front door to find Riley sound asleep in the living room.

Her younger sister, a nerd by anyone's standards, clearly
needed to get a life if she was napping on Maggie's couch on
a Saturday night.

Between helping Dad create hybrid vegetables and her
own job, Ry worked hard. If she wanted to come by for a
nap, she'd always be welcome.

Maggie gently closed the door and winced when the
snick of the lock reverberated in the quiet house. Shoot.

"Hey."

Maggie turned and found a groggy and yawning Ry
stretching her arms.

"Hey, yourself."

"I fell asleep."

"I see that."

"I came over to see if you wanted to grab dinner and a movie. Where were you? You're always home at night."

Yowzer. Riley wasn't the only one who needed a life. Maggie thought back over the last six months. Not one date. Well, there'd been one. Sort of. A friend of a friend who was so nervous about going out with a woman who carried a gun, he'd nearly wet himself.

*Sccccr*atch that one.

Riley adjusted her glasses, the cute round ones she'd gotten after returning from Costa Rica on some super-secret endurance project she couldn't speak about. Lord, one would think her sister worked for the CIA.

At the moment, her would-be-spy sister's sable hair was mashed on one side and sticking out on the other. A vision of Mom shaking her head and tsk-tsking popped into Maggie's head. A brush would be in order before baby sister left.

"I was over at Aunt Joanie's."

"What's going on there?"

"Nothing. I was meeting with Jayson Tucker."

"His Hotness?"

Mags rolled her eyes and headed down the hall toward her bedroom. She'd been renting this place since Mom and Dad returned from South Dakota and moved back into the family home.

While in the B grabbing coffee one morning, she'd overheard one of the locals filling the town criers in on her mother's broken hip and the stress of moving her to an assisted living community. Which left the poor woman's cute little bungalow, with all the furnishings, empty. Three days later, Maggie had a new home, even if it was temporary until she figured out her next move.

Before Maggie reached her bedroom, Riley fell in step behind her. "What's the scoop on him?"

I sucked his face off.

Twice.

Couldn't say that. As much as Maggie would have enjoyed a little girl gossip with her sister, Jayson's stay in Steele Ridge meant keeping him safe. Doing her job.

"You know I can't talk about it. The two incidents involving him are active cases."

"And you know that's not what I'm talking about."

She hooked the right into her room and went straight to the closet. What she needed was a hot shower, or maybe a cold one to get her mind off one Jayson Tucker, his amazing body—and tongue—and the Kingston competition-worthy meal he'd just cooked.

She opened the closet's bifold doors and peered up at the two-tiered organizer. Five of her seven uniform shirts hung on the rod, all of them washed, pressed, and evenly spaced to avoid wrinkling. Every Wednesday, Maggie dropped her uniforms at the dry cleaner and by Thursday, they were ready to roll. Shirts, slacks, ties, everything neat and tidy.

"Your closet is insane. It's like a military operation in there."

Slight exaggeration on her sister's part. "It is not. It's organized. I know exactly where everything is." Maggie ran her hand over the crisply folded T-shirts stacked on the corner shelf. Red one. It was a red kind of night. She grabbed it along with a pair of running shorts and turned back to her sister who'd flopped spread-eagle on the bed.

It brought Maggie back nearly eight years when it was just the two of them living in the family house. Both a little lonely without their parents, but making a go of it together.

On bad nights, they'd huddle in the giant king-sized bed with a tub of popcorn—Mom would have killed them—and watch B-grade horror movies together.

Maggie set the clothes on the bed and went to the dresser for underwear.

Meanwhile, Riley smacked a hand against the comforter. "Come on, Mags! Give me something juicy. I heard he works out with Reid in the morning. Have you seen him with a shirt off?"

I wish. She snatched a plain white bra and matching panties from the drawer. Jay with a shirt off. She pictured it. All his cut muscles that narrowed to lean hips and...

She closed the underwear drawer with way more force than necessary and the smacking of wood made her jump.

"Ha!" Riley said.

"What ha?"

"You *have* seen him with his shirt off."

"No." She laughed. "But a girl can dream."

She pinched Ry's toe and her sister made room for Maggie to drop next to her. She rested her hands on her belly where a steady pulsing brought memories of Jayson's lips on hers, their tongues clashing and...heat. Lots of heat.

"He's so hot," Ry said. "If he's intelligent, he'd be the perfect male."

Leave it to nerdy Riley to worry about a man's IQ. "Ry, you don't get to have a career like his without being smart. This latest crisis notwithstanding."

Riley rolled to her side, propped one hand under her head. "Tell me about him. Is he nice?"

"He is. He's..." Hmmm, how to explain this? "Mr. Calm and Cool. Charming, but soulful at times."

"Soulful? *Really?*"

"Yeah. There's a quietness to him. It's not weird, though."

She met her sister's gaze. "You know that feeling? When it's so quiet there's tension? That's not him. When he's quiet you feel...safe."

Riley's eyes narrowed. "You carry a gun. When have you ever not felt safe?"

"It's not that kind of safe."

Or was it? Whatever it was, every time Jay got close something in her brain shorted and she craved...him. His arms around her, pulling her tight like he did on the mountain earlier.

A soft sigh streamed from Maggie's throat. Dear God. Sighing? What the hell was wrong with her.

"Oh, no," Riley said. "You're crushing on this guy."

"I'm not crushing on him. What is this? High school?"

In full avoidance mode, Maggie rolled to her feet, scoffing the whole way. So she was attracted to him? Didn't mean they had to get all weak in the knees over it.

"With the way you're all sighing, it could be. And, Sis, who could blame you?" Riley sat up and moved to the edge of the bed where she peered up at Maggie. "You're the sheriff. I get that. But who says you can't have a little fun with the stud while he's in town?"

Was that what she wanted? A slam-bam affair with the football star? To be a groupie he'd picked up along the way?

She scooped the clothes off the bed. "Not interested."

"In what?"

"A fling. Or whatever the hell we're calling them these days. Not with him."

"Why?"

"Well, first of all, I'm supposed to be protecting him."

"Which you are."

Debatable. So far at least. She'd change that, though. "Second, I'm not his type."

Dammit. *Idiot, Maggie.*

"Ha!"

Again with the ha. "Riley, if you don't stop saying that, I'll hurt you."

"You know his type." She poked her finger. "You checked him out."

Her sister knew enough to badger the truth out of her, so she might as well admit it. Besides, she had the perfect excuse. "Of course I checked him out. He's in my town. It was background."

"Nice try. What's his type?"

Maggie waved the clothes in her hand. "I'm taking a shower."

Knowing Riley, she'd be off the bed and on her heels in two seconds.

"So," Ry said, "take a shower."

And, yep, by the time Maggie walked across the hall to the bathroom, Riley stood in the doorway, her foot blocking the threshold.

"Ry, I need to shower."

"What's his type?"

Typical Kingston, refusing to give up. If Maggie allowed it, they'd be squared off in front of the damned bathroom all night.

Not happening.

"What's his type?"

Grrrr. Riley and that stubborn streak. Well, fine. "Petite. Elegant. *Fragile.* I mean, my God, the man dates women who get blown over by a breeze." She ran her free hand the length of her torso. "In case you missed it, that's not me."

"Heck no."

Gee, thanks.

"Why would you want to be any of those things? You're

our Mags. You always know what to do. You can fix anything. You practically carry this town on your back. That's why everyone loves you."

Yeah, but her sister was missing the point. Underneath all that surface stuff, underneath being the go-to, always responsible Maggie was a woman who hadn't had sex in over a year. Forget that. She didn't care about the sex—not much anyway. It wouldn't hurt to have a little passion in her life, but that wasn't it, wasn't the thing she ached for.

She, go-to, responsible Maggie, wanted to be held.

By a man.

Who wasn't a family member.

She wanted to feel...safe. And damned Jayson Tucker did that for her.

But somehow, as usual, she'd never be enough. No matter how hard she worked, everyone expected more.

Heat stormed her cheeks—oh no—and Maggie whirled. A shower. That's all she needed. It had been a long few days and the fatigue finally caught up with her.

When a spurt of tears—*crap*—welled in her eyes, Maggie shook her head. Crying. Terrific.

"Mags?"

She sidestepped, tossing the clothes on the edge of the sink before moving to the tub where she cranked the ancient faucet hard enough to snap the thing off. "Ry, give me a break. Please."

"Why are you upset?"

The shower head spurted and released a steady stream of water. Seventy seconds. That's how long it would take to get the hot water flowing. Seventy seconds to avoid Riley and her questions. "I'm not upset. I'm tired."

"I know you. Are you *crying*? You never cry."

And didn't that say it all? Her family assumed she never

cried. How had things gotten to the point where people thought her a machine?

She cupped her hand under the shower spray, let the cold water refocus her whirling mind. Cold water. Her father's cure-all for tears.

Then she faced her sister. "Of course I cry. You guys just don't see it. I cry a lot actually. At silly movies, when I see little girls with their dads, when my family leaves." *When I climb into my bed alone.* "All of those things make me a little weepy. There's nothing wrong with it."

"I didn't say there was."

"Then what do you want from me?"

"I want to know why you're about to cry when we're talking about Jayson Tucker."

Ah, dammit. "Because, Ry. I like him. A lot. He makes me feel things I haven't felt in a long time. He respects me and he's not intimidated by me."

"Awesome. What's the problem?"

"I said it already. I'm not his type. He likes being in charge. We're both alphas. And our worlds don't exactly mesh. The football star and the small-town sheriff? Picture us in *People* magazine. Me in my boots and uniform. It doesn't work."

At that, her sister made a gagging noise. "Now you're being dumb. You're a sheriff. So what? It's your job. You wouldn't go to games or events in your uniform. You own other clothing, Maggie."

With the shower still running, she pushed by Riley and stormed down the hall to the second bedroom that doubled as an office. As expected, Riley followed.

Still on the printer were the photos she'd found the last two nights. Background, she kept telling herself.

She snagged the pages from the printer and shoved

them at Riley. "Here. Look at these women. Do you see anything about them that makes you think I can live in that world?"

Stubborn mule that she was, Riley folded her arms. "I'm not looking. I think you're being a goof. You like this guy, right?"

"Obviously."

"Is it, you know..."

Riley waggled a hand between them and Maggie nearly choked out a laugh. "Mutual? If his tongue halfway down my throat is an indication, I believe so."

Riley's mouth flopped open. "You *kissed* him? With *tongues*?"

"Oh, honey, I didn't just kiss him. I mauled that man."

Yow. That sounded bad.

But baby sister's eyes lit up and her lips split into an all-teeth smile. "Mags! You *have* to give me the scoop. What was that like? He's so darned hot."

Now Maggie did laugh. Riley. So funny. Never mind the crying and confessing her feelings about a total wild card of a man. Somehow they'd gotten to this extremely uncomfortable place that had Maggie, the responsible one, admitting she'd done naughty things.

And it felt...good. Freeing. Silly.

When had she been silly last? Long time.

Wasn't that the shame in all this being responsible? She'd forgotten to have fun.

What the hell? Might as well go all the way.

"It's amazing, Ry. His arms are like steel rods, but when he wraps them around you, he's gentle. I want to snuggle with him." She slapped her hands over her face. "Can you even believe I just said that? I must be insane. As soon as Grif finds him a job, he'll leave."

"But football is seasonal. He'll come back."

As smart as she was, a pure intellectual, Riley had a sweetly naive romantic side that believed love conquered all.

Maggie smiled. "We're getting way ahead of ourselves here."

"So what? If you ask me, that's what you need. If I could find a hot guy like him, who could maybe get me out of my own head long enough to actually have an orgasm, I'd never let him go. Come on, Mags. Live a little. If he's all the things you say he is, you'd be dumb to not go for it. And one thing I know about my sister. She's not dumb."

ACCUSTOMED TO CRACK OF DAWN WORKOUTS, JAY'S BODY brought him from sleep—even on a Sunday—at 5:45. Blame it on the wicked hot dream about Maggie and her hand-cuffs. Those handcuffs. There had to be some rule about not using them for recreational purposes. If so, he had no shot because buttoned-up Maggie didn't seem the rebel type.

He might have to get another pair of cuffs they could use. An unofficial pair.

He turned on his side, ignoring the discomfort of what might be the hardest, absolute granite of an erection he'd ever experienced. Maggie, Maggie, Maggie. He stared at the closed window blind while contemplating another hour of sleep.

Thanks to the dream, he didn't imagine any rest would be possible. And laying around would only force him to think about his current life situation. Out of work, drop-kicked by sponsors, and the target of a couple of attempted homicides.

Great life, pal. All because of a locker room brawl. He

threw the comforter back and set his feet on the floor. "Stupid, fucking idiot."

Somewhere down deep the nagging started. That vicious, debilitating voice reminding him where he came from, reminding him he shared his mother's DNA.

That was enough to scare the hell out of any man.

I'm not her. He ran his hands over his face, scrubbing away the morning fog and worries.

"Just fix it," he muttered.

That's all he needed to do. Fix it and get his life back on track.

He scooped his phone from the bedside table. The minute he turned it on, the damned thing would explode into another day of insanity. Calls and texts and voice mail, calls and texts and voice mail. For a guy out of a job, he was damned busy. Even on a Sunday. A day when all his friends would be on the field.

Don't go there.

The fact that he'd even turned the phone off was a stabbing indication of how much his life had changed. Before, he'd never turn it off. Maybe airplane mode or silent, but off? No way. He'd been the team's leader and as such, he'd made himself available 24/7.

No team leader.

No team.

Don't.

He set the powered-down phone on the nightstand. An hour of peace. That's all he needed. A shower, some breakfast, and then he'd let the world in.

Good plan.

Twenty minutes later, the aroma of pecan coffee drew him into the kitchen where the ticking of Miss Joan's ancient analog clock disturbed the quiet.

Tick, tick, tick.

His gaze shot to the shiny countertop where a ceramic jar held a jumble of wooden spoons, rubber spatulas, and a set of tongs. During his childhood, his mother's kitchen, normally staffed with professional chefs, had a compulsive efficiency to it. Counters cleared, utensils sorted and placed in drawers according to their purpose. All of it way too intimidating for a young kid. Jayson supposed that was the point. The insanely organized and antiseptic kitchen kept him and Sam away. God forbid they leave a fingerprint on the refrigerator when grabbing a glass of milk or a snack.

In their minds, the kitchen, a place where most families gathered, became a hostile environment.

Tick, tick, tick.

He peered at the wall and the Mickey Mouse clock Miss Joan told him she'd bought the day after she'd married her husband. It had survived six rambunctious kids.

In his mother's kitchen, the cheap clock, regardless of its sentimental value, would have been tossed. Or maybe donated to the less fortunate.

Jay walked to the sink where he grabbed a mug from the drain and poured his coffee.

Tick, tick, tick.

Somehow, the repetitive sound enhanced the peaceful energy of the house and brought him to a place of mindfulness. Being still.

When the hell had *that* ever happened?

He took a sip of coffee and held the mug up, toasting to Miss Joan and kitchens meant to be enjoyed.

10

JUST AS JAY POURED THE FIRST PANCAKE ONTO THE GRIDDLE, Miss Joan entered the room. Freshly showered and dressed in jeans, a light cotton sweater, and soft boots, she looked casual, yet put-together. His mother? She wore diamonds to the gym. Anything to hide the secrets.

"Well, look at you," Miss Joan said. "I can't remember the last time someone cooked for me in my own house. Of course, my boys aren't exactly handy in the kitchen. The girls do just fine, though."

"I hope you don't mind," Jay said. "I figured I owed it to you. I don't want you waiting on me. I've lived alone a long time." He flashed a smile. "I'm low maintenance."

Even he could see the humor in that statement. Nothing about Jayson Tucker, fallen football hero, could be considered low maintenance.

Miss Joan topped off his mug. "I can tell by the mobs of reporters."

Clearly the Steele boys inherited their mother's sarcastic wit.

He let out a laugh that damn near tickled his toes. *Thank you, Miss Joan.*

She gestured to the griddle. "You like to cook?"

"I do. When I bought my first house, I hired a chef to give me lessons. Once a week for a year."

He considered it his effort to banish the demons in his head and get over his anxiety about the kitchen. By the time he'd hit puberty, the most important rooms in a home— bedroom and kitchen—gave him nightmares.

"Oh," Miss Joan said. "I'd love that. Such fun. My sister —Maggie's mom— sure could use it. I swear, she'll poison us one of these days."

He made a show of looking over both shoulders, then leaned closer to Miss Joan as if he were about to share nuclear codes. "Don't tell anyone, but I watch Food Network."

"A boy after my own heart. What's your specialty? Besides pancakes."

"I do a decent rack of lamb. I'll make it for you one night. I'm curious what you'd think."

After retrieving a plate from the overhead cabinet, she set it next to the stove and propped one hip against the counter. "But you're my guest. I'm supposed to take care of *you.*"

He shrugged. "Cooking relaxes me. It keeps me from thinking too much."

"You've had a rough week. And, you know, you don't have to worry about that nonsense in this house. Everyone who comes here deserves peace." She paused and looked around the kitchen. "For years I loved this place. I never told the kids, but I'd drive up here and just park on the side of the road so I could sit for a while."

"Why?"

"I honestly don't know. There's something about this land. I think I was meant to be here. Even with all that craziness going on at the training center, this is my sanctuary."

He flipped one of the pancakes. "I can see why. I was just thinking how peaceful it is."

"Excellent. I want everyone who walks in here to feel what I feel. And if my son says you belong here, then we're going to make sure you have peace." She snorted. "We'll just have to keep Reid and that wicked mouth of his out."

He set one of the pancakes on the platter. "I like him. He works me hard, but I laugh a lot, too. He's a good man. Grif, too."

"When they're not fighting, they make me proud. I'm sure your mama feels the same about you. A professional athlete. That's no easy task."

After transferring another pancake, he prepared himself to give the usual speech about how his parents gave him opportunities most didn't have and how thankful he was. All true, of course.

Also the standard *get over on someone* response befitting the superstar quarterback. For years he'd been shoveling his own brand of bullshit. Protecting his carefully crafted image for the long haul.

With Miss Joan? Who'd given him a comfortable, chaos-free place to lay his head?

It all seemed wrong. *I'm a fraud.*

"My mother," he said, "isn't like you."

"Honey, if she had a personal chef, that's for darned sure."

There it was again. The humor. "Chef aside, your personalities are different."

He took a second to frame his thoughts, line up the

adjectives just right so he didn't come off sounding like a rich, spoiled kid dissing his mother. "She's...tough," he said.

And scary as shit when drunk.

"Tough can be good," Miss Joan said. "Was it?"

He moved two more pancakes to the platter and poured more batter. Then he turned to face Miss Joan, meeting her gaze head on. "She's not you. Everyone should have you. She taught me a lot, though. Made me resilient. My protective instincts and an ability to deal with crisis resulted from her. I'm also a forward thinker. For that, I'm thankful. The rest?" He shrugged. "Can't worry about it."

Because, yes, folks, he'd spent his entire adolescence thinking ahead to the day he'd leave behind his batshit crazy mother and her iron fists.

Voices sounded from the porch followed by a woman's laughter. The door flew open and banged against the wall and Miss Joan sighed. Reid stepped inside, his shoulders taking up half the friggin' doorway. The guy was huge.

Behind him, Maggie gave him a shove. "You're such a jerk."

Wisps of her honey-blond hair hung loose from her ponytail and her face had a glow that came with released endorphins. She wore second-skin tights again and an unzipped hoodie over a sports bra that displayed tight abs. The vision did nothing to dismiss the idea of his own set of handcuffs.

A welcoming smile took over Miss Joan's face. "Well, good morning you two."

"Hey, Mama," Reid said. "Superstar, you ready to work?"

Arms extended, Miss Joan took two steps toward Maggie.

"Oh, Aunt Joanie, you don't want to hug me right now. I'm seriously sweaty."

Miss Joan waved that off. "Nonsense. You know I love you any way I can get you."

She wrapped her arms around Maggie, pulling her in. And if Miss Joan's hand on Maggie's back wasn't all that interesting, the profile of Maggie's tights hugging her ass was extremely fascinating.

At least until Reid cleared his throat. Jay glanced over and got the *I will fuck you up l*ook from the badass former Green Beret.

Jayson went back to his pancakes, carefully flipping them while Miss Joan released Maggie and pulled out two chairs. "Sit. Both of you. I'll get plates. Jayson is treating me to breakfast, but it looks like he has enough batter there to stretch. How about I start bacon? We'll cheat and microwave it."

"Speaking of bacon," Reid said, dropping into a chair. "Wait'll you hear this one."

Maggie smacked him on the shoulder. "Don't even start."

"Hey," the big man said. "Not my fault he buried you. With bacon."

Miss Joan arranged bacon on a plate. "I swear, y'all speak in tongues. Is this about dinner the other night?"

Reid made a dinging noise. "The sprouts won. How she let sprouts beat sweet potatoes, I have no idea." He looked at Maggie. "How *does* that happen?"

Maggie swatted him on the head. "Cash had five pounds of bacon in there. He plays dirty! Next week, I'm giving them enough sugar to make thirty pies."

Jayson slid the last of the pancakes onto the platter and set the stack on the table. "What's this about sprouts?"

"My aunt and uncle are insane," Reid said.

Maggie dug her fork into the stack of pancakes. How he loved a woman who actually ate.

"It's more my dad. He's a major foodie. When we were growing up, he'd quiz us on spices at the dinner table. Somehow that morphed into us having family dinners where everyone makes something. Whoever has the best dish wins. To keep it fair, we all vote. Cash sandbagged me." She snatched a slice of bacon from the plate Miss Joan pulled from the microwave and held it up. "We love bacon."

Who the hell were these people who had family dinners and actually enjoyed it? The idea of it sent Jayson and Sam into convulsions. Family dinners in the Tucker household meant silence. Silence guaranteed you wouldn't get a slap or a punch or a whipping with grandad's old belt.

When the house phone rang, everyone's head snapped up.

Miss Joan reached for the cordless mounted on the wall. "Who on earth is calling so early?" She checked the ID and punched the keypad. "Grif? Are you okay? What's wrong?" A brief pause ensued until she glanced at Jayson. "Oh. Okay. You scared me, calling so early. You all right otherwise?...And Carlie Beth and the girls? Good. I love you. Come see me."

She passed the phone to Jayson. "It's Grif. For you."

"Morning, boss," Jay said into the phone. "What's up?"

"Where's your damned phone? I've been calling for an hour."

Jayson checked the counter, then the table. Nothing. Patted the pockets of his track pants. Nothing. Christ sakes, he left it upstairs. *Yeah, way out of routine here.* "Sorry. I left it upstairs."

"Dude, you're killing me."

"I know. Shocking. What's up?"

"Get somewhere private. We've got a problem."

WHILE THE OTHERS CHOWED DOWN ON HIS PANCAKES, JAY excused himself and stepped out onto the porch, settling into one of Miss Joan's Adirondack chairs.

If Grif sent him in search of privacy, this couldn't be good. "Go," he said, steeling himself for whatever news his agent had.

"I just got a call from a reporter. It's a small paper in the Village, but..."

"If he has it, someone else does. What is it?"

"Christine Webb."

The Golden Boy's wife. Maybe she'd finally talked him into getting help.

"What about her?"

"What happened at that party two weeks ago?"

That fucking party. Jay hadn't even wanted to go, but since one of his receivers was hosting, he'd put in an appearance, intending to stay only a short while.

"That's where all this shit started. I told you that."

"Well, tell me again because this reporter thinks you're having an affair with her."

With all the crap that had gone on in the last week, it shouldn't have surprised him. Still, Jay gawked as a bird dipped and looped in the morning sun. Obviously, the bird wasn't dealing with half the bullshit Jay was. "Is she saying that?"

"I don't know, but it's coming from somewhere."

"They're making like *this* is why I beat his ass in the locker room? Because I'm fucking his wife?"

"That's the gist of it." A brief silence ensued. "Jay, look, I have to ask."

Great. Now Grif was doubting him. Well, he could ask all the goddamned questions he wanted. Jay had nothing to hide. "Go ahead, Grif. I want this cleared up. It's one thing for my team to release me and lose endorsement deals. That's only money. This is my reputation they're screwing with."

"I know," Grif said, "which is why we're having this conversation. I'll get this settled. At that party, were you drinking?"

"Not a drop. I was tired and had an early workout the next day."

"Good. Did you come on to her at all?"

Jay rolled his eyes. The idea of it, that after years of working together, Grif needed to confirm Jay hadn't been hitting on a teammate's wife, well, what did that say? It said that his agent didn't know him well enough. Which was partly Jay's fault. With his family history, he kept certain things close. In doing so, it created a vast space between friend and acquaintance. Grif fell somewhere in between.

"Tuck?"

"I'm here. Thinking."

"Shit."

"Not about that. About the fact that I haven't let you know me well enough to know I wouldn't screw a teammate's wife. So, the answer is no, I didn't hit on her. At all. We did talk at that party. She asked me about him. What his mood was, how he behaved in the locker room. I knew something was up. I asked her if everything was okay and then she hit me with him abusing her."

"Shit. And then what?"

"Obviously, I wasn't comfortable. I suggested she talk him into getting help. Therapy or whatever. Discreet places. Someone interrupted us and she walked off. That was the only time I spent with her. I left right after. There were half a dozen guys outside when I left. They saw me go. End of it. The next day, Eric came to me. She'd told him what I said about them getting help. He told me to stay out of it. The following week, I almost got my head taken off by his former roommate."

"Okay," Grif said. "That's all I needed. I'm gonna get with your PR people and see what we can do. And, I hate to tell you this."

"What now?"

"Your mom."

"What about her?"

"She gave a statement."

His mother. Of course. She couldn't resist piling on. "How bad?"

"The usual. How disappointed she is and such. Ignore it. Don't answer your phone. After your workout, come to my office."

"I'll come now so we can deal with this."

"No. We want this to be business as usual. You're focused on staying in shape. Your career is the priority, blah, blah. If we do that, this other stuff will look like a minor distraction. It's a blip, Tuck. I'm out."

Jay hit the button on the cordless and rested his head back. "Hell of a fucking blip."

AFTER PUTTING AUNT JOANIE IN CHARGE OF GUARDING THE last three pancakes, Maggie stepped onto the porch, ready to warn Jay his breakfast might soon be gone if he didn't hurry up. One look at the throbbing muscle in his jaw suggested breakfast was the last thing on his mind.

"Sorry to interrupt." She held up her keys. "I'm taking

off, but your pancakes were amazing and Reid is about to eat your share."

Jay held the phone up. "I just hung up."

"Is everything okay there? Anything I need to know about?"

"Professionally? No."

"What does that mean?"

He sat forward, rested his hands on his knees and squeezed. Whatever Grif had said to him, it had sent his mood plummeting.

He stood, stared out at the trees swaying in the light wind, and after a minute walked toward her, leaving a good two feet between them.

Where oh where did playful Jayson go?

"Maggie, you're, uh, probably gonna hear some stuff today."

"About?"

"Me."

What else was new these last few days? Jayson Tucker was all anyone could talk about. "All right. What will I hear?"

He met her gaze straight on. She liked that about him. His direct manner, his willingness to be honest. In her line of work, people lied to her on the daily. As a result, she'd developed a lack of trust with strangers. With him, she sensed something different, something that put her at ease.

"Ah, dammit." He shook his head, hesitated and then forced it out. "You'll hear that I'm having an affair with a teammate's wife."

Ah, dammit, was right.

Finally a man came into her life that she wanted to get to know a whole lot better and he turned out to be an adulterer. *I sure can pick 'em.*

"I'm not," he added. "Crap. I should have said that straight away. I'd never do that. *Ever.*"

She eyed him a good long time, waiting for the flinch. For the look away, but...nothing. No sign of deception. "Good answer, Jayson. For many reasons. Why tell me?"

Tentatively, he reached out, tucked a stray hair behind her ear. "Because I like you. Because I might be here a few weeks and I'd like to take you to dinner and I don't want you thinking I'm that guy. I'm not."

He might not be having an affair, but obviously the rumor was out there and that begged questions. "Why this rumor? Why this woman?"

"She's the wife of the guy I socked in the locker room."

"Oh, boy. That's messy."

"Yeah. I think it's spin control. The team will say I'm having an affair and that's what started the fight."

Which left her once again wondering what exactly happened in that locker room. "What did start the fight?"

"It's a long story."

"Summarize."

He smiled. "See, that's what I like about you. No bullshit. Just...wham."

"Call me cautious. You just said you'd like to take me to dinner. What I hear in the press might impact my decision and I want to hear your side first."

"Okay," he said. "I'll tell you everything."

It took less than two minutes to share the whole stinking mess about Eric Webb smacking his wife around and the woman confiding in Jayson.

When he finished, Maggie nodded. "That's why the two of you got into it in the locker room? He told you to stay out of it?"

"Not totally. Prior to his wife talking to me, I'd been sidelined for two weeks with a banged-up knee. Eric played in my absence. I was due to have one more week of rest, but after Eric found out his wife talked to me, he spent two days blowing passes in practice. The night before last week's game, the coach benched him and told me I was cleared. During the game, Eric Webb's former college roommate almost shredded me with an illegal hit. That was no coincidence."

"Oh my God. That's why you attacked him. You thought he set you up."

"I lost my shit. I mean, it's one thing to be pissed at me, but he could have ended my career. Or left me in a wheelchair."

"Maybe that's what he wanted."

"Which sucks, considering the time I've put into mentoring him. I know I'm aging out. I get it. My goal was to finish my career with my team. To be remembered as the guy who helped the younger one along. That's what I wanted."

Squeaky clean Jayson Tucker. After all of this nonsense, he had nothing to lose by telling the truth to anyone who would listen. Including the media. *Something's missing.* "Why haven't you told anyone?"

"And look like a shit for putting his private business out there? They have kids and I've—"

He broke off. Shook his head.

"You've what?"

He waved it away. "Nothing. But, my mom decided to weigh in. I haven't seen the article, but the reporter must have called her and apparently she wasted no time telling him how disappointed she is. She couldn't resist, I guess."

"Oh, Jayson. I'm so sorry."

"It's all right. I should be used to this by now. She doesn't usually go to the press, but I've been ignoring most of her calls. This is her way of getting to me. She never takes a break."

The door came open and Reid stuck his head out. "Hey," he said to Maggie. "I thought you bolted."

"I'm going," she said. "Was discussing security with Jay."

Reid's gaze passed to Jay, back to Maggie, and then to Jay again. He wasn't buying any of it.

"Superstar, you done sitting around?"

Jay held his palm up and looked at Maggie. "Am I done sitting around?"

She stepped off the porch and gave him a backward wave. "Call me later about that other thing we discussed and we'll set up a time."

Dinner.

She wanted to go to dinner. For the company and to figure out just what Jayson was hiding.

AT DAWN MONDAY MORNING, JAY FINISHED REID'S TORTURE session with a few laps around the outside of the obstacle course to clear his mind and flush the lactic acid from his body. Mind-body maintenance in one shot. Couldn't beat it. He made the final turn thinking ahead to stretching, a shower, and food before another meeting with Grif.

And that would be his day. Quite a change from the over-packed schedule—and zero downtime—he'd had barely a week ago.

He needed work. Anything to get him back on the field and mentally active. Then again, he'd been the asshole who blew up his career, why would any team want him?

"Going down in flames, dumb-ass," he muttered.

He shook his head and contemplated the mess known as

his life. Adding to the drama was the crazy-assed voice mail he'd received from Eli Paskins. Apparently, his former boss was outraged over the cheating scandal. Fighting in the locker room was one thing, Eli had said, spreading rumors about marital infidelity crossed the line and Eli wanted to make sure Jay knew he would do whatever he could to squash that nastiness.

Now Jay didn't know what the hell to think. If the team had started that rumor, Eli was playing him. If they hadn't started it, Eric Webb's management must have. But how could Jay know?

Complicated situation all around.

One he couldn't obsess over too much or he'd lose his mind.

He stopped at the picnic table where Reid left him a jug of water to finish. Next to that sat his phone and keys. If he got really lucky, he'd see a missed call or text from Maggie. He'd spoken to her briefly the night before to inquire about the lab results on the cigarette butt. Yeah. Results. That's why he'd called.

Using her all-business voice, she'd informed him favors had been called in to rush the results, but even with those favors, it would take a few days.

Now he was left anticipating that moment when he'd see her name light up his screen. A feeling somewhat foreign to a guy who generally had his pick of women. Some of whom were damned pleasant to be around, but none of whom turned him into a horny teenager again.

At least until Maggie.

He tapped the phone.

Damn.

Nada. Zilch.

Yep. Going. Down. In flames.

He should have asked her to dinner the night before. Even if going out in public wasn't possible, he could have run over to her place and whipped up a meal. Or found somewhere private for them.

Because one thing was for sure, he wanted her clothes off and that tight body tucked under him. The two kisses they'd shared told him she wouldn't be shy in bed. Maggie, he imagined, would rock his world when the stress of life got to him and he wanted hard, *active* sex with someone he wouldn't break in half.

And Maggie Kingston with her toned body and aggressiveness fit the bill.

God knew he could use it right now. A change from the docile, moldable women he surrounded himself with. Easy on the eyes and zero flak about his schedule. But with all that accommodating came the flip side. The too quiet side of a woman who wouldn't tell him what she wanted in bed.

His phone rang. Ha. Maybe he'd willed her to call.

Sam.

Definitely not the female he'd hoped for, but he'd always take a call from his sister. She'd left the night before, heading back to South Carolina with a promise to check in during the week and set up another visit for the following weekend.

He tapped the video button and her face filled the screen. Her puffy, glazed eyes did nothing to hide the fact that she'd been crying. He knew his sister. And her cues.

He straightened up, pushing his shoulders back, readying himself for Drunk Marlene's latest antics. Their mother seemed to be the only person capable of reducing Sam to tears. If nothing else, the Tucker kids were a tough pair.

"Hey," he said. "What's up?"

"I..." She paused and turned her head, revealing the headrest behind her.

By now, she'd usually be in the office. "Why aren't you at work?"

She peered out the window for a few seconds, drew a long breath, and faced the phone again. "I got fired."

Fired.

Well, shit. That lying weasel Will Burns had assured him Sam wouldn't take a hit. What the fuck?

"I'm sorry," he said. "I'm not letting them fire you because of me. I'll call him."

"No," she said. "It's not...the scandal."

He didn't believe that. At all. "They're lying then, because he told me you were great at your job."

"You won't believe this."

After the last week? Not a lot would shock him. "Try me."

"The board thinks I'm embezzling. That I helped Jack siphon money."

What. The fuck? "*You're* the one who told them about the funky accounting."

"They're saying I was covering myself. You know, trying to make them think I wasn't involved by coming to them first. It has to be coming from the board."

The board. Will Burns should man-up and stop hiding behind his board. "Sam, it's crap. I'll call him."

"No. Jay, I'm not twelve. I can fight my own battles. Besides, it's too late. I'm out."

Just like that. Disposed of. Seemed to be a trend with the Tuckers. This wasn't him slugging a teammate, though. They were accusing his sister of a crime. If convicted, she'd do jail time. A dull throb thumped against the back of his eyes. "I won't call, but we need a lawyer. I'll line someone up."

Sam shook her head. How could she even argue this one? "Sam, I'm not fighting your battles. I'm finding a good lawyer to defend you against serious allegations."

"You don't think I realize that? It's my butt on the line, Jay. But Will said considering you're my brother, and with all the press, they wouldn't press charges."

"For *embezzlement*?"

"Think about it. They're a nonprofit. Any hint of impropriety could ruin them."

Jay thought back to his meeting with Will and his comment about not making their parting a focal point. "They want it to go away."

"Of course they do."

He stared up at the gray clouds overhead. Sometimes, hell, most times, he didn't understand the world. By now, given what he'd seen of a celebrity lifestyle, the backflips people did to save their own asses was commonplace.

Fix it. He looked back at the phone screen, into his sister's blue eyes. "I'm not buying it. They wanted to get rid of you because of me. The embezzling is an easy fix. A way for Will, that lying son of a bitch, to squirm out of our agreement. Sam, I'm sorry, honey. I know you liked that job."

"I did like it. But if they got rid of me because of you and instead accused me of stealing, I don't want to work there. They're not good people."

"Now what? You keep quiet? Let them pin this on you? No way."

"I have to or they'll bring in the authorities."

A nonprofit willing to walk away from an embezzler to save their reputation. None of it felt right. "How much money are we talking about?"

"I don't know. If it's what's in that account I found, it's a lot. Possibly millions."

The throbbing behind his eyes intensified. They were lining Sam up for a full-scale investigation. Buying time to make a case against her.

Lawyer.

"Sam, you need a lawyer. Just in case. Do you still have those reports you downloaded on your laptop?"

"The ones showing your supposed travel reimbursements? Sure."

"Good. Go home, get clothes, and come to Steele Ridge. We need to figure out what, if anything, they have on you."

"No way."

Maggie sat at her desk eyeballing the expense estimate for borrowed manpower from the State Police. The sun streaming through her windows should have provided warmth, but the estimate? That sucker froze her to the bone. At least she wasn't so frozen she couldn't reach into her desk drawer for an antacid.

She popped one, then another. Couldn't hurt.

A copy of the report had been sent to Grif so her cousin would see just how much money his client had to pony up. Who knew having a hunky football star in town could be so complicated?

The loss of her Bahamas trip confirmed it. She glanced down at the tear-away calendar where today's motivational quote told her to kick a door of opportunity open and wedge her foot in it. Three weeks ago, she'd drawn one of those silly cocktail umbrellas under the quote. If all had gone well, today would have been getaway day.

She'd wanted that trip. Badly. Not just for the break, but

to connect with other women. She had plenty of friends, but not women on the job, who understood the challenges of a female in a male-dominated position.

The Bahamas trip, she'd hoped, would provide a mental break from her constant looping mind. Schedules, employee reviews, reports, and budgets. Never enough time for all of it. Since taking this job, she'd gotten comfortable with to-do lists that bumped to the next day. Or the next week.

A knock on her open door sounded. Blaine—Deputy Do-Right, as Reid called him—stood in his crisp uniform, the creases in his pant legs so sharp they'd slice off a head.

"Ma'am, Jayson Tucker and his sister are here to see you."

A gentle tingle cruised down her neck. Jay. Here. After that line he'd given her about a dinner date, she had reason to feel a little girly-girl over a surprise visit. Besides, when was the last time she'd allowed herself to feel girly-girl over a man? Especially when wearing a drab beige uniform.

"Send them in," she said.

Did she have time to check her hair? Not that she could do much with a ponytail, but a look couldn't hurt. Maybe throw on some lip gloss she carried in her backpack.

Lip gloss? A light touch of makeup was one thing. Makeup meant polished. Lip gloss? Whole other affair.

One she desperately needed.

With Jay.

Girl, you need to calm down.

Except, there he was, in her doorway, all blond-haired and blue-eyed, looking like the stud he was in designer jeans and a white button-down that fit his chest just enough to make Maggie's mouth water.

What's the temperature in here?

Even if she'd had that lip gloss on, it'd have melted right off.

"Good morning," Maggie said as Sam slid into view. "This is a surprise. I thought you went home yesterday."

"I did. Now I'm back."

And something in the way she said that, the emphasis on "now" gave Maggie pause.

She pointed to the guest chairs in front of her desk. "Have a seat. Is everything all right?"

Jay held his arm out and waited for Sam to step inside. She wore a gray skirt that hit just above the knee and a cream blouse under a light blue blazer. A black mesh briefcase hung on her shoulder. Workwear.

Jay followed her into the office, allowing her to pick the seat she wanted. They had an odd rhythm, these two. Being the oldest of her siblings, Maggie understood it, but this went beyond family hierarchy. This, given what Jay had told her about their mother, was about protection.

Control.

Sam glanced at her brother, who lifted one shoulder. "Your news. You tell her."

"I went into work this morning and was promptly fired."

Okay, then. Rough start to the week. Holy moly. Maggie sat back and the spring on her chair squeaked, breaking the sudden silence. "I'm sorry. What happened?"

"Remember the other night when I mentioned I found weird accounting?"

Oh, no. Jay stared straight at her, reading her reaction. Well, he wouldn't get one. In her job, success often meant suppressing her body language. Whatever this was, she'd handle it professionally.

When Maggie didn't answer, Sam continued. "They think I was helping the CFO embezzle money."

If Jayson thought he had public image issues before, wait until the press got a hold of his sister being an alleged thief.

"I see," Maggie said. "And why would they think this?"

"Aside from the bogus marketing account that, ironically enough, I discovered, I have no idea. On Friday, I brought the accounting discrepancies to the director's attention. This morning I got fired."

Un-hunh. Maggie slid a gaze to Jay, then back to Sam. Something wasn't adding up here. "That's quite a leap. What proof did they offer?"

"No proof," Jay said. "They have a report showing some reimbursements. To me. Which never happened. I've never taken a dime from them."

"You think they set you up?"

"That's exactly what I think. Someone, the CFO I presume, threw in a couple of payments to me here and there so it wouldn't raise any flags."

"He's the one who quit?"

Sam nodded. "Supposedly. I never thought he quit. He left too suddenly. They probably gave him the same speech they gave me."

"What speech?"

"They told her if she left quietly, they wouldn't call in the authorities."

She'd seen oddball things, but major charities didn't usually let embezzlers go free. Maggie rolled her bottom lip out. "That makes no sense to me."

"It didn't for me either." Jay circled one hand. "Think about it. They dumped me over potential bad press. Imagine if people found out that donations—from folks who can barely afford their mortgages—were siphoned off by a greedy CFO. The fallout would be disastrous."

"They'd lose donors."

"Bet your ass, they would."

Maggie met Sam's eye. "So that's it? They tell you you're a crook and this goes away?"

"Pretty much."

"I don't believe it," Jay said. "I see this as them building a case while she thinks she's clear. How much evidence do they need to come after her?"

So much for the surprise visit being personal in nature. The girly-girl excitement deflated like a punctured tire. Still, of all the people Jayson could have reached out to, he once again trusted her with damaging information. For that alone, she should be grateful.

Would advising them be a conflict of interest? Maybe. They were friends, though, and for her friends, people she cared for, she'd do just about anything.

"I have limited information," she said. "I can only give you generalizations."

"Understood. I apologize if we're putting you in a tough spot. If you want us to go, say the word. No harm. No foul."

She waved the suggestion away. "We'll work with hypotheticals."

Hypotheticals, in Maggie's world, were abundant when it came to garnering information.

"Thank you."

"You're welcome. If I were investigating this, I'd be looking for checks written, electronic transfers, anything that shows money went from the charity's accounts to Jayson's." She looked at Jay. "Are you sure they've never reimbursed you for something? Even the smallest amount?"

"Never. I made sure. Celebrities can get crucified over accepting money from the charities they represent. More to the point, I didn't want it."

He'd tried to avoid the very thing happening. The life of a superstar navigating public perception.

Maggie tapped her fingers on the edge of her desk. "Then we"—We? When did this become a *we* situation?—"need to figure out what they have."

Sam reached into her briefcase and held up her laptop. "When I found the weird account, I downloaded the folder to my online storage so I could work on it over the weekend."

Oh, boy. This could be sticky. Most companies stripped terminated employees of all files and access to proprietary information. If they'd asked Sam for the laptop or any charity-related content and she lied...

Maggie held up her hand. Before she even looked at, never mind touched, that laptop, she needed to ascertain how far over the line she might be here. If Sam had lied about having company files, Maggie would be forced to step back. She cleared her throat. "That's your personal laptop?"

"Yes."

"Do they know you have the reports?"

"No."

"Did they ask you for their proprietary information?"

"No. They asked for my keycard and my company laptop. Which I gave them. They didn't ask about any files."

The line was thin, but it was most definitely there. At the very least, the charity was negligent in ascertaining whether Sam had turned over all proprietary information. They didn't ask. She didn't tell.

Maggie let out a sigh. A thin line indeed. "Let's go into the conference room and see what we can find."

11

────────

Maggie spread Celebrate Hope's bank statements, spreadsheets, and a reconciliation report across the conference room table.

She paused at one of the spreadsheets and skimmed each row. An entry with Jay's name showed a reimbursement for travel expenses totaling $4,235.00. Below that, another. This one marked miscellaneous.

$9,729.45.

That was a whole lot of miscellaneous.

Even with his wealth, would a man forget reimbursements that large?

She held up the page. "This one shows two transactions. One for travel and one for miscellaneous. Do we know what they're for?"

"Yes," Sam said. "I looked into them. One is supposedly for a first-class flight to LA."

"LA," Jay said. "When did I go to LA for them?"

"You didn't."

Maggie set the report down. "Can we prove that?"

"I absolutely can. The only trips I've made to LA were

for games. My accountant has all my credit card statements and receipts for the last five years."

"Good," Maggie said. "What about this miscellaneous one? That's the big daddy."

Sam shook her head. "I haven't found anything on that yet. I was looking for that one last night before I went to bed."

Copies of checks. If they had those, they might be able to tie them back to something. If that something even existed. Maggie said, "My department gets copies of our canceled checks with our bank statement. Does the charity's bank send copies?"

"Yes. They come with our e-statements." Sam scooted sideways in the rolling chair and opened her laptop. "What are the dates on those reports?"

"One is March and one is August."

Jay rose from his chair and cornered the table while Sam's fingers cruised the keyboard. "I had training camp in August. Nowhere near LA."

"I have March and, hold on a sec." Sam nibbled her bottom lip as she studied the screen. "Here's August."

Intent on seeing the evidence herself, Maggie joined Jay, standing beside him. His shirt sleeve brushed her bare skin, his heat pulling her a smidge closer as the three of them studied the laptop screen. Sam clicked on a PDF file and an image of a bank statement with copies of canceled checks—front and back—popped up.

"There," Maggie reached around Sam's shoulder and pointed to a check made out to Jay. Beside it, the flip side image showed the back of the check.

With Jay's signature.

WHAT IN HOLY FUCK?

Jay swiveled sideways and faced Maggie, looking straight at her. Considering what Maggie was probably thinking right about now, his next statement might be the most important of his life because he knew what he'd be thinking. That the guy in front of him was a crook. A liar to the nth.

"I did *not* sign those checks."

She held his gaze—zero movement, not even a millimeter—while she processed his words. "You're sure?"

The way she said it, that tinge of...what? Something. Not doubt, but not assurance either. Something squarely in the middle, but bottom line was she didn't believe him. Not completely. After admitting things to her he'd only trusted to his inner circle, her lack of confidence damn near gutted him.

All the years of dealing with Drunk Marlene, the compartmentalizing and visualization, the *coping* he'd done hadn't prepared him for the systematic unraveling of his career. And now this? This...this...shit...could land his ass in jail.

If it got out.

Protect, protect, protect.

Still with his eyes on Maggie, he touched Sam's shoulder. "Would you give us a minute please?"

His baby sister wasn't an idiot. She sensed the energy shift and peered over her shoulder, first at Jay and then Maggie. "Um, sure. I'll grab a soda or something."

In the few seconds it took for her to get through the door and shut it behind her, Jay put a stranglehold on his temper.

He locked his jaw, fought the wave of anger banging around inside him. Goddammit. So *fucking* tired of living in a *fucking* bubble where every *fucking* thing he said became fodder.

Well, screw that. Officially out of a job, he was done constantly running offense. Let the defense have a shot. Starting with Maggie, a woman who'd interrupted his thoughts—handcuffs and all—way more than any sane man should allow.

He pointed at the laptop. "You don't believe that's not my signature."

"I didn't say that."

"Didn't have to, sweetheart. I can read you."

"Oh, I doubt that."

She could doubt it all she wanted. "Then look me in the eye and tell me you believe me."

She looked at him. Dead straight in the eye, just as he'd asked. He waited. *Come on, Maggie, tell me.*

A long few seconds of silence dragged on while Jay's rib cage came apart. Apparently, the good sheriff couldn't grant the back half of his request.

"Great," he finally said. "I thought we'd gotten so close."

Sarcasm. The Tucker family go-to. Did it make him a prick? Sure. But from the moment she'd stepped into his world, he'd been honest. *Painfully* honest in detailing things that scared the ever-loving shit out of him if the tabloids got hold of it. And now Maggie considered him a liar.

Ironic.

"Don't be an ass," she said. "I'm in law enforcement and being as objective as possible. Do I think you're lying? Of course not. Am I willing to consider, as any good law enforcement official would, there's a chance your accountant handed you a stack of checks to endorse and these were in there? Absolutely. Anything's possible."

"I didn't. I'd know it."

"Then making sure shouldn't be a problem."

What now? His head snapped back. "What the hell are you talking about?"

"I'm talking about proving it."

Let's do it. "All for it, babe. How?"

"Knock it off with the sweetheart and babe crap. If you want my help, treat me like I have a brain. Understood?"

Damn, she had a mouth on her. "I wouldn't be here if I didn't think you had a brain."

"Then act like it. Am I clear?"

She raised her eyebrows and cocked her head. Body language speak daring him to comment. Stubborn woman. Matched with him, they'd take ornery to another level. But she had a point. He'd pushed her. "You're clear. I apologize if I offended you."

"You didn't offend me. You pissed me off. Big difference. Now, as for proving your innocence, I testified in a trial last year. A fraud case involving a resident. Prosecutors brought in a handwriting expert to verify signatures."

A handwriting expert. His life was coming apart and she wanted to bring in someone practicing a wildly imperfect pseudoscience.

He walked to the window, leaned against the frame, and stared out at the patch of lawn behind the building.

At least there were no reporters.

For once.

Jesus, he couldn't do this anymore. The hiding. Not defending himself when people called him names and accused him of rotten things. For years, he'd dealt with it. Thrived on it, even. All to save his precious reputation. His money in the bank, as he liked to refer to it, because shoe companies—the absolute gold standard of endorsement deals— liked squeaky-clean athletes.

Good Christ, had it all been worth it? All that work and the one person he actually wanted to trust him, had doubts.

He let out a laugh. Gave in to whatever kind of pain this was. "Why not?"

"Why not what?"

He turned away from the window. "Do it. Bring in your expert. Hell, bring in a truckload. If it'll prove I'm not lying to you, I'll pay for it." He had to get out of here. Get control of himself again. He walked to the door, swung it open, intent on marching out. Except, he stopped. Paused to look at her. "I'll do one better. I'll have my accountant audit my books. He'll show you every dime. Then we'll have the proof. Will that be enough for you, Maggie?"

He left. Strode right through the door, leaving her and her lack of faith behind.

At 7:00, Maggie walked through her front door and punched in the alarm code to stop the incessant beeping. Her already pounding head didn't need that aggravation. Grandma's hand-carved drum table sat wedged in the corner by the door and Maggie set her bundle of junk mail on it. As a kid, she'd sit at the table and play solitaire or set up her toy cash register with stacks of canned and packaged goods that Gram would buy. Hours and hours of play had been had there, all of them with her ever-patient grand-mother who shared stories of a lonely childhood and a girl's ability to be strong yet feminine. No wonder Mom was a corporate beast. When Gram passed, Maggie's broken heart healed a wee bit when she inherited the table. Gram's final gift to her.

She kept it near the front door so she'd see it every day and think of Gram. Currently, two days' worth of mail she should open sat on it, but it had to wait. Her raging headache took priority. It hit hard ten minutes after Jay implied doing her damned job and gathering proof of his innocence meant she didn't trust him.

Had to love it when people asked for help and then got pissed at her methods. Whatever. This would be why she had no room for men in her life. She slid off her uniform jacket, hung it on the coat rack beside the table, then yanked off her work boots and socks. She kicked the boots aside and shoved her socks into her pants pockets.

Stupid men. What did she even need one for?

Maybe she'd get a dog instead. Unconditional love right there. Dogs took work, though, and she didn't have that kind of time. Unless Reid would provide day care and let the pup hang at the training center. That might work. Plus, he'd keep a dog in shape by letting him run along the property.

Mulling over the benefits of large breeds, she yanked her shirt from the waistband of her pants and strode the short hallway to her bedroom where she threw her dirty socks in the hamper by the door. If her head didn't hurt so much, she might go for a quick run. Or call Reid and have him meet her at the obstacle course for a nighttime try at smashing his record. She had enough anger tonight to make it happen.

By the time she reached her closet, she'd unbuttoned her shirt, revealing the drab T-shirt underneath. Really, she needed to update their uniforms. Maybe switch it up and go for navy rather than bland khaki.

The doorbell rang and she stepped back from the closet, head cocked. Only salespeople rang her bell. Family and friends knocked. Or, as Riley had done the other night, let themselves in because God forbid she might be doing something her family shouldn't see.

What if she'd been standing naked in the hallway when someone barged in?

Or, perhaps, crazy as this might be, having sweaty, multi-orgasmic sex with a hunky football star?

Boundaries. Isn't that what Jay—that pain in the ass—told her? If she wanted people to respect her privacy, she'd have to tell them.

Bam, bam, bam. Whoever was at her door, wasn't going away. Damned salespeople. Still wearing her gun belt—*that'll get rid of 'em*—she made her way to the front door and checked the peephole. On the other side stood none other than the hunky superstar who'd given her the god-awful headache. Plus, he looked insanely hot in a T-shirt that stretched tight over his shoulders. The rest probably looked damn good, too, but only so much could be witnessed via a peephole.

Too bad she was still pissed at him for leaving her office before she gave him a piece of her mind.

"Maggie," he said through the door. "I saw you walk in. Open up."

Gladly. She flipped the lock and ripped the door open. "Don't you ever walk out on me in the middle of a *discussion*. Who the hell do you—"

"—I'm an asshole. I'm sorry."

"—think you are?"

Wait. *What?*

Asshole. *Well, true that.*

But the apology. Dammit! The man gets her all wound up and then has the nerve to apologize before she can even unload on him. Totally unfair.

She spun away, leaving the door open. "You. *Suck.* You really do." She moved into the kitchen, waving a hand over her shoulder. "I'm all ready to let you have it and you go and take responsibility. The least you could do is let me yell for a second. Get rid of all this"—she flapped her arms—"*frustration*."

She may have heard him laugh. If he did, she might shoot him. Right there on her doorstep.

"Can I come in?"

She opened the refrigerator, grabbed two beers, and dropped them on the counter. "The door is open, isn't it?"

Cautiously—smart man—he stepped in, closing and locking the door behind him. "You're still wearing your gun." He flashed his magazine-cover smile. "I was afraid to move."

"Save the smile, charm boy. I'm mad at you."

"I don't blame you."

"I was working the problem. We have a crime. With that crime, we have evidence. Proving your innocence starts with eliminating the endorsed checks. It doesn't mean I don't believe you." She popped the top on one of the beers. "Do you want one?"

"I want twelve."

"I have six. You'll have to make do and share."

Across the breakfast bar, she handed him the beer. Their fingers brushed on the exchange, sending a shock of heat zooming up her arm. Damn that, too. Ooh, she wanted to just stay mad at him.

Unfortunately for her, being pissed off created a need for release. And the way her body melted every time Jay Tucker came within a thousand feet, that need for release manifested itself in ways it shouldn't.

Ways that required him naked and in her bed. Because, *lawdy,* it had been awhile since she'd had some good, old-fashioned nookie.

And with a man who looked like Jay? Between the face

and his body? Total no-brainer. She slugged a gulp of beer. So, she was female. Sue her.

"Maggie, look. I've been stewing over this all day. I lost my head. I *am* sorry."

Bastard.

Already she sensed herself weakening. *I'm such a sucker.* Or maybe she'd simply made peace with her inability to hold grudges. It made more sense to relieve herself of *that* burden.

She came around the breakfast bar, meeting him on the other side. "I accept your apology. But, clearly, we had a miscommunication. You walking out doesn't tell me why we had that miscommunication. I always need the why, Jay, or whatever this is between us has no chance."

"You're right. I realize that now. I was caught up. I'd confided in you about my mother. That took a lot. I trusted you."

"And you thought my suggesting a handwriting expert violated that?"

"Yeah."

"Then you're an idiot as well as quick-tempered."

He smiled. "I guess so."

"Damn you."

"I know. It's a curse." He hooked one finger into the waist of her uniform pants and tugged her closer. So close she felt his warm breath against her neck.

He dipped his head and her pounding headache gave her a reprieve. After the day she'd had, if those luscious lips touched her right now, in her house, where the quiet let her think about all the things missing in her life, game over.

She stiffened for a split second, prepping herself as he drew closer and...did it. Kissed her. His warm lips touched her skin in that spot where the base of her neck met her shoulder and, oh, that was nice. Better than nice. Enormously nice in a completely over-the-top way that made her breasts tingle and her core light up like Christmas and the fourth of July all at once.

She tilted her head, giving him full access. Total pushover, that's what she was. In her own defense, it had been over a year since she'd had sex. And even then it had been a complete snooze-fest. The basic *let's just get to the orgasms* sex that didn't leave her in a terrible rush to do it again.

With Jay? Something told her she'd want to do it again.

And again.

He dotted more kisses down her neck. "Forgive me?"

Too smooth, this one. "If I hadn't forgiven you, you wouldn't be this close to me."

"Excellent," he said.

Smooth might do her some good.

She arched in, pressing her body against his, dragging her hands up and through his short hair. He brought his arms around her and gripped her ass and—hello, there—his erection pressed against her.

"Wow," she said, half gasping.

"Un-hunh. What are my chances of getting you out of this uniform?"

"Keep doing that thing to my neck and I'd say your odds are improving."

He brought his hands back around, pulling her shirt from her pants and his slightly calloused fingers brushed her skin, sending a zip shooting straight to her nipples. She wanted those fingers everywhere.

He broke the contact, moving to the button on her pants.

"I can do it," she said.

"Not a chance. I'm stripping you out of this uniform.

Piece by piece."

Gently, he nipped at her neck, tugging the skin just enough to heat her up another thousand degrees.

"You're going to undress me? Everything?"

"If it's okay, yeah. It's one of several fantasies."

If that didn't shock her, not much would. She rolled her eyes. "The charm. It's almost too much to bear."

"It's not..." He locked his gaze on hers. "I think about you —like this—a lot. About peeling off the uniform and seeing what's underneath. I want you, Maggie."

Before she could speak, he lifted the drab brown T-shirt over her head and tossed it somewhere in the vicinity of her couch.

That morning, considering it a day like any other, she'd slipped on her normal sports bra. When had she become such a creature of habit and gone for the comfort? Then again, who knew she'd be entertaining Jayson.

She swallowed her humiliation. "The sports bra is good for work."

Ach. Really? Did she just say that?

He leaned in, dotted kisses along her shoulder and down her collarbone. He hooked his fingers under the bra to the bottom of her breasts and ignited another shot of heat.

His fingers moved to her back and worked the hook on her bra. Then it was gone and she stood there, bare-breasted with her uniform pants and gun belt still on.

He let out a long breath. "Jesus. You're stunning."

"I think you're horny."

"I am, but it's not influencing my opinion. From the second I saw you shredding that obstacle course, I knew I wanted you. You're amazing."

He unhooked the buckle on her gun belt and brought

his lips to the rise of her breast. *God, God, God, the man.*

She let out a small moan. "The belt. Don't let it drop."

Regrettably, he backed away, holding the belt up. "I'll let you take care of it."

About to self-combust, she set it on the breakfast bar, but before she let go he spun her back to him. "Bedroom," he said. "If we're doing this, I want it done right. Not like a couple of horny teenagers trying not to get caught."

She brought the gun belt with her and he trailed behind her, the tips of his fingers lightly moving down her back as they walked. In the bedroom she set the gun belt on the dresser and turned, grabbed hold of him, and mashed herself against him.

"You've got me," she said. "I'm here. Whatever this fantasy is, get it moving because I'm ready for you and I'm not in the mood to wait."

He picked her up, tossed her on the bed, let her watch as he peeled his shirt off. The muscles, the rock-hard body of an athlete, all for her to feast on.

He kicked out of his shoes and peeled his socks off. Then his pants and boxers were gone and his erection sprang free. *Mine, mine, mine.* She sat up, ran her fingers over his hips, up his torso to his pecs, all of it hard, sculpted muscle.

He moved over her, forcing her back against the mattress and eased beside her, propping one hand under his head as his free hand explored her body.

Rather than embarrass herself with her lack of sexy underwear, she hooked her thumbs into the waistband of her pants and her cotton briefs and removed everything at once.

Efficiency. Always.

"Let's see what you've got, Superstar."

12

He'd show her. He'd show her all night long if she'd let him.

She reached down, wrapped her fingers around his monster of a hard-on, and he dropped to his back on the bed while she had her way with him.

Who was showing who?

But, damn, his fantasy had taken on a new element. Maggie. Next to him. Breasts against his bare skin. Bringing him to a climax with only her hand.

He opened his eyes, found her grinning down at him. "What are you thinking about, Jay?"

"You."

"Do tell."

That did it. He sat up, shoved her to her back, and straddled her. "Are you a talker, Maggie?"

"Sometimes." She ran her palms over his pecs and back down. "Sometimes, like now, I know what I want. Which would be you. Inside me."

He leaned down, kissed her hard with plenty of tongue that she seemed to like.

Condom.

He pulled back. "Uh, sorry to interrupt this but, I, uh…"

"Condom," she said. "Do you have one?"

"We are of the same mind." He eased off of her, reached for his wallet still tucked into his pants pocket, and took care of business while Maggie slid her mile-long leg along his back, all that soft skin waiting for him.

Holy shit. He'd screw her blind if she wanted. He'd do just about anything Maggie Kingston wanted.

Small-town girls. Go figure.

Condom in place, he came back to her, running his hand up her leg, then wedging himself between them. Maybe he'd play a little.

Except, Maggie locked her legs around his waist and arched up, apparently ready for him. "It's been a long few days," she said. "Sometimes I talk, sometimes I don't. Sometimes I want hard, fast sex. Sometimes I don't."

"And now?"

"Hard and fast."

He slammed himself inside her and she cried out—yow, that was too rough.

He stopped, held his breath, prayed she didn't push him off and kick him the hell out. When she thrust her hips, he opened his eyes. "Did I hurt you?"

"No. I'll tell you if you do."

She arched against him, urging him on and they found their rhythm, two people figuring it out, moving together, pushing each other. He drew back, entered her again and again, each thrust building on the last until the two of them were damned near off the side of the bed, but Maggie stayed with him, gripping his shoulders, digging her fingers in.

"God, please, keep going. Don't…stop."

Not in this lifetime.

His orgasm built, each thrust pushing him closer and closer to that edge, but he held on. Wanted her to go first so he could see it. The buttoned-up sheriff coming unglued under him. But...

"Maggie, I'm gonna..."

"Don't stop! I'll kill you if you stop!"

He met her gaze and the two of them burst out laughing. *Maggie, Maggie, Maggie.*

She bucked her hips and he closed his eyes because... *can't do it.* The explosion hit him hard, making his body quake as he pumped and pumped and pumped himself into her and on that last thrust, she dug her fingers in, her short nails pricking his skin and driving his orgasm to another level as her body stiffened.

She let out another cry and bucked under him one last time before the two of them collapsed into the bed with Jay on top.

"Well," he said, "holy fucking workout."

"Jayson Tucker," she said, "where have you been all my life?"

AFTER AN EARLY MORNING TEXT FROM JAY THAT REID HAD gone into town, Maggie cruised through the gate at Tupelo Hill and pulled into the training center parking lot. If she timed this right, she could do a couple of training runs on the obstacle course and be on her way home for a quick shower before 8:30.

She hopped out, entered the building, and found Gage coming from the gym looking, as Micki liked to call him, all Captain America in workout shorts and a T-shirt saturated with sweat. Unlike Reid's, Gage's body was more long, lean muscle and his short blond hair reinforced the whole Captain America moniker.

"Hey." He dabbed his workout towel over his face. "You missed Reid."

"I know. Not here for him. I'm practicing on the obstacle course. I *will* beat his time."

"I love it. You need me to time you?"

"Nope. I recruited Jay to help me."

At that, Gage cracked up. "Nice."

"Reid's always reminding us all how he holds the record. I can't stand it anymore."

"You'll have the course to yourself. He's meeting with the zoning commissioner and if it's like any of the past meetings, he'll be gone awhile."

"Excellent." They exchanged a high five and she made her way to the back door with a little skip in her step. Why not? After last night with Jay, she felt...lighter. Energized. And, hopefully there would be more nights like that.

Swinging through the back door leading outside, she found her man—her man?—standing next to the picnic table where Reid liked to sit and bark orders. That damned table was so familiar Maggie considered it a close personal friend.

Sunlight glinted off Jay's blond hair, bringing out red flecks she hadn't noticed before. Intimacy did that. Brought a level of focus that hadn't been there before.

When he left her house that morning, he'd been in jeans from the night before. Post-workout, he wore basketball shorts with a sleeveless T-shirt that showed off the tree trunks known as his arms.

Ooh, the man was jacked. "Hey, mister," she said.

He glanced up and cocked his head, watching her as she

walked. She fought the urge to break the eye contact and check her attire.

"Hey, yourself. Have I mentioned I love looking at you?"

"Last night. Several times. It doesn't get old."

"Good."

He eased his arm around her waist, his warm fingers cruising under the long-sleeved yoga top she'd thrown over her sports bra. On contact, she heated up, her body responding to the same touch that had driven her half mad the night before. He kissed her gently, gliding his lips over hers, a soft caress unlike the kisses they'd shared before. And one she liked. Very much.

So many sides to this man.

"Um," she said, "Gage is inside. And, well, you know Reid's security cameras are probably recording."

Jay shrugged. "It's not a problem on my end. Yours?"

"Not one bit. Just reminding you in case you don't want people to know."

"Why would I want that?"

"I..." Why indeed? "I don't know, actually."

"Unless one of the Steeles intends to sell the story to the rags, I'm good with it. Even if your over-amped cousin tries to kick my ass."

She laughed. "He just might."

"He'll have to wait until Grif gets done with me."

"Grif?"

"My agent isn't too happy."

"What happened?"

"He found out about Sam getting fired. I should have told him about it yesterday." He circled a hand by his head. "The day got away from me. Now, Grif'll be here in thirty to remind me that any scandal will cost me. And if it costs me, it costs him."

"It's not about money with him. He cares about you."

"I know. I didn't mean..." He shook his head. "I'm all wacked out. After he tells me to get my head out of my ass, I'll update him on the embezzlement situation."

"He's on your side, you know. He'll help."

"I know. It's still bad timing." He looked out over the obstacle course where the various pieces of equipment would kick her rear. "But we're not here for me. Let's talk strategy."

"Ah." Maggie held up a finger. "Subject change. For someone so adept at charming the media, you're terrible at avoiding personal conversations you don't want to have."

She'd experienced that twice now with him. The first when he'd walked out on her yesterday and now the subject change.

He scooped Reid's dreaded stopwatch from the table. "Let's have you run the course. On the first try, don't get hung up on time. Put it out of your head. You're a doer. Work the course. Visualize it and when I say go, shut your mind down. Your body knows this course, Maggie. Let it do the work."

For a girl whose thoughts constantly looped, it all sounded good. Too good. "What if my time is bad?"

"Don't think about that. Besides, it's only me. Who cares? The point is to relax. Put the stressors out of your mind and focus."

How lucky was she? A professional athlete giving her advice—not to mention those recent multiple orgasms. Talk about a girl with a little pep in her step.

She saluted and walked to the starting line. "Sir, yes, sir."

"Get warmed up."

Under Jay's watchful eye, she cruised through a series of

stretches and Reid's favorite inchworms and after five minutes, shook out her legs. "I'm good," she said.

"Honey, you're more than good. You're a fucking beast. You hear me?"

She peered over the obstacle course to the first element. The low log. *Got this.* "I hear you."

"Good. What are you?"

"I'm a beast," she muttered.

Then he was beside her, closing into her personal space, getting up in her grill. "I didn't hear you. What?"

She knew what this was. The superstar trying to wind her up. Get her good and motivated to kick some ass. She shoved him. Sent him sailing a full two steps. "I'm a *beast.*"

"Attagirl! Damn straight."

He smacked her on the ass and walked back to the table where he plopped his fine self on top, resting his feet on the bench. "On three, you're going."

"Got it."

She squatted into a sprinter's stance, focused on that low log. *I've got this.* And then something happened. Something light and fun and *powerful* streamed from her brain to her toes.

Usually, about now, her mind exploded. All the stress and determination coiling into a tight ball before she even left the starting line.

"Shut your mind down," Jay said.

She closed her eyes, took a deep inhale and opened them. Her gaze landed on the first obstacle.

"I'm a beast," she said.

"Yeah, you are. One, two, three. Go!"

She took off, her sneaker-clad feet flying over the moist grass. Don't think about the grass. *I'm a beast.* First obstacle. She rolled right over that sucker and cleared it.

Next up, low wall. Done.

She scrambled up the twenty-foot ladder, tripping up on one of the rungs—dammit. Keep moving. Only two more rungs and she'd climb over the top and work her way down. Halfway down, she leaped to the ground, sticking the landing and sprinting to the high wall.

Her arch nemesis.

"Don't think!" Jay shouted.

She grabbed the rope, concentrated on climbing up and —upsy-daisy—over the top.

Next element. *Get it.*

On and on it went, her mind completely dialed in on each obstacle and shutting everything else out. This must be what Reid referred to as "in the zone." Whatever it was, she'd take it.

"You're a beast!" Jay shouted, clearly enjoying his coaching duties.

She hit the ground, army-crawling under the barbed wire obstacle. The one, according to Jay, she consistently beat Reid's time on. *Go, go, go.*

Done.

Go.

She leaped to her feet and rounded the turn, flying and not even breathing as hard as usual. Her time must have sucked, but this run was like none of the others. This one was...fun. Euphoric even.

She breezed through the finish line, slowed to a light jog and lapped the table once before shuffling her feet back and forth while catching her breath.

"Well?"

"Well, what?"

She'd kill him. "How'd I do?"

He showed her the stopwatch. She slid her gaze from her time back to Jay. "No way."

"Told ya."

"That's a half second faster than my best time."

"Happens to me all the time. When I stop thinking and rely on instincts, I do better."

She angled back, stared out over the course. At that blasted wall she'd spent so much energy trying to conquer. "All along I've been battling that wall and getting more and more frustrated and you're telling me I only needed to focus on something else." She turned back, stepped a little closer. "Where the hell *have* you been all this time?"

He flashed the superstar smile and the warm buzz she'd been feeling for days now took hold. She was gone. Not just a little either. Smitten didn't cover it. This was full-blown, *I'm keeping him for myself* lust.

Period.

No sharing.

As with his visualization technique, it sounded great. Except, any minute now, Grif would find him a job and he'd leave. Off to play football and enjoy the attention of any number of supermodels.

And what if he wound up on the West Coast? Some couples made cross-country relationships work.

Maggie didn't want it.

Besides, did one night—no matter how incredible—give her the right to assume he wanted to be part of her life? That this was more than just a quick bit of fun?

"Mags?" Using her own trick, he snapped his fingers in front of her. "You with me?"

How had she never realized how annoying that was? She grabbed his fingers, bit the ends gently. His eyes flashed and he let out a low moan.

Seriously? Men were dopes. Everything revolved around sex. "Jay?"

"Yes?"

"Don't make me smack you."

"You're the one who put your mouth on me. Just sayin'."

She shoved him again and he burst out laughing before lunging at her, grabbing her around the waist and—whoopsie—swinging her into a fireman's hold.

From atop his shoulder, she smacked his butt. "Hey! Put me down."

"No."

One night and he turned caveman on her? "*No?* Are you serious right now?"

With his free hand, he scooped his phone and stopwatch from the table and shoved them in his pocket. If he dropped her, she'd hurt him. But he'd locked that big, iron arm around her and held tight. Just like the night before when she'd fallen asleep curled against him and thinking life didn't need to be so lonely.

"I won't let you fall," he said.

It might be too late for that.

JAY CARRIED MAGGIE HALFWAY TO MISS JOAN'S WHILE SHE swore at him like a truck driver and chattered on about the revenge she'd take for manhandling her. She could have at it because he wasn't putting her down. Maybe ever. He tipped his head up, let the sun's warm rays wash over him. In a couple hours, the crisp morning air would disappear and turn into a seventy-degree day.

Autumn in North Carolina. He liked it. Even more, he liked holding Maggie. Her being the independent, responsible sort didn't give a man many opportunities to beat on his chest some, so he'd take what she called a caveman stunt and consider it a win.

Ten yards from the house he stopped walking. "Sheriff, you've got a potty mouth."

Gently, he lowered her to the ground and held on while she steadied herself.

"When men throw me around like a sack of potatoes, you know it."

He smacked a quick kiss on her. "I like it. Makes me think naughty thoughts."

"Please, something tells me you think them anyway."

"When it comes to you, yes. Plus, I have to make it up to you for ruining your vacation."

She cocked an eyebrow, leaned in a little. "Now you're talking. What did you have in mind?"

"First, I'm making you breakfast. After that obstacle course run, you deserve it." He anchored one arm around her waist and nuzzled her neck. "Then if there's anything left of me after my agent gets done with me, I thought I'd let you start your day off with a bang."

"Sounds interesting. What kind of bang?"

It'd be more than interesting. He'd make sure. "Any kind you want. Fast and hard. Slow and easy. You name it. That's if you can spare me some time."

"Lucky for me, I'm the boss. And I suddenly have a meeting I can't miss. I need to take advantage of this before you skip town."

Ah, yes. His job. Any time now, he could be on his way somewhere. Anywhere. At this point it didn't matter. He needed to be back on a field. Which meant leaving Steele Ridge. And Maggie.

But football was his life right now. Being a career woman, she'd understand. Maybe they'd work something out. One thing about Maggie, she didn't need a man around. She took care of herself.

And, hell on earth, when did he become the long-distance relationship sort?

Silence muddied the air between them. What could he say? They both knew he'd go. Of course he would.

She bumped his shoulder as they walked. "Relax, Jay. I'm not about to make any demands on you. I know what this is."

What the hell did that mean? "Really," he said, trying like hell to leave the pissy out of his voice. "What is it you think *this* is? Enlighten me."

"Oh, come on. Don't be that way."

Apparently he'd failed at leaving the pissy out. "How am I being?"

She waved one hand. "Offended. All I'm saying is I don't expect anything from you. I know this is a temporary stop for you. There's no pressure here. We're having fun."

"What if it's more than fun?"

Jesus, where was he going with this?

"Is it?"

"I don't know."

"Exactly. Right now, we're having fun. Let's leave it there." She stopped walking and faced him. "I'm not usually a casual affair girl. And I absolutely don't make a habit of sleeping with men just passing through my town. This is...different."

"Good. It's new for me, too." He ran his hands over his head and blew out a breath. "My life is a shitstorm. You know that. For the first time in years, I don't belong anywhere. I'm in the middle of this embezzlement thing with Sam and could be facing criminal charges for slugging a guy."

"It's challenging, I'd imagine."

"But I like being with you. You take the edge off. You make me laugh when my life is imploding."

"The life you knew is imploding. Make a new life."

She made it sound so easy. *Make a new life.*

He tipped his head up to the sky again, felt that warm autumn sun. North Carolina. *A new life.* He smiled. "I like that idea." He dropped his arm over her shoulder and guided her toward the house. "I'm thinking waffles for breakfast."

Before Jay could get too ahead of himself on the joys of breakfast with Maggie and Miss Joan, a minivan stormed up the driveway.

Maggie let out a sigh. "I swear, I can't get used to seeing my *slick as a greased wheel* cousin driving a minivan. It defies all logic."

"But look at him go in that thing. Let's run. We'll get inside and lock the door."

The two of them sprinted to the back door, laughing like a couple of high schoolers. *Lost my fucking mind.*

They bolted into the house, found Sam and Miss Joan chatting over coffee in the kitchen, and drew up short. Barely winded, Maggie swung back and flipped the lock. "Ha!"

"Goodness' sakes," Miss Joan said, "what are y'all doing?"

Jay jerked his thumb at the door. "Grif is here. We're locking him out."

At that, Miss Joan blinked. Three times. "Setting aside the fact that you're locking my son out of my house, you do realize he has a key."

"Dang it!" Maggie snapped her fingers. "Aunt Joanie, you're totally ruining this."

Shaking her head, Miss Joan laughed. "Y'all are nuts. Sit down and I'll make breakfast."

"No ma'am," Jay said. "It's my turn. How do waffles sound?"

"I love your waffles."

This from his sister, who'd been the first to try his cooking and had never pulled a punch when it came to critiques.

Miss Joan hopped out of her chair. "I have that thick maple bacon."

A thunk near the door sounded and they all swiveled to see Grif standing on the other side jiggling the knob. He stared at them through the glass with a scowl that should have had them all running. "Really?" he said, his voice carrying through the door.

"Really," Maggie fired back.

A second later, the kitchen door lock tumbled and the fun ended. A pissed Griff entered. He wore one of his designer suits—Brioni, if Jay knew his agent—that told anyone sitting across from him that he'd take their head off and eat their brains for lunch.

Good agents.

Hard to find.

"You locked the door," he said. "Very mature."

Jay shrugged. "I know you're irritated. Seemed like a good idea at the time."

"I am *pissed*." He glanced at his mother. "Sorry, Mom."

She slapped the bacon on the counter. "I'm going to give y'all a few minutes of privacy."

Following her lead, Sam rose from her chair. "Good idea. Me too."

"No." Grif pointed at her. "You stay. Please."

"Nice try, Sis," Jay cracked.

Sam sat again. "Can't blame a girl for trying."

They waited for Miss Joan to disappear down the hallway and Grif eyeballed Jay. "What do I always say?"

I'm your first call. That's what Grif always said. "Well, you say a lot of things—"

"*Don't* fuck with me."

Playtime was definitely over. Jay held up his hands. "I know. I know. You're my first call."

"*I'm* your first call." He glanced at Sam, then came back to Jay. "What's this all about? Embezzlement? They've gotta be kidding."

"How'd you hear about it?"

"I talked to someone in the league office this morning. They're going through their books to make sure there's nothing funky happening with the funds from the joint campaign with Celebrate Hope."

"Now the league is involved in this?"

"They're covering their asses. Last year that campaign brought in two hundred million in sales. They're not risking anything."

Each year the league partnered with Celebrate Hope on sales of team merchandise. Jerseys, hats, socks, T-shirts. Whatever they could think of, they slapped the Celebrate Hope logo on and each team sold the merchandise. Once the league took their expenses out, each team received a royalty and the rest went to Celebrate Hope.

"Are they finding any discrepancies?" Sam asked.

"He wouldn't say. They're looking hard, though."

"If it helps at all, I didn't see anything regarding the campaign in that weird account I found."

"What weird account?"

Jay waved a hand. "That's what started this mess. Sam

found an account she'd never seen before. There were expenses that were supposedly paid to me."

"I thought—"

"I pay my own expenses. Which she knows. She brought it to Will and now they're accusing her of embezzlement. With the bogus payments to me, they're probably lining me up as a coconspirator."

"Well, they have to have proof for that."

"They do," Jay said.

"Come again?"

Maggie stepped forward and set one hand on his arm. "They *think* they have proof."

Whether from the placement of Maggie's hand or her statement—could've been both—Grif's eyebrows shot up. "What does that mean?"

"They have canceled checks. Allegedly, Jayson signed them."

"Terrific."

"It's not my signature," Jay said.

"Good." Grif looked at Maggie. "What do we do?"

She shrugged. "We debunk it."

We. He liked the sound of that.

"I have a call in to a handwriting expert I know from a previous case," Maggie said. "If he's available, we'll ask him to do an analysis. Jay is also having his accountant go through his finances to prove there were no reimbursements."

"With the amount of money at stake," Grif said, "the league and Celebrate Hope will try to keep this quiet. That's in our favor. While they're busy covering their asses, we'll get the evidence to clear you both and be done. Mags, what about the lab results on the bullet you dug out of that tree?"

"Nothing yet."

"And Ariel Bowman?"

Ariel Bowman. The psycho who'd pulled a knife on Maggie at the press conference.

"Still locked up," Maggie said. "She can't make bail. She'll go to trial eventually, but for now she's out of our way."

Grif nodded. "At least we know where she is. All right. What can I do?"

Jay thought it through. Couldn't come up with a damned thing. "Nothing. We've got this. You concentrate on finding me a job. Did your contact at the league say if this has filtered to the teams yet?"

"He didn't say. Why?"

The year prior, Paskins had told Jay the team's cut on the retail sales from the Celebrate Hope campaign. The amount never sat well. In Jay's mind, the team should have donated all proceeds—particularly since much of that merchandise had his name on it—not just the percentage earmarked for Celebrate Hope.

"The Knights made over four million on this campaign last year. On a good day, Paskins loses sleep worrying about ticket and retail sales being down. Now his team's quarterback might be involved in skimming money. If he knows about this, he's already taking a stroke over fans boycotting games. Forget about merchandise purchases."

Maggie cocked her head. "What's your point?"

"I could talk to Paskins," Jay said. "Let him know, being the team player I am, there's a major fucking scandal brewing that could make the team's stock price plummet."

"Whoa," Grif said. "I don't know about that."

Maggie put up a hand to silence him. "Let's think this through. Paskins will want to protect his team and in doing so, might be able to help Jay prove his innocence. A win-win."

Grif leaned back on the counter, crossed his arms, and mulled it over. "A win-win until we find out Paskins is in the loop and he throws you out of his office. Tuck, if this gets out, no team will touch you."

"I'll risk it. Staying out of jail is more important than my football career."

Grif clucked his tongue. "Okay. What else? Besides the general shit show this has turned into?"

"Nothing from me," Jay said.

He glanced at Sam. "Can you think of anything else?"

She stared at him with big doe eyes and it snapped him back twenty-five years to her watching him get a beating from Drunk Marlene. She'd stood there, in the hallway outside his bedroom, staring at him with those same spooked eyes while Marlene took her father's belt to Jay's bare ass.

Over the years, those big eyes always told Jay his sister had something on her mind. "What's wrong?" he asked.

She looked away from him. "Nothing. I'm listening."

"You're also lying. I know you. Whatever you have to say, you can say it in front of Grif and Maggie. They're gonna help us get out of this mess."

"I don't think it's anything."

Jay fought the swear word begging to be let loose. Losing his shit on Sam wouldn't help matters, though, so he held his breath a second and corralled his slipping patience. "It doesn't matter. If there's something you think is even slightly odd, it could help."

She lifted her phone off the table and put her thumbs to work. "Last night, I got an e-mail. Telling me to stop digging around about Celebrate Hope's finances. With everything going on, I didn't want to bug you with it. I figured I'd tell the lawyer you got me about it."

"No," Jay said. "I want to see it."

"I'm pulling it up."

Jay relieved her of the phone and skimmed the e-mail. Sender: Joe Smith. How very original.

The more important part was the single line of text.

Stop investigating Celebrate Hope or we'll make you stop.

What the fuck? Sam didn't think *this* was important enough to pass on to him? Rather than embarrass her in front of Grif and Maggie, he'd deal with it later, in private, where he'd set his sister straight on them being a team. One that stuck together through anything. Even threatening e-mails.

Jay read the message again, as if somehow it would make more sense. Then he handed it to Maggie. "This is definitely a problem."

After a few seconds, Maggie passed the phone to Grif. "Well," she said. "Lucky for us we have a couple of grade-A hackers in the family. Sam, forward that to me, please. I'll ask Jonah or Micki to trace it. Maybe we can get an IP address. For now, let's focus on Jay's meeting with Paskins. Hopefully, he'll tell us something that'll keep you both out of prison."

13

ON WEDNESDAY MORNING, THE SOUND OF SIRENS LEAKED through the service entrance to Jay's condo building. This is what his life had reduced him to. Standing in a narrow hallway with his ear to a door while he hid from the insatiable New York paparazzi.

The ka-chunk of a dumpster being emptied joined the mix and Jay paused, waiting for the truck to move on. A horn blast followed. Probably a pissed-off cabbie trying to cut through the alley.

None of it was foreign. All of it wrapped into sounds he'd spent his lifetime adjusting to. Had even, at some point, loved. City life, for a hotshot athlete in his prime, meant access to restaurants, shows, and clubs—and the women within them—most only dreamed of.

All of it there for his pleasure.

Until it all turned to shit and he'd been forced to enter and exit his own damn home via the service entrance. Last night, while on a private plane that landed at Teterboro airport in Jersey to avoid crowds, he'd changed into ratty jeans and a hoodie with a baseball cap pulled low on his head. He barely recognized himself. A quick call to the doorman granted him access to the service door and he slipped into the building with ease.

Since sneaking in through the alley worked, he pushed it by attempting to leave in the same manner, only this time dressed in a suit. After the Paskins meeting, he'd head back to Steele Ridge—to Maggie. Before her, he'd hated leaving the city. Now it didn't seem so bad. In fact, he found himself almost anxious. Excited to get back to her. Maggie made him laugh when he sure as shit shouldn't be laughing. The idea of leaving her behind felt like a brick to the chest.

Damn. So many complications.

Jay's phone beeped. His driver. Pulling into the alley. He cracked the door and spotted the nondescript black SUV similar to the other ten million black SUVs prowling the city. Across from the dumpster was a blue sedan. His security guy. As much as Jay understood the importance of security, he needed space. He'd compromised with security following him, rather than riding in the same car. Was it dumb? Maybe. But he couldn't live with a security team listening in on his life.

In seconds, he'd hopped into the SUV and received a welcoming smile from Saul, the retired cabdriver who'd been tooling him around New York for five years.

"Jayson," Saul said, "so nice to see you, my friend."

Jay sat forward, patted Saul's shoulder. "Thanks, Saul. You too. Just so you know, my security guy is in that blue car. He'll tail us."

"All right. Thank you."

"Now, what have I missed?"

He spent the thirty-minute ride with Saul regaling him with stories of the New York social scene. If you wanted dirt on people, New York livery drivers were the ones to call.

By the time they reached the stadium, Jay was up to speed and finding comfort in the normalcy of Saul's storytelling.

After his meeting, Saul would drive him back to Teterboro, where Jay would hop on a plane back to Maggie. After that, who knew when he'd be back in New York?

When the car came to a stop at the entrance to the executive offices on the backside of the stadium, Jay opened the door. They'd long since given up on Saul racing around to handle the job. What was the point when Jay could save a minute or two by doing it himself. Before sliding out of the vehicle, he peered up at the domed roof of the stadium. The whole of his career had been spent as a Knight and for the second time, he caught that brick to the chest. Too many emotions wrapped up in all this bullshit. He looked back at Saul, met the old man's gaze. "Thank you. For everything."

"Bah! I should be thanking you. You're a good kid. Always respectful. I'm not buying any of this garbage I hear in the news. You'll land on your feet." He waved a hand at the building. "They'll be sorry. Now go. I'm wasting gas. I'll park and be here when you're done."

In the absence of Jay's father, a man Jay learned long ago put his own ambitions and needs above all else, Saul had become the voice of reason. The protector. The one barking at paparazzi to "leave the kid alone" and coming up with alternate routes to avoid the media when necessary.

"I know you will." Jay stepped out of the vehicle. "I shouldn't be long."

The minute he closed the door, Saul hit the gas. He'd wait in the same parking spot—first row, third space from the right—as every other time Jay had a meeting.

He stood in the sunshine, dressed in his best suit. The gray one he'd bought while in Italy during the off-season.

The suit reminded him of better days and a life more complicated than most, but one he'd worked hard for.

Now, staring up at the reflective glass of the Knights executive building, Jay let out a breath. No matter the outcome of this meeting, his tenure here was over.

Time for a new life.

Despite the chaos of the last week, it didn't seem so bad.

He strode into the building, received a warm greeting from Denny, the day shift security guard manning the desk, and headed up in the elevator. In the executive suite, he received the same greeting from the receptionist and two assistants. He had friends here. Good people he'd relied on to help him navigate the trappings of fame.

Hearing the chatter welcoming Jay back, Paskins met him at his office door, extending his hand.

"Jayson," he said, "good to see you."

Jay believed him. Paskins had always been a straight shooter, a man committed to saying exactly what he thought. If he didn't like you, he made it clear. If he saw you as an asset, he made it clear. Until recently, Jay had always fallen into the asset column.

"Thanks," Jay said. "Sorry to bust in on your day."

"No problem. Come in. Doreen? Let's get Jay his coffee, please."

"On it," Doreen appeared in the hallway, her hand wrapped around a mug.

They had an espresso machine in the kitchen and Doreen made a killer cup of java with that thing. He never wanted to insult anyone, but if Doreen didn't make the coffee, he had no interest.

He took the mug and held it up. "Thank you."

"You're welcome." She paused for a second. "We miss you around here."

Whoa. He appreciated the support, but she probably shouldn't be saying that, considering this team had fired him and her boss was sitting right there.

In an effort to shut down any chance of the conversation continuing, he simply nodded.

"Jay," Paskins said, "have a seat. What can I do for you?"

Most meetings held in this office took place at the small round table in front of the floor-to-ceiling windows overlooking the practice field. The office, roughly fourteen by fourteen, was actually the smallest in the suite, but Paskins craved the view more than the ego boost that came with a large, overly decked-out work space. Jay had always appreciated that about Paskins. The man knew what he needed to get his job done.

Paskins waved him to the table and Jay took his normal seat. Well, not his seat anymore, he supposed. The thought should have meant something. Some great epiphany or heartbreak, but the brick that had been sitting on his chest broke apart. Allowed him to take a breath.

Start a new life.

Which meant tying up the old one. Jay sat back and met Paskins's eye. "I wanted to bring you up to speed on a couple of things."

"Regarding?"

"Celebrate Hope."

"Ah." Paskins gave him the solemn face. "I heard they let you go. I'm sorry about that. I know you liked those folks."

"I did. Until they accused my sister of embezzlement."

Pow. If he'd rehearsed it, he couldn't have delivered a better line. A touch of sarcasm yet casual enough that it should have left Paskins momentarily stunned.

Should have.

Paskins, though, he sat stone-faced. No outrage, no

shock, no...anything.

What the hell? "You knew," Jay said.

"I'd heard something from the league."

Jay ignored the stab of betrayal. Did he expect Paskins to give him a heads-up? To warn him? If they'd been friends, which Jay thought they were. At least prior to them firing him. Yes, he'd hoped his friend would warn him. Possibly support him.

Which meant Paskins was just a guy trying to make a buck.

"Good," Jay said, "then I'll save my breath and cut right to it. This is crap. The charity is trying to rope me into this with some bogus reimbursements they supposedly made. I have my accountant on it and I'll be able to prove by the end of the day there were no payments made to me. At all. And my sister? She's the one who brought the suspicious account to Will in the first place. If she were stealing, why would she call attention to herself? She'd keep it hidden."

"On that, I agree. The logic is...flawed."

Sure was. "My sister's boss leaves unexpectedly and then she's suddenly accused of embezzlement. Interesting timing."

Paskins remained silent.

"And why would the league be notified of that embezzlement? Given the cash the league makes on the shared antiviolence campaign, I'd think Celebrate Hope would want to get their act together, figure out what the hell is going on with their books before admitting there's a problem. Too much to lose. For all involved parties."

"Exactly why they came to us."

Us. "Who us? The league or the Knights?"

"I'm not at liberty to say who is involved. I was notified."

Of course he was. The league didn't piss without telling

Paskins. He demanded it. His team funneled enough revenue to the US Football Federation to make them fall in line.

Jay sat forward. "Here's what I know. I didn't take a dime from Celebrate Hope. If I were the league, I'd start looking real hard at joint endeavors. The money in that account my sister found was being siphoned off from somewhere and the joint campaign brought in two hundred million last year. You told me yourself the Knights' share of that was four mil. Amounts that big, who knows? Might be easy to hide indiscretions. The problem is, hardworking people don't like their donations fucked with."

Paskins's mouth lifted to a smirk. "You're threatening us."

"No. I'm trying to save my career. That means being loyal to the league and giving you—and the league—a heads-up that I'm done keeping quiet. I'm not letting my sister go to prison for Celebrate Hope and their incompetence."

"What is it you want?"

"I want what all of you want. For this to go away. They're telling Sam that if she goes quietly, they won't press charges. I think they're buying time to keep her from getting a lawyer and fighting. Hell, someone sent her a message threatening her, if she kept asking questions. If Celebrate Hope doesn't back off, I'll start talking."

"To the press?"

Jay nodded. "The league will have plenty of attention. Not sure you all want that."

"Of course not. We can't have any hint of impropriety around this campaign. That'll bring the feds in."

Bingo.

Paskins sat forward, let out a sigh. "What do you want from me?"

"Look into this. Put pressure on Celebrate Hope to figure

out what the hell's going on. A lot of people depend on them. They need to make this right. I'm guessing they got rid of Jack Hill by telling him to keep quiet. They let him walk so they could cover this up. At least until my sister discovered Hill's secret account. They're using her—and me —as the patsy and I don't like it. I'm not about to let them sacrifice my sister to save their asses."

Paskins held up two hands. "Take it easy, Jay. No one is doing anything. We're all just working through it. I'll call the commissioner this morning. See who knows what. Do I have your word you won't talk to the press?"

"I'm not waiting weeks. I'll give you two days. That's plenty of time for the league to start asking questions."

"Let me see what I can do. And thank you for the heads-up. For giving us some time."

Something Paskins, his old friend, hadn't bothered to do when he'd been informed of the embezzlement accusations against Sam's former boss. Jay nodded. "I want a job in this league. I'm willing to cooperate."

Paskins sat back, swiveled his chair sideways, toward where the stadium loomed on the other side of the practice field. "You'll get picked up. You're a good leader. We didn't appreciate it enough."

Damn right. Jay never needed a lot of stroking. Another thing Drunk Marlene had equipped him for. Praise, for him, was never expected. Or needed. He knew his worth and he'd kept the Knights' locker room in tip-top shape. "Thank you."

"It's the truth. As you know, we have explosive personalities on this team. Eric Webb can't control them."

Jay could have told him that. And what did Paskins want? Advice? *My ass*. They canned him. They could muddle through it.

"For the first time last weekend we weren't sold out. There were 2,346 empty seats. Our fans aren't happy with us."

What did Paskins want him to say? Sorry? Good luck.

Paskins swiveled back and faced Jay. "Anyway. I saw on the news you've been working out in North Carolina."

Now they'd make small talk? Doubtful. Jay stood. "Grif's brother is a former Green Beret. He's a good guy. Has a training facility for law enforcement, but he's not limited. There's plenty of land for hiking and team building. It's been good. Got me out of my routine. Cleared my head."

Paskins rolled his bottom lip out. "Interesting. You think he'd work with us?"

Jesus. How much did these people expect of him? Too much, apparently. Now he was done. And ready to get back to Steele Ridge. To Maggie.

He checked his watch. "I have a car waiting. I'd suggest calling Grif about the training center. I can't help you there."

On her way home, Maggie assisted on a domestic battery call involving a couple arguing over the correct spelling of coincidence.

What the hell was wrong with people? First of all, coincidence wasn't a particularly hard word. Second, alcohol should never be mixed with weapons. That combination added up to three law enforcement officials separating a couple of drunks wielding iron skillets. Prior to Maggie's arrival, Blaine had even been walloped on the shoulder while attempting to remove the husband from the house.

Now both were on their way to lockup, where they'd sleep off their stupor. Maybe the assaulting an officer charge against the husband and the battery charge against his wife would get them both to sober up.

Why couldn't people just play nice?

Four blocks from home, Maggie's cell phone rang. She peeked at the dashboard where the county lab's phone number flashed. So close, yet so far.

Exhausted from the day, she contemplated—only for a split second—letting it go to voice mail. *Can't do it.* She picked up the call. "This is Sheriff Kingston."

"Hey, Sheriff. It's Cole, from the lab."

"Hi, Cole. I hope you have good news for me so late in the day."

His silence told her the reverse. Dammit.

"Sorry, Sheriff. The DNA from that cigarette doesn't match anyone in the system."

Dagnabit. Longshot or not, she'd had hope. The fact that they'd even found it—a sign from the heavens for sure—convinced her they'd catch this guy. "Well, Cole, that wasn't what I wanted to hear."

"Wish I had better news for you."

"Yeah. Me, too. Thanks for turning it around fast for me. I appreciate it."

"Sure thing, Sheriff. Any time."

Cole disconnected and Maggie filled the silence by letting out a grunt. "Well, that sucks."

She'd have to come up with another angle on how to catch this guy. Maybe they'd go back to the video from Tupelo Hill. Pull everything Reid had from that entire day and see if they could spot the man or his vehicle. There had to be some other glimpses of him.

After making the left onto her street, the sight of a black Range Rover parked at the curb chipped away at her crabby mood.

Jay.

Back from New York and sending her heart pitter-pattering. When he'd left the night before, paranoia set in. Part of her imagined he'd step back into the glitz of the city, realize how much he missed its frenetic activity—along with polished, sexy women willing to let him call the shots—and she'd be forgotten. Tossed aside like the casual, *killing time with*, country girl.

What have I done?

She pulled into her driveway and there he was, sitting on the top step of her little porch, his back against the rail. Where his security was, she'd definitely like to know. The man had had two near misses in a week and he insisted on making himself an easy target. On *her* porch.

The suit he wore was a fairly solid indication that he'd probably come straight from the airport. His time in Steele Ridge, aside from business meetings, meant a wardrobe of jeans or track pants. The suit?

Couldn't be good news.

Lord, the emotional upheaval surrounding this man might do her in. *Stop.* She had to quit projecting too far ahead. If Grif had found him a job, she'd be happy for him. At least outwardly. Inside? Not so much. But what right did she have to any opinions involving his career? Staying in Steele Ridge with her—not that they'd even discussed that —meant the loss of his dream.

And they were nowhere near her being part of that conversation.

Particularly when she understood the yearning that came with wanting more than Steele Ridge.

Ready to face whatever Jay had to tell her, she pushed open the car door, grabbed her tote, locked the cruiser, and headed straight for him, her eyes on his the whole way.

If he'd be leaving, she intended to make it a good night. A very good one.

He stood and as she drew closer, something in his eyes

changed. His gaze moved over her, pausing briefly at her gun belt before snapping back to her face.

"Hey," she said, keeping her tone light.

Being the clingy, desperate female would never be her style. No matter how much she'd like to beg him to stay.

But then he was moving, reaching her in two strides, wrapping one hand around the back of her neck, dragging her toward him. Totally manhandling her in a way she'd break anyone else's kneecaps for.

But this?

Oh, yes. This, a girl could get used to.

Already feeling the charge that came with him, she crushed her lips against his while he plunged his tongue into her mouth. Were they really doing this on her front lawn?

You betcha.

She slipped her arms around him and pressed her fingers into the hard ridges of muscle. Her mind shorted. Her body, though, it knew exactly what it wanted. Him.

Right.

Now.

He brought his free hand around to her lower back, yanked her even closer so she'd feel the pressure of his extremely healthy erection. She wanted her hand there. Wrapped around him, guiding him inside her and—wowie, wow, wow—this was happening on the lawn.

My house, my lawn. So what if she was the sheriff? Sheriffs had needs, too. Sheriffs were entitled to hot, sweaty, toe-curling sex.

She broke away from the kiss, bit his bottom lip. "I need to touch you."

He dipped his head to her neck, nipping at the skin there as his hands moved over her and landed on her ass. "I came straight from the airport. Couldn't stop thinking about you all day."

"Really now? And what were you thinking?"

He smiled. "It might have had something to do with you moaning when I moved a certain way. It's a wicked loop in my head. I'm a walking hard-on."

Filthy, filthy man. Totally killing her. "Oh, my God. Inside. Right now."

"Jesus," he said. "So bossy."

"I know what I want. From the looks of you"—she pointed at his crotch—"so do you. But we're not doing it in front of my house."

She broke away and started for the house, fumbling with her keys. Searching for the one for the front door. *Where is it?*

Got it.

She jammed the key in the lock and kicked the door open. "And, where's your security?"

"I told him to take the night off. Figured you'd be home and I wouldn't need him."

"So you sit on the porch and make yourself a target?"

He paused for a second while his head removed itself from his ass. "You're right. That was careless. I should have made sure you were home."

"Lesson learned. Even small towns can be dangerous."

"Yes, ma'am."

She tossed her bag on the drum table, relocked the front door, kicked off her shoes, pulled off her socks, and headed down the hall, unbuttoning her shirt as she went. She peeled it off and tossed it over her shoulder with a laugh.

"Nice," he said. "We may need to put a pole in your room."

"Ha! Not happening."

Her T-shirt went next, leaving her in only the lacy red bra Brynne had talked her into on their last trip to Asheville. She'd worn the bra once and then shoved it to the back of her drawer. For one, it was too expensive to wear every day. Two? Why wear a bra like that when she didn't have a man to show it off to? It had never occurred to her that she should wear it for herself. To feel feminine and...sexy.

Except, this morning, something had changed and she'd dug the bra out and wore it. After the night of lovemaking with Jay, the walking around half-dressed and having him refuse to stop touching her, she felt...wanted.

"Damn, your body," he said. "Leave the bra. I want to see that from the front."

Inside her bedroom door, she spun back, let him see how her nipples poked at the sheer lace.

"You wore that under your uniform?"

"Today I did." She grabbed his suit jacket, pulled him close. "It made me think about you seeing me in it. My little secret. If you'd been here, I'd have hunted you down and had my way with you."

He flashed a smile. "I'm free all night."

He pressed his thumbs against her nipples and her body, every nerve, responded with a zapping burst that lit her skin up.

She arched against him and gave him the moan he seemed to like.

"That's it," he said. "That sound. I love it."

She loved it, too. And she sure as heck never moaned like that before.

But, God, his touch took her places, let her be Maggie, a single adult female with the same desires as every other sexual being.

With Jay, her hangups—and stress—melted away. For

once, her mind settled and allowed her to relax—to finally let go—and...and...what? *Experience it.* That's what this was. Maggie Kingston finally giving in to the ecstasy of making love.

The dreaded L word. O*h, Maggie.* She couldn't go there. Not yet. Not with this one and his career taking him heaven knew where. But he did something to her. Made her come alive in ways she'd never allowed. In ways a *sheriff* shouldn't allow.

His hands moved to her gun belt, where he worked his big fingers over the buckle.

"Don't let—

"—it drop. I know."

Gently, he worked it free, then stepped around her and set it on the dresser. "Is it okay here?"

Maybe this was how it should be.

Trust. That he'd do the right thing. That he'd let her be herself and, for a little while, put her responsibilities aside.

"I'm done," she said.

"Pardon?"

She reached up, yanked his jacket off his shoulders. "Get rid of these clothes. Now."

He kicked off his shoes, tossed his jacket on the chair, and started on his shirt buttons while she wiggled out of her pants, revealing the matching red undies. "Beautiful," he said, "but are we in a hurry?"

"We are. I've been walking around in this bra all day. It's a little itchy, I might add. I've been waiting for you, Jayson. Right here. In Steele Ridge and part of me—" She stopped, held her breath because what was she doing?

Don't. If she said it, he'd run for the door. He'd know this had gone too far, that her feelings had gone way—way—beyond a casual fling.

"Part of you what?"

Don't. She met his gaze, that pretty blue she'd spend the rest of her life, long after he left, dreaming about. She swallowed, rested her forehead on his shoulder and let out a hard breath. "Part of me thought you weren't coming back."

The panic she'd anticipated never came. Instead, more relief calmed her quaking system. A conversation. That's all this was. A moment to be honest. And vulnerable.

With a man.

She really *had* lost her mind.

He stepped back. *Yep, here we go.* But, hang on. He tucked his fingers under her chin, lifted her face to look at her with steady eyes. "I wouldn't do that. Ever. Definitely not with you. I woke up this morning and all I wanted was you beside me. That's never happened. That I want someone in my space like that. Everything with you feels...easy. Better. I don't know what'll happen when Grif finds me a job, but I want you in my life. It's not easy, though. I don't know if you want to take that on. It's..."

She grabbed his cheeks, and loving the feel of his short beard against her palms, kissed him. Anything to shut him up. To keep him from ruining this exquisite moment by talking about road trips and long distances with women throwing themselves at him.

He took his shirt off while she slid his pants down his legs. He stepped out of the pants and she took his socks off. His T-shirt went next and there he was, all smooth, cut muscle of a professional athlete and the zing happened again. Simply gorgeous. He held up a condom and she reached for the waistband of his boxer briefs, dragging them down his legs.

"You're all mine," she said.

"I hope so."

He did his thing with the condom while she moved the bra straps from her shoulders. "No," he said. "Leave it. Please. I like it."

From somewhere on the floor, his phone rang. If he answered it right now she'd hurt him. Ignoring it—good man—he moved behind her, kissing her shoulder, his lips trailing down her back and making her shiver as he guided her panties down her legs. God, the man. Every touch lit a fire.

"I've been thinking about this all day," he said.

The bed. He wanted her bent over it so he could enter her from behind. Like they'd done their first night together. A control thing, she supposed. She hadn't minded. It drove her to an orgasm she'd never experienced.

He nudged her forward, toward the bed and she braced her arms against the mattress before peeking over her shoulder. And smiling.

JAY ENTERED HER WITH A HARD THRUST THAT MADE THEM both gasp. He stopped moving and wrapped his arms around her from behind, skin against skin. "Did that hurt?"

"It felt good. Now get going. You're ruining this for me."

He laughed. Maggie. Unlike anyone he'd ever been with. Opinionated, aggressive, no-nonsense. Damn, he loved her.

He thrust again and she let out another gasp, this one followed by her moan that made him insane.

"That moan," he said. "Every time I hear it, I want to slam myself into you."

"Oh, Jay. Don't stop. Please. I'll..."

"You'll what?"

"Just...don't stop."

She dipped her head, wrapped her long fingers around

the bedspread and squeezed.

"Please…"

She moved with him, urging him on, faster and faster, and he closed his eyes as his own orgasm built. He gritted his teeth, determined to wait her out, let her go first, so he could feel her strong body go limp. For him. With him.

He opened his eyes, focused on her back and her smooth skin. Her ponytail. The woman he couldn't get enough of.

He wanted her. Forever.

"Oh," she said. "Don't…"

She gasped again. A huge rush of air as her body went rigid and she threw her head back, finally crying out. Right there with her, he kept moving. Staying on that amazing edge. He hung on to her, pounded into her again and she turned her head, looking over her shoulder at him with a wide, satisfied smile that he'd put there. *I'm gone.*

The orgasm shredded him. Broke his body nearly in two. For a second, his knees gave way, his head spinning, and he tipped forward, bracing himself against her, holding on while the waning edge of the orgasm released him.

Maggie collapsed on the bed, separating them and pulling away all her heat. A fierce cold gripped him, reminding him he'd hated being away from her. She crawled toward the headboard and rested against one of the pillows before holding her arms out in an invitation he'd gladly take.

Then he was next to her, wrapping her in his arms and recapturing the warmth.

"Maggie?"

"Hmm?"

He kissed her head. "If we keep this up, you'll never get rid of me."

14

JAYSON SHOULD BE CAREFUL.

Extremely careful.

Never getting rid of him might be the first item on her to-do list. Her new to-do list, which included staying in this bed for as long as possible. She curled into him, ran one leg against his, and hooked it over him. "If we *do* keep this up, I'll never let you out of this bed. How do you like that, hotshot?"

"If that's a threat, it's not working."

In one quick move, he rolled her on top of him. She straddled his waist and—hello, friend—a growing erection pressed against her inner thigh.

He wanted her again. Already. Between the two of them and this insatiable sexual appetite, they might literally never leave her house.

She leaned over, kissed him lightly. "It's a good thing I stocked up on groceries."

He smiled up at her, all sharp, handsome angles and oh, this man.

"I never did eat dinner," he said. "Food break? I'll cook."

A little sustenance for the night ahead wouldn't hurt. *Heh, heh, heh.* "You're on."

She rolled to her feet, grabbed Jayson's shirt from the chair. "I'm borrowing this."

Really, if they were going to do this on a regular basis, she'd need a visit to Brynne's shop for some silky bathrobes. Somehow her boxers and T-shirts didn't seem appropriate.

"Be my guest. I like you in my clothes." He shoved his legs into his pants and zipped them, leaving the button unfastened. They hung low on his lean hips and the urge to slam him down on the bed assailed her.

Tonight, he's mine. Lucky, lucky, girl.

He dropped an arm over her shoulder, then kissed the top of her head, and his scent, something rich and woodsy and expensive, filled her. A man's man all for her. These little luxuries, affection and companionship, seemed so easy with Jay. No awkward weirdness. Just...them. Two ornery people figuring each other out. "I can help with dinner. If you want."

"I'm good. Unless you mind that I take over your kitchen?"

Ha. Good one. With all the cooking competitiveness in her family, someone taking the pressure off of her would never be a problem. "Not at all."

"Good." He pointed to the breakfast bar separating the kitchen and living room. "Have a seat and let me work. How was your day?"

This was shaping up to be one heck of a good night. Should she ruin it by telling him about the failed DNA findings?

Part of her, the part that didn't want the sexual haze of the evening ruined, begged her to wait until tomorrow. Until they were done walking around her house half naked and sharing kisses that rocked her straight to her heels.

Was that selfish, considering what he'd experienced this last week? Was it fair to keep it from him? If the roles were reversed, she'd want to know.

She sat back in the stool and straightened her shoulders. "At the risk of ruining our evening, I have updates on the e-mail Sam received and the DNA."

He propped his hands on the counter and met her gaze. "This doesn't sound good."

"It's not horrible. More inconvenient. I checked in with Micki earlier about that threatening message Sam received. It came from a domain belonging to a bogus e-mail sending site. It's a dead end."

"I figured that was too easy."

"It was worth a shot. The more depressing news is that I got a call from the lab. The DNA from the cigarette we found isn't a match to anyone in the national database."

"Hunh."

That was it? After she'd been so hopeful that the cigarette would garner a lead? "That's your only reaction? No disappointment? Because it upset me. I was sure we'd get a hit."

"Of course I'm disappointed. I'm not surprised, though. Nothing with me is easy lately. But we tried. What else can we do?"

The doorbell rang and she swiveled around, cocking her head. "That better be a salesperson."

She turned back to Jay, now rummaging through her fridge, and took in his wide shoulders, the sloping muscles of a career quarterback who'd just given her the orgasm of all orgasms.

Tonight he's mine.

Ooh-wee.

The bell sounded again.

Bam, bam, bam. The hard knock jolted her. She should march over and get rid of whoever it was, but the sheriff probably shouldn't be answering the door in only a man's shirt.

Jay set a package of chicken next to the sink. "Want me to get it?"

"Nope. Whoever it is will go away."

Please let them go away.

The sound of the lock disengaging spun Maggie around just as the door came open.

Cash, her totally unexpected brother, stood in the doorway, keys in hand.

And here she was in Jay's shirt.

No pants.

Oh.

Shit.

She crossed her legs, flashed her brother a whole lot of thigh and—*oh shit again*—uncrossed them.

Cash's attention wasn't on her legs. He was more interested in the man in her kitchen.

The shirtless one.

Someday she'd find this amusing. Right now? A wicked mix of humiliation, horror, and rage spurted like a blown water pipe.

"Cash," she said, her tone sharper than her family was used to. "What the hell?"

Her idiot brother held up the key she'd given him. "You, uh, didn't answer. Are you..." He shot another look at Jay, then pressed his hand against his forehead. His head might be exploding right along with hers. "I could have gone my whole life without this moment."

Behind her, Jay let out a snort. Glad someone thought it amusing.

"Everyone relax," he said. "Let's take a breath."

Take a breath, my butt. What was it with her family letting themselves into her house? She loved them, for sure, but she was a single woman with needs. Some of which did not involve her family.

Not that she had much of a social life and they all knew that, but...grrrr.

If he'd shown up ten minutes earlier and walked down the hall, he would have gotten quite the view. Her mind tripped back to Jason standing behind her, pounding himself into her.

Oh, dear God.

Bad enough she was talking to her brother while dressed in only Jayson's shirt. True, the shirt hung longer than most skirts these days, but still, without her own clothes—her buttoned-up clothes—she felt, well, exposed.

Vulnerable.

Something she'd sworn she'd never allow.

She hopped off the stool, smoothed her hands over the bottom of Jay's shirt, making sure her crotch wasn't on full display and marched straight for her brother. "Seriously, Cash. You guys *have* to stop walking into my house unannounced."

"I rang the bell. Twice! And then I knocked."

"And I didn't answer. That should have been your first clue not to bug me."

He jerked a thumb at Jay. "After the week he's had, I show up, see your car in the driveway and his in front of the house and no one answers. What was I supposed to think after two people tried to—" He looked at Jay, waved a hand.

"Kill me?" Jay added.

"Sorry, dude, but yeah. I panicked. Under normal circumstances I wouldn't walk in, but after this batshit week? I thought you were either being held hostage or dead. What I didn't expect was—" He waved his hand again.

Maggie gave him a bright smile. "Me banging Jay?"

Cash gritted his teeth.

Yes, she was being annoying. Too bad. Her family needed to start respecting her privacy. Starting now.

"I'm a thirty-four-year-old single woman, Cash." She flapped her arms. "Here's one for Jay's publicist. I like sex. I like it even more with a hot stud of a football player!"

"Oh, boy," Jay muttered.

She whirled on him. "You stay out of this. This is between me and Cash. Don't think you're going to jump in and save me."

"Not a chance. I'd like to walk out of here with my balls intact."

"Good." She turned back to Cash and pointed to the door. "Get out."

He gawked at her, his mouth literally hanging open. "What?"

"Out. I have company. I love you, but you're intruding."

"Mags!"

"No, Cash. I'm serious." She pushed him to the door and resisted laughing when he half-stumbled. "I've spent half my life trying to make everyone happy. Even when it interfered with what I wanted. Now I'm done."

Cash halted, digging his heels in when she tried to shove him again. Her brother wouldn't be pushed if he didn't want to be. He faced her and threw his hands up. "*Well,*" he said, heavy on the sarcasm, "excuse me for doing things the way we always have. A tip here, Mags. When you want things to change, maybe you could let the people who love you know."

As exasperated as she should have been, it made sense. She peered over her shoulder at Jay who shrugged. "Boundaries, babe. If you don't set them, people don't know."

"Exactly!" Cash said.

Now they were partners? *No sir.* "No tag-teaming me in my own house." She brought her attention back to Cash. "Be on notice, I'm setting those boundaries. The first one is giving me warning when you're about to walk in on me."

"So we can't stop over now? We have to make an *appointment*?"

"Not at all. But when you saw Jay's car outside and we didn't answer, you should have called me. At which point, I would have told you we were safe and not hacked into a million pieces and that you should go away." She gave him another light shove. "Now leave."

He gave in and walked to the door, but turned back. "You know, this is gonna take some getting used to. You can't just spring this on us."

"Oh, yes I can. It's my life. I'll have a conversation with the rest of our brood, too. Boundaries, Cash. Get out."

"Jeez, something crawled up your ass."

At that, Jayson burst out laughing. Men.

Cash hit him with a hard look. "What's funny?"

She opened the door and waved her brother out. "Nothing. It's stress."

"Wait, I need your help with—"

"Whatever it is, call me tomorrow." She gave him a finger wave. "Nighty-night, little brother."

"Mags!"

"Welcome to my new world, buddy."

Then she did something she'd never imagined doing.

She slammed the door on her brother. And threw the dead bolt.

Boundaries.

THANKFUL FOR SOMETHING TO DO AFTER CASH'S UNTIMELY— and pretty fucking amusing—visit, Jay trimmed what little fat there was off the chicken and arranged the pieces in a saucepan. Cooking, once again a great distraction.

Behind him, the front door lock clicked and he glanced at Maggie on her way to her spot at the breakfast bar. "That was fun," he said.

She hopped onto the stool and cradled her head in her hands. "I won't be able to look my brother in the eye for ten years. At least."

"Could have been worse." He laughed at the image of Cash, key in hand while every ounce of blood drained from his face. "If he'd shown up a few minutes earlier, he'd have run me out of here with a shotgun."

She lifted her head, gave him the stern Sheriff look. "Jayson. *Not* funny."

"Sure it is. But, hey, at least you got rolling on setting those boundaries." He gave her the smile that made women lose their clothes. "In a big way."

"Oh. Ha. Ha. They barge in here all the time. The other night it was Riley. She let herself in and plopped on my couch. I wasn't even home. Her, at least, I can't hassle. We lived together after my parents moved. It's normal for her. It has to stop. If Cash had seen us in the bedroom? Lord, what a nightmare." She waved it off. "Tell me about your day. Did the meeting go as planned?"

Was this chicken cooking too fast? He checked the heat level on the burner—he hated electric stoves—and leaned against the counter. "Paskins is normally cagey, but today was an eye-opener."

"How so?"

"I've worked with this guy for years. I wouldn't say we were friends, but we sure as shit weren't employer-employee. We've seen each other socially. If he needed a favor, he called me. It was an easy relationship."

"And?"

"And he knew about Celebrate Hope accusing my sister, and possibly me, of embezzlement. I went in there thinking I'd knock him on his ass with that announcement and he already knew."

Maggie tilted her head, first left, then right. Apparently, her pondering action. "You expected he'd have given you a heads-up. Considering the relationship."

"I guess. I mean, that's what I'd have done. Hell, that's what I was doing. My mistake."

By now, he should know better. He'd been around professional sports enough to never expect too much from people. At least then they didn't disappoint. The aroma of burning garlic wafted from the pan. Damned electric stoves. This chicken would be rubber by the time he plated it. He lowered the heat again and flipped the meat.

"How did Paskins know about the embezzlement?" Maggie asked.

"He claims the league called him. I can buy that. He and two other owners have clout. Their teams bring in sixty percent of league revenue. The commissioner won't freeze them out. That would piss them off. And Paskins is an asshole when angry."

"Who told the league about it?"

Goddamned stove. He fished out pieces of burning garlic and hoped to hell he could save the dish. "Probably a

Celebrate Hope board member. Paskins wouldn't give specifics."

"And with Sam involved, they know you won't go to the press."

"They *think* I won't go to the press."

Maggie's head snapped back. He'd surprised her. Good. He was tired of doing the expected.

"You'd go to the press?"

He gave the heat setting one last check and turned back to Maggie. "My career is in the crapper and my major endorsement deals are going with it. What do I have to lose by defending myself? Paskins is worried about the feds coming in. I can use that as leverage."

Maggie pursed her lips. He never did like that look on a woman. It usually meant, at least in the crowd he ran with, they wanted something he might or might not be willing to give.

Or he was about to get his ass beat.

He needed a new crowd.

One that included a hot sheriff with handcuffs.

Maggie circled a finger at him. "After Sam got fired, she said her boss threatened to bring in the FBI if she talked."

"Yeah. They're supposedly trying to keep it on the down-low. I'm not sure what the hell they're doing. All I know is those pricks'll let a thief go free to save their ass. That fries me."

Speaking of. He went back to the chicken, flipped the meat again and swore at the brown edges. "Electric stoves suck."

"I know. Forget the food a second."

He flipped open the overhead cabinet. Breakfast foods. He moved to the next cabinet. Glassware and dishes. He grabbed a couple of plates and set them on the counter. "If your dinner is rancid, don't blame me." He rifled through a couple drawers, found the cutlery, and put out forks and knives.

"I think you're safe. Doesn't it strike you as odd that both Celebrate Hope and Paskins mentioned the feds?"

"The FBI handles financial fraud, right?"

"Well, yes, but so do local authorities. Why wouldn't one of them say the police? It's an interesting commonality. Don't you think?"

Jay shrugged. What did he know about financial fraud and who handled what? "Meaning?"

"Meaning, perhaps Paskins is more in the loop than we think. He insinuated the league notified him *after* Sam was fired. His comment about the feds, the same language Celebrate Hope used, makes me wonder if the league—and Paskins—were notified earlier." She crooked two fingers at him. "Come out on this limb with me, Superstar, because I think the league found out about the embezzlement when Sam's boss got fired. Maybe even *before*."

"They claim he resigned."

"That's a load of bull and we both know it. Think about it, Jay. If I'm the charity director and I have a lucrative partnership with a major sports league, the second I get a whiff of scandal, even if it's not directly related to the league, I'm bringing them in the loop. I think he panicked and called the league straightaway." She smacked a hand on the counter. "I'm calling it that the charity informed the league that Sam's boss, their CFO, was stealing and they intended to fire him. Together, they could have cooked up this threat about the feds to keep the CFO quiet."

Smart women. Total turn-on. But this was important, so maybe he should focus on embezzlement and not his growing hard-on. *Embezzlement. Paskins and the league.* Jay mulled over the timeline. "Sam blew their plan when she discovered the secret account."

"And now they have to regroup. Figure out how to back her off. They know, I'm assuming, she's good at her job and she's already tugging a thread they don't want tugged. Think about it. She brings the funky numbers to her boss on Friday. They have the entire weekend to work out a plan. Monday morning comes and they give her the same line about bringing in the feds. Why not? It worked with the CFO. How very convenient that you're in the middle of a scandal that makes you look like a *not so nice* guy."

Damned weasels. "The sons of bitches spun it."

"They sure did." In full investigator mode, she jumped off the stool and paced the length of the breakfast bar. Back and forth she went, storming a path while jabbing her finger in the air. "The league is working with your buddies at Celebrate Hope, leveraging it. They know you're looking for a new team. Any bit of additional scandal could kill your career, so what do they do?"

"They threaten my sister."

"They threaten your sister." She finished another lap, spun back, and, all riled now, threw her hands up. "Knowing, *knowing,* you wouldn't risk further deterioration of your image. Guilt by association, right? Plus, they have those bogus checks you supposedly signed. They're using your reputation, your absolute insurance policy for landing another job and future endorsements, to keep you from going to the authorities. That's just you. We haven't gotten to how this impacts the people who need their help." She finally stopped moving, drew a deep breath, and smacked her hands on the breakfast bar. "You can't let them cover this up. You *have* to call the FBI."

Whoa, now, honey. He needed to wrap his mind around it

for a hot minute. He set both hands on the counter, thankful for the cool surface that took the edge off his flaming temper. "Hang on, Sheriff. I get it. Believe me. This involves Sam's future, too. And we're not interested in our reputations being blown to hell. I've invested wisely and don't necessarily need the money, but we're both too goddamned young to not have some sort of occupation. How do either of us get a job with this hanging over us?"

Totally cornered.

Maggie pounded—*tap, tap, tap*—her finger into the countertop. "That's what they want. Don't you see? Anyone who has worked with you knows you're a freak about your image.

Celebrate Hope is manipulating you so they can salvage the millions they make on the joint campaign with the league. No one would give them a dime if people found out their money was stolen. And the league would drop them in a millisecond. They have as much to lose as you do – more, in fact."

"I agree."

"Then what's the damned problem, Jay? Call the FBI!"

The stench of burning meat hit him. Fucking stove. He whipped back, moved the pan off the burner, and shut the thing down before squaring off with her again. "Stop thinking like a sheriff. Right now, you're Team Jay. Put your Jayson hat on. I know how this league works. How these *owners* work. If I talk, they'll close ranks and blackball me. They'll use me to make a point. Not one of those fuckers will give me a job. They're pricks that way. Worse, I sure as shit won't see another endorsement deal. In the last week I've lost fifty million dollars in deals."

Her jaw dropped.

Good.

Finally, she was getting it. This wasn't just about right or wrong. This was his future. Did it suck? Sure. Instinctively, he knew he should go to the authorities. How much could he risk, though, to make things right?

"Oh, my God," Maggie said.

"Yeah. Still want me to go to the feds?"

She started pacing again. She didn't like his thinking. In her world, if a law was broken, law enforcement handled it.

In his world? It sounded good, but reality was a bitch.

She moved around the breakfast bar into the kitchen, where she placed her hands on his forearms and squeezed. Her touch, still new, but already so damned comfortable.

"Please," she said. "I know this is difficult, but you have to do the right thing here."

All she saw was a way to right a wrong. Down deep, he agreed with her. In a perfect world, the feds locked up bad guys.

"Look, Mags. I hear you."

"But."

"Paskins agreed to talk to the league."

"About what?"

"About getting Celebrate Hope to back off Sam and me. I gave him two days."

"You're negotiating with blackmailers?"

Yeah. He supposed he was. "I told him I'd go to the press."

She let go of him and stormed away, her ponytail swinging as she went. "Oh, Jayson!"

"Hey, I have to do something. This whole situation sucks. I know it's not just about me either. People who need help aren't receiving it because the money is gone. If I go to the press, maybe it'll help."

A lightning bolt of pain stabbed at the back of his eyes

and he dug his palms into his eye sockets. *So goddamned tired.* He should have gone to Grif with this. He'd see the logic.

Maggie? No way. And, shit, now that he'd brought her into this, what responsibility did she have?

He lowered his hands, found her leaning against the wall at the kitchen opening. "Should I even talk to you about this? Is there a conflict of interest for you?"

"It's fine. I want you to talk to me."

"Yeah, but you're a civil servant."

"Celebrate Hope is outside my jurisdiction. The only obligation I have is a moral one. These people should be punished. They're covering up a crime and they're blackmailing you. On top of that, I have a problem with a thief going free. But, hey," she waved one hand, "this is your life and you have to do what you think is right. I'll help you where I can, but I totally disagree with how you're handling this."

Of course she did. Props to her for saying it to his face. Aside from Grif and a few trusted others, most wouldn't. The others only cared about being in his circle. If it meant staying on his contact list, they'd go along with whatever he wanted.

"You wanna know the real pisser in this whole thing?" He didn't wait for an answer. "Reid might get business out of it. Paskins had the balls to tell me the Golden Boy is doing a shitty job with team morale. He wants to send some of the guys out here for team building exercises. I can't get away from these fucking people."

"Oh, that's brilliant."

Jayson's phone rang and he dug it from his pants pocket, remembering he hadn't checked the missed call from when Maggie had rocked his world in epic fashion.

"You gotta be kidding me," he said.

"Who is it?"

Unable to believe it, which was saying something considering the shit show he was running, he held the phone so Maggie could see the name lighting up his screen.

"Eric Webb," she said. "Fascinating."

"That's one word for it."

"Put him on speaker. I'll grab my phone and record it."

"Why not? Let's see what this douchebag wants."

While Maggie ran to the bedroom for her phone, Jay put the call on speaker. He had nothing to hide and he wanted a witness.

Just in case.

"This should be good," he said to Webb.

"Listen up, fucker," Webb said and Maggie, who'd run back into the kitchen, holding out her phone as she got to him, rolled her eyes.

"No. You listen up. If you want to talk to me in a civil tone, like a man, we'll do this. Otherwise, I'm out. Nothing to say."

"Stay away from my wife, stay away from my team. You think because you're not on a football field I can't get to you? You're done, asshole."

Jay laughed. This nutjob needed to get a life. Or some brain cells. "Now you think you're tough, rookie? Try again. I'll be done when I say I'm done. Up to this point, out of respect for your kids, I've kept my mouth shut. Keep it up, Webb, and I'll start talking. That stunt you pulled with Rajae Evans? How do you think the league will like ESPN breaking the story about how you tried to end my career? And I haven't started on the spousal abuse yet. Get your head out of your ass, Webb."

Silence drifted and Maggie raised her eyebrows.

"What's wrong, Webb?" Jay asked. "Are you out of gas already? Can't come up with anything from that scrambled brain of yours?"

Webb didn't just explode, he went nuclear, stringing four-letter words together with the added kicker of a few five-letter ones.

Jay held the phone up. "He's using more than three syllables. Stretching his vocabulary."

Maggie clamped her hand over her mouth to smother a horrified laugh.

When Webb ran out of steam, Jay nodded. "You about done?"

"You're dead!" Webb fumed. "What Rajae did to you is nothing. You hear me? You'll beg for mercy. I'll come down there and carve you up so good your mother won't recognize you."

"Okay. Great. See you then. Buh-bye." Jay punched off the call. "Did you get all that, Sheriff?"

"I sure did," Maggie said.

"Good. If he gives me any trouble, I'm shoving it up his ass and pulling it out his mouth. I'll bury him with his own words."

15

TO START HER MORNING, MAGGIE SKIMMED THE DAILY commitment report, a listing of all individuals arrested the day prior. Today's reading included four failure to reports, a DUI, three driving without a license, and a domestic battery. A relatively light day. She set the report aside and picked up the next folder Shari had left for her. This one had bright yellow caution tape wrapped around it. Her assistant's attempt at humor when it came to the budget.

"Everyone is a comedian," Maggie muttered.

Before she got the folder open, said comedian buzzed through on the intercom.

"Ma'am?" Shari said. "I have Kolten Porter here for you. He said he has an *appointment*."

The emphasis on the word appointment left little doubt Maggie had violated the *I will tell you everything* rule. "Yes. Thank you, Shari. I forgot to tell you I added him to my calendar. Please send him back to the conference room."

"Yes, ma'am."

Maggie clicked off. She adored Shari, but never allowed the lines to blur between professional and personal. They were not friends, they did not socialize outside of office functions, and Maggie certainly wouldn't apologize for managing her own schedule.

A schedule that included a sudden meeting with the handwriting expert she'd suggested to Jay. She'd spoken to Mr. Porter the day before, sending him copies of Celebrate Hope's suspicious checks, supposedly endorsed by Jayson. She also provided Jayson's actual signature for comparison. An additional charge—which Jayson would be paying—won them the honor of first priority and a fast turnaround.

Money. Always got the job done.

If that money didn't come out of her budget, even better. Hopefully, the man brought good news.

Handwriting analysis would never be the end-all, but building a case meant stacking evidence upon evidence until each element added up to a solid case.

Assuming everything went the right way.

Too many times, inconclusive results equaled a weak case that left the good guys on the losing side.

Hopefully, not this time.

Maggie grabbed her legal pad and pen and headed for the conference room near the main part of the station. No-frills, but freshly painted, this room served as the department's go-to space for meetings happening outside of Maggie's office.

As she entered the room, Mr. Porter stood to greet her. A stocky, gray-haired man at least an inch shorter than Maggie, he shook her hand, his grip firm but not obnoxious like so many men attempting dominance over the lady-sheriff. At some point, she'd simply be the sheriff. No gender designation.

After exchanging pleasantries, Mr. Porter returned to his seat across from Maggie.

Now retired from the State Police, he'd had thirty years on the job as a forensics examiner. Working the private sector allowed him to take his pension while charging the exorbitant going rate for expert witnesses. Not a bad gig for someone who'd spent a career on a civil servant's salary.

"Mr. Porter, thank you for taking care of this so quickly."

"Of course. Can't say I've ever worked with such a high-profile client."

Jay. The superstar. What a life. Nothing he did remained private. Every movement, every slip of the tongue documented or photographed. Something she'd have to remember if their affair continued. The idea of constantly being camera ready—God help her—gave her a sick feeling.

Later. She'd worry about it later.

Mr. Porter opened a blue folder he'd set on the table and arranged the contents in front of her. "Regarding the copies of canceled checks, I like to work with original documents, but I realize they weren't available."

"Unfortunately, we don't have access to those. I'm assuming, given that you're here, you've been able to draw at least some conclusions."

For what her man was paying, Porter better have something for them.

Porter pointed to the first two documents on the table. The first was a blown-up copy of the checks and the second Jayson's actual signature. Beside those sat two charts, each with the letters of Jayson's name in the first column and then copies of each letter in the second. The first row on both charts held a J.

"What we're looking for," Porter said, "is the form of the letters. Curves, size, any particular slants, et cetera."

Well, God bless on that one because Jayson's penmanship, in a word, stunk. That alone should make his signature impossible to forge.

"Next," Porter said, "I studied the thickness of the line forms. This is an indicator of the pressure and speed used when the signature was created. Also, take note of the spacing between the letters."

Maggie leaned in, studied first the endorsed checks, then Jayson's actual signature. To her? Identical.

Please let him have something for me.

"I don't see a difference."

"To the naked eye, yes." He pointed to the charts. "Ordinarily, I'd prefer to have multiple examples of all the letters in different forms. Handwritten notes, legal documents, for example. However, I studied the samples provided."

Yada, yada. *Come on, Porter.* She met his gaze. "And?"

"The Js look similar."

Similar? They were more than similar. Try exactly the same. Maggie looked again, studying the samples more closely. The loop of the Js, the cross of the Ts, the way the n at the end of Jayson dipped just below the signature line, anything she could use to prove the check endorsements were forged.

Porter pulled another document from his folder and set it on the table. "Here are two enlarged versions of Mr. Tucker's signature. The top one is the real one. Note the smooth lines and edges as the base of the J hooks around. This indicates the speed with which the name was written. It appears to be made in one stroke." He tapped the bottom signature —the endorsed check. "If you look at this one, you'll see the lines are different."

Before, without the benefit of magnification, she'd missed the form change. Now she saw it, that slight squiggle on the bottom of the J. She met Porter's eye. "The signature on the check isn't as seamless as his actual one. Right?"

"You are correct. Very good. The variation could indicate this second signature was done much more slowly."

Slowly. Un-hunh. Maggie didn't want to get ahead of herself, but she'd been around law enforcement long enough to make an educated guess. "As if someone were tracing it?"

Porter nodded. "When a signature is forged, particularly by amateurs, variations in the letters may exist. This indicates stopping and starting points—pen lifts, if you will. These lifts are a result of copying the letters slowly rather than in a quick, natural formation."

"You're saying the bottom one with the squiggly line is forged?"

The corners of his mouth dipped to a pronounced frown. The frown of noncommital. Dang it. She hated that. Had seen it so many damned times with suspects it made her nearly insane.

"Mr. Porter, all I need is your opinion. I can work with that."

"As I mentioned, with the limited number of samples, this wouldn't hold up in court, but in my *opinion,* yes, the bottom signature is forged."

Jackpot. *Yes!* Fighting to maintain professionalism, she bit her bottom lip to bury a smile. Inside though? Total happy dance.

She hadn't doubted Jayson, but having an expert concur gave her hope they'd clear him. No matter what supposed evidence Celebrate Hope had conjured.

Maggie, the orgasm-addicted female, wanted to raise her fists in victory.

The buttoned-up sheriff? No way. Total neutrality.

She met Porter's eye. "This is extremely helpful."

"I'm happy to be of service." He gathered the documents into a neat pile and slid them into the blue folder before handing it over. "These are yours."

She gripped the folder, squeezing it between her fingers. *Got it.* "Thank you."

Very, very much.

After ten minutes of shoptalk with Porter, Maggie hustled back to her office. She needed to call Jay. Right now. While her adrenaline still buzzed.

She rounded the corner of her desk, scooping up the handset before even landing in her chair, and punched out his cell number.

Straight to voice mail.

Darn it. She left him a message to call her ASAP, as in stat, as in as soon as he got the message because she had great news.

She sat and spun her chair to the window where sunshine spilled across the grass along the side of the building. That morning, before leaving her bed—eh-hem—Jay mentioned a meeting with Grif. If he was still in town, he could pop over to her office. She hit the intercom button.

"Ma'am?" Shari said.

Down deep, Maggie hated being called ma'am. She'd never correct the staff, though. Part of her power came from that one little word. If she gave it up, what other liberties would subordinates take advantage of?

"Shari, I have a message in to Jayson Tucker. If he comes by, please send him back."

"Yes, ma'am."

The red voice mail light on Maggie's phone blinked and riding on a high, she hit the button. Maybe he'd left a message while she'd been in with Porter.

First message. Not Jay. The district attorney's office regarding an upcoming trial. She'd call them back. Next message. Cameron Blackwell, the Steeles' FBI agent cousin on their dad's side, calling regarding the video she'd sent him. He'd done her a huge favor by running it through the FBI's facial recognition software.

She saved the message and moved on to the next one.

Way's voice sprang from the phone. "Hey. It's me. Way."

As if she wouldn't know her own brother. The sound of his voice, even on a recording, brought her good cheer up a notch. Way had managed to carve himself a nice little life that included custom fitting ammunition for government weapons. At twenty-nine and a restless spirit, Way had yet to get married or have kids. This left him with the ability to pick up and go between contracted assignments. On a whim, he'd hop on his motorcycle or into his truck and take off for a few days. Or, if time allowed, weeks.

That was Waylon. Maggie wasn't quite sure what drove her brother to these trips. She suspected his time as a Marine plagued him with emotional struggles he chose to sort out in isolation. For Way, Maggie imagined, moving back to Steele Ridge meant being hounded by a loving but nosey family. If the Kingstons weren't up in your business, you weren't family.

All those years away had softened Way, left him out of practice in dealing with life in the family bubble. After his military career ended, there were moments Maggie sensed something in Way. Something sad and...dark.

"I'm in Georgia," the message continued. "Heading home tomorrow for a job. Shep told me your vacation was canceled. Why this time? Call me."

As a reminder to call him back, she jotted Way's name on her notepad. He'd be after Jay and Cam.

From the stand on her desk, her cell phone rang. She glanced at it.

Cam's office number. He knew well enough that if he couldn't reach her via the office line to try her cell. She swiped the screen. "Cam, hey. Sorry. Just got your voice mail."

"Hey," he said. "No prob. I'm in between meetings. Got a second?"

"Absolutely. What's up?"

"I was able to fly under the radar with running your video."

Good news there. At least Jay wouldn't have to dig into his coffers to pay for the FBI lab. Sometimes connections got them a freebie.

"Sorry, Maggie, we didn't get a hit on this guy."

The news knocked a bit of her Porter-meeting euphoria to the curb and she sunk back in her chair. "He's not in the system."

"Not for DNA. On the facial recognition, if we had his whole face, it would have been better. With what you sent, the computer couldn't match him."

Well, shoot. "Unfortunately, I sent you the best we had."

"I figured. Is there anything else you need on this?"

Oh, she needed a lot, but so far the only thing coming together was the forged signatures. Could she have missed something somewhere? Her experience didn't compare to Cam's. He was FBI. Definitely more knowledgeable in this sort of thing. In fact, if Jay changed his mind and wanted to talk to someone about Celebrate Hope, Cam might be the better option.

"Cam, let me ask you something. Hypothetically speaking."

He snorted. "I love hypotheticals."

"I know. Let's say there's a large charity."

"How large?"

"Really large. Nationwide. Offices in every state."

He let out a whistle. "Interesting."

He didn't know the half of it. "*Hypothetically,* this charity is partnered with another high-profile entity."

"What kind of entity?"

"I can't say, but again, it's well known. Big money. The charity discovers an embezzler on staff and chooses to fire the person quietly rather than draw attention to the issue. They can't risk the scandal. However, another employee uncovers inconsistent accounting."

"Uh-oh."

"Yes. The charity, intending to avoid scandal, tells the employee who discovered the wrongdoing that if she goes to the authorities, she'll be implicated in the embezzlement."

"Right off the bat," Cam said, "we have embezzlement, extortion, and any number of possibilities regarding the cover-up. *Hypothetically.*"

Maggie smiled. "Of course. Now, if this person were to come forward, how quiet could the FBI keep the investigation?"

"Mmm, hard to say without the particulars. Are you sure this is only a hypothetical?"

He knew the answer. If it were a truly a hypothetical, she wouldn't be discussing it with him. "For now. Yes."

"Okay. Let me know if you need anything else."

"I will. Thank you."

He paused for a few seconds. "I talked to Reid a few days ago. He said you're getting closer to breaking his obstacle course record."

She sure was. And with Jay's help, look out, cuz. "Ha!

He's such a turd. I know he can't stand it and I *love* it. Love, love, love."

A deep rumble of laughter came through the phone. Cam's voice. Crazy cool. "He also said he's been working with Jayson Tucker."

Oopsie.

"And, you know," Cam said, "you'd have to be deaf and blind to not know he's a guy recently canned by a national charity."

Double oopsie.

She made a humming noise while she came up with a diversion. "Jayson's been here about a week. Causing quite a ruckus in our little town."

"I'll bet. Does your hypothetical involve him?"

Maggie stayed silent. There were hypotheticals and there were lies. At times, she'd lie if it benefited her in some way that wouldn't harm another. This time? No lying.

"Maggie?"

"I'm here."

"Did you hear me?"

Indeed she did. "Cam, thank you for your help. I'm incredibly grateful, but I'm not at liberty to comment any further."

Another long pause ensued and Maggie closed her eyes, begging whatever God available to help her get out of this conversation without betraying Jay's confidence.

"Okay," Cam said. "Obviously, you're not ready to give me details. How about this? If I should be looking into Celebrate Hope's accounting methods, don't say anything."

Maggie squeezed her eyes closed and forced herself to stay silent.

UNFUCKINGBELIEVABLE.

Jay stood in the hallway outside Maggie's office, his mind reeling over what he'd just heard. Over Maggie's betrayal.

He'd been pretty damned clear on his request to not involve anyone else in his disaster of a situation and what does she do? Bring in more law enforcement. At least it sounded like law enforcement. Either way, she'd disregarded every goddamned thing he said.

He moved into the doorway and for a second she didn't see him. Too busy reading the notes in front of her. From his spot he took in the perfect slope of her nose and soft curves of her cheeks and he got that brick to the chest. Just like every other time he looked at her.

Which only pissed him off more.

Betrayal.

He'd seen a lot of it lately.

He rapped on the door, his knuckles smacking harder than he'd intended. Then again, maybe not. She looked up and a smile lit her face.

"Hi." She popped from her chair and paddled her hands. "Come in. Come in. I just met with the handwriting expert. I have good news."

Her long legs made fast work of cornering her desk. Any other time, he'd love the sight of her rushing for him. Now, the anger fueled something primal in him. He should leave. Walk away before he said something he'd regret.

She leaned in to kiss him. Right in her office. The uptight sheriff wasn't so uptight anymore. He stood stock-still, let her peck him on the lips, just to feel her warmth. The Maggie spell that made everything in his day brighter. Except today.

Today, she'd pissed him off.

Today, she was a scheming witch.

The scheming witch was no dummy. She sensed the stiffness of his body and this time it wasn't in the crotch area.

She met his eyes. "What's wrong?"

Did she have three weeks? It'd take him that long to go through the list. And now this. "What did I ask you?"

"I'm sorry?"

"You should be."

She gawked at him and the tension, not just from him anymore, crackled between them.

"No," she said, "I wasn't apologizing. I was asking for clarification. And, frankly, what would I be apologizing for? Aside from spending every spare second I have trying to help you? *And* canceling a much-needed vacation."

The statement was delivered with such calm ease, it damn near knocked Jay back a step. Maybe he'd jumped too early on this thing.

No. He knew what he heard. Stood right in that hallway listening to her talk about a hypothetical situation involving a charity.

Should have known not to trust an outsider.

"That phone call," he said. "I heard part of it. And before you bitch at me about spying, Shari sent me back. I heard you say large charity and you can bet that sweet ass of yours I stopped to listen."

She swung around, walked back to her desk and stood behind it, her fingers tented on the flat surface. "Watch it, Jay. Do *not* talk to me like I'm some groupie who'll put up with your crap so you'll let me hang around longer."

What? His pulse went to two hundred and his ears didn't just whoosh, those suckers roared. "When have I *ever* treated you like a groupie?"

"Funny," she said, her voice carrying a tight, sarcastic edge. "I thought you just did."

If he treated her like a groupie, he'd be gone by now. "Who were you talking to?"

She shook her head, knocked one hand on her desk. "*Cameron* is Grif's FBI agent cousin. The one we sent the video to. He did us a favor. I trust him."

Cousin or not, the guy was a federal agent. "You gave him details."

"I didn't. I kept it vague. *What* is your problem with this? You knew I was sending him the video. You had to assume he'd ask about it."

"Did he?"

"Ask? Of course. He's a good agent."

She opened her mouth, but paused as if replaying the conversation. From what he heard, she'd initiated the conversation. And possibly ignited a shitstorm if Cameron decided to look into it.

"You offered me up, Maggie." He moved closer, his eyes never leaving hers because he wanted her to know just how pissed he was. "I asked you not to share this. I *trusted* you. My mistake. For the record, if I'd treated you like a groupie, I wouldn't have confided in you. And I sure as hell wouldn't be standing here feeling like an idiot who knew better."

He stepped closer. Cocked his head and focused on her luscious lips that were all over him last night. *All* over. As pissed as he was, the memories ignited a fierce need. Even now, he wanted her.

Jesus. He had to get out. Get away from her. Away from her damned body and the betrayal that made him insane. Bent on leaving, he turned and strode to the door before he said anything else that might cause him problems. Privately or publicly.

"Jayson!" she said. "Don't walk out of here. We're not done."

Now she wanted to tell him what he could do? He spun back. "Am I under arrest, Sheriff?"

Her head snapped back. "What are you talking about?"

"If you're not arresting me, I'll go wherever I goddamned please."

Now she banged both fists against the desk and gritted her teeth.

The motion, her clenched hands, and the white of her knuckles went fuzzy for a second. He blinked, tried to clear the blurriness that came with women and fists.

Never a good combination.

That combo got him feeling like a helpless twelve-year-old. A place he swore he'd never be again.

He pointed at her hands. "Stop," he said, his voice sharp and commanding.

For a second, she appeared confused, as if he'd spoken a foreign language. Finally, she looked down at her hands while the silence between them became a cement wall. Strong women.

Fists.

He'd been kidding himself thinking Maggie might be right for him. She was too headstrong. Too aggressive.

Her fingers uncurled and she looked up at him with a shocked horror he'd live with forever. "You cannot think I'd ever...Oh, my God. Please, you can't think that."

The tiny crack in her voice wouldn't fool him. No way. Been there done that. "Tell me, Maggie, are there any other secrets of mine that you've told?"

She held his gaze for a long few seconds, her eyes glistening with moisture that told him, prick that he was, he'd hit the bull's-eye and hurt her.

"And here," she croaked. "*I* thought you were a nice guy." She picked up a pen, tapped it on the desk once, twice, three times, then tossed it. She looked back at him, her deep brown eyes tear-free, but lacking the usual Maggie fire.

"You *are* something," she said. "So determined to do things your way, you don't even see when people are helping."

"You betrayed me."

"He's a federal agent! He can help you." She bit down, jerking her head. "Now I'm yelling. Great. Forget it." She waved him away. "Just...go. It'll be better for both of us."

SHE LET HIM GO.

Let him just walk right on out. What did *that* say about this supposed relationship?

Nothing good, Maggie was sure.

She sank back in her chair, taking in the empty doorway and the even emptier feeling inside her. Gutted. That's what she felt. All she'd wanted was to help him. How did she get to being the bad guy? All this effort and he couldn't see it.

Men like Jay, a man's man accustomed to people falling in line at his whim, couldn't, or wouldn't, see it. All he wanted was to be in charge. Nothing else mattered.

Better for her would be a nice, calm guy who didn't get rattled. Or pissed off. Who let life unwind on its own rather than try to bend it to his will.

A guy like her dad.

The intercom buzzed. "Ma'am?"

"Yes, Shari."

"Your mom called while you were in with Mr. Tucker. She said to call her back."

"Thank you."

Annoyed and tired of brooding over Jay, at least for now, Maggie dialed her mother's cell.

"Good afternoon," Mom said. "What are you doing?"

The woman calls the office and wants to know what she's doing. Apparently, retirement shorted the brains of brilliant people because now that Mom had retired, she assumed everyone else had also. "Um, working."

"Don't be sassy. I know that, but I'm in town. I stopped at Brynne's shop. She has a nice dress in the window and I made the assumption you haven't bought anything for her and Reid's wedding, so I picked it up for you."

Now her mother wanted to do her clothes shopping? This might be the most epic occurrence yet in Mom's retirement saga. Maggie envisioned her skull blowing open.

"Okay," she said. "Sure."

Why not? She'd try it, but wasn't holding out much hope. Dresses weren't her friend. Skirts she could deal with. Dresses always seemed too confining. It was the one-piece thing. Or maybe she was just a freak. All she knew was she'd been putting off shopping for the wedding because she needed to be mentally prepared.

And she wasn't.

"You can try it on later," Mom said, "but I thought you could take a break and meet me at the bakery. I'll give you the dress and we'll have coffee."

Maggie smiled. "And a doughnut, right?"

"Those Boston creams *are* fabulous. Can you sneak away?"

As much as Mom proclaimed herself to be a health nut, she liked to slip in a doughnut every now and again.

Maggie had skipped breakfast and after the fight with Jay, a little sugar therapy might do her good. She'd been pumped to update him on the handwriting expert's report and he'd blown it by lashing out at her. *Way to kill a girl's mood, stud.* Well, she wouldn't call him. No way.

Stubborn? Perhaps.

Regardless, she had a job to do and needed to convey this information to Camp Jay. After the doughnut break, she'd swing by and talk to Grif about the handwriting expert. "Mom, give me five minutes."

Maggie stepped out of the station, tilted her face to the sun, and decided a bit of fresh air might clear her mind. Passing her cruiser, she hoofed down Main Street, passing the dry cleaner and the new ice cream parlor. Desiree had just unlocked the door and Maggie reconsidered the doughnut in favor of ice cream.

Ice cream at ten a.m.

In the mood she was in, she might do both.

Two storefronts down, Mom stood outside the Mad Batter, where the board in front quoted Mae West.

Between two evils, I always pick the one I never tried before.

Amen, sister. At least Maggie had something in common with Mae. She'd taken the leap and entered into a steamy— hello, multi-orgasm nights—affair with a hot professional athlete she'd known from the start was a serious lapse in judgment. The man didn't even live close by. What had she been thinking? She made a grunting noise that awarded her a long look from Mrs. Johnson, who'd just left the dry cleaner.

"Sorry," Maggie said. "I was thinking."

Apologizing to the good citizens of Steele Ridge. Great. Damned Jayson.

As Maggie approached, Mom pointed at the sign. "I like this one. I took a picture and posted it on Instagram."

Oh boy. Her mother experimenting with social media. Could be dangerous.

"Mom, seriously, you need a hobby. You and Aunt Joanie should find something together. Shopping and social media are not the answer."

She pecked her mom on the cheek and gladly accepted a squeezing hug that Maggie realized she needed quite badly. A ball of emotion caught in her throat and she drew a deep breath. This wasn't her. All this negativity and angst. The neediness.

She and Jay had a fight. Big deal. They'd work it out. Or maybe not. For the second time, the man had come at her when she'd tried to help him. His attempts to control a situation, something she understood based on his family history, drove him to react in certain ways. Certain ways that strong, independent women wouldn't necessarily agree with.

If he wanted a brainless twit lacking opinions, she was so not the woman for him.

Mom pulled back from the hug and squeezed her arms. "This is nice."

"It is. I'm glad you called. I could use the break."

Mom studied her with narrowed eyes. "You look tired. Bad day?"

Fighting a burst of emotion, Maggie shrugged.

"Oh, my girl. Let's have a doughnut and you'll tell me about it."

Two minutes later, doughnuts and coffee in hand, they sidestepped a few other hungry customers and grabbed the small bistro table in the far corner of the bakery.

Anticipating the moment the sweet, sugary cake would hit her tongue, Maggie broke her doughnut in half and... dropped it. Getting hopped up on sugar wouldn't help. Misery already pinched her stomach into a ball.

She shook her head and contemplated the doughnut again. Maybe later. "Mom, I need to ask you something."

"Anything. Fire away." Mom took a bite of her doughnut and closed her eyes. "It's so good."

"You were never the traditional stay-at-home mom."

"You just noticed? I loved y'all, but I couldn't wait to get back to work. To this day I believe I'm a better mother for having worked. Your father, though, all he wanted was his babies. His babies and his plants. He dreamed of making a difference in the world, but not the way I did."

Wait. Hold on one second. In all the years her father had spent carting them around, she'd apparently missed something. "Dad had dreams?"

Mom looked at her as if she'd grown two more heads. "Of course he had dreams. He's human, isn't he? We always knew I enjoyed life in corporate America, but that wasn't him. He wouldn't invest his time in anything but his kids and making people healthier. While y'all were in school he worked on his organic produce. Did you think he was washing floors all day?"

"No. I...I don't know. Never thought about it being a dream; it was just what he did. It was always kind of weird. You know, Dad being at home and you working."

"Don't I know it. I heard the snickering around town about who wore the pants."

Steele Ridge, like every other town, had no shortage of small minds. As a kid, she'd heard the whispering, but blocked it out, tried to protect her siblings from it by telling everyone her father was a farmer.

A farmer with only a few acres.

But she'd tried. Even back then she wanted to take care of everyone. She shook her head. "People can be cruel," she said. "Did you ever say anything?"

"In the beginning, I was too embarrassed. Then I got angry. These people didn't know anything about my marriage. Or my husband. He's the strongest man I know."

"I think people misjudge him because he's so calm. And easygoing."

"But he's no pushover. Without him, I wouldn't have had the career I did. Just because a man isn't loud, doesn't mean he's not a man."

All this time, Maggie had been looking in the wrong places, choosing the wrong type of man, and winding up disappointed. "Do you think a man like Dad would be good for me?"

"What's this about?"

"I'm not getting any younger."

"Nonsense."

Maggie looked out the window at the passing cars on Main Street and the moms pushing strollers to kill a morning or woo their babies into a nap. "I'm worried I won't find someone. Quiet guys can't handle that I'm a sheriff. That I lock people up and can kick the crap out of them. The chest-thumpers can't handle it either. They want to jump in and save me. I don't need saving. I need companionship. None of them, at least the ones I've dated, know how to handle being with a strong, independent woman."

"Honey?"

"Yes?"

"Does this have anything to do with Jayson Tucker?" Mom reached across the table and squeezed Maggie's arm. "My sister isn't dumb, sweetie. And she's certainly not blind. She noticed, shall we say, a certain chemistry between you two."

"We had a fight," Maggie blurted.

"A fight. Already. Hmmm."

"It might have been my fault. But at the same time, not."

Mom held up her doughnut in a toast. "I'll need another bite for this story. Tell me everything."

Maggie gave her the recap. Her call from Cameron, the hypothetical situation, Jayson overhearing the conversation after he'd trusted her not to speak of it. *It was only Cam.* Not like she called ESPN.

"He feels betrayed," Maggie said. "I get that, but I'm also trying to help him save his career."

"Did he ask you to do that?"

"Mom!"

Mom waved one hand. "I'm not saying you're wrong for caring about him."

"But?"

"You try to save everyone. Whether they want it or not. I love that about you. You're unafraid. Not everyone sees it that way. Some might think you meddle. That's all I'm saying."

"Wanting to help is a bad thing?"

"When you're up in everyone's business it can be. Which makes me wonder why you're always so worried about everyone else."

"Other than it's my job?"

Mom scoffed. "Oh, don't give me that, Mandrell Margaret. What's the truth?"

Her mother's use of her given name made Maggie cringe. What kind of lunatics give their children the last names of country stars as *first* names?

Mom, the go-getter, the brilliant engineer, wouldn't want to hear that her oldest daughter had, well, settled. Maggie had become the good girl who always went along, who always got it right, and chickened out on her own dreams of Quantico because she'd been too afraid of failure. Disappointing people. Being strong and independent in her hometown, where everyone loved and respected her, was easy. An absolute no-brainer.

Stepping out of Steele Ridge? Totally different scenario.

Her thoughts looped and looped and looped. All this time she'd been jumping into one crisis after another, avoiding thinking too much about her own life. And the lack thereof.

After all, it was so much easier to fix other people's problems than to turn her attention on her own issues.

"I feel like I have to be a certain way. That people expect things of me. Jay says I need to set boundaries so people don't take advantage."

"To an extent, I agree. Don't let him change who you are if it's not what you want. That's where your father excels. He knows who he is and is secure enough to let me be who I am. That's the key, honey. It doesn't matter if you're both stubborn mules. What matters is finding middle ground. Jayson confided in you. In your effort to save him, you violated his trust. I'm not saying you were wrong, but he set a boundary and you ignored it."

Ugh. She, of all people, should have recognized it. People violated her privacy constantly. Hello, Cash and Riley. What right did she have to do it?

She reached across and clasped her mom's hand. "Thank you. I was too mad to see it that way. Now I get it."

"Honey, it's okay to make a mistake. You put so much pressure on yourself. You're not responsible for everyone. Your priority should be you. When you're happy, the people who love you are, too. Take some time with this. Don't be afraid to figure out what *you* want. Even if people disagree, it's not their life. It's yours. And you have a right to it."

Dressed in his workout clothes, Jay tugged on the front door of the training center. Locked. Of course.

"Son of a bitch."

Where the hell were Reid and Gage when he needed to work off some steam? Reid's truck and Gage's SUV were both parked in the lot. Here but not here.

Around back.

Probably out on the property, so they locked the doors. Fine. Whatever. He'd go around back and flip tractor tires until he could hit the weight room.

Anything to get rid of this burning, seething, absolute torture of rage tearing him up.

Damned Maggie.

He cut the corner of the building too close, bumped his shoulder and kept moving while an inferno fried his skin from inside.

"Two tenths faster!" Reid's booming voice carried on the air.

Obstacle course. He must be back there with someone running the course. Perfect.

He made the second turn and found Reid sitting on the picnic table. A slew of birds tweeted overhead, the annoying sound banging against his eardrums.

On the obstacle course, Gage crawled under the barbed wire Maggie was so good at. Sensing movement, Reid swung his head in Jay's direction.

"Superstar, what's up?"

"Need another workout."

Reid cocked his head. "This morning wasn't enough for you? Since when?"

Since a hot sheriff pissed him off. "I'm ready to go again."

"You sure? You damn near puked this morning. Can't have your pansy-ass getting injured. My brother'll kill me."

If Jay had known there'd be an interrogation, he'd have figured something else out. "You can work me out or I'll do it myself. Either way, I'm working out."

"Ho!" Gage called from the course. "I'm about to finish. Pay attention!"

Reid glanced over Jay's shoulder, waited a second and clicked his stopwatch. "You picked up a tenth. Nice job."

From what Maggie had said, Gage wasn't anywhere close to breaking the course record, but he'd suffered a brain injury in the service that he'd battled back from. His goal wasn't to break a course record. His goal was to compete against himself.

Gage huffed and puffed his way to the table and downed half a water bottle. "Hey, Jay."

"He wants to work out again," Reid said. "I don't think it's about getting a job, though. He's kinda pissy. We all know what gets under a man's skin that bad."

"Yeah," Gage said, "but since your sister is the only thing that gets me that pissed, I'm not commenting."

A wise move, no doubt, since Gage was currently living with Micki, Reid's younger sister.

Jay gave Reid another hard look. He was big and could probably kick Jay's ass with his hand-to-hand combat knowledge, but Jay was mad enough that he'd give the guy a good run.

"Thanks for the analysis, but are we working out or having a therapy session?"

"Depends."

"On?"

"Do you need a therapy session?"

"I need to kick the shit out of something."

Gage polished off the water bottle and crushed it in his

hand, the annoying crunch of plastic drowning out the tweeting birds.

"Have him run the course," Gage said. "He won't tear anything trying to lift weight he shouldn't be lifting after what you did to him this morning."

Jesus, these two. Everyone thought they could handle him now.

He turned away. "Forget it. I'll go to the gym in town."

"No, you won't," Reid said.

These fucking people in this fucking family. Every one of them was bent on annoying him today. "Watch me," Jay called over his shoulder.

Reid let out a snort that had Jay contemplating knocking him right off that goddamned table.

"Get your head out of your ass, Superstar. Might as well come back here because I'm dialing Tommy as we speak. FYI, he's the guy at the town gym. I'll tell him to barricade the door or lose his trainer. That's me, by the way. You dickhead."

Small towns. With the way his shit luck ran lately, of course the guy who owned the only other decent gym in Steele Ridge was hooked up with Reid.

Jay stopped walking, blew out a breath. If he didn't get rid of this rage soon, he'd lose his shit. In a big way.

He turned back, found Reid with a big-ass smile. So *fucking* annoying. Refusing to let Reid rattle him any further, he returned the smug grin. "Fine. Let's do this. It beats breaking my hand when I connect with that concrete head of yours."

"Oooh," Gage said. "I like it. I like it a *lot*. Unless you infants need me, I'm going back to work."

"You do that. If you order more moisturizer for the hotel, I'll strangle you. That shit is expensive. Superstar, give me some Spidermans and inchworms. You're not doing this cold."

"Wah, wah," Gage said, clearly unconcerned with Reid's threat.

Jay made quick work of his warmup, methodically going through the motions, thankful for something to concentrate on other than Maggie's betrayal.

Damned women. This would be why he never got too invested. He couldn't deal with the maintenance. Not when he had a career to tend to. The one slipping through his grip in record time.

On his last inchworm, he stood, rolled his shoulders. The brief warmup got his endorphins started, signaling his body to go to work. Already, the sharp edge of his anger dulled.

"You ready?" Reid asked.

Oh, he was ready. He nodded and squatted into a sprinter's stance. He'd blow the lid off this thing. Run the pissiness straight from his system. He had no time for female-induced bullshit when he had to find a job and get his life back on track.

"On my count," Reid said. "One."

Jay breathed in, controlled the urge to push himself too hard at the beginning and wind up burning through his energy when he'd need it at the end.

"Two."

An adrenaline dump flooded his system and a hyper-awareness set in. He focused on the first obstacle. *No sweat.*

"Three."

Jay took off, his body responding to his brain's signals. He hit the first obstacle, the log mounted on two beams. He vaulted over it and focused on the low wall. *Done.* Then came the ladder. He scrambled to the top, climbed over and halfway down leaped to the ground.

Next. High wall. Maggie's nemesis. Goddamned Maggie.

He grabbed the rope, scrambled up, and swung over the top, landing flat on his feet. Done.

Goddamned Maggie. *Forget her.* He forced her from his head, concentrated on the next obstacle. Behind him, Reid was silent. When did that ever happen?

Even the birds had shut up.

Thank you, sweet Jesus. He continued tearing up the course until he dropped to his belly, army-crawling under the barbed wire obstacle. *Maggie.*

Focus.

Clearing the wire, his body elevated to that state of euphoria that came with completing a physical task. Riding the adrenaline, he popped to his feet and sprinted to the finish line.

"Son of a bitch."

Reid stared at the stopwatch in his hand and let out a grunt.

Jay slowed to a jog, circling the picnic table as his heart pounded. He'd keep his feet moving for another minute until his breathing leveled out. "How'd I do?"

Reid finally looked up at him, his mouth twisted into a scowl. "You flaming asshole. You broke my record."

16

ONCE AGAIN, SHIT LUCK.

"Seriously?" Jay asked.

"You think I would joke about this? Dude, you fucking shattered it. A full second."

This wasn't happening. All he wanted was to blow off steam and now Maggie, who'd worked so hard to break her family's record, had his time to beat. And, really, he wasn't family. His time shouldn't count. Who the hell was he kidding? Maggie put so much damned pressure on herself, she'd never see it that way.

Jay halted. Screw keeping his feet moving. "No chance. You stopped it too soon."

"My ass, I did."

Jay snatched the stopwatch and checked the number. Dammit. He closed his eyes, then ran a hand over his face, letting out a frustrated laugh. How did these things keep happening to him?

"It's a fluke," Jay said. "Forget it."

"I will not forget it. You have the second best overall

time. Your name goes on the board right behind the SWAT guy. The top three times go on the board."

"No, Reid. I don't want it. I'm a professional athlete. I don't count."

"It counts, asshole."

He jabbed his finger. "Do not put my name on that board. Forget it. I'm not doing that to Maggie."

"Maggie? What's she got to do with it?"

"She's been working her ass off trying to break your record and I beat her to it."

As pissed as he was at her, he couldn't deal with her finding out he'd trumped her. That would make the whole mess worse. Who had the energy for that?

Jay grabbed a water bottle from the small cooler sitting on the bench and took a huge gulp. "Keep your mouth shut about this or I'll bust you up. I don't care how big you are."

"Tell your client to get his head out of his ass."

Maggie stood in the doorway of Grif's office in the Murchison building, watching her cousin pound away on his laptop. In keeping with his own version of dressing down, he wore a light blue dress shirt and no tie. The shirt alone probably cost more than she made in a week.

"Can you be more specific?" he asked. "I have a lot of clients with their heads up their asses."

Had to love her Steele cousins. She laughed and moved to the window where she liked to look out over Main Street. "I'm speaking specifically of the one in Steele Ridge."

Fully attuned, Grif stopped typing and spun his chair to face her. "Jay? That's a new one. He's one of the levelheaded ones. What'd he do?"

Not today, he's not. "He's mad that I reached out to Cam about this embezzlement thing."

Having no idea how much Grif knew about Jay's past—and his confiding in Maggie—she had to be careful here.

"He's a private person."

"And your cousin is an FBI agent. Who's Cam gonna tell?"

Grif held up two hands. "Don't get ornery with me. I'm only saying I can see his point. Mags, he's hounded day and night by tabloids. As a result, he has a handful of people he trusts."

"Yeah, well, he thinks I betrayed that trust."

"In a way, you did."

She continued to look out over Main Street and the passing pedestrians. The moms pushing strollers, the retirees grabbing coffee at the B while getting their daily steps in, all of it normal, completely carefree.

Maggie shook her head. "First my mother. Now you."

"I didn't tell you to become sheriff. Your job sucks. Sometimes you have to do things that piss people off."

"I definitely did that. He walked out before I got a chance to explain about the handwriting expert *or* the DNA results. Thus, I'm here. You can give him the results."

Griff sat back and clasped his hands on top of his head. "Do tell."

"The handwriting expert says he's fairly certain the signature was forged. He doesn't think it'll stand up in court because we don't have a big enough sample, but at least he's on our side."

"Good. We knew Jay didn't sign those checks. This only proves it. What about the video and DNA?"

Maggie sliced her hand across her throat. "Not so lucky there. No hits on either."

"Crap."

Her feelings exactly. She was upset with Jay, but he didn't deserve what was happening to him. "I knew the video was a stretch, but was hoping the DNA might get a hit. We're not giving up yet. There's one more thing we can try, but I need to talk to Jay about it. It creates a problem, since he's not speaking to me."

Still with his hands resting on his head, Grif made a face and a horrifying realization hit her. *He knows.*

"For God's sakes, Grif, don't look at me like that. I just saw my mother. I know this family well enough that if she and Aunt Joanie are gossiping about Jay and me, more than likely the rest of you are, too."

Finally, he brought his hands down and waved her to a chair. "Sit."

"I don't want to sit. I only wanted to deliver the message."

"Have it your way, but first of all, we're not gossiping. My mother raised four boys, she knows lust when she sees it."

Lust. Excellent. Maybe that's all this was.

"Mags, you're a smart girl."

"I am."

"At the risk of sounding insensitive, I don't think I need to tell you he's not staying in Steele Ridge. This is a temporary stop for him. We're talking to three teams from all over the country."

She knew all of this. Reminded herself on the daily. But hearing it, having Grif confirm it, stung like a drop of acid on her skin. "I know. And you're not insensitive. Believe me, I've been telling myself the same thing. It hasn't stopped me from getting involved. I like him, Grif. A whole lot."

"He's a good man."

"Who's not staying." She shook her head, cleared the

clog in her throat. Damned emotional clutter. "Do you know where he is now?"

"When he left here, he said he was heading back to Tupelo Hill. He's trying to help Sam figure out her next move. Did you call him?"

"Not yet. He probably won't pick up if it's me."

"Jesus, this feels like high school all over again." He hit the speaker button on his desk phone. "I think you're under-estimating him, but let's try him."

After two rings, Jay picked up. "Hey."

"My man," Grif said. "I'm here with Maggie."

A long silence filled the line. Yep, definitely still mad at her, but she'd be the bigger person here. The *not so high-maintenance* one. "Hi, Jay," she said.

"Hi."

Oh, ouch. Could he have been any more curt? For this, she'd keep it to business. At some point, hopefully, he'd become the reasonable man Grif assured her he was and talk to her on a more personal level.

"Mags has an update for you. If you'd rather talk to her one-on-one, I'll leave the office."

"I'm good," he said, still with the curt.

Grif held his hand to her.

"Thank you. Jay, the handwriting expert believes your signature was forged."

"I said that."

"I know, but having an expert verify it helps. He did say he didn't think the small sample from the Celebrate Hope checks would hold up in court, but with luck this won't get to that point. Now, the conversation this morning you over-heard part of was Cam telling me he was unable to get a match on the video we provided. Our guy isn't in the crim-inal database, but I have another idea. If you're amenable to it, we can get a warrant for the databases of genealogy companies."

"Genealogy? I don't understand."

"Yes. The larger genealogy sites offer DNA analysis so people can determine their lineage. They're private databases, though, and we'd need a warrant to access them. That means making an official request. And since the shooter was in Steele Ridge, the incident occurred in my jurisdiction. I can request the warrant."

When Jayson didn't respond, Grif met her eye. "Jay," he said, "Mags'll work with us on keeping this as quiet as possible."

"What about all the people who'd be involved at the genealogy companies? Someone, somewhere will leak it."

"It's a possibility," Maggie said. "You have to be willing to risk it."

Another long silence ensued. She'd pushed it on the warrant. *Knew it.* He'd lost his mind over her posing a hypothetical to Cam. Officially requesting a warrant would be out of the question.

Grif checked the phone's screen. "You there?"

"Yeah. I'm here. I don't know, Grif. Let me think about it. This embezzlement thing involves Sam, too. She's already worried about finding another job. If this goes public, she's screwed."

SEVEN HOURS OF THOUGHT—AND MISERY—BROUGHT JAY TO Maggie's doorstep. Where he might or might not be welcome. Dumb-ass.

He glanced at his watch for the hundredth time: 8:10. Not late. Definitely not late enough to turn chickenshit and run.

Plus, there was a classic Ford Bronco, obviously fully restored, sitting in the driveway and he wanted to know who the fuck *that* belonged to.

Granted, neither of them should be happy with how the exchange—eh-hem, argument— went down in her office, and yeah, he *probably* overreacted, which translated to the whole damned thing being his fault.

But if she had a guy inside this house, his fault or not, he'd lose his shit altogether.

He knocked, then stepped back, forcing away visuals of Maggie bent over her bed with other men. Nope, nope, nope. Not going there.

A minute later the door swung open and there she was. In the doorway in workout shorts and a yoga top that revealed the tight abs she worked so hard for. Already his body reacted. No matter what happened between them, something told him, he'd fantasize about Maggie for a good long time.

Fix this.

"Hi," he said. "Before you slam the door, can we talk?"

A few hairs had flown free of her ponytail and she tucked them behind her ears before waving him in. "I wasn't planning on slamming the door. Come in."

A dude in a long-sleeved T-shirt and hiking pants sat at her breakfast bar with an open pizza box in front of him. His hair was the color of whisky, but with random light streaks shot through it. The golden retriever lying at his feet rose to a sitting position.

"Stay, Puck," the dude said.

Puck. Great name for a dog.

The guy stood and held out his hand. "I'm Shep."

Shep. Maggie's brother. The outdoorsy one. She'd talked about him the other night. Now, with Jay's overactive and fatigued mind nudged, he recognized the Kingston family resemblance.

Jay shook his hand. "Jayson Tucker. Good to meet you."

"We, uh," Shep pointed at the door, "were just heading out."

There it was. The excuse Jay needed to turn chickenshit and avoid an uncomfortable conversation with Maggie. "No," he said. "I'll go. I should have called."

"It's all right," Maggie said, her voice carrying a sharp edge. "He said five minutes ago he had to leave. He's taking a group hiking in the morning and it's an early one. Shep, take the pizza with you. It'll spoil if you leave it here."

Her brother closed the pizza box, making sure to tuck the cover in before sliding it off the counter. "Thanks, Mags. I'll talk to you tomorrow." He nodded at Jayson. "Have a good night."

"You too."

Maggie showed her brother and Puck to the door while Jay stood in her living room. He wouldn't take it upon himself to sit. After their run-in earlier, he'd wait for the invitation.

"Sorry to bust in on you," Jay said.

She flipped the lock on the door and walked toward him. "It's not a problem. I'd say if it was. Besides, I'd like to clear the air. Have a seat."

Phew. He slid onto the stool Shep had just vacated and waited for Maggie to take the one next to him. He'd had all day to rehearse a plea and somehow he hadn't managed to come up with one decent argument for his behavior.

"Jay—"

"No." He reached for her, touched her arm lightly, and felt the ping of relief when she didn't pull away. "Don't say anything yet. Please. I thought about you all afternoon and I think—I know—I overreacted. I...never mind. No excuse. I'm sorry. I was out of line. You were doing your job and trying to help. I shouldn't have jumped all over you."

She sat for a full thirty seconds, first tilting her head one way, then the other, obviously deciding on a course of action. "A couple of things," she said. "This is the second time you've surprised me with an apology before I've had a chance to say anything. I appreciate the apology, but in the future please don't interrupt. Let me finish. Okay?"

He nodded.

"Good. Now, I agree that you could have given me the opportunity to explain myself, but I'm on the hook for part of this, too. After a conversation with my mother, I realized I may have overstepped with asking Cam about the charity. Even if I did pose it as a hypothetical, this is technically out of my jurisdiction, so I should have confirmed with you before I did anything, and should have realized that he'd connect the dots. I'm sorry. Truly, I never meant to—or would I want to—hurt you. Ever."

He shifted the hand still on her arm and intertwined their fingers. "Me neither. Look, Maggie, straight out, I'm a goner when it comes to you. Physically and emotionally and that's new. You're smart and funny and beautiful and I can't get enough. Which makes me want to tell you things I tend to not share. With anyone. Thinking about you repeating those things fried my mind."

She looked down at their intertwined hands and squeezed before bringing her gaze back to his. "Thank you. You have no idea how much of a compliment that is coming from you. Looking back on it, I see why I upset you. I think we're figuring each other out. Learning the hot buttons. In the process, I've learned some things about myself I need to change. Which really makes me mad at you. Before *you* appeared I never psychoanalyzed myself. Now? That's all I do."

He laughed. "Sure. Blame that on me, too. Why not?"

She waved it off. "It's my own fault. I shouldn't be so ready to get up in everyone's business. From now on, I'll talk to you before making any inquiries."

God, that's all he wanted. A discussion. To not be forced into something he couldn't control. "Thank you."

"You're welcome."

"I talked to my accountant earlier. He confirmed what I said about not receiving any payments from Celebrate Hope. The endorsed checks they have are bogus."

She high-fived him. "Yes! Excellent."

"Yeah. And about this DNA test, I talked to Sam. She's okay with it."

Maggie's eyebrows lifted. "What about you?"

"I think it sucks. If the reasons behind it get leaked, I can kiss any and all endorsement deals good-bye. Nobody wants a pitchman involved in embezzlement."

"But if the test'll get us answers and clear you—"

"I'll suck it up. I trust you, Maggie. I know you'll do right by us. I've been holding secrets so long, it's an automatic reaction for me. My brain screams hide, hide, hide. It's so goddamned exhausting."

She leaned in a little. Ran her free hand through his short hair, then down his cheek, gently rubbing her knuckles over his beard, and her touch, that gentle connection, gave him an odd feeling of peace. Maggie Kingston had turned his world upside down.

And right now, he didn't mind. He might even like the emotional intimacy he'd been lacking for...hell...maybe forever.

"Maybe it's time to stop hiding," she said. "You might be surprised by the results."

Could he do it? Lay his demons out there for public fodder? "I've always been afraid to admit I was an abused kid. Like people would think less of me. I mean, the big, bad quarterback who couldn't defend himself against his own mother?"

"You were a kid. What were you supposed to do? Hit her back? You're not a violent man."

"After the Webb incident, I don't think people will believe that."

"I think if you start being honest about what happened in that locker room, they might."

"What if reporters start digging and find out part of this mess involves Webb abusing his wife? I couldn't give a shit about him, but his wife and kids don't deserve it."

Maggie scooted to the edge of her seat, moving close enough to slide her leg between his, sending that intimacy up another notch.

"It's not about him. It's about you being honest. If the locker room incident comes up, you say it was a personal issue that got out of hand. At the very least, he needs to be dealt with for setting up that illegal hit. We have my recording of your phone call with him. He all but admitted it. And I guarantee if we downloaded his texts, we'd see something suspect. That might just be my jaded mind, though."

"You think I should pursue it?"

"I think you should *threaten* to pursue it. You've been so busy running from this thing, I think it's time you take the offensive." She nudged his leg. "My hunky quarterback."

He'd give her a hunky quarterback. He set his free hand on her leg, let it travel a little higher so she knew exactly where his mind had gone. "I never thought about it that way."

Her gaze moved to his hand and she pursed her lips for a second. "Stop distracting me. Believe me, you'll get lucky tonight, but we need to finish this first."

"Damn."

She laughed. "You're too used to covering up. I know it's easy for me to say, I'm not the one with reporters tailing me. I'll support whatever decision you make, but I'm giving you the flip side. The one that has you on the offensive for a change, going after people bent on destroying you."

"Do it."

"Do what?"

"The genealogy thing. I'll pay whatever the lab fees are. Maybe we'll get a hit this time. It's worth a try, right?"

"Exactly."

"And, hold on to your gun belt, babe, but if I wanted to go after Celebrate Hope, how would that work?"

Maggie fanned herself. "Now you're getting me all hot. What do you mean, go after them?"

How cute was she? He rolled one hand. "If we're going on the offensive, I need to get ahead on this embezzlement thing. The league and Celebrate Hope don't want this out there any more than I do. Let's swing back. Make them nervous."

"The charity is headquartered in South Carolina and that's out of my jurisdiction. We could take it to the FBI."

"Grif's cousin."

"I don't know. He works out of DC and what he's done for us so far has been on the downlow. Cases are usually opened based on geography, so the FBI's Columbia field office would more than likely handle that. We can call Cam and ask, though."

"Let's feel it out. See what he says."

"At the risk of this sounding condescending, I'm proud of you. You're about to do something that goes against everything you've practiced for years. It can't be easy."

A disembowelment with a dull knife would hurt less, but for freedom, for a life free of constant hiding and secrets, he'd do it. He didn't even know what that life would look like, but he wanted to try. "I'll probably puke my guts out tonight, but what I've been doing isn't working anymore. And when it's not working, you change the play. Thank you."

"Hey, I'm not the one about to spill my life to the voracious public. You did this all on your own."

"Not true. You got me there. Your strength and your damned persistence."

She smiled. "Family trait."

"Don't I know it? In this case it's a good one."

She stood and wrapped her arms around him. "I'm glad. All I want is to make sure you're okay."

"God, Maggie, you're...special. You see everything. You strip someone bare and make it feel normal. It's a gift."

"It's not hard when you listen."

"You're different. You don't need anger to feel powerful. You get your power from your brain and I want that in my life." He held on to her, squeezing even more and kissing the bare skin of her shoulder where the strap of her top ended. "I want you."

JAYSON'S WORDS FLOATED AROUND IN MAGGIE'S MIND. EVERY excuse she'd had for not believing this relationship would be any more than a fling seemed to disappear. Could they do it? Make a long-distance relationship work?

Between her long hours and being accustomed to life on her own, it might not be all that much different than what she was used to. During the season, she'd have to juggle her schedule, but if he wanted this to work, he'd have to spend time in Steele Ridge in the off-season.

"I'd like that," she said. "Logistically, it'll be a challenge."

"A lot of people make it work. Some guys are married to actresses who live on the West Coast. And I'd spend time here in the off-season. You're here, Grif's here. It makes sense."

She backed away, met his eye to make sure he wasn't caught up in the moment. That he was serious and not just telling her what she needed to hear. "You'd do that?"

"I grew up in New York and my career was there, but that's changed now. I never stopped long enough to figure out if I even wanted to be there." He smiled. "Right now, North Carolina looks pretty good. What do you say? Can we try it? See where this thing goes?"

Yes.

She wanted to say it. Let the word fly right off her tongue, but they had to be reasonable about this or one of them—more than likely her—could wind up devastated. "If you get picked up by a team out west, that's a long flight for me during the season. My schedule isn't constructed for long weekends. I have responsibilities."

"I know. And, yeah, that'd be hard. I'd want you at the games, but I get it."

"I could do some. Not all."

"I'll take what I can get."

"What about Sam? Where does she want to wind up?"

"She moved to South Carolina for the job. She wanted to get out of New York. When this mess gets sorted out, she'll go back to South Carolina and figure her next steps. If I'm spending time here, she might stay close. There's no pressure there, though. We're used to being in different places. She knows I'm here for her if she needs me."

The man had answers for everything. Darned good ones, to boot.

All they could do was try. Little more than a week ago, when Jay rolled into town with his slick smile and media circus, she wouldn't have considered it. The hotshot football star and the country sheriff. It still might be a disaster in the making. When he came within ten feet of her, though, something happened. Something light and warm and... comforting. And that was saying a lot for a girl who usually cared for everyone else.

She kissed him, let her lips linger over his while he pulled her closer and ran his hands over her hips, pulling her tight against him.

He wanted her. She wanted him.

Easy.

"Let's do it," she said. "I think we'd be really good together."

"I don't think, I know. You get me. You call me on my bullshit and you definitely aren't afraid to hang in for the ugly stuff." He laughed. "I got a lot of ugly stuff."

Ugly stuff and all, this was where she wanted to be.

JAY ROUNDED THE SIDE OF THE BUILDING FOR HIS MORNING workout and found Reid in his normal spot on the picnic bench, a cup of Miss Joan's coffee cradled in his hand. Everything about his appearance, right down to the sneakers he wore, was typical Reid. Only today, Grif was in attendance, as usual dressed to impress. The two spoke in hushed tones that immediately set Jay on edge.

Enough time had been spent with this family to know that if Grif carried good news, he'd be more animated— even at 6:30 in the morning—and trading insults with Reid.

"Hey," he called.

Grif angled back, arranged his face into a bright smile. "Morning."

"Kinda early for you, no?"

Reid held up his wrist. "Superstar, you're late."

Actually, he was right on time, but in Reid's world if you weren't early, you were late.

"Dragging today."

"You okay?" Grif wanted to know.

If he intended to keep up these early morning workouts, he couldn't have Maggie keeping him busy half the night. "I'm good. Tired is all. What's up?"

"I had a call from Paskins last night."

There's a name he didn't want to hear this early. But, speaking of that son of a bitch, his two-day deadline ended today and he'd better be giving Jay some answers on the Celebrate Hope situation or Jay would start working his contacts first thing in the morning.

"Problem?"

"No, he was impressed with the work you're doing down here. With the morale issues on the team since you left, he wants to bring some guys down for team building exercises."

"Yeah. He mentioned that. What about it?"

"Listen," Reid said, "if them being here is gonna screw up your focus, we'll tell them no. I have eighty guys coming in from Southern Cal on Sunday. We're not hard up for business."

They'd turn away a professional football team for him. Talk about loyalty.

"You don't need to do that."

"Blah, blah. We know. I got no problem turning them away." Reid looked at Grif. "Right, Pretty Boy?"

Keeping his gaze on Jay, Grif flipped his brother off. "What the knuckle-dragger is attempting to say is, the Knights were shitty to you and you're our priority. If there is any hesitation on this, just say the word."

For years, he and Sam had been watching each other's backs. They had been alone and untrusting of their own mother, emphasis on the alone. Until now. Now, Grif and his family had taken them in.

"Guys, I appreciate it, but it's not necessary. Whenever they're coming, I'll steer clear. I'll get off the property completely. I'll take a day, maybe explore the area."

And look for potential homes to buy. Because if he got really lucky, this thing with Maggie would work out and he'd become a North Carolina resident.

Grif cocked his head. "You're sure? I thought you'd be pissed."

A couple days ago, he *had* been pissed when Paskins had asked about doing this. Now? With Maggie pounding sense into him, there were more important things to get pissed over. "It's all good. Tell me when they're coming and I'll bolt."

"Game is a week from Monday night. Paskins wants them focused for the big stage. He's looking to send some starters tomorrow morning for the day. Test the waters. If it works out, they'll schedule some off-season stuff."

"All right." Jay waved a hand at Reid. "We'll do our normal morning workout—"

"Cash is coming tomorrow."

"Good," Jay said. "I could use it. Let's book extra time for Cash and a workout. That'll take us to eight or eight thirty. Give me an hour to eat and get cleaned up and I'm gone."

"I'll tell Paskins we can have them here at ten." Grif turned to Reid. "You'll arrange to get them from the airport?"

"I'll take care of it."

Jay held his hands out. "All settled. Now, I'm gonna warm up."

"When you're done," Grif said, "come see me. There's an offer on the table I didn't anticipate. I was gonna say no, but I want to run it by you."

"Will do, boss. Now get the fuck out."

He needed to stay sharp and game-ready. And with Maggie agreeing to give their relationship a shot, even with this bullshit embezzlement crap, he was starting to feel good about his life again.

At 9:00 sharp, Jay walked into Maggie's office. All buttoned up in her uniform, she sat at her desk, tie perfectly straight, badge in place, and her hair pulled back in a slick ponytail. A definite contrast to the woman who'd wrapped her long legs around him last night and let her hair go wild while telling him *exactly* what she wanted from him. Yow. He needed to stop thinking about that.

Wicked turn-on though, this all-business Maggie versus the sex goddess Maggie.

She peered up at him with her big brown eyes and a sly smile slid across her lips. Tonight, he'd get her out of that uniform and they'd see about her handcuffs.

"Hello," she said. "How was the workout?"

"Good. You're not gonna believe this one."

She widened her eyes and took a breath. "What now?"

"Paskins wasn't blowing smoke up my ass about training with Reid. He's really doing it. He called Grif last night and wants to bring the guys down tomorrow."

Her head lopped forward. "On a *Saturday*? Don't they have a game on Sunday?"

"It's a bye week. They're not playing until next week. A night game. Ton of pressure with national coverage. Knowing him, he wants to get them sharp for that. Reid and Grif were gonna tell him no. They'd turn away what could turn into not just the Knights, but the entire league training down here. Can you believe that?"

"Of course I can. That's my family. We take care of our own."

Our own.

Maggie's family stood behind each other, shoring up, adding energy and strength to the united front. Something he'd only had with his sister and suddenly, experiencing it from Maggie and Reid and Grif, he wanted more. Wanted to be part of it for as long as his twisted life would allow.

"For me," Jay said, "it's weird. My family is so screwed up, we never had that. It was me and Sam. No one else."

"Well, that's changing, isn't it?"

"I guess it is."

He took the seat across from her, slouching enough to appear casual, but they both knew better.

She eyed him for half a second. "You ready?"

Never. "Yep."

"Are you lying?"

"I am."

She laughed. They'd talked for a long time last night, debating the pros and cons of a warrant for the private DNA database and calling Cam about the mess with Celebrate Hope. If Jay made the call, his nasty secrets would be out there. Maybe, Maggie had argued, the feds could keep it quiet.

Maybe not.

After so many years of shielding his image and hiding the miserable truth of his upbringing, this felt…foreign. Like driving in a foreign country. On the wrong side of the road. With no navigation.

In the end, after weighing every option either of them could toss out, he'd told her he'd sleep on it. Which he did. As of 5:30 this morning when he rolled out of her bed to head back to Tupelo Hill, he'd informed Sheriff Kingston she could get the warrant and they should call Cam. It scared the ever-loving shit out of him, but he was tired of running. And with radio silence from Paskins, deal or no deal, it was time to take matters into his own hands.

He pointed at her desk phone. "Let's do it."

She nodded. "Good, because I already have the wheels rolling on our warrant. My favorite judge is in court this morning, but I should hear something from her by lunchtime."

"What happens then?"

"Then I send the warrant over to the genealogy sites and we run the DNA through their databases."

"That fast?"

"They could stall, but I'll put pressure on them." She smiled. "I can be convincing."

He snorted. "Don't I know it?"

"I took the liberty of texting Cam that I might be calling around now. He said he'd be at his desk."

She pointed at the door. "Want to close that while I dial?"

Jay hopped out of his chair and gently shut the door.

The snick of the locking mechanism reverberated in his head, shifting his hypervigilant system to protection mode.

Don't do it. He could leave. Open the damned door and walk right out.

That, however, would make him the worst kind of coward. The one who couldn't face his own past.

He ignored his slamming pulse and turned back to Maggie.

She tapped a button on the desk phone, sending a dial tone blaring into the room. "You're doing the right thing. I'm sure it doesn't feel like it, but you and Sam are being set up here. And worse, they're blackmailing you. You shouldn't be forced to accept that. Not for an image. This embezzlement has to be addressed. Particularly for the folks Celebrate Hope should be helping."

Don't do it. The panic hit him like a freight train, stealing every ounce of air from his body. *Can't breathe.* Jesus.

Maggie hit the button again and the room went silent. "Jay?"

He should haul ass. Right now. Forget the whole goddamned thing. He snapped his gaze to her fingers still on the keypad.

"I'm here for you, Jay," she said. "Whatever you need."

Damn, this woman could read his mind. He inhaled hard, forcing oxygen into his body. Maggie. Even with his career in flames, she was right here with him.

He took three more breaths and focused on the task. On doing the right thing, no matter the consequences. "Thank you," he said. "Now let's do this."

Maggie nodded and dialed. The line connected and rang twice.

"Blackwell."

His voice was deep. Rough. Like Maggie's all-business voice. Might be a cop thing. Who the hell knew?

"It's me," she said.

"Hey, Mags." His voice eased to a more casual, less clipped tone. "What's up?"

"I—" she glanced at Jay. "*We* need your help with something."

"We?"

"I have Jayson Tucker in my office. He has information he'd like to share. About Celebrate Hope."

17

ON SATURDAY MORNING, THE MORNING THE KNIGHTS WERE set to arrive, Jay stood at the stove in Miss Joan's kitchen throwing together a Denver omelet. Miss Joan had broken his heart by choosing to leave on a day trip with Eddy rather than joining Jay for breakfast. A day trip. Really? Must be what older folks called it when they wanted to get laid.

Day trip, my ass.

The heartbreak was probably meant to be because he hadn't factored in time to prep the food and cook when he'd given Reid his timeline for clearing out of Tupelo Hill. The wall clock tick-tocked and he glanced up: 9:15. *Shit.* Paskins and crew would be arriving at 10:00. Giving himself a cushion meant peeling out by 9:50—or sooner unless he wanted to risk running into his former teammates. Some, he wouldn't mind seeing, but he wasn't sure who all would be in the group and he wasn't risking it.

Paskins, though, he needed to see, or at least talk to. Jay had left him a message the night before regarding their deal and the blown deadline. Jay had yet to hear back. The son of a bitch was ducking him, testing Jay on his threat to go to the press. At this point, Paskins shouldn't push it. The only thing keeping Jay from reaching out to a few well-chosen reporters was the fact that Cam Blackwell had asked him to hold off.

As of last night, Cam had spoken to the Columbia, South Carolina, field office regarding opening an investigation into Celebrate Hope. The public needed to know where their money went and an investigation would, in Jay's mind, clear Sam as well as himself.

His cell phone rattled against the counter and Reid's name flashed. Jay tapped the screen. "What's up?"

"You got company heading your way," Reid said. "A couple of your buddies from the team."

Crap. He glanced at the clock again, knowing full well he hadn't suddenly fallen into a fugue state and lost forty minutes. "*Now?* What happened to ten o'clock?"

"A couple of the guys came down last night. They got here early to catch you. I told 'em you were staying up at the house, but might be gone already. Feel free to not answer the door. I wasn't making that decision for you. Your friends, your decision."

"Who is it?"

"Dirks and Rothstein."

Ah, jeez. Two of his closest friends. How the hell could he ignore them? "All right. Thanks for the heads-up."

Jay punched off the call and slid his omelet from the hot pan. Rather than sit, he stood at the counter, shoving in forkfuls of food before his friends knocked. He polished off half the omelet and took a slug of water before the *bam, bam, bam* occurred. Front door.

Was he ready to see them when the stab of disappointment over being ousted from the team was still fresh? Even when it came to his friends, it seemed too damned soon. But these guys had had his back from the get-go, deflecting questions from reporters and leaving him messages of support.

The knock—pounding, really—sounded again. He'd have to answer it. What kind of chickenshit asshole leaves his friends at the door? He wiped his face and hands with a napkin and tucked it under the plate.

Bam, bam, bam.

Friggin' animals might knock down that door banging so hard. "Ho! Keep your goddamned shorts on."

No chance Sam might still be sleeping after that racket. He strode to the door, set his hand on the knob, and took a second to breathe. He ripped open the door. "You two dumb-asses almost broke the door down."

Dirks shoved him aside and let himself in.

"By all means," Jay said, "come in."

On his way past, Rothstein lightly smacked Jay's cheek. "Dude," he said, "whassup? Do you miss us?"

More than you know.

"Dream on, douchebag. I finally got some peace and quiet."

Dirks stopped in the living room and spun back. "Quiet? Who needs that shit. I say it's overrated."

"You'd be surprised."

As much as he'd like to act pissed off about these guys busting in on him, seeing his friends brought on a smile. Because, yeah, he'd missed them. "But, you know, you assholes do grow on a guy."

Rothstein made pistols with his fingers and clicked his tongue. "Exactly why we're here. Whatever this wargaming shit is, you're doing it with us."

Hold on now. "Thanks but no thanks. It's team business.

You might have missed it, what with the reporters and psychos trying to kill me, but I'm not a Knight anymore."

Dirks waved that off. "Who gives a crap? You're our guy. We want you up there."

Awww, sweet, but...no. "No way, boys. Not happening."

"Come on. There's only eleven of us. All the senior guys. *Your* guys. Paskins told us to check it out before he sent the whole team."

Now this was interesting. "Which guys?"

Rothstein rattled off the list of names. All men Jay had played with over the last few years. Guys who'd shown loyalty to him before and after the Eric Webb shit show.

"That's why you came in early? To talk me into this."

Dirks held his hands wide. "We love you, man!"

"Plus," Roth said, "we got the rundown from the swol guy."

"That's Reid. He owns the place."

Roth waggled his hand. "Whatever. He said he's letting us loose in the woods for team building. Paintball guns and shit."

Reid had bounced his plan off Jay during his workout that morning. He'd come up with a fictitious hostage situation where the guys would be split into teams, competing to be the first to find and rescue the hostage.

Roth circled his finger. "You know the layout of the place. We'll put you on our team and ace this thing."

Jay snorted. If only it was that easy. "There's about twenty acres out there I haven't seen, so don't count on me to bail your asses out. Is Paskins here?"

Dirks shook his head. "Last I heard, no. But we weren't on the plane."

"I gotta meet with him about something."

Rothstein set his hand on Jay's shoulder and shoved. "Even more reason for you to hang around. Don't be a pansy-ass and run. Stick around. Meet with Paskins and then war-game. It'll be fun. Christ knows you haven't had any of that lately."

Not true. Media chaos, would-be assassins, and embezzlement issues aside, he had Maggie. That right there? Fun with a capital—and bold—F.

"It's not bad here."

"Hicksville?"

Now Roth was pissing him off. "It's not Hicksville. Yeah, it's quiet. But the fresh air is...pretty fucking awesome. I'm thinking I'll buy a place here."

His friend's jaw fell open. "No way. You?"

Jay laughed. "Wait'll you see the property. And if I do buy a place, I'll let you idiots rent a room from me."

"Generous," Dirks said.

"It's in my nature."

Rothstein wrapped his *thick as an oak* arm around Jay's neck and added enough pressure for him to feel it in his throat.

"Give in," he said, "or I snap your pencil neck. Pretty boy quarterbacks and your skinny necks."

"I may have a skinny neck, but I got a free hand that can twist your balls until they break off."

To add drama, Jay held his hand out and wiggled his fingers.

"Shit." Roth let go. "Don't touch my junk, man. That's dirty."

Dirks got in the middle of them. "You two about done horsing around? We're on the clock here. Come on, Tuck. What have you got to do that you can't stomp around in the woods with us?"

When Jay didn't answer, Roth shoved him to the door. "That's what we thought. Go. Let's kick some ass."

JAY'S REUNION WITH HIS FORMER TEAMMATES LASTED ALL OF seven minutes. After which, Reid turned into a drill sergeant sending his troops to stow their personal belongings, including cell phones, in lockers.

There'd been no sign of Paskins. Either he hadn't made the trip or he was locked in an office somewhere doing business. Later, Jay would ask Reid about it.

For now, a bunch of grumbling, electronics-free football players assembled behind the training center where a grinning Reid set equipment out on rolling tables. Nothing Reid loved more than getting under the skin of guys who'd like to kick the crap out of him.

Judging body size by eye, Reid and Gage outfitted everyone with protective clothing and headgear and then lightened the mood considerably by handing them all badass-looking paintball guns.

At least Jay assumed they were paintball guns. Faded splotches of color on the handles told the tale.

Paintball.

This *would* be fun.

Reid stood before them, legs wide, hands clasped behind his back, waiting for the group to settle down. With this crowd he'd be waiting awhile.

"Gentlemen," he finally said, his voice booming above the hooting and general savagery a dozen professional football players could create. "Our first exercise of the day is a rescue operation. A United States aid worker—otherwise known as my sister, Evie—has been taken hostage and is being held in the mountains of—" He turned to Gage. "Where should she be?"

Gage shrugged. "Istanbul."

Reid went back to the group. "Istanbul. Evie is heavily guarded and located in a structure no bigger than a backyard shed. Gage will review the terrain with you and answer questions, but our information is limited. You will have ninety minutes to complete your mission. After which, we'll review, make adjustments, and try again. Any questions?"

"Uh," Roth said, "how the hell do we find her?"

Reid grinned. "It's a team building exercise. Figure it out." He turned to walk away, then snapped his fingers. "Oh, and stay sharp. There are Kurdish separatists out there and they don't like visitors. In addition, our hostage can be combative. She will most likely mistrust and fight you. Believe me, I know."

"How many separatists?" one of the guys asked.

"Enough to get one of you shot. Ninety minutes, gentlemen. Good luck."

Gage stepped forward, handed the men maps, compasses, and a photo of Evie. "Your suits have GPS transponders sewn into them. If your group doesn't return in ninety minutes, we'll locate you and ensure everyone is safe."

Steiger held up his map. "Why can't we use our phones?"

Gage eyed him. "What fun would that be? The point of the exercise is to work together. We're doing this old-school, gentlemen, but we've helped by marking the maps with probable areas where Evie might be held."

Jesus. No social media or cameras? This crew would slide into withdrawals that might require hospitalization.

After a brief review of the map, Gage had the men count off and all even numbers step forward. Jay was number eleven. Since Roth and Dirks stood on either side of him, they were both even numbers and, therefore, on the other team. There went the whole bonding thing.

Whatever. It'd still be fun.

No doubt, Reid and Gage would be the so-called separatists, which would give Jay an opportunity to exact his revenge for the week and a half of abuse he'd been dealt by Reid. A definite perk.

"You six," Gage said to those in the front row, "are Team Blue. The rest of you, Team Red." He pointed to a red canopy tent at the southwest side of the training center and then to the blue one on the southeast side. "Those are your home bases to plan strategy. The clock starts now. The team that returns with Evie first is the winner. Good luck."

Talk about motivating a bunch of athletes. Make it about winning and losing and see how fast they get their shit together.

The two groups moved to their respective tents, voices already reaching elevated decibels over who the team leaders should be.

Jay hung back. He was no longer their quarterback. If they wanted him to run this show, they'd have to ask or vote or do whatever it was teams did to establish their leader.

Three minutes later, with Jay elected team leader, the men set out on their search.

"Okay, boys," Jay said, walking toward a clump of trees, "let's do this. I haven't been up on that part of the property, but I can tell you there are sheds and small cabins scattered throughout. We may find some that are empty. And Reid is a filthy weasel. Plan on at least five tricks that might get us eliminated."

His teammates nodded, a few of them swearing under their breaths. They didn't know the half of it.

"We'll make the initial hike together and then split up to surround any structures we find. Then we search them and move on. If we get split up, remember, Reid has GPS on us. He'll identify anyone separated from the group and come at us. Hard."

MAGGIE SAT AT HER DESK, SCROLLING THROUGH E-MAILS WHEN the ding of a new message sounded. Minutes earlier they'd had a call about disorderly conduct on the edge of town, but the deputies hadn't notified her of needing backup so she'd stayed put, hoping to catch up on administrative tasks. She glanced at the preview of the message from one of the genealogy websites she'd contacted. DNA Results.

The report was in.

Oh. Goodie.

Yesterday, after speaking with her favorite judge and explaining how she came to possess a cigarette butt with their possible shooter's DNA on it, she'd been granted a warrant. Said warrant gave her permission to seize genetic information from the genealogy website's database. Already, they had an answer. The private sector. Sometimes so much easier to navigate.

She clicked the e-mail and scanned the message. Each person, two genetic markers, blah, blah. One for the mother, one for the father. Blah, blah. She knew that. She scrolled down, skipped over the explanation of locus and chromosomes and DNA indexes. She'd heard all of it before and still didn't understand, but she didn't need to. All she needed to know was if they'd found a match.

Below the second paragraph was a chart with numbers and the Combined Paternity Index. In the DNA testing world, if the CPI wasn't zero, a person couldn't be excluded as a match. That's what she wanted here. Someone, anyone, who could possibly be a familial match to the sample they'd submitted.

With that, they at least had a starting point and could follow the thread to finding their shooter.

CPI Indexes. All above I.

Not zero.

A blood rush set her cheeks on fire. *Not zero.* Which meant... "Oh, my God."

Heart slamming, she continued reading, skipping over more genetic-speak she didn't understand.

"Come on. Give me the damned name."

Summary paragraph. Finally. *Not an exact paternal match.* Paternal match. *Ninety percent certainty.* Excellent. They'd better be giving her a name. She'd heard about another case where someone used the genealogy website's database and the company, in an effort to protect their customers, refused to release the person's name. At least until a second warrant was issued and specifically demanded the name.

Not willing to risk the time suck and legal wranglings, Maggie had included the request for any potential names in the warrant and she got one that was a 90 percent match.

Ninety percent.

Hot diggity!

There it was. The name. She read it once and her excitement plummeted. Hoping she'd read it wrong, she blinked and blinked again. Coincidence. Had to be. Right?

"Oh, no. Oh, Jay."

She shot out of her chair, sending it tipping backward as she snatched her phone and keys and ran for the door. She hit Jay's name on her phone screen. *Please, let him pick up.*

Voice mail. She punched off. She'd try again when she got to the car.

She bolted down the hallway, reaching the bullpen in seconds. "Shari, find me Grif. Tell him to call me. Immediately. When the deputies are done with that disorderly, tell them to meet me at Tupelo Hill. We've got a huge problem."

THIRTY MINUTES INTO THE EXERCISE, JAY'S TEAM CAME UPON multiple structures. All would have to be searched and with only an hour remaining to complete their mission, time was not their friend.

So far, they'd found and searched two small cabins that didn't take long to clear, but every second counted. Jay checked his map, found other buildings to the west. How the hell would they get this done?

After a slug from his water bottle, Troy Bennet paused beside Jay. "What're you thinking, boss?"

"We need to split up or we'll never get done."

"Is that smart? Considering Team Blue is probably up here somewhere?"

"It's not smart. At all. But it's at least a twenty-minute hike back to base, once we have her. That leaves us just under forty to find Evie." He held up the map and pointed. "Four of you take these three cabins and Bennet and I will search these others."

He scanned the group, received nods from all. "Good. Let's hit it."

Jay and Bennet left their teammates behind and marched through a thick clump of trees, their feet crunching over twigs and leaves and rocks. Late morning sun broke through a cloud, instantly knocking the final edge off the cool air. In another hour, a perfect seventy-degree day would be had.

Jay pointed to a tree root sticking up. "Watch that."

He swept his gaze over the thick brush in front of him. If his map was correct—and not an attempt on Reid's part to screw with them—the other two buildings should be just beyond the trees.

They trekked another three hundred yards before the first cabin came into view. Huge oaks fanned behind it and sloped downward. Jay moved quickly, scanning the area, checking for Reid's *separatists*. As hard as it was to admit, Jay didn't have a chance in hell at beating Reid, the former Green Beret, at this game, but he wouldn't lie down, either. If nothing else, Reid—or his separatists—would find themselves covered in paint. A lot of it.

Refocusing on his task, Jay scooted under the window on the far side of the house and duckwalked to the back edge where a steep incline—had to be forty feet—led to an oversized shed. Jay's pulse kicked. If he wanted to take a hostage, that shed would be perfect. *Perfect.*

Or, more likely, if he were Reid, that's what he'd want the amateurs to think.

Ambush.

Had to be. He inhaled and the moist air coupled with the earthy scent brought his mind to a dangerous calm that might lose this game for him.

A twig crackled behind him and, still in a squat, Jay spun, weapon at the ready.

Bennet threw his hands up. "Yo, it's me."

"Sorry. Something isn't right." He gestured to the shed. "That's too convenient. I think Reid is screwing with us."

Bennet dropped to his knees and craned his neck to peer over the drop-off. "Sharp incline. How the hell do we get down there?"

Good question. If they tried to walk straight down, one of them would wind up ass over elbow. And probably snap something. Not good for a professional athlete. Jay peered through the thick clump of trees and foliage. Fifty yards to his right the terrain flattened enough for them to carefully make their way down.

They'd wind up scratched to all hell from walking through bushes. God knew what might be poisonous in there. Fucking Reid.

"Swear to God," Jay said, "if I get a rash, I'll kill that son of a bitch."

Bennet laughed. "Tick-tock, dude. What's the plan?"

Jay checked his binoculars, searching the area for Team Blue or any separatists ready to pounce.

Nothing, but rustling branches, birds yapping, and the gentle hum of a light wind.

No voices, no crunch of footsteps, no swish of clothing. Everything that wasn't there nagged at him. But they now had barely forty minutes left to rescue Evie and he couldn't get hung up.

"Okay." Jay jerked his thumb. "We're short on time. You check this place while I make my way down to the shed. And, don't go in the door. See if you can hear anything. Or maybe look in the window first. I think this might be an ambush, but we don't have time to go back and get the guys. I'd rather be covered in paint than lose by a deadline miss."

"Agreed."

"I'll check the shed. If it's clear, I'll meet you back here."

"Got it. Call me on the radio if you need me."

"Ditto."

Jay kept low while he crept along the tree line, his hiking boots catching and rolling on loose rock and downed branches. He wouldn't consider his walkway a path, but it offered enough space for him to work his way through with minimal damage. At least he'd worn a long-sleeved shirt for this excursion. A tall, thick shrub dead ahead blocked his path so he veered around it, pushing twigs away only to get smacked on the helmet by a rogue branch.

"Pop, pop," a familiar voice said. *"Pop."*

Caught. He hadn't been sprayed with paint yet, though, so he might have a chance here. Jay turned and faced Eli Paskins, who stood in the brush, a half smile on his face. He wore jeans and a black sweatshirt, something Jay had never seen on the man before.

Great. Eli was a goddamned separatist.

How appropriate.

Except he wore jeans and a sweatshirt. No paintball suit. Maybe he'd ditched it? Who knew what kind of mind games Reid had conjured. The guy was a master at the mindfuck.

Jay made a move for his weapon, but Eli raised his own. This one a handgun.

Hang on, here. Reid had only given out rifles. Then again, if Eli was the enemy, Reid probably gave him different weapons.

Yep. Master mindfucker.

"Jayson," Eli said, "let's head inside and talk."

18

MAGGIE STORMED THROUGH THE FRONT DOOR OF THE
training center screaming Reid's name. Her cousin rushed
out of his office, meeting her in the hallway with a *where's
the fire* look?

"What's wrong? You okay?"

"Where's Jay?"

Reid's shoulders dropped. "You come in here screaming
like there's a murder and you're only looking for the superstar? Jesus, don't do that." He slapped his hand over his
chest and blew out a breath. "He's out on a training exercise.
Why?"

Oh, no. Please, no. "Is Eli Paskins out there?"

"Yeah. He wanted to play. He's a Kurdish separatist."

Maggie stared at him for a few seconds. "A Kurdish—
what?" She shook it off and pushed around Reid. "Never
mind. We need to get to them. Fast."

"Whoa." He latched on to her arm, holding her back.
"They're in the middle of an exercise. What do you need?"

She broke away from him and started for the back door

before he could stop her again. "I'll tell you on the way. You have to trust me on this one. Can you locate them?"

"Sure." He fell in step with her, holding his phone up. "They all have GPS units sewn into their suits. We can track them on the app."

"Good. And, cuz, you'd better grab your sidearm."

In the thirty seconds it took Reid to grab his weapon, Maggie had already jumped on one of the ATVs parked behind the building to the right of the exit. Reid hustled out the back doors and swung his leg over the seat on the adjacent ATV.

"Mags, what the hell's going on?"

"I ran the DNA from our shooter's cigarette butt. The one I found on the road."

"You got a hit?"

"I did. The shooter's name is Theo Paskins. I believe he's the brother of Eli Paskins. I have Shari running it down now."

"Shit." He tapped his phone. "Jay is on the move. Near Digger's Ridge. He's not even close to Evie."

Evie? What did she have to do with anything? "Is Paskins with him? And why is Evie up there?"

Reid looked over at her. "She's playing hostage. And, according to the GPS, Paskins is nowhere close to Jay."

But she knew her cousin too well, and his dipped mouth —Reid's worry face—gave him away. "What's wrong?"

He fired up his ATV and spoke over the growl of the engine. "GPS has Paskins stationary. And alone."

"Meaning?"

"I told him where Jay and his team were. He's supposed to be ambushing them."

A fresh wave of panic blasted her. They had to get up there. Fast. "He ditched the suit."

When Reid didn't respond, Maggie had her answer.

CAPTURED BY PASKINS PLAYING A KURDISH SEPARATIST. JAY nearly laughed. After the Knights and Celebrate Hope and his sponsors had dumped him, this might be the ultimate flip-off. Consider it a lesson learned about Reid's ability to take the mind games to another level.

"I'll give you credit, Eli. You got the jump on me."

He made a tsking noise. "I couldn't announce myself, could I?" He whipped the handgun to the shed. "Inside. Before the rest of your team comes looking."

For a few short seconds, Jay considered cracking wise about these boys not being his team any longer, but Eli's jerky movements suggested this might not be the optimum time for sarcasm.

Jay slid his finger to the trigger of his rifle and Eli's gaze shot to it. He leveled the handgun on Jay. "Drop that. Right now. The radio too."

"Eli, I have less than forty minutes to rescue Evie. You can bet your ass I'm not going to drop my weapon."

Eli stepped closer. "I think you will, Jay."

"Why is that?"

"My gun." He held the weapon straight up for a split second, then pointed it at Jay. "Real bullets. Now drop your rifle and the radio and move your ass."

Jay took a second, his gaze moving from the gun to Eli. Could it...?

Eli jerked the gun again and Jay's body tensed. If Eli didn't stop jabbing that thing around, it would go off. If it was real? Game over. Literally.

Had to hand it to Reid on this one. He knew how to screw with a man.

No. Nuh-uh. There was no way Reid gave an untrained man a loaded handgun. No way. Which meant...

White noise filled Jay's mind. He focused on the gun, forced himself to think. To break the situation down into usable parts.

Eli had twenty-five years on him. And Jay was bigger, faster, and stronger. He could easily relieve him of that weapon. *If* he could get to him before he got a shot off.

If he couldn't and that gun *was* real?

Shit. He'd have to try another way. Maybe try and talk Eli down enough to get closer and overpower him. Or use his helmet as a projectile and possibly knock the gun from Eli's hand. Jay set his rifle and the radio on the ground and then removed his helmet, tucking it under his arm. "Eli, what are you doing?"

He lifted the gun higher, aiming it directly at Jay's face. "Inside. Where we can talk."

Jay stalled while weighing his options. Bennet had to be done with his search of the cabin. By now he'd be waiting by the path Jay had taken. Jay could yell out, but if this *was* all part of the training exercise, he'd give away his location and more than likely be eliminated by any Team Blue members —or would-be separatists—in the area. If it wasn't an exercise, he'd be risking getting Troy shot.

Or he could go inside with Eli and figure out a way to get that weapon, real or not, out of his hands. All while the clock ran down on this mission.

Jay started walking.

MAGGIE ROARED TO A STOP ON THE WEST SIDE OF A CLUMP OF trees that, if her memory served, led to a small shack and a cabin. According to Reid's app, Jay and one of his team members were straight through the trees while the rest of the squad congregated on the higher ground just east of them.

If her hunch was correct and Paskins was up to no good, she couldn't risk the other players getting injured.

Or worse.

"Reid, let's radio those men and tell them to stay where they are. If something goes sideways, we don't want them in the middle of it. If Paskins has a radio, keep it vague so we don't tip him off."

"On it."

Maggie hopped off the ATV. Without a path through the woods, they'd have to walk the rest of the way. "Once we get to the other side, we'll split up and see if we can locate Eli."

He held up his phone. "Jay is by the shed, I think, and Bennet near the cabin. He's on the move."

"Well, tell him to hold position, also."

Reid spoke into his radio again, but received no response. "Goddammit."

"Is he still moving?"

"Yeah. He probably thinks it's a trick."

What a cluster. Right now, she wasn't even sure what was simulated and what was real. For all she knew, Bennet could be working with Eli.

She left Reid messing with his phone and headed for the trees, using the larger ones for cover because God knew who else was out here. This whole thing with Paskins was mind-boggling. Did he have Theo hiding somewhere? And why?

Reid caught up to her and held a skinny branch back before she got smacked with it. "Nothing from Bennet."

"Okay. We'll assume he thinks it's part of the exercise."

"It might be, Mags. We don't know."

"It's better than thinking he's in on this mess with Eli. Either way, something tells me we're about to find out."

"Tuck?"

Bennet's voice. Outside the shed.

Crap.

Jay swung his head to Eli, who still held his gun on Jay but had angled his body so he could easily watch the door and Jay without too much effort. The shed was empty. Just four battered walls illuminated only by light through the small window and open door. The place left Jay nothing to use as a weapon or for cover in case Eli decided to shoot.

A good jump.

That's all Jay needed and he'd be on top of him. He'd wait for Eli's gaze to shift to the door again and go for it. *Come on, come on.*

"Drop that helmet," Eli said. "Don't think you'll get to me when I'm not looking."

Jay held on to the helmet and Eli jabbed the gun at him.

His former boss gritted his teeth. "Goddamnit, I said drop it."

"Okay." Jay set the helmet down. "Relax. Don't get worked up. Tell me what this is about."

"You and your damned sister not staying out of my business."

And there it was. Eli was most definitely not a Kurdish separatist. Jay's heartrate exploded, all that energy firing straight to his head, making it pound. He inhaled, held his breath for a long second and exhaled. Slowly, the pounding gave in enough for him to focus. On Eli and the gun.

When Jay didn't respond, Eli shook his head. "You

people have no idea what it takes to run a publicly owned team. Every shareholder has an opinion."

Well, yeah. That's why they're owners. "They're shareholders, they have a right to protect their investments."

"Please. Most of them have zero business knowledge. They own less than a percentage point because they think it's"—he made air quotes—"cool. Imbeciles. They have no idea." He shook it off. "Between the bad press and this Celebrate Hope situation, you and your family are in the middle of it and Webb isn't helping. I never liked that kid."

"Now it's my fault the fans are pissed? You should have handled it better."

Eli poked the gun again. "I've already had enough of you. Don't push it. Besides, you can make it up to me."

Make it up to *him*? The man had gone off his goddamned stone. Waving that gun around wasn't helping either. But Jay would keep him talking, maybe get him on a roll and distract him.

He held up his hands. "Relax. We've always been able to talk. What do you want from me?"

"You're gonna back off on that threat to go to the press. I need more time. I've worked since I was ten years old. My success is *earned*. You had money. *You* don't understand hustling for a meal or for a pair of shoes. Living with rats crawling around. I've worked for everything I have. And I'm not losing it."

This couldn't be about ticket sales. What kind of moron throws his life away over that?

"This mess is about *ticket* sales?"

"Don't be stupid. Ticket sales is the least of it. Stock prices and cash flow are king."

Ah. Now they were getting to it. Jay hadn't checked the

stock prices, but they must have been free-falling to have pushed Paskins this far. "Eli—"

"Shut up. If you go to the press about Celebrate Hope and the embezzlement, I'm done. The board will remove me faster than I can come up with an argument. I'll be ruined. And broke. And since I knew about the CFO embezzling and the deal the board made with him, I'll probably be on my way to prison. Ruined, broke, and locked up. As long as you've known me, what makes you think I'd stand for that? Not after I worked to get free of that life."

As if any of it were Jay's fault? Eli already admitted he'd known about the embezzlement; he should have come clean and gone to the authorities immediately. Instead, he'd kept his mouth shut. And here they were. Standoff.

"All you have to do," Eli said, "is stay quiet. Protect your team."

"*My* team? Not anymore."

"Okay. Fine. Not your team. My team. But I can make this embezzlement go away and clear your sister. I'll talk to the other owners, get you a nice fat contract to finish out your career. Just keep your mouth shut. Give me a chance to clear it up."

"And if I don't?"

Paskins snorted and his eyes took on a wild glow. Something feral and crazed. Something on the cusp of coming apart.

"Jayson, I thought you were smarter. Look what I'm wearing."

Jeans. Black sweatshirt. No suit. Which meant, no GPS.

"Reid Steele thinks I'm sitting in a tree waiting to pick you all off. And no one knows I have this gun. I'm too far in now. Got nothing to lose. I'll take out you and Bennet, run back to the tree, put the suit on, and wait. Perfect alibi. As far as your sister, she'll be dealt with."

Sam. He'd spent his life protecting her from predators. This time? This situation? Too big for him. Too much.

"Tuck? Is that you?"

Bennet's voice. Closer this time. Jay needed to get rid of him. Clear him out before he got pulled into the middle of Eli's twisted plan.

Eli glanced at the door and Jay took a step. The gun came up and he halted.

"Get rid of him," Eli said. "Unless you want me to shoot him."

That was all Jay needed to head for the door. Eli grabbed the back of his paintball suit and shoved the barrel of the gun into Jay's back. "Don't be a hero. We can still work this out and no one gets hurt."

A MALE VOICE YELLING JAY'S NAME CARRIED THROUGH THE trees and Maggie and Reid exchanged a look before checking the GPS app on Reid's phone. Based on the proximity of Jay's team members, the one yelling had to be Bennet. Unless someone else was nearby. And not wearing GPS-enabled clothing.

Nearing the edge of the woods, Maggie spotted the roof of the shed.

"Bennet, I'm all good here."

Jay's voice. Just yards away. Maggie ducked low in the brush, buying herself a few seconds as relief washed over her. Behind her, Reid dropped to a squat.

"Bennet," Jay repeated. "There's a locked trunk I'm trying to bust open. I don't think our hostage is in there, but I gotta check it. Go meet up with the team and I'll catch up."

Maggie turned to Reid. "What's in that shed?"

"Nothing. I cleaned it out last spring."

"Then he's stalling. Why?"

"Beats the hell out of me."

"If Paskins did ditch the suit, he could be in there with him. Check the app. Make sure Paskins hasn't moved."

Reid checked his phone. "According to this, he's still nowhere near here."

Beyond the trees, the twigs snapped—crap. Someone was *right* there. Maggie ducked lower.

"I'm not leaving you," Bennet called, his voice close enough for Maggie to realize he was the one snapping twigs.

"Yeah, you are," Jay said. "We're losing time here. I'll search the trunk and catch up. It's the only way."

Maggie needed a better visual. Still squatting, she inched to her left, taking care not to make too much noise. She hid behind a fat oak tree and peered out to where Jay stood in the doorway of the broken-down shed talking to Bennet.

Reid appeared beside her, his footsteps as light as possible in the middle of heavy woods, where snapping twigs like the ones under Bennet's feet could betray them.

"Something is off," she whispered. "I'll break away and sneak around the back of the shed. You cover the front."

Reid nodded. She'd half expected an argument, but being the more compact of the two of them, Maggie was less likely to be seen.

"There's a window around back. Too small to climb through, but you'll be able to see."

Raised voices between Bennet and Jay covered the sounds of her movement as she crept along the tree line. Assuming someone was in the shed with Jay, she'd need to bolt through roughly ten feet of open space to the shed.

This entire thing seemed...weird. For all she knew, this could be part of the game. A Kurdish separatist holding Jay hostage until time ran down on the exercise.

Then again, there'd been two attempts on Jay's life since he'd been in Steele Ridge.

Focus, Maggie.

The sun slid behind a cloud and she drew a long pull of late morning air. Rain coming. Her internal divining rod told her.

"Awright," Bennet finally said. "I'm going, but I don't agree with this shit. At all."

Maggie watched as Jay jerked backward. What the heck?

That was unnatural movement. Unless someone had tugged him backward, clearing the doorway.

Go, go, go.

An adrenaline burst propelled her forward into the open area while she swept her gaze left and right. Focus.

That's all she needed to do. Stay centered on her task and get Jay to safety. And so help her, if this was all part of the training exercise, she'd murder someone.

Her boot's edge landed on a rock, sending it crunching against some loose gravel and she one-hopped the last step, pressing her body flush against the side of the cabin while her pulse slammed. *Go, go, go.* She rested her head back, waiting a few seconds, listening for any movement around the side. Nothing but tweeting birds.

Still safe.

She eased out a breath and navigated over loose gravel. She made the turn and there it was. The window. Two steps.

One.

Two.

Muffled voices came from inside. Jay and...who?

Something about celebrate, but the words trailed off.

Had to be Celebrate Hope. Could this be Eli Paskins's brother? Or, if her guess was correct, maybe Eli himself.

She had to look. If she knew who Jay was in there with, she might have an idea of what was going on. Was that crazy? Doing a quick peek to see?

Probably.

But as the late sheriff used to say, nothing focused the mind like an oncoming train.

She closed her eyes, pictured that oncoming train, and swung left, peeping in the window. Light poured into the otherwise dark cabin via the open door. Jayson stood in profile, his tall form silhouetted against the far wall, while a much smaller man, also in profile, held a gun on him. Handgun. Real or a paintball gun?

From this distance, impossible to tell. She focused on the man. Her Internet research on Jayson had gifted her with hundreds of photos of him with various Knights executives. Including the much smaller Eli Paskins.

Had to be him.

Her guess that he'd dumped his suit so the signal would show him in another location proved right.

As if sensing her, Eli's head moved a fraction. He swiveled and...

"Maggie!"

Jay's voice.

Whoa. She lunged right, away from the window.

Pow!

A bullet pierced the window, its high-speed momentum sending chunks of glass flying. Maggie whirled, protecting her head and eyes from the explosion.

She charged around the shed. Another gunshot sounded, then another. Both splintering the wood where she'd just been standing.

Three shots. And all three came through the window and side wall. At least she knew Jay hadn't gotten shot.

Another four steps brought her to the front of the building where she turned the corner and spotted Reid, about to bust through the doorway.

No, sir. She jammed her finger into her chest. That asshole had just taken a shot at her. Three shots. If anyone brought him down, it'd be her.

Reid shook her off—damned alphas—but she pointed to the rear of the shed. She'd have him cover the window while she went in the front.

When he didn't move, she tapped her badge. "Go!" she mouthed.

Clearly not happy with her, he disappeared around the side. The sun disappeared behind a cloud, eliminating the risk of throwing a shadow, so Maggie did another quick peek in the doorway. Eli stood near the window, his gun still on Jay. Maggie pivoted into the open doorway, bringing her weapon up and aiming center mass at Paskins.

"Drop it."

Jay took a step and Eli's head snapped around. "Don't move," he said. "Either of you."

"Jayson," Maggie said, "I've got this."

Barely four feet away, Paskins froze, his wild, spooked gaze bouncing between Maggie and Jay. Back and forth, back and forth.

"I'll shoot him," he said. "Then you. I've got nothing to lose. Everyone thinks I'm sitting in a tree far from here."

If he intended on shooting them, they'd be dead already. At least, that's what Maggie told herself. He might be scared. Sometimes a scared man was more dangerous—and unpre-dictable— than an evil one.

"Eli," she said, her voice calm but firm, "put the gun

down. You've already taken a shot—three actually—at me. There's no way I'm letting you take another at Jayson."

The stubborn rat didn't move and sweat formed on the back of Maggie's neck. She needed to end this. Fast. All she had was the DNA and the name Theo Paskins. She wasn't even sure what the relationship between Theo and Eli might be. They might be related, but she didn't have enough information yet. She had some, though, and she could make it work.

"Eli, this is over. I know about Theo."

That got his attention. "What about him?"

"He's a smoker. Made the mistake of dropping one of his cigarette butts in the road after he took that shot at Jay on Saturday. DNA, Eli. It's all the rage with the genealogy sites. We got a paternal match on one Theo Paskins."

Eli shook his head. "You're lying."

"If I'm lying, how do I know about Theo? Or that he's a smoker? I have the evidence. And, like all things, it's just a matter of who talks first. How good is your relationship with him, Eli? Because one of you will turn on the other. When it comes to life in prison, someone always flips. Who's it going to be, you or Theo?"

He stayed quiet, staring at Maggie with eyes that no longer had that shiny, crazed wildness. In the course of her little speech, he'd gone from indignant to...something. Something dark and sad that sagged his cheeks. He flicked a gaze at Jay, the dead last thing Maggie wanted.

"Please, Eli," she said, drawing his attention back to her.

If one of them had to go down, it would be her. It had nothing to do with bravery and everything to do with not seeing a man she was more than likely in love with getting shot.

Eli lifted his hand. Pointed the gun straight at the ceiling.

Jesus, God, thank you.

Then he moved his hand again—*no.* Brought the gun right under his chin and the explosion of panic filled her again. Insane energy crackled and pulsed in the small shed and Maggie's skin tingled from head to toe. No way could she let this man kill himself in front of them. No way.

Focus.

Her weapon still pointed, she kept her eyes trained on Eli. "Don't!"

Jay, his instincts more than likely kicking in, stepped forward.

"Jay, no!" Maggie yelled.

Eli faced her, shaking his head hard enough to scramble his already stressed brain.

The sun decided now would be an exceptional time to reappear from behind the clouds. A beam of sunlight streamed into the cabin, hitting Eli straight on. Blinded, he squinted against the intrusion and, despite her warning, Jayson was on the move, his body flying through the air with the ease of a career athlete.

At least until the next shot sounded.

THE FAMILIAR THUD OF BODIES COLLIDING REGISTERED IN JAY'S mind the split second before the shot went off. *Jesus, Jesus, Jesus.* Did he get shot?

There was no pain, but that didn't mean anything. Sometimes, it took a few minutes. Right now? No pain. Just a rush of adrenaline—nature's gift to the human body— firing his system.

He hit the floor with Eli under him, serving as his cushion.

A beam of light shined down from right above him. How could that be? Unless...

Son of a bitch. Dying. On his way to whatever form of heaven awaited. If he was lucky.

Leave it to him to get shot by his former boss in this broken-down shed where he would die in front of Maggie. Where he'd leave Sam to deal with Drunk Marlene on her own. This was *not* the way he figured his death to go.

"Ohhhhh."

The groan came from under him. Who the hell was groaning while *he* was dying on a dirty fucking floor?

He stared up at the beam of light, hoping to see Saint Peter at those pearly gates, waving him forward, welcoming him to paradise.

All he saw was light. Bright, blinding, annoying light.

Through a hole in the ceiling.

No Saint Peter. No gates. WTF?

"Jay, where's the gun?"

Maggie's voice. The all-business one. He lifted his hand and she grabbed it, squeezing tight. He angled his head toward her, away from the light and there she was, her sweet face, the brown eyes that mesmerized him. She snapped her fingers in front of his nose. No declarations of love or gentle support.

How rude was *that* when he was dying?

She snapped again. "Are you hit? Where's the gun?"

Behind Maggie's head, Reid's mug appeared. If this was heaven, it sucked. The woman he loved being pushy and Reid, his tormentor, grinning that shit-eating grin Jay wanted to pummel off him.

And then the groan again. And something moving under him.

Eli. *Gun.*

Not dead. At least, he was pretty sure he wasn't dead.

Where's the gun?

Maggie's question floated in his mind and—wait. The gun. They didn't have the gun. Shit. A zapping current blasted him from his heels to his head, locking his mind into the situation. He rolled, popping to his feet. Eli lay sprawled on the floor, blood oozing from the side of his head, and Jay's stomach heaved.

"Got it," Reid said, carefully nudging the gun with his foot, putting it out of reach of Eli.

"Did he..." Jay swallowed, fought the rising bile in his throat. "The shot?"

But Maggie was focused on Eli as she dropped to her knees. His woman. Look at her go. Cool and calm under fire. Literally.

"Hold him, Reid," she said.

Reid gripped Eli's wrists at his waist, while Maggie shined her flashlight on his head. "It's his ear. The idiot clipped his ear with the bullet."

Reid peered up at the ceiling. "It went through the roof." He shook his head and brought his gaze back to a still groaning Eli. "You can't even shoot yourself right. Plus, you shot up my shed."

19

At nine o'clock, Jayson broke away from the Steele-Kingston family dinner taking place in the Tupelo Hill dining room and made his way out to the porch. These people were gatherers. In crisis, they came together, something Jay wasn't accustomed to. It had always just been he and Sam, who now sat next to Miss Joan being force-fed enough protein to sustain her for three days. After hearing the day's events, his sister still wore the pale, blown-out look of someone in shock.

Who could blame her?

He was suffering from some weird version of it himself by floating through the day, his ears ringing with the sound of gunshots.

And now he wanted Maggie.

She'd left him in Miss Joan's hands and followed the ambulance carrying Eli to the hospital. He hadn't seen or heard from her since. Getting answers was more important than coddling him.

He opened the kitchen door, felt the blast of cool mountain air, and sucked it all in. Cold night by North

Carolina standards. For a football player, it might as well be spring.

"Hey, mister."

Maggie stood at the base of the porch, one foot on the bottom step and God, his heart damn near exploded.

By the time he reached the top step, she was already there, rushing toward him. *Thank you, Jesus.* He caught her in his arms and wrapped her up tight and hung on. Maybe he did need that coddling. Or at least the stability that came with a hot sheriff.

She slid her hands around his waist and propped her forehead against his chest. Even after her long day, he caught the clean, no-fuss scent of her shampoo.

Maggie.

She tipped her head up and the porch light illuminated the dark circles under her eyes. His girl was tired.

"Are you okay?" she asked.

"I'm great now that you're here."

"I'm sorry I was gone so long."

He shrugged. "It's your job and it's important."

Her shoulders dipped and she leaned in, her body sagging against him. What the hell? Was she okay? An owl hooted, shattering the weird vibe suddenly filling the air.

"Hey," he tucked his fingers under her chin and lifted her head so he could look at her. "Were you actually worried I'd be mad you were gone so long?"

"I didn't have a chance to call. In the past it's been a..." She shook her head.

"Maggie, you were brilliant today. Amazing. You probably saved my life. What kind of man could be mad at you for that?"

She smiled up at him, slapped her hand across the back of his neck and hit him with a lip lock that made him think, yes, they would finally use those handcuffs tonight. But first, he wanted to hear about Eli.

He patted her ass and dragged himself from her lips. "How about we finish this later? In private?"

She dropped another quick kiss on him to seal the deal. "*That* is a date."

"Can you tell me about Eli? Where is he?"

"County lockup."

"Is he talking?"

She smiled up at him. "He sure is. Gave the whole thing up. When Celebrate Hope notified the league of the embezzlement, they called Eli."

"Not surprised. They'd want to bounce it off him."

"He panicked because the league and Celebrate Hope had agreed to let Sam's boss go without prosecuting. You were right about them not wanting the media to get a hold of it."

"I know how they operate. If people knew about the theft, they'd lose faith in the program. With all that money floating around, the league couldn't have that."

Maggie stepped back—too bad—and sat on the edge of the porch rail. "Thanks to sales of all those limited edition Jayson Tucker jerseys, the Knights brought in the most revenue for the charity. The drama surrounding your release created chaos, which would only worsen if the embezzlement story went public. The perfect storm to tank stock prices."

"Which meant even more pissed-off shareholders."

"Yes. And then Sam discovered the embezzlement."

The owl hooted again and Maggie broke eye contact. Apparently in search of the owl. But in the blackness, she'd never find it and they both knew it.

Stalling. Whatever else she had to say, she needed a minute to get her thoughts together.

"Maggie? You can tell me anything. I hope you know that."

She faced him again. "I know. I just..." She raised a hand, let it drop. "I hate to break your heart, but you're going to find out anyway and I want it to come from me."

What could this be now? Had to be something with Sam. That would be the only thing in this mess that would destroy him. He pushed his shoulders back, readied himself for the hit. "Tell me."

"It was Sam they were after, that day we were hiking. Remember that first bullet? It was closest to her."

Sam. He knew it. Somehow, twisted as it seemed, relief took hold and he bent over, propped his hands on his thighs and let out a strangled laugh.

"Jay?" Maggie's feet came into view and she set her hand on his back. "Are you okay?"

He nodded. "I thought you were going to tell me my sister was a crook. Somehow someone taking a shot at her is a relief. What's wrong with me? Jesus, I'm a mess."

"It's okay. You've been through a war this week."

But he'd also found Maggie. For that alone he was grateful. He straightened up, entwined his hand with Maggie's, and led her back to the porch rail where they both sat. "Is Theo Eli's brother?"

"He is. The NYPD nabbed him an hour ago trying to board a plane at Kennedy. I pulled his DMV photo. I won't know for sure until I see him in person, but he looks like our shooter. Plus, when I first saw Reid's security video of the suspect, something looked familiar about him. I think I saw him in the Triple B that night we were all there. He was standing against the wall by our table. He probably overheard us talking about going to see the wolves. Add to it that he's a sharpshooter."

"Seriously?"

"He's not military or law enforcement. Just a gun enthusiast who likes to hunt. He's spent years practicing and entering competitions. I guess he has financial trouble and owed some not so nice people money. He'd been begging Eli for help, but was cut off."

"Until Eli needed him."

Maggie nodded. "Yes. They made a deal. Eli would give him the money if he'd scare Sam off. Eli says they weren't trying to kill her."

"You believe that?"

"I don't know. I want to. Eli is also the one who sent her the threatening e-mail. He set up a dummy account so we couldn't trace it back to him."

He'd worked for this guy for years and had never seen the evil. Astounding. "How did we get to this place?"

"I know. Greed does it to people."

The back door came open and Grif stuck his head out. "Everything okay?"

Still holding Maggie's hand, Jay met his agent's eye. "Yeah. I needed air."

"And probably some quiet," Maggie said. "Go inside, Grif. Keep the masses at bay while our quarterback gets his head about him."

"Will do. Let me know if you need anything."

He made a move to close the door. "Grif?"

"Yeah, Jay?"

"If you're still looking for a way to sue the Knights, forget it. I want this over."

"You sure?"

"Yeah. But thanks. For everything. Your family is amazing."

"They are that." Grif smiled. "Most of the time, anyway."

The door closed and Jay waved Maggie to one of Miss Joan's Adirondacks, where they'd hopefully sit in peace for the next hour. That's all he wanted. Maggie, the hominess of Miss Joan's porch, and quiet.

Jay rested his head back. "Have you seen the news?"

"Nope." She smiled. "Been a little busy."

"After what went down with Eli today, Dirks and Rothstein went nuts. Totally off their rockers. They got on the phone with every network they could think of and broke ranks. Laid the whole thing out there about Webb setting me up."

"Even the spousal abuse?"

"No. They left that part out. No sense in Webb's wife and kids suffering any more than they're going to, with this being revealed. They blamed the incident on professional jealousy and claimed Webb circulated the rumor about me sleeping with his wife to cover his own ass. He was trying to make me look bad and figured everyone would believe him."

"Webb didn't count on your friends outing him."

In the distance, a wolf howled and Jay wondered if it could be one of Britt's precious pack. Tomorrow, Jay would ask Britt to take him back there so he could see them without them getting spooked by gunfire.

"I asked them not to," Jay said. "That first night after I was released, they both came to me and said they'd start talking. I told them no. That it wasn't worth blowing their careers over and that I'd handle it. They taught me something, didn't they? I almost screwed the whole thing up."

"Nah. We'd have gotten there. That's what friends do. We come together and find a way."

He reached over, cupped his hand on her cheek. "Thank you. I think you're amazing."

"Hey!" The silhouette of a very large man stalked around the side of the house. "You two, what are you doing?"

Why would Jay have even considered the possibility that Reid wouldn't obliterate his few minutes of rest? Still, he had to smile. "So much for Grif keeping the masses at bay. The fucker snuck out the front door."

Maggie let out a laugh and looked over at him with warm, loving eyes that made him think of handcuffs.

"Welcome to Steele Ridge, Superstar," Maggie said.

AT EIGHT O'CLOCK SUNDAY MORNING, MAGGIE PARKED HER SUV in the training center lot under clear, blue skies and a bright sun that she was sure meant today would be the day. Today, she'd beat Reid's obstacle course time and break the family record.

Why else, after the forfeit of her vacation, would Mother Nature bless her with weather suited for paradise?

Assuming the front door of the training center was locked, she walked around the building to the rear, where Reid barked at Jay as he flipped a five-hundred-pound tractor tire.

He'd left her place at six for an early morning workout and then a meeting with Grif. On a Sunday.

The man might be obsessed, but to his point, football players worked on Sundays.

"Morning," she called.

Jay heaved the tire and smiled his wicked smile. "Good morning."

He'd already greeted the day with her in exquisite fashion.

"Hey, cuz," Reid said. "Get warmed up."

"Okay. But I want to run the course before we work out."

Reid shrugged. "Sure. Superstar, focus here. You're slowing down."

"My fault," Maggie said. "I distracted him."

And if that gave her a little sick satisfaction, she'd be the only one to know because, yes, the football star couldn't concentrate on his workout when she entered his orbit.

Oh, she could definitely love him.

Maggie started in on her inchworms, watching Jay move, his solid legs squatting, the flex of his biceps and back muscles as he lifted. The man's body was proportioned perfection that she craved the minute he left her. And lucky her, today was her day off and after Jay's meeting, he'd be free.

On a beautiful morning like this, she'd steal him away for a hike.

And other things that would get their heart rates up.

Heh, heh, heh.

"You're done," Reid said. "Run a lap to cool down and then stretch. Good work today."

"Next victim!" Jay called.

Ha, ha. Funny man.

Reid took his spot on the picnic table, swinging the stopwatch around his fingers while she warmed up. She hopped to her feet, did some butt kicks, and then a series of karaokes while Jay did his lap around the perimeter of the obstacle course. She knew he'd run the course himself a few times, but he hadn't shared his time. A clear indication that he must have broken Reid's record but didn't want to tell her.

Which was fine. As he was a professional athlete, she'd expect him to do well. Her? The spirit of competition with her cousin kept her going.

Simply put, she needed to break that record and shut Reid up.

Jay cruised to a stop in front of her, barely breathing heavily after his quick run. He waved a hand at the course. "You ready?"

"I guess we'll see."

He cocked his head. "I'll ask again. Are you ready?"

Ah, more of his mental psyching her up. It had worked last time, so she'd play. She looked out over the course, took in the various obstacles, and pictured herself shredding them. Even the high wall. Her gaze wandered to Reid messing with his phone. Could she do it? Beat his time?

She thought so. She nodded. "I'm ready."

"Good. What are you?"

"I'm a beast," she whispered.

"You know," he said, "you sound about as excited for this as a dead man walking. Now what are you?"

"I'm a beast!"

Reid's head snapped up. "Damn straight, girlfriend."

Aw. That was sweet. "Thank you, cuz."

Jay rolled his eyes and waved her forward, heading to the start.

"I could use a good cardio push. I'll run it with you."

Maggie gawked at him. Here she was, all ready to do this and he wanted to mess with her head by running alongside her? She'd never beat him. Ever. How would that help her? "Wha...uh, *why*?"

Reid looked up from his phone again. "What's happening?"

"I'm gonna run it with Maggie."

Her cousin snorted. "This'll be fun."

For him maybe. Not for her. She'd be sucking in Jay's dust. She grabbed his arm. "I don't understand what you're doing."

He faced her and folded his arms across his amazing chest. "God," she said, "I can't wait to get you naked again."

"Ditto. But if you want to break his record today, you need to get your mind right. I can tell already you're not dialed in."

"And you think running this course against a professional athlete will do that?"

"You're competitive. Highly motivated by a challenge."

True that.

"I didn't want to tell you this," he said, "but I've run this course. Three times. I beat Reid's time on each."

She knew it! "When you wouldn't tell me your time, I figured. I'm okay with that. It's the family record I want."

"Good. Because we're gonna run this bitch together. You're going to focus on each element and me running it next to you. When you start to think about your time, you'll know I've beaten Reid and if you're keeping up with me, it's a good time."

"A nice thought, but I can't keep up with you."

"Not with that attitude you can't."

Now he wanted to motivate with insults? Not going there, fella. "Look, hotshot, I'm not being negative. You're a professional athlete."

"And you're a beast."

Maggie shook her head, then eyed Reid, who pretended to be fascinated with his phone but was completely eavesdropping. She lowered her voice and dragged Jay a few feet away. "This isn't about me being a beast. This is about me trying to top Reid's time and running this with you will freak me out."

"Baby," he said, cupping his hands on her cheeks, "it won't. I promise. Please, trust me on this. You'll perform better on a team. You and I, we're that team. Now, what are you?"

She peered out over the course, visualized running beside Jay, having him coach her along the way. Having his support while she went for something he knew was important to her.

A team.

The two of them, together.

Huh.

"You really think it'll work?"

"I do."

She twisted her mouth, mulled it over. Jay knew about these things. Maybe he was right. It might work.

No.

It *would* work.

She faced him again and gave him exactly what he wanted. "I'm a beast." She shoved him. Hard. "Let's do this."

"Attagirl."

"Reid," she said, "are you going to sit there or start that damned stopwatch?"

"Waiting on you." He gave her his annoying grin. "You beast."

Maggie and Jay stood at the starting line while Maggie shook out her arms and legs. *I've got this.* All she needed to do was keep up with Jay. If she could stay with him, she'd beat Reid's time.

"Don't think too much," Jay said. "Remember, we're working with muscle memory. Shut down your mind and let your body do the work. You're ready for this."

"Counting down," Reid said. "Three."

I've got this.

"Two."

Got it, got it, got it.

"One."

She took off, her feet light as she got the jump on Jay. Whoot! He might be bigger and stronger, but she had the speed and on the straightaways he'd never outrun her. She scrambled over the log while Jay performed a perfect vault and sailed over. Didn't that piss her off? Grrrr.

Ahead, the low wall begged her to do that vaulting move. She picked up speed, readied her arms for the push off the wall and—whoosh—over she went, her body in perfect unison with Jay's.

"Nice!" Reid called from his spot on the table.

Lord, she was doing this. Actually keeping pace with Jay.

They reached the high ladder and he leaped, catching a higher rung and shooting straight up. Dammit. He had her on this one.

"Don't think about me," he huffed. "Focus!"

The reprimand snapped her mind back to her task and she flipped herself over the top of the ladder. Three rungs down she took a flier—literally—and jumped to the ground. She landed on her feet, managing not to shatter a knee, and spun into a sprint toward her nemesis. The high wall.

Jay had a full stride on her, but she closed the gap quickly.

"You've got this, Maggie. Grab and climb. Grab and climb."

Got it. They reached the wall together, Jay using his strength to pull him up the rope and over.

Dammit.

"Don't think!" he shouted from the other side.

She scrambled over the top, once again dropping to the other side and sticking the landing. Done. *Whoot.* A burst of adrenaline propelled her forward. The hardest part was over. On the rest of the course she'd gain time. More running, fewer obstacles, and the barbed wire. She kicked ass on that one.

A good six feet in front of her, Jay swung across the monkey bars. "Push yourself! Get moving!"

She hit the bars, swung on through, and focused on the expanse of grass in front of her. Here she'd make up time and catch him. *I've got this.*

Once on the ground, she pumped her legs and arms, allowing them to drive her as she landed on the front of her feet and pushed off from her toes.

Three steps behind.

Get it, girl.

Coming into the barbed wire, she'd just about caught up, but her heart slammed from the exertion. Almost there. She inhaled, forced herself to slow her breathing and not hyperventilate because—Lord Almighty—the man was in good shape and nearly killing her.

Don't think. In less than a minute, she'd be done and she could do anything for a measly forty-five seconds.

Barbed wire.

She dropped to her belly

"Damn, girl," Jay said as she cruised by him and resumed the lead.

How much farther? She raised her head and—*shit*—her hairband caught on the wire, snagging for a precious few tenths of a second before she broke loose of it.

"Crap," she said.

Beside her, Jay huffed his way along. "Let it go. Nothing to be done about it. Focus. You've got this."

And then they were clear of the wire, both of them scrambling to their feet and heading toward the finish line.

"Push, Maggie," he said.

She squeaked out another burst of energy, but Jay pulled away, besting her by a few steps, his longer legs capitalizing on her fatigue.

She pumped her arms harder, concentrated on firing off of her toes and...finish line. Jay got there first, a good three steps ahead, but the time. That's all that mattered. And he'd beat Reid each time he'd run this, which meant...

Maybe.

Reid sat on the picnic table staring at the watch while Maggie jogged a lap around him to slowly bring her heart rate down. "Don't just sit there," she said. "Give it to me."

When her cousin refused to look at her, she stopped and shuffled from foot to foot. Such a bastard. Frustrated with his antics, she snatched the watch from his hand and checked it.

Ohmygod.

She stared at the number, blinking dripping sweat from her eyes. Wait...

Jay stepped up beside her, his hand settling over hers and tipping the watch so he could see the number. "How'd we do?"

"Ha!" Maggie said, her voice carrying in the quiet air. "Ha! Ha! Ha!"

She threw her arms up and did a victory lap around Reid, who laughed at her and shook his head.

"Don't get cocky," he said. "It's only four tenths faster. I can make that up and the record is mine again."

Who cared? For now, she'd beat his time. No one else in the family had. Not even Cash. She did a little happy dance, swinging her hips and arms. "Go, Maggie, go, Maggie, go, Maggie," she sang.

"Really?" Reid said, twisting his mouth to hide a grin. "I mean, talk about being a bad winner."

"Ha!" Maggie said again.

She turned to Jay, held her arms high and charged him, launching into him and knocking him back a step as he caught her. He steadied them and she wrapped her legs around him, kissing him hard on the mouth for a full three seconds while Reid cleared his throat behind them.

Once again, who cared? Jayson Tucker. She might love him.

She peppered his lips with kisses. "Thank you," she said. "Thank you, thank you, thank you."

He patted her butt and gave her the magazine-cover-worthy smile. "You're welcome. I told you we were a good team."

20

Post congratulatory smack talk with Reid, her cousin lumbered off, leaving Maggie and Jay by the dreaded picnic table.

Jay picked up his gym bag and slung it over his shoulder. "How does it feel?"

"To beat Reid? It feels great."

"Good. I was worried you'd be mad that I broke the record first."

"Nah. You're on another level than the rest of us. If you didn't break that record, I'd say you needed to work harder." She angled back, waved a hand toward the course. "This was a goal for me and, with your help, I reached it. Makes me realize I have other goals I need to work toward."

"Like?"

Ooh, tricky business here. Saying it aloud added pressure. Confiding in him, a man who'd fulfilled his dream of professional sports, was the equivalent of throwing down the gauntlet. A daily reminder of something she wasn't quite sure she'd thought through yet. Or was that another excuse? "The FBI."

There. Said it. Done. Done. Done. And, even better, surprisingly painless. Freeing even to finally admit what she'd been hanging on to for so long.

Jay's head snapped back. "Really? You want to be an agent?"

"I do. Always have. Life got in the way, though. Now I think it's time to at least try. Don't you think so, Superstar?"

"I'd rather try and fail than spend my life wondering."

She bumped him with her shoulder. "Exactly. I have to do it before I get too old. Once I turn thirty-seven, I'm ineligible. So, no time like the present. Can't hurt to try."

"I agree. Maggie, after what I've seen you do, it's a no-brainer. In my humble opinion."

"And what about you? Any news to report on the job front?"

He hesitated, looked down at his feet while they walked, and her stomach flipped. She'd been prepping herself for his departure, but...Dang it, she didn't want him to go. Why had she even asked the damned question when she didn't want the answer? She'd all but had herself convinced this was it. That he was leaving. Probably back to New York or some other major market too far from her.

But this was the life of a professional athlete. She adored him and would have to deal with it. If she was accepted into the FBI academy, who knew when and where they'd see each other?

He stopped walking, slid a document from the side pocket of his duffle, and faced her. "I wanted to show you this."

She eyed the paper, but refused to touch it. "What is it?"

He held it out. "Look at it."

"No."

He laughed. "No?"

"I don't want to look. If it's what I think it is, it's going to mean you're leaving."

"And you don't want that?"

"Uh, not after all the amazing orgasms, no. Plus"—she waved one hand—"I'm kinda attached to you now. You grow on a girl." She flicked her fingers at the paper. "But since you're so bent on me knowing what this is, why don't you tell me."

He stepped closer, brought his lips to her ear and his warm breath heated her already stirred-up system. "It's a draft of a contract," he said. "Grif's been working on a deal. I didn't want to say anything until we worked out all the particulars."

Then he smacked a kiss on her cheek. For a man about to break her heart, he was awfully playful.

"Are you happy?"

"Yes and no. I wanted to finish my career with the Knights. This is...different. It's a good deal. Less money, but it gives me three more years to play on a young team that needs an old man's leadership."

"Do you like the coaches?"

"Yeah. I've heard good things and talked on the phone with them. Seems fine."

"You don't sound excited."

"I am. I don't want to leave you. I'm hoping we can work something out. Maybe you can come to a couple of games and there's the off-season. And, you know, I think I owe you a vacation."

He reached into the side pocket of his gym bag again. A second later, he held out a rumpled cocktail umbrella.

"I picked this up the other day," he said. "Been carrying it around waiting for the right time. If you can wait until my season is over, I'll take you somewhere. Anywhere you want."

Her heart did a little leap at the thought of seven days alone with Jay, but depending on the new team's location, was it even possible to make this work? She had to try. With the way he made her feel, she couldn't walk away. Not now. She owed it to herself to finally do what she wanted.

She took the umbrella, spun it between her thumb and index finger. "We can definitely work it out. You can tell all the women who hit on you that your girlfriend carries a gun."

"I will do that. It may not be all that necessary, though."

"Why?"

"I might be spending a lot of time at home." He leaned in again, kissed the tip of her nose this time. "With you."

What was with him acting so oddly? She cocked her head. Where exactly would he be playing ball? "Jayson, what team are you going to?"

He held up the contract. "Well, if you'd read the contract, you'd know. Turns out, the United States Football Federation has a team in North Carolina. Go figure."

North.

Carolina.

She ripped the paper from his hand and quickly unfolded it, accidentally tearing it a little. "No way. Are you kidding? If you're teasing me, I'll never forgive you. I'll never have sex with you. Ever. Do you hear me?"

He laughed as she turned the contract right side up and started reading. Ninety minutes away. That's how far he'd be. Even on workdays she could drive it with no problem. The citizens of Steele Ridge would have to adjust to her not being at their mercy. Plus, there was the whole FBI thing.

"Oh my God," she said, almost too overwhelmed by it all.

She threw her arms around him, smacked kisses over his face as he scooped her up, tucking her legs around him. She held on, squeezing tightly and loving the feel of his solid shoulders under her hands.

Finally, a man who understood her, who wasn't intimidated by her strength and independence. A man who knew exactly how to take care of her.

"So," he said, "what do you think, Mags? Want to help me shop for a house in Steele Ridge?"

THE STEELE RIDGE SERIES

Steele Ridge: The Kingstons

Craving HEAT, Book 1

Tasting FIRE, Book 2 (September 2018)

Searing NEED, Book 3 (October 2018)

Striking EDGE, Book 4 (Coming 2019)

Burning ACHE, Book 5 (Coming 2019)

―――――

Steele Ridge: The Steeles

The BEGINNING, A Novella, Book 1

Going HARD, Book 2

Living FAST, Book 3

Loving DEEP, Book 4

Breaking FREE, Book 5

Roaming WILD, Book 6

Stripping BARE, Book 7

Enduring LOVE, A Novella, Book 8

TASTING FIRE

BY KELSEY BROWNING

Enjoy an excerpt from Kelsey Browning's *Tasting FIRE*, Book Two in the Steele Ridge: The Kingstons series (Coming in September 2018):

Emmy and Cash stopped in front of the Murchison Building, and she gestured up toward her apartment windows. "I want to be here. I love my hometown."

"Which you showed so eloquently by leaving."

"Yes, I had to leave to become a doctor, and I won't apologize for building a successful career, but..."

"But what?"

"I wasn't building a life I really wanted."

"You are a piece of work. Never satisfied, are you? And now you think you can find the life you're looking for here, in Steele Ridge?"

"Yes." She risked putting her hand against his cheek, savored the prickly feel of short scruff. Her pulse sped up at the simple contact.

"At one time, I wanted to build a life with you," he said, his voice edged with bitterness.

"We were young. Naive," Emmy whispered. "But the last thing I wanted to do was hurt you."

Cash took a step, moving closer until Emmy was forced to back up. The bricks of the Murchison building caught the fabric of her shirt, the rough texture at her back making her skin ripple. She lifted her hands to his chest, and her fingers curled into the softness of his T-shirt.

He leaned in, lowering his face until their lips were within breathing distance. "Pain is a helluva teacher. I've gotten some smarts since you left, Emmy. But apparently not enough, because I still want to kiss you."

Standing right here on Main Street, Emmy had the impulse to loop her arms around Cash's neck and jump into his arms. Squeeze her thighs around his waist and plaster her front to his. That was the kiss she wanted.

But that was too much, way too soon.

Still, she couldn't resist touching him, so she lifted to her toes and pressed her mouth to his. Their long-overdue kiss was just a touch of lips. A sweet slow slide that was supposed to soothe away his anger. Instead, it yanked the very breath out of Emmy. Every millimeter of her skin was suddenly clamoring for his touch, simply because she was holding back the torrent of need inside her.

Then Cash skimmed the tip of his tongue along her bottom lip. Thank goodness the wall was at her back or her knees might've been in trouble.

She grasped for his waistband to steady herself and hooked two fingers inside, against his hot skin. But when she tugged, he didn't budge, just slowly heated up the kiss, degree by degree.

Good Lord, he'd learned a thing or two since the last time they kissed. And he'd been a knock-her-socks-off kisser then.

When Cash finally opened his mouth over hers and took the kiss to tongues, hot breath, and heaving chests, Emmy's brain stopped thinking and turned everything over to her body.

This. This was the passion and yearning and need that had been missing from her life. She'd been without it for so long that she hadn't realized what she was missing until the night Oliver had executed his clinical proposal.

Go away, Oliver.

One hand in his waistband, she grabbed hold of Cash's hair with the other and yanked. Oh, God. A brick wall at her back and a hard man at her front.

The perfect kind of trapped.

Cash obviously thought so too, because his erection was hot against her stomach even through the fabric of their clothes. Sure, they'd *done it* a few times when they were dating their senior year, but those had been quick, furtive encounters the few times they could find privacy.

Not easy in a small town.

Once down at Deadman's Creek in the front seat of the truck he'd driven back then.

Once on her couch when her mom had taken Kris to see a play in Asheville.

They'd had plans, though, for sharing an apartment one day. Sleeping and loving together in their own bed. But she'd rejected all that.

Cash's hands came up and framed her hips, pulling her up the wall and tilting her pelvis against his. It made Emmy want to claw at him, tear at their clothes until they were skin to skin and he could slide inside her. Fill up the places she'd recently discovered were so empty.

She even went so far as to flip open the top button of his jeans, but before she could shove her hand fully inside his pants, something whooshed past them and crashed through one of the Murchison building's front windows.

ACKNOWLEDGMENTS

Writing a book is always a labor of love and I couldn't do it without the help of some very generous people. Thank you to my dear friend, Milton Grasle, who somehow always manages to help me battle my way out of the nasty corners I write myself into. Thanks also to John Leach for answering my law enforcement questions, no matter how silly even I think they are. A big thanks also to Jeff Rinek for helping me with FBI procedural details. I've done my best to get it all right, but any mistakes I've made are mine.

Thank you to my cowriters on this series, Tracey Devlyn and Kelsey Browning. Sharing a world with other writers takes an enormous amount of attention and I'm thankful to be working with such highly organized women. I must, must, must also acknowledge Misty Evans for constantly answering the call when I need plotting help.

Thank you also to Amy Remus and Liz Semkiu for taking the time to read an advance copy of *Craving Heat*. I appreciate it!

As usual, thank you to my guys who make sure I smile every day.

And finally, thank you to the readers who have embraced the Steele Ridge series and shared it with friends. I'm humbled by the love you've shown for the series. Muhwah!

-Adrienne

ABOUT THE AUTHOR

 **Adrienne Giordano** is a *USA Today* bestselling author of over twenty romantic suspense and mystery novels. She is a Jersey girl at heart, but now lives in the Midwest with her workaholic husband, sports-obsessed son and Buddy the Wheaten Terrorist (Terrier). She is a cofounder of Romance University blog and Lady Jane's Salon-Naperville, a reading series dedicated to romantic fiction.

For more information on Adrienne, including her Internet haunts, contest updates, and details on her upcoming novels, please visit her at:
www.AdrienneGiordano.com
agiordano@adriennegiordano.com

Lightning Source UK Ltd.
Milton Keynes UK
UKHW021126120220
358606UK00009B/1728

9 781948 075060